TURNING THE TABLES

I closed the door as quietly as I could, and turned to face the household, my hands gripping the doorknob so the so-called ghost couldn't get back into the kitchen if she took it into her head to do so.

"Daisy!" Mrs. Bissel shoved Mrs. Cummings out of the way and hurried into the room. When she saw me, she stopped running and stood still, panting, her huge bosom working like a bellows, and her arms held out at her sides to prevent anyone else from entering the room. Her household staff piled up behind her, no one willing to leave the shelter of her largeness for fear of what might befall her without the protection of the mistress of the house. It would have been funny, had I been in a mood to be amused.

I wasn't. I did, however, get my spiritualist aura to come back and help me out, thank heaven. Holding one arm out, palm up in a gesture cops make when they want to hold up traffic, I said in my best mystical murmur, "Stay back. This is not a matter for those unversed in the ways of the spirits. Danger lies below."

BOOK YOUR PLACE ON OUR WEBSITE AND MAKE THE READING CONNECTION!

We've created a customized website just for our very special readers, where you can get the inside scoop on everything that's going on with Zebra, Pinnacle and Kensington books.

When you come online, you'll have the exciting opportunity to:

- View covers of upcoming books
- Read sample chapters
- Learn about our future publishing schedule (listed by publication month *and author*)
- Find out when your favorite authors will be visiting a city near you
- Search for and order backlist books from our online catalog
- Check out author bios and background information
- Send e-mail to your favorite authors
- Meet the Kensington staff online
- Join us in weekly chats with authors, readers and other guests
- Get writing guidelines
- AND MUCH MORE!

**Visit our website at
http://www.kensingtonbooks.com**

FINE SPIRITS

Alice Duncan

ZEBRA BOOKS
Kensington Publishing Corp.
http://www.kensingtonbooks.com

ZEBRA BOOKS are published by

Kensington Publishing Corp.
850 Third Avenue
New York, NY 10022

All Kensington titles, imprints and distributed lines are available at special quantity discounts for bulk purchases for sales promotion, premiums, fund-raising, educational or institutional use.

Special book excerpts or customized printings can also be created to fit specific needs. For details, write or phone the office of the Kensington Special Sales Manager: Kensington Publishing Corp., 850 Third Avenue, New York, NY 10022. Attn. Special Sales Department. Phone: 1-800-221-2647.

Zebra and the Z logo Reg. U.S. Pat. & TM Off.

First Printing: July 2003
10 9 8 7 6 5 4 3 2 1

Printed in the United States of America

*For Jan Rotondo and Virginia Majesty,
who very kindly allowed me
to borrow their last names.*

One

First off, it must be clearly understood by one and all that I'm not a priest. I think you need to be a Catholic or an Episcopalian, not to mention a member of the male gender, in order to become a priest, and I'm none of those things. I'm female, and my family has always attended the First Methodist Episcopal Church, North, on the corner of Marengo Avenue and Colorado Street, in the fair city of Pasadena, California.

Therefore, when Mrs. Griselda Bissel (relict of the late Mr. Francis Bissel, and as rich as Croesus but nowhere near as regal) called me on the telephone at my own modest family home on South Marengo Avenue in Pasadena from her mansion on Foothill Boulevard in Altadena and asked me a rather startling question, I hesitated. The reason I did so is that, as stated above, I am not a priest. In point of fact, I'm a spiritualist medium; but more about that later.

My name is Daisy Gumm Majesty. Most people who know me think Daisy is short for Desdemona, but it's not. When I was ten years old and first started playing around with various forms of spiritualism (to wit, at the time, an old Ouija board), I decided Daisy was too pedestrian a name for a spiritualist. I opted to become Desdemona. It stuck, although no one calls me anything but Daisy unless they don't know me.

As mentioned, I am a spiritualist by trade, and it's a

darned good one. Mind you, I wouldn't object to being supported by my husband Billy. However, since the Great War Billy's been confined to a wheelchair. His war experience, which occurred shortly after we were wed, has affected our lives and our marriage tremendously. Not to mention catastrophically.

I'm not complaining. Many lives were altered far more tragically than ours. My own aunt Viola lost her only son, which left a gaping hole in her life that will never be filled. Losing a child has got to be worse than having a crippled husband.

Still, I sometimes got the feeling that Billy believed he'd have been better off if the Huns had killed him outright instead of leaving him in the pitiful condition that passed, after the war, for his life. Truth to tell, sometimes I thought so, too.

No matter how much I loved him, and I did, life was hard for both of us because of his terrible injuries and the pain and depression they engendered, again, in both of us. They call it "shell shock" in soldiers. I don't know if there's a name for what the shell-shocked soldiers' wives suffered from, but I had a bad case of it, whatever it was.

Billy hated how I earned our living, even though I hauled in more money than if I were to work as, say, a clerk at Nash's Department Store or as a housemaid in a rich person's home. There were lots of rich people in Pasadena back then. The only reason my family lived there was because the rich folks needed people to work for them, and we were them. The workers, that is to say.

We (Billy and I) lived in a bungalow on South Marengo Avenue which we'd bought primarily by using the proceeds from my spiritualist business, so you'd think he'd have been more appreciative of my efforts. He wasn't. He hated it that I earned the money in our marriage, even though his inability to do so wasn't his fault or mine.

The fault lay with the be-damned kaiser and his miserable soldiers who gassed Billy out of his foxhole in France, then shot him when he tried to crawl to safety. When Billy finally came home to me, he was more dead than alive and crippled for life. Which just goes to prove (if anyone doesn't know it already) how fair life is, which is not at all.

My parents, Joe and Peggy Gumm, lived with us, as did my aunt Viola Gumm, the one who lost the son and who was widely acknowledged to be the best cook in Pasadena, if not the entire United States. Aunt Vi worked as a cook for Mrs. Madeline Kincaid, who owned a gigantic mansion on Orange Grove Boulevard, but we got to eat her cooking, too, which meant that my entire life at the time wasn't a total wreck, just the marriage part.

Anyhow, when the telephone in the kitchen jangled on that dreary, late November day in 1920, Billy and I were alone in the house. Ma had gone to her job at the Hotel Marengo, where she was head bookkeeper. Aunt Vi had gone to work at Mrs. Kincaid's place. I had no idea where Pa was. He had been a chauffeur for rich Hollywood actors, directors, and producers and the like, but heart problems had kept him idle for a couple of years. Still, he was a sociable man, and he enjoyed visiting friends. Pa had never met a stranger, so his sources for fraternizing were plentiful.

Our telephone number was Colorado 13, and the ring was ours, as defined by the length and number of rings. In 1920, even in so sophisticated a place as Pasadena, most of us shared the telephone wire with several other families. These "party" lines were good for the telephone company, I guess, but they could be hard on those of us who shared the wire.

One woman in particular on our party line was a dedicated pain in the neck, a snoop, and a gossip. She always tried to remain on the wire during my own personal telephone calls. In a way I couldn't blame her, since my calls were unquestionably more interesting than hers, if only because my calls usually featured people wanting me to summon up their dead relatives for a chat and things like that.

I recognized her voice as soon as I picked up the receiver. "Mrs. Barrow?" I always tried to be polite, even when I wanted to shout at her. "This call is for me, I believe. That was our ring."

"Daisy? Daisy Majesty? Is that you?" It was Mrs. Bissel. I could tell it was she because I heard her pack of dachshunds baying in the background. Any time anyone talked to Mrs. Bissel over the telephone, the hounds barked a backup accompaniment to the conversation. Mrs. Bissel claimed her dogs were like children in that regard: as soon as your attention swerved away from them, they started acting up.

"Yes. How do you do, Mrs. Bissel. One moment, please." I sucked in air and told myself to be calm. "Mrs. Barrow, hang up your telephone now. I won't be long."

Mrs. Barrow said, "Humph," in an indignant voice and slammed her receiver in the cradle. You'd have thought I'd recommended she go outdoors and shoot herself—a suggestion that had occurred to me more than once, but which I'd not offered the unmitigated magpie thus far. I believe this consideration shows a good deal of restraint on my part.

After trying and failing to repress a sigh, I spoke to Mrs. Bissel again. "How do you do, Mrs. Bissel?"

"What? Oh, I'm well, thank you. Or . . . No, I'm not well."

"I'm sorry to hear it."

All right, I'm going to say something now that may be perceived as mean-spirited by some. But the fact is that every now and then, when I was dealing with rich matrons who'd never been forced to do a day's work in their lives, who had all the time in the world not to do it in, and who forgot that the rest of us weren't so lucky, I became a trifle irritable. In fact, I occasionally became downright short-tempered, although I exercised extreme self-control and never let it show.

Those of us who have had to work for a living most of our lives don't have time to dither. Darned near every single one of the wealthy women who availed themselves of my spiritualistic services in those days were ditherers. Usually this didn't bother me. That day it did, mainly because Billy and I had been quarreling. Again.

"Actually, it's not that *I'm* ill," Mrs. Bissel went on. "It's something else." Her voice dropped to a sepulchral whisper on the *something else* part of this speech.

This time I was successful in suppressing my sigh. In the time it would take her to tell me her problem, I'd probably have been able to sweep the kitchen and vacuum-clean the living room rug—or resume bickering with Billy. But instead of doing something useful, I had to stand in the kitchen with the telephone's earpiece jammed against my head, the black mouthpiece sticking out of the wall, and listen to a woman who wasn't accustomed to thinking think. Can you tell I was in a really bad mood?

"I'm glad you're not ill," I said pleasantly. I was always pleasant to the clients, even those whom I'd have preferred to strangle. To be fair, Mrs. Bissel wasn't one of my imaginary stranglees. She, although daffy, silly, and a general waster of my time, was a very nice lady.

Besides, I had designs on one of her dogs. Her female dachshund, Lucille, had, with the help of her male companion Lancelot, just given birth to four of the most adorable puppies I'd ever seen in my life. They were black with little tan spots over their eyes, tan feet and muzzles, and were as shiny as the seals I'd seen in the Griffith Park Zoo in Los Angeles. I wanted one. What's more, I suspected that Mrs. Bissel would be willing to trade one of the pups for a séance if I worked on her just right.

Mainly, I wanted the dog for Billy. He often got lonely and angry when I left home to work as a spiritualist. Since he claimed it was *what* I did, rather than the fact that I had to work at all, that bothered him, I was supposed to understand that he wouldn't have cared if I'd left him every day to work at Nash's or as a typist for an attorney or to do something else "normal."

I didn't buy it. I think he'd have hated my having to earn our living no matter how I did it. In a way I could understand his attitude. Until the war, Billy had never been one to sit idle and let others do for him. He'd done all sorts of things to earn money before he became a soldier. He was a whiz at automobile mechanics, and he'd had a job waiting for him at Hull Motor Company after the war . . . if he'd still been healthy and whole.

It was hard on his masculine pride to be unable to work. Heck, it was hard on me, too, although in my case pride had nothing to do with it. I hoped that a dog, especially one as sweet and funny-looking as one of those dachshund pups, would keep him company. At that point I was willing to try anything to make Billy happy. Well, except give up my work, because I couldn't afford to do that.

"It's something else," said Mrs. Bissel, still sounding as if she were buried in a tomb and attempting to communicate with a living entity, or vice versa.

"Ah," I said mysteriously. Sounding mysterious had become second nature to me years earlier.

"It's because my house is *haunted.*"

That took me aback, which was unusual, given my line of work. "Um, I beg your pardon?"

"Oh, Daisy!" Mrs. Bissel wailed. Being fair again, I must confess that Mrs. Bissel didn't wail at me very often. Mrs. Kincaid, my aunt Vi's employer and one of my very best customers, was a first-class wailer, but

Mrs. Bissel generally remained calm when speaking to me. "My house is being haunted! By a spirit. Or a ghost. I don't know what it is, but it's belowstairs, and the servants are all terrified, and so am I, and I don't know what to do about it, so I called you. I need you to get rid of the spirit—or maybe it's a ghost—that's haunting my house!"

Ah-ha. Very interesting. As I mentioned earlier, however, I'm not a priest. The fact of the matter is that I'm no sort of ministerially sanctioned exorcist. To tell the absolute, unvarnished truth, I don't even believe in spirits, or "hants," or ghosts of any variety. I use them for my work, which is mainly conducting séances and pretending to chat with folks raised from the Great Beyond with the help of my spiritual control, a Scottish fellow named Rolly, but I don't believe in them.

I told Mrs. Bissel the part about my not being an exorcist. "Um, as much as I'd love to be of service to you, Mrs. Bissel, I don't think I'm the one to help you. Don't you need a priest to conduct an exorcism of your house? I'm not a priest."

"Of course you're not! But I trust you, Daisy. You're the *only* one I trust to do the job properly."

This flattering declaration sailed through the telephone wire and landed in my ear even though I'd just told her I was not equipped to do the job at all, much less properly. Rich people have always confounded me. "Er, I'm not sure, Mrs. Bissel. I've never done anything like ridding a house of a spirit—"

"Or a ghost," she supplied.

Right. "—before."

"Nonsense. You speak to the spirits all the time. You understand how to communicate with them. You can persuade them to do what you want them to do. I'm sure you can do something to rid my home of this one tiny little demon. You have the gift, Daisy. Everyone knows it. This thing hasn't been there long, and it's just the one little spirit. Unless it's a ghost. Well, you know, it probably doesn't matter."

Not to me, it didn't. It could have been a warthog, and it wouldn't have mattered to me, although a warthog would probably be easier to get rid of than a spirit. Or ghost.

I continued to waver, mainly because I knew that whatever had taken up residence in Mrs. Bissel's basement, it wasn't anything I could tackle with a clear conscience, with or without help from the fictitious Rolly, and might even be dangerous. I supposed a lunatic or an escaped criminal could have decided to hide out there, although that seemed almost as far-fetched as a haunting.

Then I recalled the puppies. My resolution not to become involved in this affair started to totter a bit. Billy is always telling me that what I do for a living is wicked and evil and bad for my overall moral constitution. I guess my vacillating in this instance might be considered proof of his contention, although I'm usually an upstanding Christian woman who tries her best to be good. I even sing alto in our church choir, for crumb's sake.

I took a deep breath and thought fast. "Well . . . the thing is, Mrs. Bissel, that I can't guarantee results. As I've already told you, I've never done anything like this before. I may have to experiment." That was putting it mildly. "I'm almost sure it would take more than one visit."

"Of course. That would be fine, dear. Come as often as you like. I only want you to try. I'm sure you can do it."

It was nice to have a cheering section, although I couldn't help but wish mine were closer to home. In actual fact, it would have been nice if Billy, who was at the time sitting in his wheelchair in the living room and probably fuming because I'd run off in the middle of a fight, had appreciated me. Ah, well.

"I'm not so sure," I told her bluntly, because it was

the truth, and also because I didn't want her to hate me once I'd failed to do the job. "I can but try my best. The spirits are often stubborn. They come from a plane far removed from our own, and have their own ways—ways that transcend our mortal ken—you know." I'd become so accustomed to speaking such folderol that this ludicrous speech danced off my tongue like a prima ballerina.

"I know it, dear. That's why I want *you.*"

Still I hesitated, and not merely because I knew I could no more rid a house of a ghost than I could speak Mandarin Chinese. My hesitation this time centered around my automobile, a 1909 Model T Ford that didn't take kindly to climbing hills. Mrs. Bissel lived on the corner of Foothill Boulevard and Maiden Lane in Altadena. That was *way* uphill from our house on South Marengo Avenue in Pasadena.

Of course I could always take a red car. The electric railroad (we just called them the red cars) went uphill and down on a regular schedule, and there was a stop right at the corner of Lake and Foothill. From the redcar stop, I would only have to walk one short block to get to Mrs. Bissel's house.

The other reason for my hesitation sat in the living room, just waiting to hear about this call so he could rip my character and morals apart some more.

Poor Billy. I really did love him desperately. It's only that he'd come back to me from that awful war in such terrible shape, and neither of us knew how to cope with his new self. He was in almost constant pain and had to take morphine more and more often to keep his suffering under control. His lungs had been ruined by the Kaiser's mustard gas. He was, in short, a wreck of himself. He hated being crippled.

When we married in 1917, we'd known each other all our lives. I'd expected to stay married to the happy-go-lucky, cheerful, true-blue Billy Majesty who had looked so handsome in his soldier's uniform on the day of our wedding. I hadn't anticipated living the rest of my life with the wreck the Germans had made of him: the ravaged, heartsick, shell-shocked, debilitated Billy.

It broke my heart every day that I saw him in his present state. It broke his, too, but his unhappiness took the form of rage and helplessness, both of which he unleashed on me, and I really don't think I deserved it. He didn't deserve it, either.

To make a long story short, there was no easy answer to the problem of Billy or of our marriage. My insides ached almost all the time because of it.

"Um, I'm not sure, Mrs. Bissel . . ." I let my voice trail off, not for effect but because I was honestly struggling with my conscience about accepting a job I knew darned well I couldn't do.

"Oh, but Daisy, you *must!* You're the only one I trust."

Yeah, yeah, she'd said that before. Her trust didn't alter the fact that I wasn't fit to do the job. I was no kind of exorcist. Nor was I, if her problem was rats or mice or cats or opossums, an exterminator.

I made up my mind. "Very well, I'll do my best, although I can't guarantee results."

A long sigh on the other end of the wire almost blew my eardrums out. "Oh, *thank* you, Daisy. I'm sure you will prevail against this spirit. Or ghost."

"Thank you." I wished I was as sure as she was.

"And if you think it would be better, you may stay here for the duration of the job. That would spare you traveling back and forth if it takes more than one session to get rid of the spirit. Or ghost."

Oh, boy, wouldn't Billy love that? "Thank you for your kindness, Mrs. Bissel, but I think I had better not stay at your house. My husband, you know . . ." Again, I allowed my voice to trail off, this time on purpose. Everyone knew about poor Billy.

I felt like a traitor to him when I had a sudden, piercing urge to take Mrs. Bissel up on her offer to live at her place for a while. I could have used a good rest.

Mrs. Bissel sounded guilty when next she spoke. Her guilt made mine rear its ugly face and stick its tongue out at me. Billy was right about one thing: I did use my well-honed spiritualist act to manipulate people. If that was wicked and evil, I guess I was.

"Of course, Daisy dear. I shouldn't have asked. You have such burdens to bear for such a young thing."

Darned right, I did. Heck, I'd only turned twenty the day before, yet I was supporting a whole family. Well, with the help of my mother and my aunt, but gosh, you'd think Billy would respect my situation at least as much as silly Mrs. Bissel.

I knew better than to expect it. After I'd made an appointment for a first visit that afternoon and hung up the telephone receiver (leaving Mrs. Barrow free to talk all afternoon with whomever she chose), I returned to our living room. Sure enough, Billy sat in his wheelchair, glowering, looking as if he was spoiling for a fight. I tilted my head a little and gazed at him, wondering if I looked as hopeless and helpless as I felt.

"Who was that?" he demanded.

"Mrs. Bissel. She's the one with the frankfurter dogs."

"What did she want? A séance?" He sneered.

I was used to it. "Not this time. She wants me to rid her basement of a spirit. Unless it's a ghost."

"She *what?*"

Every now and then, when my life and job got truly bizarre, Billy's anger evaporated into surprise. That's what happened this time. I hoped it would last.

I sighed and sat on our comfy old sofa and put my elbows on my knees and my chin in my hands. I was wearing one of my most comfortable wrappers, a pink-and-white checked one that probably clashed with my dark red hair, but I didn't care. I dressed up for my work; at home I relaxed—except when clients came over for a palm-reading or to consult the Ouija board or to participate in a session of table-turning. "She claims a spirit or ghost has taken up residence in her basement, and she wants me to get rid of it for her."

"You've suddenly turned into a—what do they call it? A minister who gets rid of ghosts?"

"An exorcist. Yeah, I guess so. Mrs. Bissel claims she doesn't want a priest. She wants me."

"Good God, Daisy, your business is crazy. And you're crazy to take a job like that. It's bad enough that you pretend to raise dead people's ghosts and gab at them for money. This is going too damned far."

I gazed at my husband and felt like crying. We Gumms are made of sturdy stuff, though, and I didn't. *"You* tell her that, then. I told her, and she chose not to believe me. I told her I wasn't qualified to do the job and almost certainly wouldn't succeed. She wants me to try it anyway."

Billy shook his head in amazement. I knew exactly how he felt, because I'd been feeling the same way ever since Mrs. Bissel ignored everything I'd tried to tell her and begged me to take a job for which I was totally and admittedly unqualified.

"Rich people are strange, Billy."

"You're telling me."

"Do you want to fight with me some more, or can I change clothes and go up to Mrs. Bissel's house and study her basement?"

His lips straightened into a flat line, and he glared at me for several seconds before he gave it up. "Aw, Daisy, you know I don't want to fight with you." He'd have sighed, but his lungs wouldn't let him.

Sometimes I hurt for my poor husband so much it was all I could do to keep from screaming at God for letting something like this happen to so good a man as my Billy. I still felt like crying—and still didn't. "I don't want to fight with you, either, Billy. I love you."

His smile went lopsided. "Do you?"

I moved from the couch to his chair and threw my arms around him. "I love you more than anything, Billy Majesty, and you know it."

His arms went around my waist and I sank down onto his lap, wishing we could have a real marriage. I knew Billy would have made a wonderful father, had the Germans allowed him to come home to me a whole man. Too late for that now. As much as I tried not to, and as much as I knew the feeling to be irrational, I hated the Germans.

"I just wish you didn't have to do what you do, Daisy. That's all."

Darn it, he was *so* unfair about my job! I didn't want to spoil the mood, so I murmured, "I know it, Billy. I'm sorry."

And, after a short round of smooches, which was as much lovemaking as we were able to accomplish thanks to the damned Germans, I went off, drooping, to change into my spiritualist costume and catch a red car up to Altadena so I could pretend to exorcise a spirit (or ghost) from an addlepated rich lady's basement.

Merciful heavens, but my life seemed strange sometimes.

TWO

Even though my mood was as gloomy as the weather, I looked swell when I was through transforming myself from a simple everyday housewife into a spiritualist medium. I'd recently had my hair bobbed at the barber shop Billy and Pa frequented, and the new hairdo suited me fine. I'd resisted cutting my hair for a long time because I was afraid people wouldn't accept a spiritualist with short hair. However, since I almost always wore hats when I worked, it probably didn't matter much.

So far, nobody seemed to be appalled by my short hair. Only a couple of years earlier, if a woman cut her hair short, the whole world thought she was a lady of the night or a Bolshevist or something else equally awful. Not anymore. Nowadays even prim and proper ladies were getting their hair shingled—and not at hair salons, either. Rich and snooty ladies went to barbershops, just as I'd done.

As an added bonus, the bob was easy to care for. All I had to do was wet my hair, comb it out, make finger waves that lay flat against my cheeks, and my hair was "done" for the day. Not only was it easy to care for, but I have thick, heavy hair, and when the barber cut most of it off, I felt at first as if I were going to float up into the sky, I was so light-headed.

I kissed Billy as I walked to the front door. "I'll be back as soon as I can be."

He looked up at me and gave a half-hearted smile. "You look beautiful, Daisy."

"Thanks, sweetheart." I was wearing a black wool dress that I'd sewn on Ma's White side-pedal rotary sewing machine. The dress had a long waist that tied with a sash on the side of my hip. I also wore black stockings and pretty black leather short-heeled shoes that tied over my arches, and I carried a black handbag. I topped it all off with a black cloche hat I'd remade from last year's model. When I threw on my black wool coat (which I'd also made myself), I looked as if I were going to a funeral. That suited me fine, because it worked both for the job I was headed toward as well as my mood. "Wish me luck."

As I might have expected, that was the wrong thing to say. Some days, everything I said was wrong, and if I kept my mouth shut that was wrong, too.

Billy frowned. "I can't do that, Daisy. You're lying to people, and I can't wish you luck doing it. Not with a clear conscience."

"I didn't lie to Mrs. Bissel," I protested, stung. "I told her I couldn't do this job. She wants me to try anyway."

He shook his head in disgust. "That's ridiculous."

"Maybe to you," I said, my voice hard.

Before we could tangle further, I left the house. I had to stand on the front porch and take several deep breaths to make sure I wouldn't cry. The day was as gray outside as I felt inside, and I wondered if I should have taken an umbrella with me. Because I couldn't bear going back into the house and facing Billy again, I decided *to heck with an umbrella,* and began walking the few short blocks to Colorado Street where I could catch a red car.

It didn't take more than forty-five minutes for the red car to get to Foothill Boulevard and Lake Avenue. There was still no hint of rain—and no hint of sunshine. The orange groves that took up a lot of Pasadena land looked as if they didn't enjoy the gray weather any more than I did, and every time the red car chugged its passengers past a weeping willow, I felt as though it was weeping for me. The air was thick and cold, and I hugged my coat around me in the car, feeling miserable and oppressed and generally lousy. Not even the appreciative glances I got from the conductor and several of my fellow passengers cheered me. I wanted my husband to value me, not a bunch of strangers.

When we came to the end of the line and I got off the car, I noticed the conductor staring at me as if he was worried about me. "Is anything the matter, Miss?"

"Not a thing," I lied. "But thanks for asking." I gave him a quick smile to let him know I was fine, even though I wasn't, and commenced walking briskly to Mrs. Bissel's mansion.

As mansions go, Mrs. Bissel's was kind of small. I mean, Mrs. Kincaid's mansion on Orange Grove Boulevard had a huge iron fence around it, an electrically operated gate, and a man to guard it. I don't know how many acres of prime Pasadena property Mrs. Kincaid owned, but she had an entire orange grove in her backyard.

In contrast, you could walk right up to Mrs. Bissel's front door from the street. Of course, it was a long walk. She owned all the property from her house on the corner of Maiden Lane and Foothill to Lake Avenue, and everything behind her house as far as a street called Las Flores. She owned a hunk of land. I guess it didn't look as impressive as Mrs. Kincaid's property because there was no iron fence surrounding it.

The house itself was smaller than the Kincaid mansion, too, although it was still huge. It was a three-storied, stucco, beige-colored house with brown trim. A balcony on the second floor looked out over the big, rolling lawn in front. Mrs. Bissel's backyard featured a circular drive surrounding a monkey-puzzle tree she'd imported from Australia.

Behind the tree, on the other side of the circular drive from the house, Mrs. Bissel had a rose garden that looked and smelled wonderful during the summertime. Some stairs led from the rose garden up to a little picnic area where Mrs. Bissel entertained friends during the warm months.

That day I was glad I didn't have to go through the back door, because I'm sure looking at the bare, brown rose garden and the empty picnic area would only make me feel worse, if such a thing were possible.

Mrs. Bissel also owned a couple of horses, both of which were grazing in the field between her house and Lake Avenue that day. I blessed her for those horses. They looked so pretty, and I desperately needed something pleasant in my life just then. One of them was brown and the other had brown and white spots, and I could imagine red Indians riding them across the plains in a Zane Grey novel. I didn't know what variety of horse they were, although I knew they must have had better pedigrees than our own old horse, Brownie, who lived in back of our house, and who was getting lazier and more cantankerous with each passing day.

Heck, they had better pedigrees than Billy and me, if anybody cared to check. Whatever their ancestry, those horses looked swell, and watching them made me feel a tiny bit better, although not much.

The lawn in front of the Bissel place had three sloping hills on it. Her front porch ran the entire width of the house. The grass was green and well tended, although it was getting a little yellow because it was that time of year. A row of bird-of-paradise had been planted in a garden running the length of the porch, and there were a bunch of rosebushes in front of the bird-of-paradise.

Nothing was blooming on that depressing fall day, but the rolling lawn still looked pretty. Fortunately for my shoes, there was a concrete walkway running from the street to the porch, so my heels didn't get stuck in the dirt on my way to the house.

As soon as I neared the doorbell and even before I pressed it, I heard Mrs. Bissel's herd of wild dachshunds indoors go into their announcement act. They cheered me up even more than the sight of the gorgeous horses in the field had.

I don't know what it is about dachshunds. They're so short and funny looking, yet they think they're such tough cookies. Perhaps I identified with them because I felt so puny and yet acted so tough myself. Who knows? Probably Dr. Freud could tell me, but I don't speak German and never want to, so his diagnosis wouldn't help me much.

Mrs. Bissel didn't have a butler, as did Mrs. Kincaid. She did, however, have a live-in housekeeper and a couple of housemaids. It was one of the maids, Ginger Sullivan, who opened the door to me. I knew Ginger from school.

I grinned at her, but she didn't grin back. I considered this reaction strange, since Ginger and I had always been friendly. "Hi, Ginger. How are you?" I could hardly hear myself for all the barking.

Evidently Ginger was accustomed to the dogs, because she didn't seem fazed in the slightest. "Scared to death," she said flatly, opening the door and allowing me entry and several of the dogs outlet. "This place is haunted. I hope you can get rid of it, Daisy, because I'm about to quit."

"Golly, Ginger, I didn't know it was so bad."

She shivered. I knew she wasn't faking it, either, because I saw the gooseflesh on her arms when she rubbed them. "I've never been so scared in my life."

Now, this was an ominous declaration, for certain. It wasn't good for anyone, including Ginger and me. Jobs weren't as easy to come by as they had been before the war, and the whole country had sunk into a depression.

Ginger wouldn't be talking about quitting her job for no good reason, because there was no guarantee that she'd be able to find another one.

As for me, I could almost imagine Mrs. Bissel being frightened about nothing, but if Ginger confirmed her employer's estimation of the basement situation, it meant there truly was something down there. And I was expected to get rid of it. I wondered if Pa or Billy had a gun somewhere. Not that I knew how to shoot a gun, but still . . .

I'd have liked to ask Ginger some questions, but Mrs. Bissel emerged into the huge entry hall from the front room, her arms outstretched, managing somehow to avoid stepping on any of the dogs frolicking at her feet and mine. She was clad in a shocking maroon day dress (shocking because it was such a vibrant color for so large a woman). She looked like an ambulatory purple whale. If I ever get fat, I'm sticking to basic black.

Some of the dogs jumped up on me, digging their sharp little doggie claws into the skirt of my beautiful black dress, but I only bent down, spoke softly, and gently disengaged the claws. Not even for a lovely handmade black wool frock would I alienate a client by hollering at her dogs.

Fortunately, Mrs. Bissel hollered at them for me, so my skirt was spared except for one tiny snag that I knew I could fix in a jiffy. She also clapped her hands, which seemed to affect the dogs. They all stood back, sat down (it was difficult to tell whether they were standing or sitting because their legs were so short) gazed up at me, and a chorus of tails swept the floor. Gee, those dogs were cunning! I *really* wanted one.

"Daisy's here, Mrs. B.," Ginger announced informally (and unnecessarily). At Mrs. Kincaid's house, nothing was informal. Mrs. Kincaid's butler, Featherstone, probably wore his butler suit to bed at night. I preferred Mrs. Bissel's more relaxed standards.

"I'm so glad you could come, Daisy!" Mrs. Bissel beamed at me and gave me a small hug. "Sorry about the welcoming committee."

"I don't mind," I told her honestly. "I love your dogs." I glanced at the floor and tried to count, but the dogs kept moving around. "How many do you have now? It seems there are more than there were the last time I was here."

Mrs. Bissel loved anyone who loved her dogs. "I have a grand total of ten glorious dachshunds at this minute, Daisy, dear. Of course, I'm counting Lucille and Lancelot's pups in the grand total."

"Ah." Ten dogs. The mind boggled. At least these dogs were small. Can you imagine if they were Great Danes? "I see you have some brown ones along with the black-and-tan ones, too."

"Yes." Mrs. Bissel sighed happily. "I bought two red dachshunds from a gentleman in Arizona and plan to breed them." She took me by the arm and started leading me kitchenward. "I'm hoping that one of these days, I'll have a Westminster winner."

Okay, here's the thing about rich people and their dogs. Most people like dogs. *I* like dogs. But people who have a lot of time on their hands, and most of them are the rich ones because the rest of us have to work all the time, like to enter their dogs in dog shows. There's a big dog show at Tournament Park in Pasadena every year, and I know Mrs. Bissel "showed" her dogs there.

I'd learned from various clients over the years that the Westminster Kennel Club Dog Show, held annually in New York City, was the be-all and end-all of dog shows, and the one everyone wanted to be entered into and win. If your dog earned enough points at other dog shows during the year, it could go to Westminster. More than one Pasadena dog owner has told me it's an honor for dogs even to be entered into the Westminster Dog Show. I say, more power to them, especially if they're dachshunds.

Another rich lady of my acquaintance, Mrs. Frasier, bred feisty, frenetic little dogs she called miniature pinschers. Her main goal in life was to get these miniature pinschers recognized as a legitimate breed at the Westminster Kennel Club. I'm not sure what that entailed, but it sounded strange to me. I mean, since I'd met Mrs. Frasier, I could identify a miniature pinscher when I saw one. I didn't understand why the Westminster folks had trouble recognizing them. I could conceive of someone mistaking a miniature pinscher for a Chihuahua, but only until you looked at him more closely. Then you realized the pinscher had longer legs, less bulgy eyes, and a short, stubby tail. Both breeds were small and noisy, but they didn't really look *that* much alike.

But I digress.

"Would you like a cup of tea or anything before you confront our phantom?" Mrs. Bissel asked.

"No, thank you. I'd best get to work at once."

"Good." This short, pithy comment came from Ginger. "The sooner the better."

"Yes, that's probably the best thing. But do take Daisy's coat, Ginger. She won't need it, I'm sure."

"Sure thing, Mrs. B." Ginger took my coat. The house was warm enough. "I'll hang it in the hall closet."

"Thank you, Ginger." Mrs. Bissel gestured for me to follow her as Ginger went to hang up my coat. "There's a door to the basement from the kitchen," she told me as we walked through the huge dining room and into the pantry. The kitchen lay straight ahead. "I'll take you downstairs from the kitchen."

"That's fine, Mrs. Bissel."

"We never hear anything during the day," she went on. "So I don't think there's any danger right now, although the household help have taken to going downstairs in pairs or trios because they're all so frightened." She glanced at me and I saw her lips quiver slightly. "So am I."

"I'm awfully sorry," I said. And I was. Shoot, I didn't want to tangle with a *real* problem. Maybe it was just a cat. Or maybe it was a bear. Mrs. Bissel's house was right there up against the foothills. I suppose there were bears in the foothills. Or mountain lions. I *really* didn't want to meet a mountain lion face-to-fang.

I realized I was scaring myself and gave myself a mental shake.

Mrs. Bissel's housekeeper was also her cook, I guess, because she was in the kitchen, cooking something. I knew her slightly, so I smiled and said, "Hello, Mrs. Cummings."

"Hello, Mrs. Majesty. I sure hope you can help us."

Golly, everybody in the whole house was spooked. Something puzzled me about all this, though. When Mrs. Bissel went to the door leading to the basement and unlocked it, I asked her about it. "What about all your dogs, Mrs. Bissel? Can't they help you find out what's down there? They certainly let you know when someone's at the door. Don't they bark at the thing in the basement?"

"That's true, but the only doggies who sleep in the house at night are Lucille and Lancelot and their pups, and I carry them all upstairs with me when I go to bed."

"Ah. Have you considered allowing a few of the others to sleep in the kitchen or on the service porch?"

"I've thought about it," she said, "but I don't want them going down into the basement."

"Oh? Why is that?"

"It's not good for them to climb up and down the stairs," said Mrs. Bissel. "Their legs are too short and their backs are too long. They might hurt themselves. Besides, I'd not risk a hair on any of their backs if the spirit or ghost turns violent."

Which meant she was perfectly willing to risk my hair. I didn't object. I supposed ridding houses of spirits could be viewed as an aspect of my job, although I kind of resented not being judged to be as important as a dachshund. Anyhow, she was right about their legs and backs. Someday perhaps someone could design a dachshund with an extra pair of legs in the middle. But no. That would make them look even sillier than they already do.

"They do bark sometimes in the night," Mrs. Cummings said. She shivered, as had Ginger, and I saw that she had gooseflesh, too.

Obviously, there was *something* in the basement. I wasn't happy to know it.

"I'll go down with you," announced Mrs. Bissel stoutly. She took a deep breath, as if to brace herself.

"Be careful," said Mrs. Cummings.

I saw Ginger hanging back between the kitchen and the pantry, looking frightened. "Yeah," she said. "Be careful."

"We will be careful."

Mrs. Bissel squared her shoulders and straightened her back, and I got the impression she felt as if she were forging onward into battle. Naturally, this made me think of Billy, and of how frightened he must have been when the Germans were shooting at him. I shook my head hard in order to rid it of the mental image of my poor husband on that bloody battlefield.

"Yes," said I. "One must always be careful when dealing with the spirits."

Not to mention when dealing with escaped lunatics, criminals, bears, mountain lions, or maddened house cats. I tried not to think about it.

But not thinking about it was impossible. Mrs. Bissel, tiptoeing downstairs ahead of me, clutched the banister so hard her knuckles turned white, and she pressed her back against the wall at the same time. She was a stout woman, and well-corseted, but I saw her bosom quiver.

Her terror was obvious, and suddenly it irked me. If

she was so darned scared of whatever was down there, why the heck didn't she call the police instead of me? Policemen *chose* to risk their necks for other people's sake, a choice I'd never made.

I tried to keep my temper in check. It had been awfully short in recent days. In fact, the last time I'd been in a good mood had been earlier in the month when I'd pushed Billy in his wheelchair down Colorado Street in Pasadena's annual Armistice Day Parade. The cheers from the crowds as we rolled along had made us both feel as if Billy's sacrifice had not been in vain. He'd been only one among many wheelchair-bound ex-soldiers, too, some of them missing arms, legs, and even eyes, so he didn't feel like a freak for once.

Our life together had gone downhill fast after that. Probably the lousy weather had contributed to its downward rush. Also, I wasn't happy that I hadn't been able to vote in the recent election. It was an historic occasion, since it was the first national election in which women were allowed a voice.

Except me. Nobody cared about twenty-year-old me or who I'd have voted for. I'd have to wait until I was twenty-four before I could have a say in anything, darn it. The fact that my man, Harding, had won didn't alter the fact that I hadn't been allowed to vote.

But that was neither here nor there. At issue now was my ability to maintain my composure, and I was a mistress at that. I had to be. If I allowed my annoyance to show every time one of my clients did or said something stupid, I'd be yelling all day, every day, and nobody'd hire me anymore.

"You've got to get rid of this thing," Mrs. Bissel said in a stage whisper. "We're all so frightened."

"I can tell." I don't think I sounded sarcastic. "And I'll do my very best."

"I'm sure you will."

She didn't sound sure to me. She hesitated at the foot

of the stairs, still pressing her rotund self against the wall.

Because she didn't look as if she were going to be of any use in my search of the basement, I asked, "Is there a light switch?" If she expected me to poke around in the dark, I'd have to decline the job. Not even for a dachshund puppy would I chance getting bitten by a black widow spider or a snake or a rat or anything else poisonous or rodentine.

"A light? Oh, yes. Let me pull the cord."

She did, and the basement flooded with light. It looked like an average basement to me, although it was a lot bigger than, say, ours on Marengo. That's because this was a mansion. "Ah," I said. "Thank you."

"Take as much time as you need." Mrs. Bissel's voice shook slightly.

I took stock of my surroundings. Mrs. Bissel's basement was pretty nice, for a basement. It had been painted white in the recent past, and housed the family's laundry equipment: A big wringer washing machine that looked brand-new, a mangle for ironing sheets, and an ironing board upon which sat an electrical iron. I'd never used one of those before. We still had flatirons spread out on the range in our kitchen on Marengo. An electrical iron sounded like a good idea to me. I wasn't particularly adept at the domestic arts, and I burned myself quite often on those darned flatirons.

Canned goods were stored in the basement, too, and against the far wall I saw a wine rack. Somehow, I'd never pictured Mrs. Bissel as a wine drinker, although I don't know why not. Maybe it was her dogs. I pictured wine going with people who owned poodles, not dachshunds.

"About how long have you been bothered by noises in the basement?"

"I think it's been two weeks now."

"And how does the spirit manifest itself?" That

sounded *so* silly. Still and all, something was bothering the people in the house, and if Mrs. Bissel thought it was a spirit (or ghost), so be it.

"There are bumps in the night," Mrs. Bissel said with a shudder. "And it sounds like scraping noises sometimes. As if it was dragging chains."

Egad. "Chains? You mean, the noises are loud?" I most especially didn't want to encounter a criminal swinging a chain. Did they have chain gangs in California? I couldn't remember.

"No, no. They're soft noises. As if whatever it is was trying to be quiet."

I'd never heard of soft-sounding chains, which was minutely encouraging. "Um, perhaps it's not a chain, but a chair or footsteps or something along those lines."

"Maybe. I suppose that's possible."

Shoot, she sounded disappointed. You'd think she'd be glad not to be threatened with chains. I didn't argue with her. "Do any of your staff live down here, Mrs. Bissel?" Stepping away from the staircase, I steeled my nerves for an inspection.

"No. They used to, but the whole place flooded in nineteen-fifteen, and I moved all the servants up to the third floor. We only use the basement to store things in now, and for doing the laundry and so forth."

"But there are still bedrooms down here, I see." Brilliant deduction, and one based on my appraisal of the two closed doors on the far wall.

"Yes. The rooms are still here, but they aren't used for anything. Mrs. Cummings was the last to move out. She liked living down here because it's closer to the kitchen than the third floor."

Sensible woman, Mrs. Cummings. "When did she move out?"

"About two months ago. She decided she didn't like being so isolated from the rest of the household staff."

"Ah."

Because I knew myself to be a sensible woman and not one to be scared by ghosts, especially since they didn't exist, and since I'd do anything to avoid acting like an idiot, Mrs. Bissel's overt fear was making me feel better. That and the light. It was difficult to imagine anything bad happening in this bright, white, well-lighted room full of laundry products, wine, and preserved food.

Nevertheless, using my best wafting technique, I explored the basement's nooks and crannies. There actually weren't many of them. The room was a huge rectangle, and the two rooms on the far side were spare and clean.

Both rooms contained small, bare beds. When I stooped to glance under one of them, I found something interesting: an empty tin of Franco-American spaghetti. I picked it up and peered inside. It looked to me as if someone had scraped it clean recently, because the little bit of Italian sauce sticking to the tin's sides was fresh. I set the empty can down on the tiny bedside table and thought hard.

Now who, wondered I, would be eating spaghetti out of a tin can in Mrs. Bissel's basement? No answer occurred to me, and I decided to keep the empty tin to myself for the time being. If it had been Ginger who'd suffered a craving for canned spaghetti in the middle of a hard day, I didn't want to get her into trouble for stealing food.

I also got the weird feeling that this particular room had been occupied recently, and not by a spirit or a ghost. I'm not claiming to have any sort of relationship with the Other Side, whatever that is, but I have become sensitive to feelings as part of my trade. I sensed recent occupancy of this one room. When I went to the other room, I sensed nothing but emptiness.

That being the case, I returned to the first room and did a more extensive search. There wasn't a whole lot to search. The room was equipped with a cupboard, which was bare. Hooks on the wall had been used for the servants' clothes and held nothing now. A washstand, holding a pitcher and bowl, sat in a corner. The bowl had recently contained water; it was still wet on the bottom.

Mrs. Bissel's grating whisper came to me from where she cowered at the foot of the staircase. "What do you think, Daisy? Have you found something? Do you sense anything?"

Yes, indeedy, I sensed something, all right. I sensed that somebody was using Mrs. B's basement as a hideout, but darned if I knew who or why. "I am receiving certain vibrations," I told Mrs. Bissel cryptically. Ridiculous, but I didn't want to tell her about my other findings yet. For all I knew, they meant nothing.

"Oh, my goodness," she whispered as if in awe. I was used to this reaction to my occult gibberish.

When I exited the room, I saw her sitting on the bottom step of the staircase, her bulbous maroon breasts heaving in fear. She stared at me, chewing her lip, and giving every appearance of a woman in grave distress.

To ease her worries, I offered her one of my stock of gracious smiles. Gracious smiles, along with my wafting walk, were part of my act. "There is no danger now, Mrs. Bissel. You need fear nothing in the daylight." As for the rest of the time, darned if I could tell her anything at all.

"I'm so glad." She expelled a gusty sigh.

I puttered around in the basement for a while longer, searching for any sign other than the empty Franco-American spaghetti tin and the damp bowl that someone had been residing there. Don't ask me why I lifted the lid of the washing machine and peered inside, because I don't have an answer. All I know is that I did lift the lid, and I peered inside.

"Is your laundry done on one specific day of the week, Mrs. Bissel?"

"What? Laundry? Why, yes, the laundry is done on Monday. Cynthia Oversloot comes in to help Ginger every Monday."

"Ah. And is the dirty laundry kept somewhere in particular until Monday rolls around?"

"The dirty laundry? Why, yes. The maids throw it down the laundry chute, and it lands in a basket." She pointed to a big wicker basket set against the wall, above which a black hole loomed. "See? There's the basket and the chute."

I wafted over and saw that the basket held almost nothing, probably because today was Wednesday. "I see."

"Why? Have you found something?"

"No," I fibbed. "I just wondered. You say no one uses the washing machine except on Mondays?"

"No. I mean, yes. No one uses it except on Mondays. Not unless there's a special need. Say, if someone gets sick overnight or something."

"Ah." So why, then, was there a neatly folded sheet and blanket sitting in the washing machine? I didn't ask Mrs. Bissel, primarily because I was pretty sure she wouldn't have an answer for me. Also, if the sheet, blanket, damp water bowl, and spaghetti tin signified a mortal presence in her basement, and if I managed to get whoever it was to move out, I didn't want Mrs. Bissel to know it hadn't been a spirit. Or a ghost. I wanted to get paid, and I wanted to get paid in dachshunds.

Anyhow, I didn't know for sure that my surmise was correct. After searching for another few minutes, I decided I'd learned all I could learn from the empty basement. "I'll have to go home and meditate about this, Mrs. Bissel." I made sure I sounded extremely serious and mystical. "This is a knotty problem. I doubt that there will be an easy solution."

"I feared as much."

For so large a woman, she could move in a sprightly

manner when she chose. She popped up from the bottom step and charged up the staircase, heaving a huge breath of relief when she shoved the door open and escaped into the security of her kitchen. I wasn't far behind her. There's something about basements, even in the daytime, that makes me feel creepy, as if there might be ugly, hairy monsters lurking down there behind, say, the mangle, ready to grab me by the ankle, yank me downstairs, run my body through the wringer, and eat my liver for lunch.

When I stepped into the kitchen after Mrs. Bissel, I saw Mrs. Cummings, Ginger, and Susan Farley, the other housemaid, all huddled together at the sink and all gaping at us as if we'd just returned from beyond the grave itself.

Mrs. Cummings spoke first. "Wh-what did you find?"

"I'm not sure," I said. It almost wasn't a lie. Sure, I'd found an empty spaghetti can and a sheet and a blanket, but I had no idea what they meant, separately or together. I knew that's what Mrs. Cummings' question had meant, even if she hadn't expressed it exactly that way.

"Daisy says it's going to take a good deal of thought and meditation in order to discover the best way to deal with it," confided Mrs. Bissel, taking care to lock the door to the basement, as if a lock could keep a spirit (or ghost) confined. It seemed to me that she got along with her household staff almost as if they were family. I thought that was sweet.

"I hope you can meditate fast," Ginger said, sounding a speck tart. "Whatever's down there is scaring us all to flinders."

"Now, Ginger," said Mrs. Cummings. "Daisy will do her best."

"Of course, she will," affirmed Mrs. Bissel.

"Well," said Ginger, "better you than me, Daisy. I wouldn't go down into that basement alone to save myself."

Who said anything about me going down there by myself? I didn't ask the question, certain it would reflect poorly on my abilities to exorcise the demon below-stairs. Not that I had any such abilities, even it *was* a demon, which I doubted.

Rather, I chose to appear arcane and to speak in my best mediumistic voice. "The spirits can be difficult. Yet they may listen to reason from one who knows their ways."

After having a cup of tea and a piece of gingerbread, I left Mrs. Bissel's mansion, wondering how the devil I was supposed to get rid of whatever was living in her basement. I suppose I'd have to figure out who or what it was first, and then decide what to do.

I have a very good imagination, a characteristic I inherited from my father (my mother has no imagination at all). All the way home on the red car, I thought about Mrs. Bissel's basement's possibilities. First I pictured myself being attacked and brutalized by a huge, vicious escapee from some prison or other.

I didn't know if there were any prisons nearby, so when I'd wrestled that mental image into unlikeliness, I featured an escaped lunatic brutalizing me instead. Crazy people could be living anywhere. For all I knew, hundreds of families in Pasadena and Altadena kept their insane relations confined to attic rooms in their houses. Any of them might have escaped and might now be seeking shelter in Mrs. Bissel's basement, and might also object to my interference with their living arrangements.

That thought frightened me more than the notion of encountering a bear or a mountain lion, although I don't know why it should have. I suppose that in reality bears and lions are more dangerous even than lunatics.

At any rate, by the time I got home again, night had fallen, the weather was cold and windy, and I was thoroughly scared and out of sorts. It was all I could do to keep myself from running from Colorado Street to our cozy little house, but I didn't do it. I'm a Gumm, after all, and we Gumms are tough.

My mood didn't improve when I walked through the front door and saw we had company. This particular company wasn't the good kind. This wasn't a long-lost friend or a relative visiting from San Francisco and bearing gifts and candy. Nor was it Reverend Smith from our church, paying a social call on the family. It wasn't my pal Harold Kincaid dropping in to invite me to a premiere of one of the pictures he'd done the costuming for.

No. This company was nothing like that, more's the pity. When I entered our snug little bungalow that evening, I saw that Billy and Pa were playing gin rummy with Detective Samuel Rotondo, from the Pasadena Police Department.

Nuts, I thought. If my luck wasn't running true to form— that is to say, uniformly bad—I didn't know what was.

Three

Detective Sam Rotondo and I had met a few months earlier at Mrs. Kincaid's place, first when Stacy Kincaid, Mrs. Kincaid's awful daughter, had run amok, and later when Mr. Kincaid had stolen several thousand dollars' worth of bearer bonds and tried to hotfoot it out of the country. His plan hadn't succeeded, primarily because I had forced Sam to listen to my well-reasoned theories. He hadn't wanted to. He'd resisted my suggestions at every turning in the road. Eventually my theories had been proved absolutely right. He still hadn't gotten over it, either.

We didn't get along, Sam and I. It was my rotten luck that Billy and my own father, whom I'd always considered a true gem of a man until then, had decided they liked Sam a lot. I had once hoped that Billy's friendship would soften Sam's attitude toward me, but it hadn't happened.

Sam was always coming over to our house to play gin rummy with them and eat my aunt Vi's good cooking. I didn't think he deserved Aunt Vi's cooking any more than I thought he deserved Pa and Billy's friendship.

To be fair, I was glad for Billy's sake that he had a friend who treated him as if he wasn't a cripple. For my own sake, I wished Sam Rotondo would take a long walk off a short pier.

Sam's profession and mine were destined to collide,

no matter what. I'd known from the minute I met him that he had no use for fortune-tellers (because he'd told me so). When I'd explained that I wasn't a fortune-teller, but a spiritualist, he'd rolled his eyes. He and Billy were as one on the spiritualist issue, darn it. The fact that Pa liked him, too, made me feel left out and abused even in my own home.

Because I'd be slowly roasted over Mrs. Bissel's barbeque pit before I showed Billy how little I wanted Sam there, I sauntered over and surveyed the card table. "Who's winning?"

Billy grinned up at me. "Me."

It was an effort, but I grinned back. "Glad to hear it."

I know it sounds petty, but I resented the fact that Sam Rotondo, a man who didn't like me and whom I didn't like, was able to cheer Billy up when I couldn't. All I ever seemed to be able to do was irritate my husband. The sad, not to mention foolish, truth was that the situation made me want to cry *again*. I wondered if my monthly was due. I'm not a weepy person as a rule, and only get moody during that time of the month.

"Will you boys just look at my beautiful daughter," Pa said, winking at me. "That's a pretty dress, Daisy. Did you make it yourself?"

"Sure did, Pa. Thanks."

"You look like you've just been to a funeral."

I glared at Sam, from whose lips the above comment had issued, annoying but not surprising me. "Thank you."

"She's been up to Altadena," Billy told Sam. "She's turned into an exorcist. She's trying to get rid of a ghost in some rich lady's house."

"It's Mrs. Bissel's house. And it's not a ghost," I said, pushing the words through clenched teeth.

"What is it?"

"I don't know yet."

"Good God," said Sam.

He laughed. So did Billy and Pa. I wanted to conk

someone over the head—maybe three someones. Instead, I said sweetly, "I'll go change clothes. Have you fellows had supper?"

"We're waiting for your aunt," said Pa. "She called to say she's bringing leftovers from Mrs. Kincaid's house."

This news cheered me up. Every time Aunt Vi cooked, no matter where she did it, we ate well. "Does she know there's an extra person to feed?" I shot another good glare at Sam. He wasn't looking at me, which figured, not that my glares ever seemed to affect him to the least degree. He might as well have had elephant hide, his skin was so thick.

"Pa told her," Billy supplied. Ever since his own parents died during the influenza pandemic of 1918–1919, he'd called my father "Pa."

I guessed that left nothing more for me to do, so I took myself off. I stopped to chat with Ma, who was in the kitchen looking confused as she gazed at a recipe card. "What's up, Ma?"

"I don't understand this." She pointed at the recipe card. It was a good thing Aunt Vi lived with us, because neither Ma nor I could cook worth beans. "I was trying to make a raisin pie using this recipe that Vi copied out of the last issue of *Good Housekeeping*, but I don't understand it. What does a capital T mean?"

I looked at the card. "Um . . . I don't know. Teaspoon?"

"I think that's a small t-s-p."

"Oh. Tablespoon?"

"I think that's a capital T-b-s-p."

"Oh." I read the rest of the recipe. "Sorry, Ma. Beats me. The pie sounds good, though. Did you have to buy a lemon?" The recipe called for a cup of lemon juice and a teaspoonful of lemon rind.

"No. Mrs. Longnecker gave me a lemon from her tree."

"Ah. I'm surprised she had any left."

We both stared at the recipe card for a couple of moments, neither of us knowing what the heck a capital T stood for.

At last Ma spoke. "Well, I guess I'll put in a tablespoon-full of baking powder and see what happens."

"Sounds logical to me." It sounded as if the pie filling was going to take the lid off the oven, actually, but I was too depressed in spirits to question Ma's judgment on the recipe issue, especially since I knew my own was just as bad, or worse. All I wanted to do was change into something comfortable, crawl into bed, and pull the covers over my head. But such a blessed escape was not in the cards for me that evening.

Sometimes I got to wondering if Billy was right about me. Maybe what I did for a living really was evil and wicked. I know for absolute certain that I wished I *could* communicate with spirits and read the future in the tarot cards or communicate with Rolly through the Ouija board. I'd have liked to know if life was ever going to get better for Billy and me.

Of course, if the spirits, the cards, and Rolly all told me I was doomed to remain unhappily married to Billy for as long as I lived, I don't know what I'd have done about it. Resigned myself to a miserable future, I suppose.

Nuts. There was no quick answer to my problems. I decided to make the best of them, at least for the evening. Then I told myself I was being stupid, and that it didn't matter what I decided or didn't decide; my circumstances were what they were, and whatever was destined to happen would happen.

Brother. Sometimes I wondered if my job wasn't getting under my skin a bit too much.

I was in a truly blue mood when I hung up my pretty black dress, eyed the puppy-claw snag with disfavor, put my hat away, rolled down my stockings, stowed my shoes, threw on my pink-and-white-checked housedress, stuffed my feet into a pair of floppy slippers, and went back to the kitchen. The pie was in the oven, and I hoped the capital T had meant "tablespoon," but it didn't matter a whole lot. If the worst thing to happen in the world was a bad pie, life would be good.

Aunt Vi had just arrived with jars and plates of food, so I got to help her unload. The thought of food made my stomach growl, and I realized I'd forgotten to eat lunch, which tells you what kind of state I was in, because I *never* forget to eat. Virtually never. Clearly, I'd forgotten that day.

"Go on with you, Daisy," Vi said. "You've been working all day, too. Go set the table while your mother and I get the food heated."

Aunt Vi was trying to be nice. Vi knew, and Ma knew, that the cooking gene had missed me. I could boil a fair pot of water, but that was about it as far as my culinary talents went. Because of my lousy mood, I felt as if she were kicking me out of her kitchen because I was no good. Telling myself not to be an idiot, I said, "Okay," and went to the dining room.

Billy rolled in as I was laying out the silverware. I glanced over at him and produced a smile from a reserve stock I kept for such occasions. I didn't feel like smiling. I still felt like crying. "How much did you win, sweetie?"

"Fifteen cents." Billy grinned at me.

"Wow. Don't spend it all in one place."

"I won't. I'm adding it to the fortune I've already won from Sam."

The only good thing about this day so far was that Sam Rotondo was apparently a very bad gin rummy player and Billy kept winning pennies from him. I was pretty sure Sam wasn't letting him win, either, because Billy wouldn't have stood for that.

"I think your husband cheats," came a grumbly voice from the living room.

When I glanced over Billy's head and into the living room, I saw Sam and my father folding up the card table and putting the cards away. I'm sure Sam was joking, but I took instant exception anyway, which again shows what kind of humor I was in. "My Billy would never cheat," I said coldly.

"Heck, I don't *have* to cheat when I'm playing with Sam," Billy added, laughing.

I scolded myself for being a drip. I ought to be grateful to Sam for taking Billy away from his pain and misery for a few hours a week. I tried to produce a smile, failed, and said, "There you go," which meant nothing.

Pa and Sam trooped into the dining room just as I'd laid out the last plate. I was reaching for glasses when I felt a large presence behind me.

"Here, Mrs. Majesty, allow me."

I felt stupid when Sam's voice, so close at my back, made me jump. I pretended to be simply moving out of his way. "Thanks."

My Billy was a tall man when he stood up, which wasn't often because he was so badly crippled. He'd always been lean and lanky, though, and had never, even when he'd been in perfect health, made me feel small.

Sam Rotondo was big. He was not only tall, but much more heavily built than my Billy. He made me feel small no matter where he was in relationship to my shortish self. That day, I resented his bigness almost as much as I resented Vi for kicking me out of the kitchen, and chalked up another score for the bad guys.

I'm usually a light-hearted, optimistic person. Honest Injun, I am. It's only that life had been batting me around fairly savagely in recent weeks that I was in such sorry shape that day. I suppressed a powerful urge to kick Sam Rotondo in his big, hairy shins, and retreated to the table, where I sat and awaited events. If nobody needed me, fine. I'd just stay out of the way.

"What are you doing, Detective Rotondo?" Ma. Glancing askance from Sam to me. "I thought you were setting the table, Daisy."

I felt my mouth pinch into a wrinkled bud of its normally serenely shaped self. "The good detective took over for me."

"Oh." Ma looked blank for a second, shrugged, and set a steaming bowl on the table.

Sniffing, I detected the aroma of mashed potatoes. I love potatoes. Sometimes, when I'm feeling low or sick, I'll even make potato soup. I'm sure there's a better recipe somewhere, but my kind of potato soup only requires potatoes, onions, water, salt, pepper, butter, and milk. Not even I could mess up potato soup. Well, except for the one time I forgot about it, and it burned, and we had to throw the pot away because we couldn't get the burned parts scraped off its sides and bottom.

Aunt Vi appeared at the dining room door with another platter. She smiled broadly. "Roast pork. I know that's Billy's favorite."

"Anything you cook is my favorite, Vi," said my darling Billy. See? He was still my darling Billy, in spite of our differences.

Roast pork was my favorite, too, but obviously nobody cared about me.

As soon as *that* thought floated through my head, I knew I had to do something, and fast, to repair my sense of proportion, not to mention my mood. In an attempt to accomplish this goal, I smiled at my aunt. "I *love* roast pork, Vi. It's my favorite, too. Along with your pot roast, roast lamb, and various other dishes, especially some of the ones with chicken."

"Go along with you, Daisy. I can't understand why you're not as plump as I am, the way you like to eat."

I shrugged. "I'm not going to get fat as long as I keep forgetting to eat lunch, I guess."

Both Aunt Vi and Ma turned to stare at me. "Are you

sick?" Ma rushed over and put a palm against my forehead. "You don't feel hot."

"I'm not sick." This was embarrassing. "I just forgot to eat lunch, is all. It's because I got a call from Mrs. Bissel and went to her place before lunch. Once I got there, I got busy and forgot all about food. Anyhow, she fed me a piece of gingerbread."

"I've never understood how people can forget to eat," said Pa musingly. "You'd never catch *me* forgetting food."

One of Pa's troubles, in fact, according to Dr. Benjamin, was that he enjoyed his food too much. He'd recently suffered a small heart attack, and we all worried about him. All of us except Ma tried not to bother him with comments about food, though. He knew what he was supposed to eat and what he wasn't, and if he chose to eat it anyway, no matter how much we wished he wouldn't, we didn't complain. Besides, Ma complained enough for all of us.

Ma said, "Pish-tosh, Joe. You know you're supposed to be cutting down."

See what I mean?

"I know, I know," said Pa. He didn't mind about Ma pestering him. I guess he figured it was part of her job as his wife. "But I still never forget to eat."

"Me, neither," said Sam.

I could believe it. Sam Rotondo wasn't fat, but he was perhaps the least little bit on the hefty side. I bit my tongue to keep myself from saying something unkind.

"Of course," Sam continued, smiling winningly at Aunt Vi, "I don't usually get to eat such delicious meals."

"Aunt Vi's the best cook in Pasadena," said Billy matter-of-factly.

"In the United States," I amended. For the life of me, I couldn't make myself smile at Sam. I have a feeling the look I gave him was more like a glower or a grimace, because he appeared slightly startled. To heck with him.

The roast pork was delicious, as were the mashed potatoes and gravy, green beans, applesauce, and salad. Ma's pie turned out okay, too, which was a surprise to me. I think Ma was a little surprised herself. Like I said, neither one of us could hold a candle to Vi when it came to cooking.

Conversation around the table was lively. Billy asked me about Mrs. Bissel's spirit (or ghost), and I told everyone my suspicions about stray cats or mice. I left out the spaghetti tin and the sheet, blanket, and wet bowl. I also left out my fears about bears, lions, lunatics, and escaped criminals, although I did ask Sam if he knew of any escapees who might live in the Pasadena area. He grinned at me.

"Not that I know of." He shoveled another bite of pie into his mouth. "If we knew where an escapee was living, he wouldn't be an escapee for long."

Billy and Pa laughed.

"Good." His news didn't make me feel appreciably better, although it was rather comforting to know I was safe from any known criminals. Then again, the only way a body becomes a known criminal is to be nabbed and jailed. Who knew how many unknown villains were skulking about Mrs. Bissel's neighborhood? It was a good neighborhood and full of rich people and mansions, but that's the logical place for a criminal bent upon theft or worse to hang out, isn't it?

"But," Billy said, grinning, "one of Pasadena's finest families has misplaced a daughter."

We all stopped chewing and gazed at Billy. "I beg your pardon?" I didn't really want any raisin pie, which is a little rich for me. I wanted more roast pork—so I had seconds.

"It's true," said Sam. He was grinning, too. He passed a plate full of pie to Billy.

I didn't think losing a daughter was anything to grin about, although I didn't get nasty yet. I'd learned that a hasty temper often led to embarrassment, and I didn't want to jump the gun. Besides, I figured they were teasing me in an attempt to make me get mad and then feel foolish. I resented that. Lately, I resented everything.

"There's got to be more to the story than that," I said. Then, to make sure I didn't holler at Sam for being snide and uncaring, I jammed more roast pork and gravy into my mouth and chewed viciously.

"There is," said Billy. "But Sam had better tell you about it. I can't remember it all."

"My goodness," said Ma, fascinated. "How can a family misplace a daughter? I'm sure I never misplaced Daisy or Walter or Daphne." Walter and Daphne are my siblings. They were both married and rearing their own families in 1920. "Children are too important to misplace."

Have I mentioned my mother's lack of imagination? She also doesn't have much of a sense of humor. Although she's probably the sweetest, nicest human being in the entire world, she can't appreciate nonsense the way Pa and Aunt Vi and I can. "I think Sam was joking, Ma," I told her gently.

"Oh." She looked blankly from Billy to Sam to Pa, who winked at her. She colored slightly.

This exchange between my parents made me want to cry some more. Shoot. I knew I was in bad shape when I got mushy and sentimental because my parents loved each other.

"I didn't mean to be flippant, Mrs. Gumm," Sam said, sounding chastened, although I didn't believe it. Sam Rotondo didn't give a rap about other people's feelings. Except maybe Billy's. I know for a certified fact that he never once had a thought to spare for my own personal feelings.

I said, "Hmmm," and ate more pork. I was making up for my missed lunch and then some. "I thought you coppers weren't supposed to talk about your cases until they were solved." I'd gleaned this information from the detective novels I loved to read.

"That's true, for the most part," said Sam after swallowing a bite of pie. "This time, the entire city of Pasadena's going to know about it tomorrow, because the family's placing an item in the newspapers."

"My goodness." I shoveled up more mashed potatoes and gravy, interested in spite of myself. I think I even forgot to frown at Sam.

He turned toward me. "Do you know a family named Wagner, Mrs. Majesty? Dr. and Mrs. Everhard Wagner?"

I swallowed my potatoes, surprised. "The Wagners? Sure, I know them . . . kind of. Well, I don't really *know* them. They've attended parties at Mrs. Kincaid's house when I've been conducting séances. Aren't their children all grown up? Don't tell me one of them is missing."

"I can't not tell you that, because one of them *is* missing."

"Good grief." I was so shocked, I forgot to take another bite of my second helping of everything. "Which one?"

"Their youngest daughter, Marianne."

"How awful." Ma put her napkin to her lips, and for a minute I was afraid she might burst into tears. She might not have any imagination or a sense of humor, but she was a gracious, sensitive woman, and she hated to hear about stuff like this.

"Do they have any idea what happened to her?" I tried to place Marianne, but she wouldn't come into focus in my brain.

Dr. Wagner, whom I didn't like upon our first meeting because he was pompous, supercilious, and domineering, had definitely been the head of his household. Mrs. Wagner was your average doormat. She acted as though she was scared of her husband, which seemed sensible, actually. I know I wouldn't want to get on the doctor's bad side, and I suspected his bad side was his largest.

I sort of began to remember Marianne, although from what I recalled of her, she was a silent, shrinking thing who was forever trying to fade into the wallpaper. Her brothers were dreadful young men. I got the feeling they'd been taught bullying techniques from their father, and had been good pupils. None of the Wagners were exactly my cup of tea.

After eating another bite of pie, Sam resumed his story. "At first, they thought she might have been kidnapped for ransom."

"Good heavens!" Now it was Aunt Vi who looked shocked and worried.

"But," Sam continued, "no ransom note has been received. Therefore, we've pretty much ruled out kidnapping for ransom. That's why they're placing a notice in the papers."

"How long has she been missing?" I wanted to know.

"A little over two weeks."

"Two *weeks?* And they're only just now trying to find her?"

"They've been trying to find her ever since she failed to return home from the library one evening." Sam gave me a fair imitation of one of Dr. Wagner's supercilious sneers. "As I said, at first they feared she'd been kidnapped for ransom and they didn't want to advertise her absence or let the presumed kidnappers know they'd contacted the police department. The police have been searching for her ever since her disappearance was reported."

"But wait a minute here," I said, deciding to ignore his sneer, since I had a feeling no one else at the table would deem it supercilious, I being the only one present who considered Sam a fiend. "This doesn't make any sense to me. Marianne Wagner is a rich girl. Rich girls don't disappear for no reason. I think the ransom idea is the only one that makes any sense. Surely she couldn't just vanish off the face of the earth on purpose."

Sam shrugged and scraped up the last of the pie filling on his plate with his fork. "She seems to have done exactly that, although I'm not sure about the *on purpose* part."

"Hmmm." Gee, I wasn't even hungry anymore, which demonstrates how good a juicy bit of gossip is for one's various pangs. The pork roast probably helped, too.

Silence settled over the table, the only noise being the soft chewing and swallowing sounds coming from some of us. After a moment, Sam sat back in his chair and looked my way again, unconsciously patting his stomach. "How much do you know about the Wagners, Mrs. Majesty? If I'd known you were familiar with them, I'd have asked you sooner."

"I don't know much." Concentrating, I tried to recollect everything I knew or had ever heard about the family. "I can't imagine Marianne running away from home. Now, if it were Stacy Kincaid . . ."

"But it isn't," said Sam, and he added, "Unfortunately."

"Right," I said. "That is too bad."

Everyone at the table knew that Mrs. Kincaid's daughter Stacy was a stinker. In contrast, Stacy's brother Harold and I had become close friends since Mr. Kincaid took it on the lam with a pile of bearer bonds. Billy didn't like my friendship with Harold, naturally. He didn't like anything I did. But it was my opinion that Billy ought to be glad Harold wasn't one of your so-called "normal" men.

In fact, Harold was a homosexual. That had shocked me at first, but now I appreciated Harold a lot. It was wonderful to be able to talk to a man I could trust in every way. Billy, Sam, and all the other "normal" men I knew called men like Harold "faggots." Don't ask me why.

But enough about the Kincaids. After another moment of thought, I went on to say, "I get the feeling Dr. Wagner is a cruel lout. Maybe a wife-beater."

"Good heavens!" Ma's eyes popped open wide.

In fact, everyone's eyes widened as they stared at me. Sam only frowned, which was typical. "What do you mean, a wife-beater?"

I shrugged. "He seems to have his wife in a pucker all the time, and his kids walk on eggshells around him. They all seem to be trying to stay out of his way and not make him mad. Mrs. Wagner is the most unmitigated sissy I've ever met. And then there are those sons of theirs." I grimaced as I contemplated the two Wagner boys. "Both of them are just like he is: stuck-up, condescending, spiteful, and mean."

"That's quite a catalog of sins, Mrs. Majesty. Would you care to elaborate? Let's see now. The sons are . . . what are their names?"

"Gaylord and Vincent," I supplied. "They're both terrible boys. Or men, I guess they are now. They remind me of a couple of characters out of that F. Scott Fitzgerald novel. You know, they're bored with the world, drink too much, play fast and loose with women—"

"Daisy!" Ma cried.

Darn it. I hadn't meant to say that in front of my mother, even though it was the absolute truth. I sighed and offered an elucidation I thought the whole family— and perhaps even Sam—could understand. "Do you remember a few months ago when I told you that Mrs. Kincaid's husband was trying to take advantage of Edie?" Edie Applewood, formerly Edie Marsh, worked as a housemaid in Mrs. Kincaid's mansion. Mrs. Kincaid's louse of a husband had pestered her for months before his nefarious career was nipped in the bud, thanks in part to yours truly.

Ma pressed a hand over her mouth and gasped.

Aunt Vi said, "Good Lord."

Pa said, "In other words, they're spoiled rich boys playing at being part of the 'lost generation' and preying on girls who have to work for a living?"

"Exactly." I beamed at Pa, who understood everything.

"In other words, they're scoundrels, is what you mean," Billy muttered. Squinting at me in a way I'd come to recognize and dread, he said, "Has either one of them ever bothered you, Daisy? Because if they have—"

"No!" I cried, not wanting Billy to threaten the Wagner boys, even from so removed a spot as our own dining room. Before the war, I'd have bet money that Billy could have licked both of the Wagner brothers, together or separately, but not anymore. Now I just wanted my husband to keep himself safe at home. "I wouldn't stand for it if they tried. I think they only go after women who can't defend themselves for fear of being fired from their jobs." I sniffed to let the assembled eaters know what I thought of *that* state of affairs.

"How do you know this?" Sam asked, his black eyebrows slanting into a V over his eyes.

"I talk to the servants, detective. They're not shy about sharing their opinions of people, believe me. I've heard things about the Wagner boys."

Sam sighed. "You're probably right."

"I know I'm right, and I suspect they take after their old man. Children learn to emulate their parents, don't forget. Dr. Wagner's a pompous blowhard who thinks he's clever and desirable because he's got lots of money. I wouldn't trust him alone in a room with a defenseless female."

"Well, that lets you out," said Sam. "I've never met a less defenseless female in my life than you, Mrs. Majesty."

"Amen," muttered Billy.

"That's my girl," said Pa.

"You're probably right," said Vi.

Ma only looked confused.

I said nothing, but hoped my killing look would teach Sam a lesson in manners. I should have known better.

"So, I take it you don't like Dr. Wagner," he said.

"Perceptive of you, Detective Rotondo. I think the man's an ass."

"Daisy!"

"Sorry, Ma, but he's conceited and nasty, and I wouldn't trust him to doctor my dog. If I had a dog. I'll bet he kicks dogs for fun." I thought about Dr. Wagner for another second or two and had a sudden inspiration. "In fact, it wouldn't surprise me if you found out that poor Marianne riled him one day, and he beat her to death in a fit of pique."

Pa's eyebrows arched so high, they almost got lost in his hairline. "I can't imagine a father doing such a thing to a daughter. I know I had to whip Walter a couple of times when he was growing up, but I'd never actually *beat* a child, male or female."

Looking grim, Sam said, "I wish all fathers were like you, Joe. Unfortunately, they aren't." He swiveled his head in my direction again. "But I can't feature a prominent doctor killing his own daughter, Mrs. Majesty."

"So maybe Gaylord or Vincent did her in," I offered, trying to be helpful.

Sam shook his head and smiled faintly. "I think your imagination is running wild again."

"What do you mean *again?*"

"Er . . . nothing."

Like heck. "Huh." Turning to my aunt, I said, "May I please have a piece of pie now?"

"Of course, dear." Aunt Vi handed me a plate with a thick slice of Ma's pie on it.

"Thanks." Eyeing my pie doubtfully, I said, "I think I've made up for my missed lunch."

"I think so, too." Pa laughed, which made Billy grin, which pleased me, because I hadn't really meant to horrify my family by voicing my suspicions about Dr. Wagner.

That did not, however, negate the fact that I thought Sam and his police cronies should start searching the doctor's gardens for freshly turned earth. It wouldn't have surprised me if they'd found poor Marianne's mutilated corpse planted behind the dahlias.

Four

Sam left our house shortly after dinner. I was in the kitchen helping Ma and Aunt Vi clean up, so I didn't see him go.

I'd have liked to have spoken with him alone. Even though the thought made my stomach ache (unless that was my huge dinner), I'd have told him a few more little things I'd heard about Dr. Wagner. Then I'd have made him promise to search the bad doctor's gardens and trash receptacles. Not to mention the foothills. Dr. Wagner wouldn't have been the first crazed murderer to throw a body away in the foothills as if it were no more than trash. Terrible, but true.

The wretched detective probably wouldn't have listened to me. He hadn't listened to me during the Kincaid affair, either, even though my suggestions had eventually been followed, resulting in the capture and arrest of Mr. Kincaid.

As I dried plates, I must have scowled, because Aunt Vi noticed my expression. "Good heavens, Daisy, what are you frowning about?"

"What?" I glanced from the plate to Aunt Vi. "Oh. Sorry, Vi. I was thinking about Marianne Wagner. I hope she turns up. But . . . after two weeks?" I shook my head. "I don't know. It seems to me that if she was still alive, they'd have found her by this time."

Ma sighed. "I'm afraid you might be right, Daisy.

What a tragedy it would be to lose a child." She glanced quickly at Vi, whose son Paul had been killed in the war. "Oh, Vi, I'm sorry. I didn't mean . . ."

But Aunt Vi only smiled sadly. "It's all right, Peg. I know what you mean. It is a tragedy, but at least my Paul volunteered to fight for his country. That poor Wagner girl didn't."

"I can't imagine Marianne volunteering for anything, much less running away from home, although I wouldn't blame her if she did."

"She's shy?" Ma glanced at me, her eyebrows lifted.

"I always got the impression that she's scared to death of her old man. I guess that's not exactly shy, but it was as if she didn't dare move without his permission, just like his wife. Now if it were Stacy Kincaid who'd disappeared, that would be something else. I can definitely imagine Stacy running away from home, probably with a man."

"Daisy!"

Shoot. I'd shocked my mother again. I couldn't win that night, no matter what I said. "Sorry, Ma, but it really wouldn't surprise me if Stacy ran off. Not Marianne, though. She's too . . . too . . . I don't know. Afraid of everything, I guess."

Aunt Vi tutted sympathetically. "Poor dear thing." Aunt Vi was a dear thing herself, and always compassionate regarding other people's problems.

"I hope some dangerous lunatic didn't get hold of her," I said, thinking of a few of the crime novels I'd read. My mother and my aunt both turned to stare at me in horror, and I became defensive. "Things like that happen, you know. Mashers and kidnappers and so forth *do* nab young women from time to time. People like that surely must be crazy or they wouldn't do such things, but from what I've read, they don't often look it. Crazy, I mean."

"Daisy! For heaven's sake!"

The fact that I'd managed to shock my poor mother three or four times in a single evening demonstrates better than anything else how black my mood was. I usually tried to spare Ma's sensibilities. That evening, it was like a demon had taken possession of my brain. Or maybe just my tongue. I snapped, "They exist, Ma. Ravishers of young women and kidnappers and even child murderers. You might not read about the cases in the *Pasadena Star News* or the *Evening Herald*, but that doesn't mean horrors like that don't happen."

"Good heavens." Ma clutched the back of a chair, presumably because she felt faint. I hadn't meant to stun her so badly. It irked me that she didn't share what I considered to be my reasonable concerns regarding Marianne Wagner's disappearance and possible explanations for it.

"Whether they happen or not, we don't need to chat about them at the dinner table or while washing dishes, Daisy Majesty."

Aunt Vi sounded as stern as she was able. She was a firmer disciplinarian than my mother, but that didn't mean much. Her asperity in this instance annoyed me. Darn it, it wasn't *my* fault the world contained demented people who thought it was a good idea to snatch women and assault and murder them.

I wanted to slam my dish towel on the rack and stomp off, then throw myself on my bed, have a temper tantrum, and cry for an hour or two. Fortunately, even *I* could recognize such an urge as unusual and unproductive, and I stopped myself before I could explode. I shook my head hard in an effort to loosen my bad mood from its moorings. As I might have expected, given the rest of my evening, shaking didn't help.

That being the case, and hoping to preserve peace in the family, I said stiffly, "I'm sorry, Vi. You're right. I beg your pardon." I didn't want to apologize. I wanted these two women, who were the most important females in my life, to understand and value my point of view. Fat chance.

Vi patted me on the back with a wet, soapy hand. "Fudge, Daisy, don't worry. I know you have too many burdens to bear. I don't blame you for being short-tempered sometimes."

"Of course, dear." Ma gazed thoughtfully at the cup she was drying. "But I *do* wonder what has happened to the poor Wagner girl. Even if you don't care for her father, her parents must be desperately worried about her."

"I'm sure her mother's worried, anyhow." I didn't reiterate my suspicions of Dr. Wagner, because I didn't need another lecture from Vi.

Ma and Aunt Vi glanced at me as if they thought I was being unreasonable, but I knew better. Some angel of sanity seized me, thank God, and I didn't say so.

After I'd put away the last dish, I felt as though I'd been whipped, so I wandered, yawning, into the living room, where Pa and Billy were chatting. As I walked over to my husband, my usual wish that he was still a whole man flitted through my head. Stupid head. Stupid thought.

"Ready for bed, Billy? I'm bushed."

He glanced up at me. "Rough work getting rid of ghosts, is it?"

Pa chuckled.

I gazed suspiciously at my husband. He didn't look as if he was trying to start an argument, so I didn't blow up. "Yeah. But I think skipping lunch is what really made me tired."

"Let's go to bed then, sweetheart. Good night, Pa."

I bent and kissed my father. He looked more wan and pasty-faced than usual that evening. I feared he'd overtaxed himself during the day. "You'd better stay home and rest tomorrow, Pa. You know what Dr. Benjamin said."

Dr. Benjamin had told my father to stop eating so much, give up cigars, and rest as much as he could. Pa hadn't done any of those things, although I didn't smell any traces of cigar smoke lingering on his clothing that night.

"Pooh," said Pa, chuckling some more. "I want to enjoy what life I have left to me, Daisy. No sense sitting around, waiting for the Grim Reaper to pay me a call. I'd rather go out and meet him head-on."

I think I gawked at him. I'd never heard Pa talk about dying before, and it scared me. "Nuts," I said. "You're going to outlast us all."

"You're certain to outlast me, at any rate."

I turned my gawk upon Billy, who had a lopsided, cynical grin on his face. "Billy! Don't talk like that."

He took my hand. "Sorry, sweetheart." After a pause, during which I could swear I could see the tension crackling like electricity in the air around us, he said, "Would you really miss me if I died, Daisy?"

I couldn't help it. My eyes filled with tears, and I felt a couple of them slide down my cheeks. It had been a truly ghastly day, and this was no way to end it. "How can you even ask me that, Billy?" To my deep chagrin, my voice quivered. I absolutely *hate* acting like an emotional woman, even though I am one, albeit not often.

He shrugged. "I don't know. Seems like all we do is fight lately."

This was, sad to say, all too true. "That's only because you don't like what I do for a living."

Pa, who didn't care for strife in any form, even the mild sort Billy and I were displaying, yawned theatrically and rose from his chair. "Think I'll turn in now. As you just said, Daisy, Doc Benjamin told me to get lots of rest."

God bless my father. His diversion worked. Billy chuckled. "Since when have you done what the doctor tells you to do?"

Pa winked at the both of us. "Since it serves my purpose in this instance." He left us alone in the living room, and I heard him say something to Ma in the kitchen. After supper, she and Vi always sat at the kitchen table for a cup of tea and a gossip session.

"Are you really ready to go to bed, Billy?" I decided not to resurrect the topic we'd been discussing before Pa left us. It was too touchy a one, and I wasn't up to another fight with him. "You don't have to retire just because I'm dead-beat."

"I guess I'm ready."

"I'll push you to the bedroom."

Normally Billy didn't like people pushing his chair for him. The chair was one of those newfangled ones with wheels so big, the person sitting in it could propel himself around. But Billy didn't object when I occasionally pushed him on walks. That night he didn't object, either.

We said good night to Ma and Aunt Vi as we rolled through the kitchen to our bedroom, which was directly off the kitchen. Our bungalow had two nice, private rooms upstairs that would have been swell for a young married couple to live in. Since Billy couldn't climb the stairs, Aunt Vi used them.

Pa had built us a sun porch, or deck, outside our bedroom, and on fine nights Billy and I would sit out there and chat or just watch the stars. On that bleak November night, it was too darned cold to go outdoors so I shut our bedroom door to get some privacy. I knew that Ma and Aunt Vi would take their tea into the living room because that's what they always did, out of consideration for Billy and me.

I had lots of reasons to be thankful for my family. Ma and Pa and Aunt Vi were three of the best, most praiseworthy people in the universe. The three of them almost made up for the reasons I had to wonder why God had played Billy and me such a dirty trick.

But that was nonsense. Even in my foul mood that night, I recognized nonsense when I thought it. I firmly believed then, and I still believe, that God endowed human beings with free will and the brains to use it wisely if they chose. Therefore, I don't really believe it was God's fault the wretched Kaiser had decided to use the gifts God had given him for a wicked purpose. It was our bum luck that Billy had been caught in the Kaiser's evil scheme. And if mustard gas isn't evil, I don't know what is.

I helped Billy change into the pajamas I'd given him for his birthday the summer before. He hated night-shirts, since they made him feel even less like a man than he already did. After changing into my nightgown, I climbed into bed after him. He snuggled close to me and wrapped me in his arms, and as much as I hate to admit it, I cried again. It had to be time for my monthly, because that was the only time I became at all emotional. Thank heaven, Billy didn't notice my tears.

It rained the next day. As I stared out our bedroom window at the water pelting down from the sky, I decided it was just as well. It was much easier to abide a filthy mood if the weather cooperated. Heck, if the sun had shone down upon our little place in the world that morning, I might have cheered up a little. And that would never do.

Every once in a while, I got to feeling cynical. That morning was one of those whiles.

"At least the rain will keep Pa indoors," I muttered to Billy as I hung up my nightgown and tried to decide what to wear. A crown of thorns seemed appropriate, but there wasn't one in any of my hatboxes.

"I doubt it." Billy was already dressed.

For some reason, his being dressed encouraged me slightly. I entertained the perhaps foolish hope that as long as he continued to get up and dress in a shirt, collar, tie, jacket, and trousers every day, all was not lost.

I'd read about men who became so down in the dumps, they wore their nightshirts and robes all day and all night, no matter what. While I knew there was no cure for Billy's ailments, as long as he cared enough about life to look as spiffy as he could, there might exist the chance of a mental recovery, if not a physical one.

Also, the fact that he'd dressed before me that morning meant that his pain wasn't so bad that he'd had to struggle through the agony of moving his ruined legs before getting out of bed. This wasn't as heartening as it might seem, since it probably meant he'd had to get up in the middle of the night and take a dose of the morphine syrup he got from Doc Benjamin.

Billy's morphine use had increased during the past year. I feared he'd become addicted to the drug, if he wasn't already. But he needed relief from his pain, and morphine gave it to him. Therefore, I tried not to worry too much. Even though it was stupid and fruitless, I couldn't stop wishing there was another answer to Billy's pain. But I feared that as long as he still lived, there wasn't.

At least he hadn't awakened in the night crying out, thinking he was still in a foxhole in France and being shot at by the kaiser's army. I've read that terrible nightmares are another symptom of shell shock. It seemed to me that Billy had enough to bear without nightmares, but nobody'd asked me.

Mrs. Bissel called bright and early that morning, before I'd donned more than my combination underwear. I threw on a robe and dashed to the kitchen, hoping I'd beat our other party-line friends (I use the term loosely) to the telephone. I should have known better. Mrs. Barrow had the fastest pick-up in the West. I swear, the woman sat next to her telephone twenty-four hours every day, just waiting for the phone to ring so she could eavesdrop.

After I'd shooed her and a couple of other people off

the wire, Mrs. Bissel asked breathlessly, "Did you determine anything during your meditations, Daisy?"

Gosh, I'd forgotten all about telling her I'd meditate on the matter of her haunted basement. Not that I ever meditated on anything, but I might at least have done some hard thinking about her problem and come up with a plan of action. But lack of thought had never stopped me before, and it didn't stop me then.

Rather than flat-out lying to her, I said, "I need to visit your home again, Mrs. Bissel. The spirits can be elusive." And I could be forgetful.

"Of course, of course. I expected you to come again today."

The chorus of houndish woofs in the background made me smile, which made me perk up slightly. Until I looked out the kitchen window and saw the rain again. Thanks to heavy winds, the torrent's downward path had been pushed sideways. It was darned hear horizontal at the moment.

I sighed, wondering if the Model T would make it up the hill. Then again, why bother with the automobile? It wasn't a closed-in machine; I'd probably drown if I tried to drive it all that way in this hideous rain. I knew from experience that the Model T didn't like rain any more than it liked hills, and I'd have to drive on at least one unpaved street. Asking it to tackle rain, hills, and mud together might prove fatal to the motorcar, if not my humble self.

Perhaps Brownie could take me in the pony cart. I could rig up some sort of cover for it. Maybe. Then again, Brownie was a recalcitrant beast at the best of times. I wouldn't put it past him to sit down in the middle of Lake Avenue and refuse to move at all if I asked him to pull me uphill in a storm.

It would be better to take a red car. At least the cars weren't completely open to the elements, and if I took Pa's big umbrella, I might stay moderately dry, except for my feet, but I could wear rubber boots. They weren't exactly fashionable, but sometimes elegance had to bow to practicality. And, as an added benefit, I wouldn't have to crank up the Ford and pray it would start, or coax a balky Brownie to do his duty and pull the pony cart. The red cars ran up and down the various hills in Pasadena and Altadena on their little tracks, and all I had to do was hand the driver a nickel to avail myself of their services.

Mrs. Bissel must have sensed my thoughts, because she said, "I'll have Henry run down and pick you up in the Daimler. I don't want you having to walk in this terrible weather."

"Thank you. That would be very good of you, Mrs. Bissel."

"Nonsense. I do so appreciate what you're doing for me, Daisy."

What I was doing for her was, so far, absolutely nothing, but I didn't point it out to her. Nor did I reiterate that I wasn't an exorcist. I'd learned long since that people believed what they wanted to believe. If Mrs. Bissel wanted to believe that I could help her rid her home of a spirit (or ghost), so be it.

Her call made my choice of costuming for the day easier. I put on one of my spiritualist dresses, a dark blue gabardine number that had white trim around the collar, cuffs, and belt, and had a hem that ended a tasteful six inches above my ankles. A dark blue hat, black stockings (in those days, one wore black or white stockings, unless one wanted to scandalize everyone, and I definitely didn't want to do that), and black shoes. A black handbag completed my ensemble, and I'd wear my good black woolen coat. Another funereal ensemble, and appropriate to the weather, my mood, and my profession.

By the time I was dressed, Billy had made himself some toast and was eating breakfast with Pa in the kitchen. Pa looked up from the newspaper he'd been reading and smiled at me. "You're looking very nice today, Daisy."

"Thanks, Pa." I smiled at him and at Billy, who didn't smile back. I gave a hefty internal sigh, and waited for him to say something rotten to start my day right.

He surprised me. "You look great, Daisy." He gave me a sad grin that made my heart ache.

My poor heart took more abuse than any such organ ought to be forced to take. Which didn't matter any more that morning than it ever had. "Thanks. It's nice to know the men in my life appreciate me."

Pa appreciated me. Billy didn't. I didn't say so. Nevertheless, I twirled in front of them as if I were a model at Nash's Department Store, walking down that runway-thing they put up when the society ladies attended fashion shows there.

"Going to Mrs. Bissel's?" Billy asked, sounding wistful, as if he wished I were going to stay home and keep him company on that lousy rainy day.

I wished I were, too, but I had to work—not that he'd ever thank me for it. Maybe he'd like my job better when I brought him a puppy. I still had to ask Mrs. Bissel about that. "Yes. That was her on the telephone."

"Going to use some kind of anti-ghost poison?" Pa asked, chuckling. "Like ant powder?"

Good old Pa. He could always make me giggle. "Wish I had some. It might come in handy in Mrs. Bissel's basement."

Billy said, "Huh," and chomped on his toast.

I didn't snap at him, but instead put another piece of bread in the toast rack and lit the burner. We had a pretty nice gas range (bought with money I earned as a spiritualist, I might add), and it was much easier to regulate the toasting of bread than it had been when we used a wood-burning stove. Ma and Aunt Vi were always thanking me for getting such an up-to-date stove. Pa probably would have thanked me if he'd thought about it.

Billy had never thanked me and never would, because of his feelings about my spiritualist business. That morning, I tried not to get indignant at him for it. Didn't work. Never did. As far as I was concerned, Billy was pigheaded and unreasonable about my job. Even if he was a wounded war hero, he didn't have to be so darned illogical.

He was wrong when he said what I did was wicked. Through my work I helped people cope with their grief. Many's the woman who's thanked me after a séance during which I'd told her that her son or husband or cousin or lover was at peace on the other side of life and still loved those he'd left behind. I don't consider easing people's heartaches wicked. I consider it pretty darned nice.

Billy would never admit that he thought so, too. To my credit, I didn't allow my frustration to show that morning.

I took my toast over to the table and buttered it. "Are there any oranges already picked?" We had a navel orange tree right next to the back steps that produced oranges in the fall. Another orange tree closer to the back end of our yard, this one a Valencia, produced oranges in the springtime. Therefore, we had fresh oranges almost all year round: another splendid reason to live in Pasadena.

"Sorry, sweetheart. I ate the last one." Billy was honestly rueful that I'd have to go outdoors and pick an orange if I wanted one.

"That's okay." I glanced at the window again and decided I was sorry, too. Still raining. I decided I could live without an orange for breakfast. "Mrs. Bissel's sending her car to pick me up today, so I won't have to get soaked walking to the red-car stop."

"Glad to hear it," said Pa. "I was afraid I'd have to

stand in the rain and crank the Model T for you." He chuckled again.

Billy didn't. As usual. "At least you won't have to drive in the rain," he said, sounding as if he would have liked to scold me for going out in the rain but didn't dare do so in front of Pa.

"Right." To make up for Billy's lack of enthusiasm, I added a brightness to the word that I didn't feel. "She's got the best dogs, Billy. You'd love them."

"Hmmm," said Billy.

"What kind are they?" asked Pa.

"Dachshunds."

"Aha! Little sausage dogs, eh? I'll bet they're cunning."

Have I mentioned that Pa was the greatest guy in the world? Well, he was. He knew exactly what ailed Billy. He also knew what Billy put me though every day as I tried to earn our bread, but he never once talked about our problems. He only tried to smooth over the bumps when they occurred.

"They are," I said around a mouthful of toast. "They're the most precious puppies I've ever seen."

I almost added that I was going to ask Mrs. Bissel to give me one in payment if I succeeded in getting whatever was living in her basement to move out, but I caught myself before I could blurt it out. I wanted to surprise Billy. I didn't think even Billy could resist the charm of a dachshund puppy—although who knew? Billy was an expert at resisting those who tried to help him.

Still and all, and as discouraged as I'd been in recent days, not all my faith in miracles had died yet. And although it was a big task to ask of a tiny puppy, I prayed a puppy could help us out. We sure needed something.

A knock came at our door, and I got up to answer it. Henry, Mrs. Bissel's chauffeur, stood on the porch, holding a big black umbrella. "Put the umbrella on the porch and come on in and have a cup of something, Henry. I'm just finishing breakfast."

"Thank you, Miss Daisy."

Henry Pettigrew, as brown and wrinkled as a walnut, was a nice fellow and I liked him a lot. He and Pa knew each other from the days when Pa used to be a chauffeur for rich moving-picture people. Henry and his wife and two children lived in an apartment off Mrs. Bissel's garage. Mrs. Pettigrew was a very good seamstress, and lots of ladies in Altadena and Pasadena availed themselves of her talents.

As I ran to get my coat and hat, Pa poured Henry a cup of coffee and made him sit down and warm up. I was glad of it, because Billy seldom said nasty things about my work when nonfamily members were present. I figured the more the merrier, at least for me.

It didn't take me long to complete my toilette. Henry, good employee that he was, jumped to attention as soon as I walked into the kitchen. "You sure look pretty today, Miss Daisy. You're a sight prettier than the weather."

"I think so, too," said my Billy, not caring to be upstaged by a chauffeur, I guess, because he didn't usually compliment me more than once per day.

"Thanks, Henry. And you, too, Billy."

I bent down and kissed Billy on his forehead, not deeming it appropriate to demonstrate too much affection in front of others. Not for me the loose morals running rampant among the young people of the nation in those days.

Even if I'd felt like being loose, which I didn't, I wouldn't allow myself to be because it might hurt my business. Working as a spiritualist medium was tricky enough, even for a proper, moral young matron who sang in the church choir. If people thought I was one of the free-and-easy girls everyone deplored back then, my goose would have been cooked.

"When will you be home?"

Billy's question came out sounding tight and not altogether pleasant, and my heart sank into my sensible, moderately low-heeled shoes. If his mood didn't improve before I came home, I'd be in for it tonight. I should have been used to it, but I wasn't.

"As soon as I can be. It probably won't take me long." Primarily because I didn't have the faintest idea what to do about Mrs. Bissel's problem. Which set me to thinking, as I should have done the night before.

I supposed I could bolt the door leading from the basement to the out of doors in order to trap whoever was living down there inside. Then I could get rid of it myself or call on the local law enforcement people to do it for me.

No. That wasn't any good because it would clue Mrs. Bissel in to the fact that it wasn't a creature from the netherworld hanging out in her basement, but a living entity. I wasn't sure she'd pay me even in money, much less in dachshunds, if she knew the truth—whatever the truth was. Heck, I didn't know for sure there was anything at all down there, much less a human being.

Henry helped me into the back seat of the Daimler, holding the umbrella over my head the whole time, and I felt kind of special. Maybe it's not so bad being from the working classes, because we appreciate stuff like being driven around in Daimlers more than people who are accustomed to such luxuries.

The only problem with the arrangement was that it was more difficult to chat with Henry when he sat up front and I sat in the back. That being the case, and since I still felt gloomy and depressed, I didn't try to talk to him, but stared out the window at the rain.

It's a funny thing about our weather. Sometimes it didn't rain for months on end. At other times it would rain so hard, houses slid down hillsides. You'd never catch me building a house on a hill in Southern California, even if I could afford to.

The downpour must have started sometime during the night, because already the streets ran with water. Henry had to drive in the middle of Colorado Street in order to keep us from getting waterlogged in the huge puddles that had built up next to the curbs and made small lakes in the street. Luckily, all of Pasadena's main streets had been paved. When Henry turned north onto Lake Avenue, the street looked like a river running downhill. I began to wonder if we'd make it to Mrs. Bissel's house even in the Daimler, which was a darned good machine.

But Henry knew what he was doing, and although it took a good deal longer to drive from our house to Mrs. Bissel's place than it would have done had the weather been sunny, eventually we made it. After turning right from Lake onto Foothill Boulevard, Henry drove north up Maiden Lane, which was running with mud at the time, turned left into the circular driveway in back of the house, and pulled up next to Mrs. Bissel's flagstone patio.

I'd been to her house during the summertime when she'd entertained guests back there, and I loved it. She had a shrub called a daphne that had glossy green leaves and pearly white blossoms that smelled so wonderful, I could shut my eyes and fancy I'd died and gone to heaven.

On that ghastly autumn day the daphne was dripping and dreary like everything else, and nothing smelled like anything but mud. Even Mrs. Bissel's monkey-puzzle tree looked as if it had been dunked upside down in a bucket of water. It drooped as if it had caught cold in the lousy weather and ought to be lying down and resting with a hot-water bottle on its head and its roots resting on a footstool.

Henry ran from his door to mine, the umbrella held

high, and opened my door. I thanked him for it, and he walked me to the back door, still holding the umbrella over my head and his. I thanked him for *that,* too. It's kind of nice to be treated as if you were worth taking care of once in a while.

Approximately a thousand dachshunds, all barking hysterically, greeted me as I walked into the sun porch off the patio. Henry laughed as he shook out the umbrella. Mrs. Bissel was close on the dogs' heels, holding out her hands in greeting, and hollering at her dogs to shut up. They didn't, of course

Five

It took approximately twenty minutes for the dogs to calm down enough for Mrs. Bissel and me to hold a conversation.

"It's because they've been cooped up all day," said she. "The rain, don't you know. Their little legs are so short, I'm afraid that if I let them go outdoors, they'll just float away downstream and end up in San Marino."

I wouldn't mind ending up in San Marino. It was a great place, full of mansions and rich people, including Harold Kincaid. I didn't mention my thoughts, although I must admit that the mental image of a bunch of little sausage-shaped hound dogs floating downhill was an amusing one. In fact, I almost laughed, which was an improvement over the glumness that had been my companion from my house to Mrs. Bissel's.

"Come into the breakfast room and have a cup of tea to warm you up, Daisy. There's plenty of time to work on the spirit belowstairs. I need to tell you what happened last night."

I perked up a tiny bit more. "Something happened last night? Something out of the ordinary?"

"Yes." Mrs. Bissel's voice had sunk to a whisper. "Oh, Daisy, I do *so* hope you can help us. Whatever's down there is becoming more bold."

"My goodness." Rats. This sounded bad. If there was

anything I didn't need, it was a bold spirit—or criminal or lunatic or mountain lion. "What did it do?"

She drew her chair closer to mine and leaned toward me. Mrs. Cummings must have been warned to bring tea and cakes as soon as I arrived, because that's what she did.

"Good morning, Mrs. Cummings," I said politely.

"Is it?" Mrs. Cummings replied, which I thought was odd.

"Oh, Daisy, you just can't imagine how frightened we all are!" exclaimed Mrs. Bissel.

"That's the God's own truth," affirmed Mrs. Cummings.

Golly, this didn't sound good at all. In fact, it sounded like a job for someone other than a phony spiritualist. I'd never say so. "What happened?" I asked again.

"Whatever's down there made something crash."

I glanced from Mrs. Bissel, who'd made this pronouncement in a voice that would have done the spirit belowstairs proud, to Mrs. Cummings, who nodded her head and looked grim. "Um . . . It made something crash? What did it make crash? You mean, like a glass or something?"

"That's just it," Mrs. Bissel said in a harsh whisper. "We don't *know!*"

Mrs. Cummings nodded some more.

"Ah . . ." Crumb, what did this mean? I wasn't even sure what they were talking about. "Do you mean you heard a noise like that of breaking glass? And it came from the basement?"

"It came from the basement, all right. It was probably a mirror," said Mrs. Cummings gloomily. Her aspect went well with the horrible weather. "I understand them spirits and so forth don't like mirrors."

"Ah. Of course. A mirror."

Mrs. Bissel nodded and looked thoughtful, as if she were considering Mrs. Cummings's comment and agreeing with it. "Yes. It might have been a mirror smashing."

"Are there very many mirrors down there?" I asked, just curious as to how Mrs. Bissel's resident spirit might have gotten its transparent hands on a looking glass. Most basements of my acquaintance weren't heavily endowed with mirrors.

"I don't know of any," admitted Mrs. Bissel.

She peered questioningly up at Mrs. Cummings, who shook her head. "I never seen one down there."

I made the brilliant deduction that the paucity of mirrors belowstairs let mirrors out as the crashing device. Whoever lived there probably broke a glass by accident. "Did you investigate this morning, to see if there were shards of glass or anything like that left on the floor?"

"We all four of us—Mrs. Cummings, Susan, Ginger, and me—went downstairs together." Mrs. Bissel's voice dropped again, and again she sounded as if she were speaking from a tomb. "We didn't find anything, Daisy. Not a single thing."

Tidy ghost. "Ah."

"So it must have been a spirit," Mrs. Bissel concluded with impeccable illogic. "Or a ghost. What else could have made the mess from a crash like that disappear?"

Beats me. I gave her another cryptic "Ah." What in the name of goodness was *I* supposed to do about her mirror-smashing fiend? Easy answer. I was supposed to exorcise it. Crumb.

The cakes were delicious. Mrs. Cummings's culinary skills weren't quite up to my aunt Vi's, but those little breakfast cakes were wonderful. When I asked, Mrs. Cummings said they were applesauce-spice cupcakes, and she'd iced them with a frosting made from Philadelphia Cream Cheese. I decided to tell Aunt Vi about using cream cheese in frosting. She appreciated getting these little tips every now and then, even from me, who could barely cook an egg, although my potato soup was tasty.

"So you found nothing that might indicate where the crash came from or what caused it? No broken windows or anything of that nature?"

The two women exchanged another look before Mrs. Bissel said, "I don't think we looked at the windows."

"No, we didn't. If it was a window, that basement's going to be flooded if this rain keeps up."

"But we'd surely have noticed glass on the floor," said Mrs. Bissel, brightening.

"We would," agreed Mrs. Cummings.

I wasn't so sure. I could picture the four women, arms clutching each other, so scared, they wouldn't notice a hippopotamus if it were hiding in a corner. I'd have bet anything that no one had thought to look inside the two rooms down there, although I didn't ask. If *I* found the broken window, the discovery would make me look as if I knew what I was doing. Maybe.

That ended our brief sojourn at the breakfast table, darn it. I wanted another cupcake.

Since I planned to go with them, Mrs. Bissel and Mrs. Cummings said they dared to enter the basement sans a fourth member of the party. I would have rolled my eyes, except that I didn't do things like that when I was working. The customer, as they say, is always right. This axiom held true even when you made your living doing something as outrageous as raising spirits from the dead and chatting with them, or exorcising demonic ghouls from basements.

Taking the lead in our expedition, I said, "I'll go first." Brave little thing, aren't I?

"Thank you, Daisy."

Mrs. Bissel's thanks sounded heartfelt, and I scolded myself for inwardly sneering at her. I'm sure I would have been frightened, too, if something had decided to live in our basement. The notion that it might be a skunk, of which there were plenty around, struck me, and I decided not to be snide anymore. I think I'd rather face down a lunatic than a skunk. I'm not sure about the criminal or the bear or the lion.

I walked softly but assuredly down the basement stairs. When I glanced over my shoulder, I saw Mrs. Bissel and Mrs. Cummings, arms encircling each other, trying to walk downstairs side-by-side. Since both women were large, this didn't work, but they managed to stay close to each other in spite of their respective bulks.

"Why don't you remain at the foot of the stairs," I said. "I don't want to overwhelm the spirit or ghost."

"Are you sure? Don't you think we ought to stick together?" Mrs. Bissel's objection didn't come from the heart. From her apprehensive expression, I knew she'd have been glad if I'd told the two ladies to go back up to the kitchen. Still, it was nice of her to offer to accompany me.

"I don't believe it would serve any purpose," I said.

A thought had just struck me, sort of like a bolt of lightning. I almost let an exclamation of surprise escape, but suppressed it before it leaked out.

After calming down a bit and pretending to investigate the laundry basket closely, I asked, "Did you say this spirit or ghost has been down here for two weeks?"

When I glanced over my shoulder, I saw the two women silently consulting one another. Mrs. Cummings nodded first, and Mrs. Bissel turned to answer me. "Yes. It's been about two weeks. Maybe two and a half."

"Ah."

Marianne Wagner had been missing for a little over two weeks, according to Sam Rotondo. Was it possible that timid little Marianne had run away from home and was now hiding out in Mrs. Bissel's basement? The notion was preposterous on the face of it, but I wasn't certain it was wrong.

If I were Marianne, I'd have skipped town years before, but I wasn't Marianne. Marianne Wagner seemed to me to be a girl who'd been beaten into submission so early and so often, she'd lost any spirit (so to speak) she might once have had. I imagined, from what I'd seen of her and the rest of the Wagner clan, that she didn't dare do anything the least bit daring, much less something as outrageous as running away.

Still, even the meekest lambs among us have our limits, and if she *had* run away, she probably wouldn't go far. She'd be too scared to walk boldly into a train station and buy a one-way ticket to New York, say, or tell her parents to go to hell and then get herself a job.

Yet the notion of her eating spaghetti out of a tin can in Mrs. Bissel's basement was kind of . . . loopy, I guess. As I poked into corners, visited the mangle, peered inside the washing machine—the sheets and blanket were there again, or still, I didn't know which—I thought hard about Marianne. She was so good at self-effacement that she tended to blend in with the scenery, so it took me some cogitation to recall her to mind.

The first time I'd seen her, she'd been sitting in a corner of Mr. and Mrs. Wright's sublimely lighted and decorated ballroom. It was at a Halloween party. I was there because Mrs. Wright, whose husband had become wealthy producing chewing gum, had hired me to read my crystal ball for her guests. I loved attending these parties because when I wasn't busy, I got to look at all the ladies' fashions. I gleaned scads of great ideas that way. It had been kind of disappointing to me that so many people had availed themselves of my service that night.

I didn't really mind, although my crystal-ball readings were less effective at overawing people than my séances. But this was all in fun, and Mrs. Wright was collecting money for a worthy charity: the Pasadena Humane Society, which had been established in the late

1800s (Pasadena was a very progressive city). Besides, lots of the women for whom I normally worked were there, and lots for whom I didn't, and I always garnered new customers when I entertained people at gatherings like that one.

Several of the young ladies at the party had come to me for a crystal-ball reading. They acted just like most people do: they adopted an air of doubtful good humor, but they couldn't help but wonder if maybe I might have some sort of link to the Great Beyond. Of course I didn't, but I was so good at my line of work that almost all of them left believing I'd actually seen the things I prophesied.

It's always puzzled me that nobody's ever come back to inform me that nothing I'd foretold for them had come true. I guess they either forgot about it or aimed to give my prophecies more time. I was careful not to put time limits on my predictions.

At any rate, I'd sort of expected Marianne to drop in to my fortune-telling tent, which Mrs. Wright had her servants set up in the ballroom, but she didn't. Mrs. Wright kept coming to the tent and telling me I needed a break—she was a nice woman—and every time I took advantage of her kindness, which wasn't often, I'd see Marianne sitting in the corner, her hands strangling each other in her lap. I got the impression she was trying to hide from everyone, as if people scared her. It sounds silly, I guess, coming from me, a person who's grown up poor but proud and hard-working, but I felt sorry for her, a girl who had everything money could buy. I could feel her terror from my tent, and I didn't understand it.

That was before I met her father, mother, and brothers. When Mrs. Wright introduced us, I thought I might have met the source of Marianne's stifling fear.

Her father was an overbearing, dictatorial ass. Her mother was as colorless as a worn-out bedsheet, and she had the same terrified look about her as Marianne. I hate bullies, and I took an instant dislike to Dr. Wagner. I'd met Marianne's two brothers once or twice before, and knew them to be worthless sons of dogs. I figured they took after their father, except that the doctor was rich. I presumed Gaylord and Vincent just leeched from their old man.

I deliberately walked past Marianne that evening and smiled at her. My nature is outgoing and friendly, probably because I'd always been too poor to develop neuroses, or whatever it is the psychiatrists call them. Even my friendly smile seemed to frighten poor Marianne, and she shrank farther back in her chair. I got the impression she'd have liked to disappear altogether.

So I felt sorry for her. Then I forgot about her.

Until last night when Sam Rotondo told us she was missing, and again that morning in Mrs. Bissel's basement, when I remembered what Sam had said about her disappearance. I kept telling myself I was being stupid, that no wealthy young lady would take refuge in, of all places, a basement, but I couldn't get rid of the notion.

Marianne had never struck me as the adventurous or imaginative type, and she might have become lost and chosen the basement out of sheer terror. Or maybe somebody had chased after her and she'd taken refuge from him under Mrs. Bissel's house and didn't dare leave. In the time it took me to inspect the basement, I'd come up with all sorts of scenarios that would account for a timid creature hiding out in a rich lady's basement.

After my tour of the main room, I entered the bedroom in which I'd found the empty spaghetti tin. There was no such incriminatory evidence to be found today. Was that because Marianne had swept up the jar she'd dropped and broken the night before?

A trash container sat next to the washing machine, so I wafted over and peered inside. Nothing. Not even a scrap of paper or lint. Hmmm.

"How often is this trash container emptied, Mrs. Bissel?"

"I beg your pardon? The trash container? I . . . I don't know."

She looked inquiringly at Mrs. Cummings, who provided an answer. "We generally toss the trash on Mondays, when Ginger and Cynthia Oversloot do the laundry."

"Ah," I said mysteriously.

Shoot, it was Thursday. Surely, *some* trash must have accumulated since Monday. "And do your servants have business in the basement every day, Mrs. Bissel?"

Again the two women exchanged a glance. Mrs. Bissel spoke up this time. "They used to, until the haunting started. Now they try to bring everything upstairs that they think they'll need for the whole week."

"The whole month's more like it," grumbled Mrs. Cummings.

I gave them another enigmatic "Ah."

This was very interesting. If whoever was living down there had broken a jar, swept up the glass, and thrown it in the trash, he or she had taken the trouble to empty the trash receptacle so that nothing of the accident remained. I shivered involuntarily, thinking about how sloppy and muddy a slog that must have been. Mrs. Bissel's outdoor trash bins sat beside the garage and were at least a hundred yards from the house. I wondered when the rain had started, and felt sorry for the intruder.

I stood in the little room, thinking, trying to decide what to do next. If Mrs. Bissel's "spirit" was Marianne, and if I could get her to come out of hiding and return to her parents' home, I might earn a fee from both Mrs. Bissel and the Wagners. That was an enticing prospect. I hadn't looked at the *Star News* that morning and now wished I had, because Dr. and Mrs. Wagner had, according to Sam, placed an item about their daughter's disappearance in the local newspapers, and it was supposed to run that day.

Had they offered a reward? Probably. Even though Dr. Wagner was, in my opinion, a certified meanie, he wouldn't want the world to know it. Besides, he had more money than God. Surely he considered Marianne worth a few dollars of that fortune. Or maybe not. But he cared about his reputation; I was almost certain of that.

Thinking about Dr. Wagner (I honestly wasn't sure he gave a rap about anyone at all other than himself), I wandered over to the pitcher and bowl. The bowl had a teeny puddle of water in the bottom again. This was all very strange. I tried to keep my imagination from going wild, but it was a difficult thing to do, since my imagination was like a runaway train at the best of times.

I also tried to keep from becoming too set on the Marianne idea. After all, I had no proof it was she living down there. It would be a capital error to become so enthralled with the Marianne idea that I failed to consider other options. This basement-haunting problem might still prove to be nothing. Or a skunk. Or an escapee from an insane asylum. Or a criminal.

In fact, the only thing I was sure of was that no spirit or ghost inhabited Mrs. Bissel's basement, because such things didn't exist. That struck me as kind of funny, although not funny enough to laugh about.

With a sigh, I left the bedroom, closed the door, inspected the other room, found the same nothing that had been there the day before, and went over to the two women huddled together at the foot of the staircase. As I did so, I tried to think of something worthwhile to do to resolve the situation. No luck.

"Did you discover anything, Daisy?" Mrs. Bissel had her hands clasped in a tight, white-knuckled knot at her waist.

"I sure hope so," said Mrs. Cummings, who patted

Mrs. Bissel on the shoulder in a comforting gesture. The two women treated each other as friends, rather than as mistress and servant. I approved of this egalitarian state of affairs. Not that anyone cares what I thought.

"I'm not sure," I said in my most mystical spiritualist voice. "Would you mind going upstairs and leaving me here alone for a few minutes?"

Mrs. Cummings's eyes darned near popped out of her head. "No!"

Mrs. Bissel gasped. "Oh, but Daisy, it's not safe! Please don't stay down here by yourself. Anything might happen."

True. Even I wasn't altogether happy about the prospect of being left alone in her basement. But I knew darned well that if her so-called spirit was Marianne Wagner, I'd never be able to roust her unless I was by myself down there. Alone, I might be able to persuade her to come out of hiding. The idea of returning her to her parents didn't appeal to me much, but heck, she couldn't live in a basement for the rest of her life, could she?

I said, "Please. I am accustomed to dealing with the spirits. They can be extremely elusive." And if *that* wasn't true, I didn't know what was. In actual fact, they were so elusive, I'd never encountered one in my life.

"Well . . ." Mrs. Bissel was still doubtful.

Mrs. Cummings, on the other hand, had no doubts at all. "I think you're crazy, Daisy Majesty."

I offered the two women one of my best, gently gracious smiles. "Recall, please, that I'm familiar with the ways of the Other Side. The spirits won't appear unless they feel comfortable. They don't care to have strangers around them."

"You're more of a stranger in this house than we are," Mrs. Cummings pointed out, darn her.

"Perhaps in this case, but in the overall scheme of things, I deal with spirits every day." I attempted to look modestly competent. Try it sometime. It's not easy, especially when you want to holler at an unbeliever.

Mrs. Bissel and Mrs. Cummings gazed at each other for a few seconds. Then Mrs. Cummings shrugged. Mrs. Bissel let out a huge breath, as if she'd been waiting for approval from her housekeeper. "Yes. I see what you mean, Daisy. We'll just wait at the top of the staircase. Please call out if you need help, dear."

"I will."

Boy, I could just imagine *that* scenario. Everybody in the entire household was afraid to go down to the basement even when nothing was wrong. I visualized how they'd panic if the spirit (or ghost) decided to do something horrid to my personal self. They'd probably rush around until they found Henry and send him down, and by that time I'd be dead.

I told myself not to think about such a possibility.

Once I was sure Mrs. Bissel and Mrs. Cummings were out of the way and the door was shut, I inspected it to see if I could lock it from within. I couldn't. After contemplating the situation for a moment or two, I decided it might be better this way. If, say, a mountain lion should happen to leap out at me from a ceiling rafter, at least I wouldn't have to fight to unlock the door to the kitchen—if I managed to get that far.

Not exactly a comforting thought, even though it was slightly better than death by spiritual possession. I'd much prefer Marianne Wagner to a mountain lion or a crazed ghost.

Descending the basement staircase once more, I pondered how to begin inducing a reluctant and assuredly scared-to-death runaway girl to show herself. No serviceable thoughts struck me, so I opted to start with her name.

"Marianne? Marianne Wagner? Are you here?" I pitched my voice to its most comforting, mediumistic tone.

Nothing. Not even a rustle of skirts or an indrawn breath.

I tried again. "Marianne, if you're hiding down here, please show yourself. I only want to help you." Because I'd met her father and disliked him, I decided it wouldn't hurt to add, "I won't tell your father." My conscience told me I'd just lied to the girl, but I told my conscience to shut up and be still.

Nothing.

"Marianne? Marianne, are you here?"

More nothing.

"If you're afraid to show yourself, please don't be. I won't hurt you."

Yet more nothing.

I elaborated, feeling increasingly stupid, "Nobody will hurt you."

Nobody answered, either. Bother. Either it wasn't Marianne, or she wasn't there, or she was too frightened to let her presence be known, even to me, who was relatively harmless.

On the few times I'd seen Marianne, she'd struck me as a girl who was afraid of her own shadow. If she'd somehow drummed up enough courage to flee her home, she might have exhausted her modest stock of gumption. I could envision her in my mind's eye, huddled somewhere—say, on a rafter or behind the furnace—terrified, shaking with apprehension, too appalled by her own mutinous behavior to reveal herself to me.

I stayed down there for another ten minutes or so, trying every persuasive word I could think of to lure the basement-dweller out of her (or his; I still didn't know if it was Marianne) lair. The result of my persuasion was a whole lot more of absolutely nothing.

Darn it, how could I earn a puppy if the person in the basement wouldn't cooperate with me and come out of hiding? Feeling a good deal less than sure of myself, I gave up for the day.

We Gumms are tenacious cusses, however, and I determined to keep trying. If I went down there alone for several days running and talked to Marianne, I might manage to crack her resistance. Or she might just up and get sick of me. Marianne couldn't possibly be as stubborn as I was, mainly because she'd never done anything the least little bit outré before in her life, and I earned my living at it.

Of course, if it wasn't Marianne, whoever it was might get sick of me, too, and heave a knife at me, but I'd take the chance. I was agile. I could probably dart out of the way of a knife, providing I saw it coming and the one throwing it was kind of slow.

Darn it, I was scaring myself.

With a sigh, I walked up the stairs to the kitchen. All of Mrs. Bissel's household staff had huddled together at the door, and every one of them appeared apprehensive when I shoved the door open and stepped into the room. When they saw me, they let out a collective gasp.

Then Mrs. Bissel took a step forward. "Well? What happened, Daisy? Did it speak to you?"

I shook my head. "Nothing happened today, I'm afraid. But I'm not giving up. I'll try again tomorrow if it's all right with you, Mrs. Bissel. I did sense something down there, and I'll need to meditate upon it." I added the last sentence because I didn't want her to give up first.

"Of course!" she cried. "I know you can do it, Daisy."

That's more than I knew. Nevertheless, when we chatted over peanut-butter cookies and tea, I made arrangements with Mrs. Bissel to exchange my services, providing they proved successful, for the little male puppy to whom I'd taken such a shine.

I felt moderately better that afternoon than I had in the morning. As Henry motored me home, I noted with approval that the rain had stopped, the sun had come out, and even though the weather was still as cold as a witch's heart, my mood had lifted. Tomorrow I planned to bring a rodent trap to Mrs. Bissel's house. We had one in our basement on Marengo, and it couldn't hurt to set it up. I wasn't sure how I'd sneak it past Mrs. Bissel and into her basement, but I was going to catch whatever was down there or my name wasn't Daisy Gumm. I mean Daisy Majesty.

Six

I have to admit that my mind took to wandering that
night at choir practice as we in the alto section were
learning our part. The choir director, Mr. Floy Hostetter, became exasperated with me.

If it came to that, I was exasperated with myself.
After promising myself that I wouldn't, I'd managed to
conclude positively that it was Marianne Wagner in
Mrs. Bissel's basement. My brain didn't seem to have
room in it for consideration of another possibility.

Was this my renowned spiritualistic instinct rearing
its precognitive head? No. It was because I'd managed
to fix on Marianne and was worrying the poor girl in
my mind as if she were a bone and I were one of Mrs.
Bissel's bull-headed dachshunds.

"Mrs. Majesty," Mr. Hostetter said, sounding grim.
"Where are you this evening?"

"What?" I jumped a little in my chair and felt guilty.
"I'm sorry, Mr. Hostetter."

"Hmmm," he said. I knew he wanted to yell at me,
but wouldn't, because we were in church. Thank heaven
for that. "You failed to come in on the chorus. I fear
the other altos follow your lead, so if you do the same
thing on Sunday, we're going to sound ludicrously thin."

"I'm really sorry. My mind's wandering this evening,
I'm afraid."

"I should appreciate it if you would please call it back

to the here and now. We have only another half hour to whip this hymn into shape."

Mr. Hostetter was not sarcastic as a rule, so I knew he was genuinely peeved with me, and I regretted it. "Yes," I said. "I'll do that." And I tried. Unfortunately, the hymn, "I Want a Principle Within," was one I'd always considered mind-numbingly boring, and Mrs. Bissel's basement-dwelling fugitive kept calling to me.

Her fictitious spirit or ghost *had* to be Marianne Wagner, I told myself. One would have to account for far too many coincidences for it to be anyone else. Sam Rotondo had once told me he didn't believe in coincidences, and I'd told him to tell that to Charles Dickens, but now I found myself thinking the same thing.

Even if it wasn't Marianne, I told myself, it had to be a human being down there. Skunks and mountain lions didn't eat Franco-American spaghetti. The possibility that the can might have fallen out of a trash container and rolled across the floor occurred to me only to be rejected. Even full cans of spaghetti can't open doors, and the empty one I'd found had been lying beneath the bed in a room with a closed door.

Again I considered the possibility that Ginger or Susan had snitched the spaghetti and eaten it in that bedroom so as not to get caught, but I doubted it. Mrs. Bissel was too kindhearted an employer to begrudge her housemaids enough to eat. And if her kitchen was anything like ours, there were always leftovers lying around, calling out to be eaten.

Crumb. I was driving myself crazy. And I hadn't been paying attention. Again. When I guiltily glanced up, I saw that I was driving Mr. Hostetter crazy, too, and swore to myself that I'd forget about basements and sing.

When I left choir practice to return home, we'd managed to whip "I Want a Principle Within" into submission. The hymn was still, in my estimation, as dull as dirt, but at least I'd learned my part. I have a feeling poor Mr. Hostetter was going to need to take a powder when he got home, and it was probably all my fault.

I woke up the next morning to weather well suited to hauntings. Fog had rolled in overnight, and it enveloped our little bungalow in a thick, swirly, surly-looking gray blanket, through which I couldn't even see to the street in front of the house.

When I staggered out of bed, threw on a robe, dragged myself through the kitchen, dining room, and living room, opened the door, and went outside out to get our morning newspaper, one of our neighbors, Mr. Longnecker, emerged out of the gray mist like an apparition and nearly scared the stuffing out of me. I managed to smile and wave at him without showing that he'd startled me. Who'd hire a medium who was afraid of the fog? Nobody, that's who.

If I were a ghost, I'd have loved weather like that. Since I wasn't, it only made me feel gloomy, which was a normal state of affairs.

I *really* wanted that little dachshund puppy. If it didn't cheer Billy up, I was almost positive it would cheer me up.

With that in mind, I made short shrift of breakfast, dressed in another one of my spiritualist costumes (a gray wool dress, and my standard black shoes, hat, handbag, and coat), kissed Billy good-bye, and headed to the red-car line on Colorado Street. Billy hadn't been pleased when I'd told him I was going to Mrs. Bissel's house again, which was also a normal state of affairs.

At least Mrs. Bissel, Ginger, Susan, Mrs. Cummings, and Henry, who was in the kitchen drinking a cup of coffee and chatting with Mrs. Cummings, appreciated me. I don't know why. It's not as if I'd done anything for them.

After giving my coat and hat to Ginger and greeting one and all, I tripped down the basement steps, propelled by a renewed sense of confidence. Darn it, it *had* to be Marianne Wagner down there. Nothing else made sense. In any case, I'd forgotten to bring the rodent trap, so it had better not be a skunk.

My optimism lasted approximately five minutes. Marianne didn't respond to any of my cajolery. In fact, nothing responded. What's more, I didn't find any more empty Franco-American spaghetti cans. The sheet and blanket were neatly folded and resting in the washing machine, the pitcher and bowl in the tidy little bedroom were both slightly damp, and that was it.

This was getting downright discouraging. Since I've always had more persistence than brains (according to my beloved husband), I sat on the basement steps and thought hard. There had to be a way to find out who had taken up housekeeping in Mrs. Bissel's basement.

Whoever it was needed to eat, and evidently *had* been eating, as illustrated by the empty spaghetti tin. Hunnicutt's, a small grocery market, sat on the southeast corner of Foothill Boulevard and Lake Avenue, next to the fire station. I suppose a transient basement-dweller might buy food there, although it would be risky. Marianne Wagner's picture had been printed in both the *Star News* and the *Herald*, although she probably didn't know it. Also, I didn't suppose she'd taken much money with her. I doubted that Dr. Wagner allowed her a huge allowance, since he had two worthless sons to support.

Plus, there was that fire station next door to Hunnicutt's. I've always heard that firemen are a particularly watchful and alert bunch. If any of them spied Marianne buying food, they'd assuredly notify her parents or the police.

It followed, therefore, that Marianne must be sneaking into Mrs. Bissel's kitchen at night and snatching foodstuffs. She couldn't have been stealing much, because Mrs. Cummings hadn't noticed any losses. She'd have told Mrs. Bissel if the larder had been raided, and neither lady had announced signs of a shrinking food supply to me.

Naturally, if Mrs. Bissel's unwelcome visitor turned out to be an escaped lunatic or criminal, he or she would also probably be raiding the kitchen at night. I didn't like that idea, but at least I'd more or less eliminated mountain lions and bears from my list of suspects. And skunks. That was a good thing, if not awfully useful.

Nuts. I had to try a different approach. Sadly, I couldn't think of one. So I sat there with my elbows on my knees and my chin in my hands for several more minutes. My mind kept wandering off the topic of basement-dwelling spirits for lack of any more rewarding thoughts to occupy it.

I was in the middle of deciding whether or not I wanted to get an Oldsmobile or a Chevrolet should a bounty of dollars magically fall on my head when an idea interrupted me. I don't know why I hadn't thought of it before, because it was about the only way to achieve results. If I spent the night down there, I'd be sure to see Marianne if she emerged from wherever she was hiding in order to scrounge for food.

I glanced around the basement and shivered. Maybe it wasn't such a great idea. The notion of hanging out in Mrs. Bissel's basement after dark when everyone in the whole household, except the being hiding in there, had gone upstairs, leaving me absolutely alone without even a dachshund to warn me if somebody decided to sneak up on me with, say, a huge butcher knife in his fist, didn't really sound like a lot of fun.

But I could spend the night in Mrs. Bissel's kitchen, couldn't I? That wouldn't be quite so spooky, and it would be just as effective, providing Marianne actually *was* sneaking food at night.

Of course, if it wasn't Marianne, whoever it was

might kill me with that big, ugly butcher knife, but that was a chance I was willing to take, mainly because I could run really fast when scared out of my wits. Besides, I felt in my bones that it was Marianne. Which just goes to show what a deep thinker I was. Instead of my brain, I trusted my bones. No wonder my third-grade teacher, Miss West, had made a habit of whacking my knuckles with her ruler.

Because I'd occasionally found that some of my brilliant ideas weren't so great upon closer inspection, I remained at the foot of the stairs and mulled it over for several minutes more. I thought so much and so hard, in fact, that I darned near fell asleep.

Finally I concluded that I'd thought enough for one day. Billy would be happy if I came home early, and there clearly wasn't anything more I could do downstairs.

I guess Mrs. Bissel's household staff had become accustomed to me calling on the specter in the basement and surviving the experience, because they'd ceased waiting for me at the head of the kitchen stairs in a terrified clump. When I opened the door, only Mrs. Cummings was there to greet me—or she would have done so had she been watching the door.

At least she cared enough to utter a shriek of fright and whirl around when she heard me. When she saw me, she gasped and slapped a hand to her heart. She was wielding a butter knife as if she aimed to stab me with it. "Merciful heaven, Daisy Majesty! You frightened me to death!"

"I'm sorry, Mrs. Cummings." Golly, I guess I'd better start announcing my presence before opening the basement door from now on.

"Did you find anything?" Mrs. Cummings put down the butter knife.

"I may have," I lied. "I need to meditate upon several aspects of this situation."

Mrs. Cummings blinked a few times and said, "Oh."

I've never figured out why poor people, like my relations and Mrs. Cummings are, as a rule, so much less gullible than rich ones. Probably because they had to do all the things rich people didn't want to do. Hard work has a habit of clearing one's mind of irrelevancies. Like, for example, spirits and ghosts.

Because I figured Mrs. Cummings would only become more skeptical if I tried to explain myself, I asked, "Is Mrs. Bissel around somewhere, Mrs. Cummings? I need to talk to her."

"She's out back with those dogs of hers." Mrs. Cummings evidently didn't share Mrs. Bissel's and my own appreciation of dachshunds. "Always underfoot, those dogs. They're pigs, Daisy Majesty. Worse than pigs, because they're so cunning, and you can't resist 'em. They're apt to eat a body out of house and home."

"I'm hoping to get one for my Billy. He needs something to keep him company when I'm working."

Mrs. Cummings eyed me sympathetically. Shaking her head, she went back to what she'd been doing before I interrupted her, which looked like washing dishes. "It's a crime, what happened to your Billy, Daisy. So many young men lost, and so many hurt, damn the Kaiser to perdition."

"My sentiments precisely," I told her. "Thanks, Mrs. Cummings." Worried that I'd start crying if I stayed there and received any more of her sympathy, I went in search of Mrs. Bissel.

As soon as I opened the door to the sun porch and stepped out onto the patio's still-wet flagstones, I heard where the kennel was. Following the sound of uproarious barking, I found her a minute later, talking to a man in work clothes and a cloth cap.

She saw me before he did, and her smile made me feel guilty. "Daisy! What's happened?"

I couldn't say "Nothing" again. Rather, I equivocated. "The emanations are coming closer, Mrs. Bissel. I believe I'm on the verge of discovering exactly what type of spirit or ghost is inhabiting your basement."

"I'm so glad!" She remembered the man standing with her. He'd listened to my little speech with widening eyes. "Daisy Majesty, please let me introduce you to Robert Dembrowski. Robert keeps my kennels for me. I was afraid they'd flood during that awful rain yesterday, but they didn't."

Good Lord. She'd hired a guy to take care of her dogs. It used to boggle my mind that so many rich people could afford to hire butlers and housemaids. But a man to take care of the dogs? It was hard to take it in. Nevertheless, I smiled at Robert Dembrowski and stuck out a hand. "How do you do, Mr. Dembrowski?"

He whipped his soft cap from his head and stammered, "I'm fine, Mrs. Majesty, and hope you are the same." He took my hand and dropped it again almost instantly. I got the impression he was afraid of me. Obviously, he'd heard stories about me raising the dead during séances.

I got that reaction sometimes from people who were either afraid of what I did, or who considered it somehow unholy or eerie. With an internal sigh, I turned back to Mrs. Bissel, knowing I wasn't responsible for other people's opinions, even though they sometimes bothered me. "May I speak with you for a minute, Mrs. Bissel? I believe I'm at the point where more direct action needs to be taken."

She gasped. Mr. Dembrowski took a step backward. I really didn't enjoy scaring people, although I guess it went with the territory. "It's nothing bad," I said, trying to reassure both of them.

If people acted more like dogs, I decided on the spot, the world would be a better place. None of her dachshunds were afraid of me, and they were supposed to be the ones without big brains. In spite of my gray dress, I stooped to pet the dogs. I couldn't help myself.

This spontaneous show of affection for her dachshunds reassured Mrs. Bissel, who squatted beside me. Her joints made quite a racket, although the noise from the dogs was slightly louder.

"Do you wuv Miss Daisy-Wazey?" she asked the dogs in a silly, baby-talk voice. "Yes, you do-ums."

I hate to admit it, but I talked that way, too. I'd singled out Billy's pup, and was holding him close, muddy paws and all. What the heck. I could always wash my dress when I got home. "Yes, and I wuv him back," I cooed.

After several more minutes of that nonsense, although it didn't feel like nonsense at the time, I sighed, put the puppy back on the ground, and stood up, trying to brush the mud off my bodice, which didn't work very well. I'd forgotten all about Mr. Dembrowski. When I glanced at him, he didn't seem to have discerned anything out of the ordinary in my behavior. Apparently most people turned into blithering idiots around puppies.

He helped Mrs. Bissel to her feet, accompanied by barks from the dogs, creaks from her knee joints, and grunts from her mouth. Have I already mentioned that she was a very large woman? Rather like an overstuffed chair? Well, she was, and Mr. Dembrowski was plainly accustomed to assisting her in this way, even though he probably weighed half as much as she did.

"They're so adorable, Mrs. Bissel. I can't wait to take one home to Billy."

"Why don't you take him today, dear? I'm sure I don't mind."

Oh, boy, was *that* a temptation. However, in spite of Billy's opinion of my overall moral worth and character, I operated by a strict code of ethics, and I never accepted payment until the job was done and the customer was happy. "Not until I've fulfilled my obligations to your satisfaction, Mrs. Bissel, but I do thank you."

"But Daisy, I don't mind. Truly. You're doing me such a favor."

I hadn't done a thing so far except hang out in her basement for a couple of hours. I didn't point this out to her, but only said, "Thank you, but no. I never accept payment until I've done the job to the customer's satisfaction." I was beginning to remind myself of an automobile salesman. Or a broken phonograph record.

As we walked back to her house, she continued to argue, and I continued to refuse. It wasn't a heated battle, and she gave it up as soon as we got to the patio.

The fog had lifted, but the air was chilly. A breeze had begun to blow, and I looked toward the San Gabriel Mountains, wondering if it would snow up there. It was pretty early in the season, but I always loved seeing the mountain peaks covered in white. We'd probably get winds instead; we usually did.

In November and December the "devil winds," or Santa Anas, would blow, knocking over trees and power lines and fences and the occasional windmill that still remained in Pasadena or Altadena. Since we'd already experienced cold, rain, and fog, I figured it was time for the winds to wreak havoc in the vicinity. I supposed the winds were better than fire, famine, and a plague of locusts, but they made everyone itchy and bad-tempered. Since poor Billy was already both of those things most of the time, the notion of the Santa Anas arriving to aggravate his condition didn't appeal to me one little bit.

There was nothing I could do about the weather, so I forced myself to pay attention to Mrs. Bissel and my next step in the solution of her haunting problem. When we were both seated at the breakfast-room table (which, by the by, was larger than our own dining-room table on Marengo), I said, "I think it would be a good idea for me to stay overnight in the basement one of these nights."

She paled visibly. I'd never seen anyone do that before, although I'd read about the phenomenon in novels. She slapped a hand over her gigantic bosom as she did it. "No!"

Mrs. Cummings, walking into the breakfast room with a tray in her hands, stopped in her tracks. "No, what?"

Mrs. Bissel turned to her housekeeper for support. "No, Daisy can't spend the night in the basement. It's far too dangerous."

Staring at me as if I'd lost what was left of my mind, Mrs. Cummings snorted, regained her footing, and set a plate of iced cakes on the table between Mrs. Bissel and me. "You're daft, Daisy Majesty. There's no way on God's green earth that you'll be allowed to sleep in the basement. If the ghost don't get you, the damp and chill will."

Comforting thought. "I'm sure that's not so, Mrs. Cummings. I deal with the spirits all the time, don't forget."

"Tush." With the one pithy word, Mrs. Cummings set a flowery teapot and two flowery cups down on the table so hard, I feared for their continued health. Nothing broke, and I breathed more easily.

"Exactly," said Mrs. Bissel, pouring tea into a cup and pushing it at me. "It would be the height of folly for you to remain belowstairs after dark. I don't care how much experience you've had in dealing with spirits."

I'd been hoping for such a reaction, although I hid my delight. I was a mistress of my craft, as one of my friends had told me on more than one occasion. I pretended to be unhappy. "But how else can I exorcise the spirit? I need to be in your home when the spirit is active, Mrs. Bissel." If neither woman brought up the kitchen, I aimed to do so. Darned if I'd sleep in her basement; the mere thought gave me the willies.

Mrs. Bissel shook her head so hard, her chins wobbled. "Nonsense. I won't allow you to do so risky a thing, Daisy. There has to be another way."

"Absolutely." Mrs. Cummings placed the cream pitcher and the bowl of sugar on the table more gently than she had the teacups. "Even thinking about spending the night down there is insane, and you'd be a blockhead to try it."

I didn't enjoy being called a blockhead. It didn't go with my carefully constructed appearance and demeanor. I held my frown in check, but it was an effort. I did, however, say, "I don't believe that's the case, Mrs. Cummings. I deal with the—"

"I know, I know," she interrupted gruffly. "I don't care how many spirits you talk to in your séances, this one's bad, and I won't let you do it."

"Nor will I."

I sipped my tea, pretending to contemplate the ladies' words. It was nice of them to worry about me. I guess Billy worried about me, too, but not like this. He mostly just resented me.

After several moments passed and it looked as if Mrs. Bissel and Mrs. Cummings were becoming confused and unhappy, I said slowly, and as mysteriously as possible, "Perhaps there's another way."

"There'd darned well better be," muttered Mrs. Cummings. Evidently feeling that it was safe to leave me alone with Mrs. Bissel, she stomped back into the kitchen. "A night in the basement, my hind foot."

"What other way is there, dear?" Mrs. Bissel asked, popping a piece of cake into her mouth and following it up with a sip of tea into which she'd dumped four lumps of sugar and half a cup of cream.

I bowed my head and tried to appear innocent and cryptic at the same time. "Perhaps I can stay overnight in the kitchen."

Mrs. Bissel brightened up immediately. "Why, Daisy, that's a perfect solution! That way, you'll be close to the basement when the spirit or ghost is active, but you won't be directly in its path."

"My thoughts exactly." It occurred to me to ask how she expected me to get rid of her haunter if she wouldn't allow me to confront it directly, but I'd long since stopped trying to figure out how some people thought.

I left shortly after that, making a short detour into Hunnicutt's Market. In order to disguise the purpose of my visit, I bought a pound of peanut butter for Aunt Vi. Truth to tell, it was for me, too. Aunt Vi made the most delicious cookies with peanut butter; Mrs. Cummings's cookies had reminded me.

A stack of newspapers rested on the counter. As I rooted around in my handbag, I motioned at the top one. "It's too bad about that girl who disappeared, isn't it?"

Mr. Hunnicutt, scooping peanut butter out of the barrel and into a jar, nodded. "Probably buried in the foothills."

"I thought exactly the same thing," I said, wondering how many other people in the area read detective novels. "What a tragedy that would be."

"Sure would."

"I don't suppose you've seen her since she disappeared, have you?"

He gave me an odd look. "Nope. Can't say as I have."

No one else there had seen anyone resembling Marianne Wagner either, as I discovered after a few more minutes of chitchat. I got the impression Mr. Hunnicutt thought I was nuts, but at least I learned what I'd visited the store for. Then I tried to decide if I was disappointed or not, couldn't, caught a red car, and rode it down to Lake and Colorado, where I transferred to a car on an east-west route that let me off on the corner of Marengo and Colorado. It was only a short walk home, and, as I had expected, Billy was happy to see me.

"Hey, Daisy, Sam called and invited the whole family out to eat at the Crown Chop Suey Parlor and to a picture show afterward tonight."

He was more enthusiastic than I'd seen him in ages, so I put on a show of being pleased. Under the circumstances, I didn't want to be anywhere near Sam

Rotondo. He was too darned smart, and I wouldn't put it past him to figure out that I expected to find Marianne Wagner in Mrs. Bissel's basement.

However, the prospect of dining out, and on Chinese food, which was my favorite (truth to tell, all kinds of food are my favorites), was a nice one. "Sounds good. What picture are we seeing?"

"Knickerbocker Buckaroo. It's got Marjorie Daw and Douglas Fairbanks in it."

"Ah. Good." I'd have preferred to see *Anne of Green Gables*, but I knew the men would have objected and called it a "girl's" movie. Anyhow, it was always a pleasure to see Douglas Fairbanks in anything. Or Mary Pickford. I envied her those blond ringlets. Redheads never got treated like fragile flowers the way blondes did. Of course, this particular redhead (me) didn't act much like a fragile flower, either, but that's another story entirely.

Seven

The picture was pretty good, but first I had to endure eating a Chinese dinner with Sam Rotondo. If it had been anything but Chinese, the meal would have been much more trying.

Even before we got to the restaurant on North Fair Oaks, driven there in his car, a closed-in Hudson that had given me an appreciation of Hudsons, I didn't like the way he looked at me. Piercing. That's what his eyes were that evening, and they made me nervous. I always got the feeling Sam Rotondo knew more than I wanted him to about my business.

With Sam's support, Billy walked into the restaurant. He couldn't walk very far, even with help, and he hated me to assist him in public. It galled me that he'd accept assistance from Sam, a man who considered me some kind of lower lifeform. Billy was probably afraid I'd drop him—and I might have, since his weight was difficult for me to balance, as small as I am. Sam was a big man. Maybe it was only sensible that he be the one to help Billy, but I still didn't like it.

In an effort to make Sam think I had nothing to hide—which I didn't, actually, since I had no idea if the Wagner girl was hiding in Mrs. Bissel's basement—I decided to strike the first blow instead of waiting for him to blindside me. As the waiter led us to a table, I asked, "Have the Wagners had any results from the notice they placed in the newspapers?" I smiled as innocently as I was able.

I think the innocent smile was a mistake because Sam's eyes got squinty. "Why do you ask, Mrs. Majesty?" His own smile reminded me of a cobra about to strike. Not that cobras smile. Oh, you know what I mean.

I blinked, again innocently, since I couldn't think of anything else to do. "Why, because we're all worried about the poor girl and her parents." My troublesome sense of honesty got the better of me, darn it, and I added, "At least I feel sorry for her mother."

"I see." He held a chair for my mother. I didn't wait for anyone to perform the gentlemanly gesture for me, but pulled out my own chair and plunked myself down on it. When I glanced up, I saw him eyeing me as if he'd like to haul me out back and take a blackjack to me until I confessed to something. Doggone him, anyhow.

"My goodness, yes," said Vi, for whom Pa pulled out a chair. I was the only female present who didn't deserve masculine courtesy, I guess. "Her parents must be frantic."

"They're upset all right," said Sam. "Can you blame them?" He stared at me as he said it, and took a seat across the table from me. He would. The better to spy on me, I suppose.

Billy sat next to me at the table. I felt more comfortable with my husband at my side; don't ask me why. "No," I said. "I can't blame them at all. It must be awful for them, not knowing if their child is alive or dead."

"Daisy," my mother said softly in a mildly reproving tone of voice. I guess she didn't want me talking about the possibility of death as concerned Marianne Wagner.

Oh, brother. We hadn't even been given menus yet, and already I'd disappointed my mother. Because I couldn't seem to win, I decided to remain mute unless forced to talk. It was going to be tough, because I'm not shy and I generally love to blab.

"I guess the police have to take such things as possible death or suicide into consideration when it comes to missing persons."

This declaration of support came from the throat of my own husband, thereby shocking *me* for a change instead of Ma.

"After all, people don't usually drop off the face of the earth as this Wagner girl seems to have done, unless they have help or they've run away. From what Daisy's told me about the girl, she's not the type to run away."

"Exactly," I said, smiling upon my husband.

"I suppose so." After giving me one last long look, Sam glanced around the restaurant as if he expected to find Marianne hiding underneath a chair.

Upon a sudden and (I thought at the time) brilliant inspiration, I said, "Or maybe she committed suicide." I knew the suggestion had been a mistake as soon as the word *suicide* hit the air. Everyone looked as me as if they'd been delivered of a brutal and communal blow from the Almighty.

"My goodness," murmured Ma, her eyes as round as baseballs, "I hadn't considered the possibility of suicide. How awful."

It sure was. I swallowed, for the first time thinking about what I'd said. It was a bad habit of mine to speak before thinking, I know. I sure hoped Marianne hadn't taken that way out.

A smiling Chinese waiter walked up to our table and handed out menus. I love Chinese food, and as much as I mistrusted Sam, I still had to admit that it was nice of him to take us all out, even though he could undoubtedly afford to. Besides that, he was probably trying to make up for all the free meals he'd mooched off Ma and Aunt Vi. Not that they minded. I was the only member of the family who minded when Sam came over, primarily because he drove me nuts. I already had one man driving me nuts in Billy. I didn't need another one.

The meal was delicious. I was especially fond of the spareribs they served.

After we'd all eaten more than we should have, and finished off several pots of tea and a dozen or more almond cookies, we went to the Crown Theater. There, as mentioned before, we saw Douglas Fairbanks and Marjorie Daw in *Knickerbocker Buckaroo*. A one-reel comedy accompanied the featured picture. I wasn't actually in the mood for a slapstick comedy, mainly because my mind kept dwelling on how I was going to tell Billy I aimed to spend the following night away from him. It wasn't going to be easy. I'd never done anything like it before.

I think what was really bothering me was the thought of suicide. Ever since I'd spoken the word in connection with Marianne Wagner, I'd been thinking of it in connection with Billy himself.

He'd never commit suicide, would he? I couldn't imagine it, although I knew he was unhappy and in terrible pain. The truth was that he wouldn't have been the first shell-shocked veteran of the Great War to kill himself. What an abysmal legacy from an atrocious conflict. Even during the picture, I couldn't drive away the notion of my Billy taking his own life. It kept spinning in my head until I wanted to cover my ears and scream in order to drive it out.

As Sam ushered us all into his automobile—he had supported Billy into the theater, as he'd done into the restaurant—I knew I should be grateful to him. After all, it was a real pleasure for Billy when we got to go out. Since it was so difficult for him to get around, when we went to the pictures we usually visited the two motion-picture theaters that were within walking distance of our house, and I'd push him in his wheelchair.

This outing must have been like an exciting adventure to poor Billy.

Which brought my stubborn mind back to the subject of suicide, exactly as I didn't want it to. Because I couldn't stand it and hoped to divert myself, I said, "Anybody want to go back to our house and have some cocoa and cookies?" We always had cookies, thanks to Aunt Vi.

"We can do better than cookies," said Vi, bless her heart. "I brought half of a chocolate layer cake home from Mrs. Kincaid's house today, since she and Mr. Pinkerton are going to be away for a few days."

"Sounds great to me," said Sam.

"Me, too," said Billy.

Pa, Ma, Aunt Vi, and I all agreed to it, so we traipsed back to our house on Marengo. The hot cocoa was comforting on that cold fall evening, and Aunt Vi's chocolate layer cake couldn't be beat.

After downing a cup of cocoa and a thin sliver of cake, I slumped back against our old sofa and sighed, feeling sleepy and tired and better than I'd felt during the rest of our evening out. There was something about chocolate layer cake and cocoa that could drive even worries about suicide away. I savored the feeling, because I knew it would only last for however long I could keep from telling Billy my plans regarding Mrs. Bissel's kitchen.

It was Sam who brought up the sore subject of Marianne Wagner's disappearance again. He did it in a roundabout way that was more disconcerting than if he'd come right out and asked me if I suspected her of hiding out in Mrs. Bissel's basement. I should have expected it. Sam never did anything I wanted him to, and he was forever doing things I *didn't* want him to do.

With a resumption of his squinty-eyed stare, he said, "So, Mrs. Majesty, have you managed to remove the ghost from that lady's house?"

I heaved a huge sigh and steeled my nerves. "Not

yet." Hoping to divert him—which never worked, but I couldn't not try—I asked generally, "Anybody want more cocoa?"

Nobody did, blast them.

"She keeps going up to her house, though," Billy said. His tone was light, but I sensed the disapproval in it. I suppressed another sigh.

"Do you really think something's living in her basement?"

Sam had asked the question, and it sounded innocent on the surface, but I knew better. Nothing about Sam Rotondo was innocent. When I glanced around our living room, I saw all eyes fixed upon me. With as much nonchalance as I could summon, I said, "Sure, there's something there. I think it's probably a stray cat. Or maybe an opossum. I meant to bring a trap with me today, but I forgot it."

"You're going into the extermination business?" Sam again.

Nuts to him. "Who said anything about exterminating it? If it *is* a wild creature living down there, I don't aim to kill it. I'll trap it and then figure out how to move it from Mrs. Bissel's basement to the foothills. Or something." I felt like sticking my tongue out at him, which pretty much shows the effect he had on me. I reverted to behaving like a three-year-old every time I was in his company.

"If it's a skunk, I doubt that you'll want to drive it up to the foothills," Billy said.

Glad for this diversion, I laughed and lied, "Golly, I hadn't even thought about skunks. You're right, though. It would probably object, and when a skunk gets mad at you, you don't want to linger in its vicinity."

Everybody laughed except Sam, who was still looking at me with his piercing brown eyes. Darn it, what did he think, anyhow? That I'd spirited Marianne Wagner out of her parents' home and into Mrs. Bissel's basement all by myself? Probably. He was like that, and he *always* suspected me of wrongdoing. I'd managed to work myself into a pretty good self-righteous state of annoyance when the irritating man finally rose to leave.

Just as I was congratulating myself on enduring another session with Sam without the two of us coming to physical blows, he asked, "May I speak to you for a moment, Mrs. Majesty?"

I'd joined Ma and Aunt Vi in picking up plates and cups, and I darned near dropped my favorite teacup when I heard the question. Swirling around, I stared at the detective, feeling guilty. Darn it, I *hated* that. Knowing I was, as yet, innocent of keeping anything at all from the police, I mentally smacked myself and told myself to calm down. "Sure," I said. "How come?"

"I just have a question or two about Miss Wagner."

"But I don't even know her."

He smiled, and I decided I'd best just let him ask his questions. Maybe it's because of how we met, but I always felt like a criminal around Sam in those days, even when I had nothing to be condemned for, which was the case in that instance.

Feeling mistreated as well as misunderstood, I left Ma and Aunt Vi to finish cleaning up and walked out to the front porch with the detective. "What do you want to ask me?" I said, adopting a faintly hostile attitude, which I deemed appropriate.

He didn't beat around the bush. "Do you have any reason to suspect that Marianne Wagner is living in Mrs. Bissel's house?"

I managed to look shocked. I *was* shocked, although for a reason I wasn't about to admit to Sam. I hadn't expected him to jump to the conclusion I'd jumped to, much less come right out and voice my suspicions aloud. "What? Why should I believe that, for Pete's sake?"

He eyed me without speaking for several seconds. It

was darned cold out there on the front porch, and I hadn't bothered to put on a sweater. "Well?" I demanded. "What makes you think Marianne's in Mrs. Bissel's house? Do you know something I don't know? Anyhow, it doesn't make any sense. Why should she be there? Is Mrs. Bissel a friend of the Wagners?"

After several heartbeats, Sam said, "I don't know. I just think the timing is awfully coincidental."

"The timing?" I hugged myself hard, hoping to warm up some. "What about the timing? What do you mean by timing?"

"She disappeared, and all of a sudden one of your clients has a ghost in her basement. The two events strike me as too strangely coincidental to be unrelated."

"Shoot, Detective Rotondo, you've been working too hard. You're beginning to see suspicious things everywhere."

He grunted. "Maybe. But if you know anything— anything at all—about the disappearance of Marianne Wagner, you could be arrested for obstructing justice if you don't tell the police about it."

"Oh, for heaven's sake! I don't even know the girl, and I'm certainly not keeping anything from the police." That was the truth, as far as it went, and I was grateful to be able to exhibit honest indignation. "How come you always think I'm doing something wrong, anyhow?"

His mouth screwed up into a moue of frustration. "I don't always think that. I'm only concerned about the Wagner girl. And I know you to be a woman with somewhat—shall we say flexible?—ethics."

"No, we shall not! I am not a woman of flexible ethics!" Now I was *really* angry. "That's not fair! My morals are not flexible at all!"

He looked up into a tree in supercilious disbelief, and I had a hard time not shouting at him. "What I do for a living helps people. Anyhow, *my* business is none of *your* business!"

He grunted again. I wished I really *was* a hardened criminal so I could kick him.

"I apologize," he said unapologetically. "I'm sure you're a woman of the highest moral caliber." I could tell he didn't mean a word of it.

"Darn you! I don't know why Billy likes you so much. You treat me like dirt!"

"Your husband is a good man, Mrs. Majesty."

"Yes, he is. And so am I. A good woman, I mean."

"Hmmm. At any rate, the police are very concerned about Miss Wagner's welfare. So are her parents. You can understand that, can't you?"

I didn't buy the part about her parents being concerned about her. Not her father, at any rate. I'm sure her mother was frantic. "Well, I don't know anything about her, so you can stop worrying on my behalf. Anyhow, if you think she's in Mrs. Bissel's house, why don't you go up there and search the place for yourself? Get a search warrant or whatever they call it." I might lose a dachshund pup if he did, but who knew? Maybe they wouldn't be able to lure Marianne out of hiding any better than I could. If she was there at all, and I didn't know that she was.

"We have no reason to do so."

"Then why are you accusing me of concealing her?"

"I'm not accusing you of anything."

"You are too!"

"Huh."

"Huh, yourself."

He sucked in a deep breath, and I could tell he was irked. He'd probably have liked to strangle me, which was fair, since I'd have liked to strangle him, too. "If you do hear or see anything, you'll tell me?"

"Of course, I will!" I tried to keep my voice down, but it was difficult, mainly because I was cold and furious and beginning to feel a trifle panicky. I mean, gee whiz, I didn't want to be arrested for obstructing justice. That sounded dreadful.

But I was jumping the gun. For all I knew, Marianne Wagner was alive and living in Paris, France, with a husband nobody knew about. Or she might have been murdered and buried in the foothills. It was a terrible thought, but it wasn't the first time I'd had it.

"Very well," Sam said, overtly unsatisfied.

"Thanks for the dinner and the picture," I said stiffly. I didn't want to thank him for anything.

He slapped his hat on his head. "You're welcome."

Even though it was cold and I was about to freeze solid, I watched him walk to his car and drive away. Darn him. I turned and stormed back into the house. Ma and Aunt Vi had already washed up the plates and cups, so I kissed them both good night and went to the bedroom, still fuming.

The evening had already been stressful, so I decided to postpone what was surely going to be a disturbing scene with Billy until Saturday morning.

I was right about the scene. Billy was so angry when I told him about staying overnight at Mrs. Bissel's house, I feared for his blood pressure.

Pa had built a ramp from the back porch to the back-yard, and we were there at the time. I was picking up the oranges that had blown down during the night and pil-ing them into a bushel basket. Billy, unable to be of much help, was fuming in his wheelchair as he carried branches and twigs to the trash barrel next to the garage. I knew it was hard on Billy to be so helpless, and I tried always to remember that. Sometimes when he was being particularly unreasonable, as he was that day, I forgot myself and got mad at him.

"What do you mean, you're going to spend the night in Mrs. Bissel's kitchen?" he roared.

Ma only worked a half day on Saturday, and Pa had taken our old, cranky horse, Brownie, out for a walk. Aunt Vi had the day off because her employer was away for a few days. She had taken a red car into downtown Los Angeles to do some shopping with two of her friends, so Billy and I were alone at the time of our scene.

He never roared when there were others at home with us, and I regretted having slept late that morning. But I'd had a hard time falling asleep the night before because thoughts of Marianne Wagner, Sam, and the obstruction of justice kept plaguing me.

And then, after I'd finally dropped off to sleep, the wind had awakened me, howling like a banshee around our house, rattling the windows, and ripping branches from trees. Every time I was about to drift off, I'd hear a tremendous crackling and rending sound, and my eyes would pop open as I imagined the big oak tree in the front yard toppling over and crushing us all as it smashed our house flat.

My skin itched, my nerves jumped, my head ached, and I knew we were in for it. The Santa Anas were blowing again, and life would be even crazier than usual for however long they lasted.

"It's only for the one night, Billy. I've got to trap whatever's living there when it's moving around, and it only moves at night."

"That's nonsense."

"It isn't, either. It's the only way I'm going to earn any money from this job!"

After a trip to the trash barrel, he wheeled himself closer to the orange tree. "You have no business pretending you're exorcising a spirit if it's a 'possum. You have no business pretending to deal with spirits at all. You're earning money by lying to people, and it's a wicked thing to do."

I'd picked up the bushel basket, but at that, I slammed

it back down. "If you hate it so much, why don't you divorce me?"

Never, in spite of the anguish we put each other through every day, had either one of us ever mentioned divorce. Nobody in my family had ever been divorced for as far back as anyone could remember. The same held true for Billy's family. Therefore, when the ugly word popped out of my mouth, it shocked me as much as it did Billy. I remember that I even slapped a hand over my mouth.

Billy slowly turned his wheelchair around. His face was white and pinched. I knew he'd had a restless night, because I'd had one, too. As I looked at him that Saturday morning, I wished I'd ripped my tongue from my head before I'd said what I'd said.

"Is that what you want, Daisy?"

My throat was so tight, I couldn't talk, so I shook my head, my hand still pressed over my mouth. I was horrified to have said something so vicious to the only man I'd ever loved, even if our life together hadn't been exactly blissful. It sure bore no resemblance whatever to the average fairy-tale happily-ever-after marriage. But the fact was that even if I'd ever considered divorcing my husband, I couldn't have done it. I'd loved Billy my whole life. I'd sooner die than divorce him and leave him alone in the world.

"I'm no kind of husband to you," he said. "You could do better. You could have a real marriage with another man."

My hand fell away from my face and I swallowed hard, trying to dislodge the huge, painful lump in my throat. I shook my head again and managed to say, "Stop it."

He cocked his head, and an ironic grin twisted his lips. "Stop what, Daisy?"

I felt something snap. I guess it was my restraint, because I flung myself at my husband, sobbing. "Stop talking like that! Oh, Billy, I'm so sorry! I didn't mean it!"

His arms closed around me. My shoulders were heaving so hard, I knew I was probably hurting his legs, but I couldn't let go of him. "I love you so much, Billy! I hate fighting all the time!"

"I do too, Daisy."

My nose began to run, and I managed to pull away from him as I dug in a pocket for a handkerchief. I know I looked a fright as I mopped my face and blew my nose. "Then let's not fight, Billy. Let's be nice to each other."

He sighed. It wasn't a big sigh, because his lungs had been ruined by the Kaiser's mustard gas. I felt so guilty, I wrapped my arms around him again. "I'm so sorry, Billy. I don't know why I said that."

"I do," he said.

My heart sank. I knew he thought I wanted out of our marriage, but I didn't. "No, you don't. I love you, Billy. I'd never, ever leave you."

"Huh."

"But I get so angry when you carp at me about my job. It's not fair, Billy. I do what I have to do in order to earn money for us to live. I think you're unfair to me."

Silence.

"It's not evil, what I do," I said, becoming desperate and defensive. "It helps people cope with their problems and losses."

More silence. It was almost like I was back in Mrs. Bissel's basement, trying to lure Marianne Wagner out into the open.

"It's the truth, Billy." I wondered if I was protesting too much. But in spite of all evidence pointing to the fact that he would remain steadfast in his opposition to my spiritualistic career no matter how much good sense I used on him, I persevered. "People need to know that their loved ones are content on the other side of life, and that the ones they left behind aren't forgotten."

"Christ, Daisy, do you know how loony that sounds?"

I withdrew from him and wiped away more tears. "I don't want to argue, Billy. I think you're unfair. I'm using the only skill I have to support us, and it's a better living than I could make as a sales clerk or a typist."

He looked at me for a long time, his face expressionless. Only his eyes held a world of pain, and I almost broke down again. "I should be the one supporting us," he said at last.

"But you can't!" I sucked in approximately an acre of cold, cold air. The wind had picked up again, and I knew we were in for a rough day. His legs couldn't support my weight without hurting, so I eased myself from his lap. "I know you hate it, Billy."

I brushed his dark hair from his brow—the brow that used to be tanned and glowing with health and was now sickly white and furrowed with pain. My heart broke every time I thought about the Billy who used to be, the Billy I'd married. Our wedding day seemed like decades ago. I could scarcely remember that Billy.

"Yeah," he said. "I hate it."

"Then why can't you be a little nicer about my work?" I asked. "I know you'd rather be the one supporting us, but I don't mind, Billy. Truly, I don't. If I could heal you, don't you think I would? But I can't. The only thing I can do is try to earn as much money as I can, and I can make much more money as a spiritualist-medium than I ever could if I worked as a clerk at Nash's."

His shoulders hunched. "I know it."

And he hated it. Because Billy could no longer sigh very well, I heaved a big one for both of us. I contemplated saying something more, but there wasn't anything we hadn't both said a million times before. I figured one more "I love you" wouldn't hurt, so I gave him one.

"I know it, Daisy. I love you, too."

If anyone ever asks you if all a couple needs is love, you can tell them from someone who's tried it that the answer is a firm and absolute *no*. Billy and I loved each other, and look at us. We were both as unhappy as we could be. Worse, we hurt each other all the time for no reason.

A gust of wind lifted the skirt of my housedress and blew my straw hat right off my head. I ran to fetch it, glad for the diversion, calling back over my shoulder, "We'd better get back indoors, Billy. It's going to be a nasty day." And I didn't want his lungs to suffer from the cold. Because I didn't want to add any more insults to his injuries, I refrained from saying so.

"Right," he said. "I'll take the basket indoors."

I caught myself before I could shout out a horrified "No!" The basket was heavy, and if he tried to lift it from his wheelchair, his lungs were going to give out. Scooping up my hat, I raced back to him. "I'll pick it up," I said, one hand clamped to my hat to hold it on.

"I hate being a damned cripple."

It was unusual for him to admit that his physical problems were the cause of his ill tempers. I put the basket in his lap and patted him on the shoulder. "I know, Billy. I know."

I'd just started pushing him, one-handed, trying to keep my hat from blowing away again, when I heard a voice that darned near made me shriek, I was so startled and had been thinking so hard about family problems.

"Here, Mrs. Majesty, please allow me."

Sam. I spun around, gasping. "What are *you* doing here?"

Okay, I know it was impolite, but gee whiz. The man always seemed to pop up out of nowhere when I least wanted him to.

"Just thought I'd drop by to see if you two wanted to go to the Griffith Park Zoo with me today."

He wasn't wearing his copper clothes today, but had on a casual outfit consisting of brown tweed trousers and jacket, a soft-bosomed shirt with an attached collar, and a sporty tie. He stood there, smiling, his hands in his trouser pockets, and I'd never seen him looking so relaxed. Naturally, I figured he was only trying to lull me into revealing something about Marianne Wagner, which just went to show how much *he* knew about anything. I didn't know a single thing about Marianne Wagner, except that she was missing, her father was an ass, and her mother was about as useful as hair on a basketball. The fact that I suspected several things about her wasn't any of Sam's business.

"The zoo?" Billy tilted his head back and peered up at me. "What about it, sweetheart?" I guess he'd forgiven me for the divorce remark, although I hadn't forgiven myself.

I didn't want to go anywhere with Sam Rotondo. I also knew that Billy wouldn't go without me.

"I attached a trailer to my machine to carry your wheelchair," Sam said, as an added inducement, I guess.

It was nice of him to think of Billy's wheelchair. I'd never admit it.

Because I knew Billy loved getting out and about, and because I knew it would be grossly selfish of me to object to such an outing, I offered only one flimsy objection. "What about the wind?"

Sam shrugged. "What about the wind?"

"That's right," I said, recalling conversations I'd had with him months before, "you haven't lived here very long, have you?"

Sam had moved from New York City to Pasadena because his wife was ill with tuberculosis. She'd died shortly after their move west, and Sam had stayed. The latter was unfortunate for me, although I couldn't honestly blame him for preferring the west coast to the east. Pasadena must have been heaven compared to New York City.

"Sounds like fun to me," said Billy.

I knew he meant it because Billy seldom expressed a solid opinion about anything (except my work and me).

The fact that he had done so on that blustery Saturday morning meant he definitely wanted to go on the outing.

"Well, then . . ." I frowned at Sam, who lifted his eyebrows, innocent as a baby. Ha. I knew better. "I'll have to change clothes."

"Great." Sam rubbed his hands together. "I'll push Billy's chair into the house while you get ready, Mrs. Majesty."

I gave up. There was no good reason for me to resent Sam Rotondo for offering Billy a day out—after giving the whole family an evening out. Billy enjoyed the animals at the zoo, and I did, too, if it came to that. It was just that I dreaded a day spent dodging Sam Rotondo's doubting glances and ironic comments. It's petty and shameful, but I also disliked the fact that Sam could make Billy happy when I couldn't.

After that "divorce" crack, however, I owed Billy, so I acquiesced with fair grace, and we spent the day being blown to bits at the Griffith Park Zoo. I'd made the mistake of wearing a day dress with a fuller skirt than was usual for me, and it was all I could do to remain modest in front of the lions and bears and elephants. Sam bought us lunch, and he helped push Billy's chair over the largest bumps in our way.

That day I discovered that the wind is bad for headaches and that I dislike monkeys and love elephants. I don't know what the psychologists would make of that.

When we got home, I took a powder and a nap while Billy and Sam played gin rummy in the living room with Pa, who'd finally become fed up with Brownie's bad mood and returned the horse to his stable in the backyard. Aunt Vi hadn't come home from Los Angeles yet. She was really making a day of it—unless the red cars had blown off their tracks and left Vi stranded somewhere between the Broadway Department Store on

Fourth Street in downtown L.A. and our house. Ma fixed a simple supper (the only kind she knew how to fix; I think I inherited Ma's cooking ability).

After eating a meal of sandwiches and Campbell's tomato soup, I declined Sam's disingenuous offer of a ride to Mrs. Bissel's house, ignored Billy's sullen stare, kissed Ma and Pa good-bye, assured everyone that I'd be home in time for church on the morrow, and drove the Ford to Foothill Boulevard and Maiden Lane.

The Model T creaked and groaned and protested, but if the night progressed as I hoped it would, I was going to need the automobile. And if the machine rebelled and wouldn't start once it got to Mrs. Bissel's house, I was pretty sure I could coast it down Lake Avenue if I had to, in order to carry Marianne Wagner back home.

The notion of money and dachshund puppies kept my spirits from spiraling into my shoes as I drove to Altadena.

Eight

My head had almost stopped aching when I rang the back doorbell, having parked the Model T in the circular driveway. It looked out of place there next to Mrs. Bissel's Daimler—sort of like a poor relation.

The wind hadn't let up. It whipped the skirt of my sober black dress against my legs, and I nearly lost my black, small-brimmed hat a couple of times as I stood there, waiting for somebody to open the door. It also hurled a spiky limb from Mrs. Bissel's monkey-puzzle tree at me. The branch stabbed me in the calf as if I'd been the wind's target in the first place. The poor daphne bush looked like it had been thrashed to within an inch of its life. I found myself longing for summer, even though I often longed for autumn when the weather soared into the upper nineties during the summer months.

Eventually Ginger opened the back door and let me in. She looked down at my stocking, which had been badly vandalized by the monkey-puzzle branch. "Gee, Daisy, those monkey-puzzle things are dangerous. Do you need a bandage?"

"Maybe some iodine," I said. "And maybe a needle and thread."

So, as I didn't care to face Mrs. Bissel with a snagged stocking, Ginger led me up three flights of stairs to her room where I darned my black stocking and applied iodine to my leg. It seemed an inauspicious start to my evening's work. I told myself not to borrow trouble.

When I'd finally doctored my wounds and showed myself downstairs, Mrs. Bissel and her dogs welcomed me with open arms (on the part of Mrs. Bissel) and wagging tails and deafening barks (on the part of the dachshunds). "I'm so glad you've come, Daisy. I can't wait to get rid of that thing."

"I hope I can help," I said demurely. I was always demure when I was working. It was part of the act.

"I'm sure you can," cooed Mrs. Bissel.

That was considerably more than I knew, but I let it pass.

Mrs. Cummings patently disapproved of my agenda for the night; her severe frown told me so. Ginger and Susan looked as if they considered me nuts for even attempting such a perilous method of ghost-removal. I had a sinking suspicion they were right.

It wasn't time for bed yet, although I was exhausted and still mildly headachy, so I dealt out a tarot hand for everyone in the household. I made sure the cards predicted happy times for one and all, and everybody (except Mrs. Cummings and yours truly) was feeling pretty jolly as they trooped up to the second and third floors to consort with the sandman.

After providing me with a tray piled with more food than a family of eight could eat in a month, showing me where to get more food should I run out, and making sure I had plenty of blankets and pillows, Mrs. Cummings reluctantly left me alone in her kitchen. "I still think you're daft," she said before she departed.

"You're probably right," I said with one of my gentlest, most gracious smiles.

As soon as my tray of food and I were alone in the room, I sagged into a chair, rested my head on my arms at the kitchen table, and closed my eyes. Why couldn't something go right for a change? Why was every day a constant battle with Billy? I loved him, and I think he still loved me; why couldn't we get along? Why couldn't I have a normal life?

No answer occurred to me, although I did indulge in an imaginary conversation with God, who told me to stop whining. Big help.

With a gigantic sigh, I decided I might as well settle in for the night. With this purpose in mind, I surveyed the kitchen with an eye to hiding places. There weren't any. But I knew that as soon as I turned out the light, the room would be dark, and any marauding ghost or runaway would be unable to see me any better than I could see her. Or him.

Therefore, I settled a kitchen chair in a corner across from the basement door and next to the large icebox, cushioned the chair with a pillow, and sat down, cradling another pillow in my arms and covering myself with the blanket.

Then I searched for a nearby light switch. There were two of them, and both were across the room from me in different directions. With a sigh, I got up, poked around in kitchen drawers until I found the stub of a candle, lit the candle, traipsed across the room to turn the light off, and went back to my chair. As soon as I blew out my candle, darkness engulfed me.

I'd known it would, of course. That was the whole point of this exercise: to lure whoever hid in the basement into believing the kitchen was empty of human occupancy.

What I hadn't known was that it would be so creepy, sitting there in the dark, waiting for a spirit (or ghost) to show itself. If the wind hadn't been making that giant of a house creak so much, I probably wouldn't have been so ill at ease. And it would have helped, too, if the room hadn't felt so cavernous. When Mrs. Cummings, Ginger, and Susan were all rushing around in it, performing their daily duties, it seemed a bright, friendly room, full of good smells and friendly people.

Not now. Now it was a black hole of a place, fraught with weird sounds and too darned many creatures of my own imagining. Generally speaking, I cherish my imagination because it helps me in my work. As I huddled in the corner of Mrs. Bissel's kitchen, I wished my imagination would go away and leave me alone for a while.

No such luck. Although I'd pretty much discarded notions of mountain lions and bears as potential campers-out in Mrs. Bissel's basement, both possibilities now loomed large in my mind as eminently possible. And then there were the escaped criminals and lunatics I imagined creeping up the dark basement stairs. They'd know I was in the kitchen alone. And they'd get me.

The wind didn't help, as I've already mentioned. Leafy tree limbs outside the kitchen windows scratched on the panes like desperate things trying to get in. The wind got sucked down chimneys and moaned and groaned like assorted souls in torment. I heard skittering noises, like those of mice hurrying across floors—only they weren't in the kitchen. I didn't know where they were. A tree branch tore away from its moorings and slammed against the service-porch door. Somewhere in the house or out of it, something thumped heavily, causing me to jump in my chair and my heart to speed up until it was racing in my chest like a hamster on a wheel.

And cold? Oh, my goodness, that room was cold! I felt every single breeze that managed to wriggle through cracks in windows and doors. Memories niggled at my consciousness of books I'd read when I'd studied spiritualism and fortune-telling. All the books said that when ghosts are present, they bring with them the cold of the grave. I'd like to believe my teeth were chattering merely from the chill and not from sheer terror, but I'm not sure. Darn it, this was no fun.

And Marianne Wagner didn't show up. My headache had come back to keep me company, however, with a vengeance.

After what seemed like hours and hours, I fell into an uneasy slumber, my head resting on my arms, my arms folded on the pillow I'd settled on the kitchen table. Sounds made by the wind and its victims plagued my dreams. I wasn't sure whether I was asleep and dreaming or awake and exhausted when the slightest of noises penetrated my fuddled semiconscious state. I blinked, not sure where I was. And then I remembered everything and darned near fell off my chair. Dread crashed through me like a rampaging tornado.

Someone was in the room with me. Lord, Lord, someone had come up from the basement and entered the kitchen. And I was stuck in a corner with no weapon—and no light. I'd forgotten all about making sure I had matches with which to light my candle.

There was no good to be had in contemplating vain regrets. I could chastise myself for being an idiot later, if I survived the forthcoming encounter. As quietly as I could, I shoved the blanket away from me and stood up. My heart was beating so hard, I was sure the interloper could hear it as I tiptoed to where I knew the light switch to be.

When I got to the switch, I paused, trying to collect my wits and my courage, neither one of which was cooperating. Deciding *to heck with it,* I braced myself and pressed the switch. The sudden burst of light nearly blinded me, but I experienced a moment of triumph when Marianne Wagner spun around, let out a terrified shriek, and dropped the supplies she'd foraged: a can of tuna fish, a can of spaghetti, and a jar of jam. Apparently, she'd become adept at pilferage in the two or so weeks she'd been doing this. The cans and the jar fell to the kitchen floor with a hideous clatter, and I knew Marianne and I weren't going to be alone in the kitchen for long. Fortunately for both of us, the jar didn't break. It bounced on the soft linoleum and rolled a couple of inches my way.

The poor girl stood stock-still, bug-eyed, hands pressed to her cheeks, staring at me as if she suspected *me* of being a ghost. My heart still rattled like a machine-gun, and when I opened my mouth to try to subdue her fears, my voice didn't work.

"Oh my God," she whispered. "Oh my God. Oh my God. Oh my God."

Suddenly I heard footsteps pelting down the main staircase from the upper stories, and I snapped to attention. "Don't say another word," I whispered urgently. I darted over to the girl and picked up her foodstuffs; she was still too stunned to move, much less do anything useful. Shoving the tins and jar into her arms, I then grabbed her shoulders and turned her around. "Get back downstairs. Hurry! And don't say a word. Not one word. I'll help you. Just get out of the kitchen quick!"

She must have been in a state of absolute panic, because she didn't object to my peremptory commands or even try to pull away from me. Rather like a docile lamb heading to the slaughter, she allowed herself to be shuffled to the basement door and shoved inside. I closed the door as quietly as I could, and turned to face the household, my hands gripping the doorknob so Marianne couldn't get back into the kitchen if she took it into her head to do so.

"Daisy!" Mrs. Bissel shoved Mrs. Cummings out of the way and hurried into the room. When she saw me, she stopped running and stood still, panting, her huge bosom working like a bellows, and her arms held out at her sides to prevent anyone else from entering the room.

Her household staff piled up behind her, no one willing to leave the shelter of her largeness for fear of what might befall her without the protection of the mistress of the house. It would have been funny, had I been in a mood to be amused.

I wasn't. I did, however, get my spiritualist aura to come back and help me out, thank heaven. Holding one arm out, palm up in a gesture cops make when they want to hold up traffic, I said in my best mystical murmur, "Stay back. This is not a matter for those unversed in the ways of the spirits. Danger lies below."

"But what happened?"

I wish I could have taken a photograph of Mrs. Bissel and her staff. They all stared at me as they clutched each other, and no one dared step out from behind Mrs. Bissel's bulk. I guess they figured her body would stop any projectiles directed at them by evil-intentioned ghosts or fiends. The idea tickled me, and I calmed down some more.

I didn't budge from the basement door, though. "You must leave me to deal with this alone." I lowered my voice to a thrilling whisper. "The spirit walks."

"It did more than walk," Ginger said, sounding more than slightly miffed. "It must have tripped over something to make that awful noise."

Darn her. Here I was putting on one of my best extemporaneous performances, and she had to get all practical on me. I eyed her with disfavor. "Please. I know what I'm doing."

Very slowly, Mrs. Bissel began backing away from me, toward the swinging door to the pantry, making her staff back up or risk getting squashed under her tread. "We'd better get back upstairs, girls. Daisy's right. She knows what she's doing, and we'd only be in the way."

God bless her. Not only did she have the best dogs in the world, but she trusted me. I nodded. "Please, all of you. Go on back upstairs. I'll deal with the spirit belowstairs."

As if she were unsure about any of this, Mrs. Bissel said, "Will you let me know what happens, Daisy?"

"Of course." What did she think? That I'd run away, like Marianne Wagner, never to be seen again? Not very likely, no matter how much I sometimes wanted to. But more than that, I wanted Billy's puppy—and it was beginning to look as though I'd get it, too, if these people would only go away and leave me to deal with Marianne.

Unless she'd escaped through the other exit down there as I dealt with Mrs. Bissel and crew. Darn. I wished I hadn't thought about that—or better, that I'd thought about it sooner, so I could have locked the other door from the outside. Impatient now, I repeated, "Please. All of you need to go back upstairs so that I can finish my job here."

"I don't know," Mrs. Cummings said doubtfully.

Frustration gnawed at me. I looked imploringly at Mrs. Bissel. She was the boss, after all. "Mrs. Bissel?"

"What?" She blinked several times before she understood, then she jerked. "Oh! Yes, of course, Daisy."

She turned and made herding motions with her arms. I must say her appearance was quite . . . remarkable, I suppose is the best and least insulting word for it. Clad in a bright purple dressing gown with a matching purple sleeping cap covering her tightly curled gray hair, she resembled a gigantic eggplant with a growth. Mrs. Cummings, Ginger, and Susan, after sending me a variety of last glances—Ginger rolled her eyes—obeyed their mistress.

Mrs. Bissel was the last one out the door. I tried to reassure her. "I'll let you know the result of my work as soon as I can, Mrs. Bissel, but that may be sometime tomorrow. Please don't come into the kitchen until you hear from me."

"Of course, dear. Please be careful."

"I will be. Thank you."

I gave them plenty of time to get upstairs. I didn't want anyone barging in on Marianne and me. When I was pretty sure we wouldn't be interrupted again, I grabbed the untouched tray of food Mrs. Cummings had left for me, opened the door, noted with gratitude that Marianne had turned on the light, and charged down the basement steps as fast as I could. By that time, I was positive Marianne had escaped.

You can imagine my elation when, panting from my headlong dash, I paused at the foot of the staircase to catch my breath and saw her sitting on the mangle, her hands covering her face, sobbing as if her heart was broken. I gulped air and told myself to proceed with caution. Not that I believed Marianne would harm me, but I needed her cooperation, and she wouldn't give it if I handled this wrong.

"Marianne?" I stayed near the staircase and spoke softly so as not to spook her. "My name is Daisy Majesty, and—"

"I know who you are," she interrupted, her voice thick with grief.

"Mrs. Bissel and her staff thought the basement was haunted and asked me to get rid of the ghost. But the ghost is you. You gave everyone quite a scare."

Lifting her head from her hands, she wiped her tears with the hem of her dress. "I didn't mean to."

She sounded utterly miserable. Looked it, too. She'd tied her blond hair back from her face with a ribbon before she left home, I guess, but it now straggled from its confinement. It also looked as if it hadn't been washed since before she ran away. Her dress was stained and wrinkled, and her black cotton stockings had ladders as big as my thumb.

I took a step closer to the mangle, and when she didn't move, I dared come even closer. I didn't want her to bolt. "I have some food for you, Marianne. I'm sure you haven't been eating well."

Her glance slewed from my face to the tray I held. She looked as if she'd lost weight since the last time I

saw her. Never robust, at the moment she looked as if
she were about to expire from starvation. Making no
sudden movements and walking slowly, I finished my
trek to the mangle and laid the tray down next to her.
Then I stepped back a pace or two so as not to worry
her. She swallowed as she surveyed the tray.

Mrs. Cummings had provided me with a variety of
small sandwiches (with their crusts removed. Now, I ask
you: what's the point of that?), a banana, three apples,
an orange, a cluster of fat juicy grapes, and at least a
dozen cookies and tiny iced cakes. Because I hoped to
soothe her, I took three of four more steps back from the
mangle and gestured at the food. "Dig in," I suggested.
"You can eat while we talk."

She eyed me sharply for three of four seconds before
she reached for the grapes, plucked one from the bunch,
and popped it into her mouth. Her eyes closed, and I
heard her stomach growl. I felt really sorry for her.

"Eat up, Marianne. Have a sandwich."

Without speaking, she did as I suggested, stuffing a
cream-cheese-and-cucumber sandwich into her mouth
as if she hadn't eaten for weeks and weeks, which was
almost true.

After watching her jam food between her lips for a
minute or two, I said, "Will you please talk to me, Marianne? Your parents are worried about you."

She swallowed several more grapes and said, "Ha," in
a dispirited tone.

Because I thought I understood the nature of her disbelief, I said, "Your mother is worried, anyhow."

She heaved an enormous sigh. "Poor Mother. I'm
sorry to have worried her."

Taking a chance, I said softly, "Your mother has
enough burdens to bear, I imagine, without being frightened on your behalf."

Her head jerked up, and her eyes widened as she
stared at me. She'd have had pretty eyes if they weren't

so sunken and tired-looking, with huge black circles under them. "What do you know about my family?"

Okay, here's the thing: When I'd first considered the possibility that it was Marianne Wagner hiding in Mrs. Bissel's basement, I hadn't thought further than finding her and taking her back to her parents. When she stared at me with those huge, petrified eyes, as round and blue as robin's eggs, I began to rethink my plan of attack. If she was this scared of her father, maybe I'd have to come up with something else to do with her, rather than returning her to the family manse.

Oh boy. I visualized my poor little self being taken into custody by Sam Rotondo. Wouldn't he just love that? And Billy; wouldn't he feel justified? In case you harbored any doubts: Yes. He would. They both would.

I could scarcely bear to *think* about Billy's reaction if I should continue to hide Marianne from her parents.

That being the case, and because I honestly didn't want to incur the wrath of the Pasadena Police Department or my beloved but ever-cranky husband, I decided to question Marianne about her family before I did anything rash. People tended to hide their skeletons and dirty laundry, not wanting to have them flaunted to the world, but this was a special case. I aimed to get the whole truth, even if it was appalling, from Marianne.

In any case, it couldn't hurt to ask. Because I hoped to make her relax, I hiked myself up onto the mangle beside her, leaving the tray of food between us so as not to spook her. "I don't really know anything about your family, Marianne, although I must admit your father doesn't act like a very nice man. I'm sorry if that offends you."

"It doesn't," she said dully.

"And your brothers, too, never appeared to me to be full of the milk of human kindness. I never got the impression they were especially fond of their fellowman. Or woman."

"Ha." Still not a trace of animation. "They're not."

"That being the case, and because I want to do what's best for you, it would probably be a good idea to tell me about your family. I gather you ran away from home."

"Yes."

Gutsy of her, and unexpected. I'd have been less surprised to find out she'd been murdered. "Then I assume you're not eager to return to them." I shrugged and smiled gently. "Heck, you ran away from them. There must have been a good reason."

She took a tuna-fish sandwich and ate it before she broke off a small bunch of grapes and put it in her lap. She looked as if she was guarding them. Obviously, she hadn't been eating well lately. I assumed she still wore the clothes she'd run away in, too, because her dress, which had started out in life an expensive number made by a skilled seamstress, was a total loss unless somebody could work miracles. So was she. Well, she wasn't a total loss, but she hadn't bathed for a long time, although I knew from the tiny puddles she'd left in the washbowl that she'd at least tried to keep her hands and face clean.

After eating two grapes, she turned and looked directly into my eyes. "I hate my father." At this shocking confession, her own eyes filled with tears that overflowed and trickled down her face again. "He's cruel to my mother and me."

Because I was pretty sure she'd run away unprepared for life, even when it came to the tiny things, I dug in my pocket and pulled out a clean handkerchief. "Here," I said gently. "Use this."

She did. "Thank you." Her voice was tiny.

I waved her thanks away. "Tell me about it, Marianne. Maybe we can think of some way to prevent your having to move back to your father's house."

For the first time since I'd caught her in the kitchen, she appeared minutely hopeful. "Really? You'd actually help me?"

"Of course I will," I said, committing myself without a second thought. Billy would have said I never gave anything a second thought, but that's not true. Not entirely, anyhow. "If you're afraid of your father, I'll do my best to find something else to do with you." That didn't sound right. "I mean, do you have any relatives you can stay with? Do you have friends who could put you up?"

She shook her head and slumped, her one tiny flame of hope extinguished before it had time to grow into a full-blown fire. "No. He'd get me and make me go back. My father, I mean."

"I know who you meant." Tilting my head, I studied her for a couple of moments. "Does he hurt you? Hit you? Beat you?" I kept my voice gentle and low.

She nodded. "He uses a strap. Always on my back and legs so that the bruises and welts don't show. And he does . . . other things."

I stared at her, not understanding. "Er . . . what kinds of things?"

She drooped a little more, blushed, and shook her head again. "I . . . I can't tell you."

Understanding struck. At least I thought it did. "Good Lord! You don't mean to say that he . . . he touches you in—in secret places."

Nodding disconsolately, she said, "He says it's for my own good and that it's because he loves me, but I don't believe him. He told me never to tell anyone because they wouldn't understand and wouldn't believe me."

"Well, that tears it. You're not going home." Once my indignation was roused, any remaining shreds of caution flew out the window. If I got arrested for assisting Marianne Wagner to elude her bestial father, so be it. I thought of something else that might help the two of us to collude effectively. "How old are you, Marianne?"

"Eighteen." She sniffled unhappily. "If I were twenty-one, I could do anything I wanted, and my father wouldn't be able to touch me ever again, but I'm not."

Darn. "True. That's a real shame."

"And if I go home again, he's going to make me marry Marcus Finch."

I cast about in my memory, trying to place Mr. Finch. Couldn't do it. "Who's he?"

"An awful man. All he cares about is money."

Money is a handy commodity, especially if one doesn't have enough of it, but I didn't point out this salient fact to Marianne, who wouldn't have been able to appreciate it. "I see."

"Father wants me to marry him because Marcus agreed to give him a lot of money."

"Good heavens, you mean to say he's *selling* you to this man?"

She heaved a huge sigh. "That's what it amounts to, I guess."

"That really stinks, Marianne."

She absently popped an iced cake into her mouth, chewed, swallowed, grabbed an apple and crunched into it. "You're telling me."

"Well, there's no use in crying over something that can't be helped." Suddenly I remembered Harold Kincaid, who, because of his own experiences with life, was likely to take a more sensible view of Marianne's problem than most "normal" people. Sitting up straight, I said, "I have it!"

She eyed me uncertainly. "You have what?"

"I know what we can do." I gave her a reassuring smile. "I have a friend who'll be happy to hide you in his house—"

"No!"

I winced because she'd screeched. "Shhh. Don't bring the gang down on us again, or you'll be shipped back to your father quicker than you can say Jack Robinson."

She didn't holler again, but her voice was urgent when she next spoke. "No! Don't tell anyone else. Please, Mrs. Majesty! Nobody must know about me!"

Deciding a soupçon of common sense wouldn't hurt in this instance, I looked her square in the eye. "Heck, Marianne, the whole of Pasadena knows about your disappearance. Altadena, too. And probably San Marino and Alhambra. Your parents placed an item in all the local newspapers, and your picture has been posted all over everywhere. Unless I can get Harold to help us, it's only a matter of time until you're discovered and sent back home."

She buried her face in her hands once more and slumped tragically. "Oh my God."

"That being the case," I went on, trying to boost her morale, "we need to find someplace to put you until we figure out what else to do with you. You can't stay in Mrs. Bissel's basement for another three years until you're twenty-one."

"Oh my God."

"Harold is a very nice man, and I'm sure he'll be able to assist us. If he agrees to hide you, you'll be living in the lap of luxury, because he has a beautiful home in San Marino."

"Oh my God." She still had her face buried in her hands.

I was beginning to get the feeling that Marianne wasn't going to be of much help when it came to rescuing herself. She'd grown up a pampered rich girl, except in certain perfectly ghastly ways, and probably nobody'd ever bothered to teach her how to take care of herself. If it had been I who'd run away, you can bet I'd have taken as much money as I could with me. And I'd have gone a whole lot farther than three or four miles north into an Altadena basement. Out of curiosity, I asked, "Why'd you pick Mrs. Bissel's basement, out of all the basements in Pasadena and Altadena?"

She shrugged. "I was tired. I didn't know where else to go or what else to do. I couldn't stand it anymore, and when I found the outside door to this basement open, I climbed in."

"Hmmm. I guess I can understand that, but . . . well, never mind." The poor girl didn't need my criticism on top of everything else. She had enough on her plate. We were silent for several minutes. Marianne started eating again, and I sat on the mangle, thinking.

After formulating a plan, more or less, I spoke again. She'd polished off the sandwiches and was working her way through the last of the cookies and iced cakes. "What we need to do first is get you out of here."

"Where will I go? That man's house?" Her words were mushy because she'd spoken with her mouth full. It was probably the first time she'd done such a thing since her mother taught her manners, and I wondered if Billy was right about me and if I really *was* a bad influence.

"We can't go there until I talk to him about you. I'll do that as soon as I can tomorrow morning."

I could have driven her over there that night, but I didn't want to butt in on Harold if he and Del Farrington were having a tête-à-tête. Although Marianne had been through a lot with her father, I didn't trust her not to frown on Harold's way of life.

People were odd that way. Let a man do something horrid to a woman, and people shake their heads. Let a man so something wonderful with another man, and people lock them both up and call them perverts and criminals. I'll never understand human nature, even though I've made my living by exploiting it.

"What will I do in the meantime? Stay here?"

"No. You can't stay here any longer. Mrs. Bissel's staff is getting too edgy, and they might find the courage to come down here and confront you. Right now, they still think you're a spirit. Or a ghost."

"Oh."

"The thing is, the only place I can think of hiding you until I can talk to Harold is in the basement of our house on Marengo." I scanned Mrs. Bissel's basement. "It's not as commodious as this one, I'm afraid."

For the first time since I'd discovered her in the kitchen, she smiled. "I don't mind."

I thought of something else that might throw a monkey wrench into the works. "Nuts," I said. "I have to go to church tomorrow, because I sing in the choir."

"That's very good of you, Mrs. Majesty."

"For heaven's sake, call me Daisy."

"Daisy," she said obediently.

At least the girl was manageable. That was a good thing at the moment. As far as ultimately getting her to be responsible for herself, her strict compliance to other people's orders and evident inability to think for herself might not be such a useful quality. "I guess you'll have to stay in our basement until we get back from church. I'll try my best to make arrangements before I leave the house in the morning, but I can't guarantee anything."

"As long as I don't have to go home again," she said, her voice trembling.

"You won't have to go home again," I promised. I only hoped I wasn't lying to the poor child.

Nine

The rest of that night was pure hell. I don't think I got more than an hour's worth of sleep altogether.

First I had to sneak Marianne out of Mrs. Bissel's house and into the Model T. That wasn't too difficult, since the rest of the household was upstairs, although they probably weren't sleeping. Not since Marianne and I had startled them out of their collective wits.

I threw my blanket over her, hoping that if anyone was looking out the window, maybe they wouldn't see her. I know it sounds stupid, but I was desperate. Besides, the night was a dark one, and the wind was still howling like the devil's choir in hell. I didn't think anybody would notice a black lump huddled near me as I walked to my automobile. The wind darned nearly blew both of us to perdition before we got to the Model T and I gestured for Marianne to squat next to a back tire.

Marianne did as I'd told her to, staring at the driver's side of the car. "Where's the door?" She pointed, her whispered question almost blown away before it reached my ears.

I whispered, too. "There isn't one on that side."

"Oh."

"I'll have to crank it up. You'll have to wait until I get it started and get in. Then you can get in, too."

"I've never seen a car without a door on this side."

That's because she was rich and didn't have to get

around in an old Model T Ford. I didn't say so. "I'm hoping to buy a new machine soon. Do you know how to handle the choke wire?" I was hoping for the best but prepared for the worst, which turned out to be a good thing.

"What's a choke wire?"

"Never mind."

Cranking the Model T to life was difficult even in the daytime. In the dark of night, with the wind trying like mad to whip me away, it was even worse than usual. I couldn't see a blasted thing. I persevered, as I always did back then no matter what I was doing, and eventually the motor coughed to life. And I didn't even break my arm, which was perhaps the first truly good thing that had happened all evening.

The Model T didn't have headlights like cars today have, and it was hard to see anything by squinting into the blackness as windblown dust made my eyes water. Marianne sat next to me in the machine, shivering, although she was still wrapped in the blanket.

Once I got the automobile on the road, I asked, "Are you all right?" If she took sick from eating such a poor diet for two weeks, I didn't know what I'd do. If she visited a doctor, there was no way in heck her presence in my life could be kept a secret.

I think she nodded, although I couldn't see her very well. "I'm just scared."

Perfectly understandable. I was scared, too, for that matter. Sam's warning about the obstruction of justice kept clanging in my head like an alarm bell. Darn him, anyhow. Trust Sam Rotondo to make my job more terrifying than it already was, even when he wasn't present.

"Try not to worry," I advised. She might as well relax, since I was worrying plenty enough for the both of us.

"I'll try."

Boy, was she easy to manipulate. Her father must have whipped her into obedience when she was a baby.

I don't think she had a backbone to call her own—not unlike her mother. I decided to work on her, maybe get her to respect herself and stand up for her rights. She'd better learn how to take care of herself, and quick, if she expected to remain independent of her family.

All at once the task facing me loomed up like a mountain in my mind's eye. I couldn't do this. I was being an idiot. I was wrong and bad, and Billy was right about me. And so was Sam.

"Thank you, Daisy," Marianne said in a small but sincere voice. "Nobody else has ever understood or tried to help me before."

Okay, maybe I wasn't a total failure. The poor thing needed somebody on her side. She *deserved* for someone to be good to her for once. Smothering an internal sigh, I said, "I'll do my very best to help you, Marianne." I'd never expected rich people to be so much trouble before I took up spiritualism as a profession.

"Thank you."

I heard her sniffling and sighed inside again.

I managed to get Marianne inside our house on South Marengo Avenue in Pasadena without making too much of a racket. Tiptoeing around the house like a thief in the night, I brought her bedding, an old nightgown and robe, and some slippers. Her feet were bigger than mine, but she didn't complain. By that time, if she *had* complained, I'd probably have carted her straight back to her family, no matter how much I sympathized with her.

Hiding a daughter from her parents was a frightening and perhaps illegal proposition, and I was in an anomalous position. Actually, it wasn't anomalous at all. I was doing something both the law and everyone else would consider wrong. But I couldn't abandon her. Not now that I knew the hell she suffered in her home.

I couldn't stop having mental visions of cutting her father's privates off, but I kept them—the visions, that is—to myself. Even Marianne, who had good reason to wish her father a eunuch, would likely have been appalled.

After I got her settled, and after reassuring her approximately six hundred and fifty times that I'd be back as soon as could be, I left her in our basement and drove the Model T back up the hill to Mrs. Bissel's house. The car objected strenuously to being driven uphill twice in one night, but I forced the issue, praying all the while that it wouldn't break down or that I wouldn't run into anything in the dark. Because I figured I'd asked enough of God for one night, I thanked Him once I was safely parked in the circular driveway.

Then I trekked back down to the basement, cleaned up the crumbs, grape stems, banana peel, and apple core left over from Marianne's meal, carried the tray upstairs, and searched around until I found paper and a pencil. I wrote a note to Mrs. Bissel, telling her that I believed I'd solved her problem and would return to her house later that afternoon (it was almost dawn by this time), and I'd talk to her then. Fortunately, I remembered I'd told her not to return to the kitchen until she heard from me, so I left the note attached to the telephone in the pantry.

When I got back home, I checked once more on Marianne. She'd made herself snug on top of an old desk Pa had carted down there a couple of years before. He'd planned on making an office for himself, then decided he didn't need an office, which was true, but the desk remained.

I held a candle, since if she'd fallen asleep I didn't want to awaken her, and I saw her eyes, glowing like a cat's in the dark. "Don't be afraid," I whispered. "It's just me. I only wanted to see if you needed anything else before I went to bed."

She sank back into her nest on the desk. "Oh my! I was so frightened. I was afraid somebody'd heard me and decided to check the basement."

"No, I think the household's asleep. Try to sleep,

Marianne. My family will be leaving the house about nine in the morning to go to church, and there's always lots of coffee cake left over. My aunt Vi is a wonderful cook. You'll find plenty to eat in the kitchen. There are eggs in the icebox and bread and so forth."

There was a lengthy pause before Marianne said, "Thank you."

I surmised the reason for her hesitation. "You can't cook, can you?"

"No."

"Don't worry about it. Just eat things you don't have to cook. You can make toast, can't you?"

"Um . . . I don't know."

Again I wondered how this was going to work. It was as if the girl had been trained to be helpless. "Just eat the coffee cake, then, and maybe an orange. All right?"

"Yes. Thank you."

"You're welcome."

When I finally trudged upstairs from the basement for the last time that night—or morning, I mean—I was done in. It was all I could do to remove my dress and shoes, and I fell into bed with my combinations and stockings still on.

And I couldn't get to sleep to save myself. I kept envisioning myself being handcuffed and hauled off to the pokey by Sam Rotondo.

When I finally did get to sleep, it didn't last long. Billy woke me up around 6:00 a.m. with one of his nightmares.

"Joey! Joey! Oh, God, no!" he shouted, all but scaring the life out of me. "Oh, Jesus! The blood, the blood. Joey! God, Joey. No. He's gone."

I jerked to a sitting position and blinked to get my bearings. After no more than a second or two, I understood what had happened, so I lay back down and wrapped my arms around my poor, ruined husband. "Hush, Billy. It's all right."

Every time this happened, the crack in my heart grew wider, and I loved him more. Life had been so darned hard on Billy. He deserved better. Before the war, he'd been a cheerful, happy-go-lucky man, with a good start on a career as an automobile mechanic.

Not any longer. Now he was a shell-shocked, shot-up, gassed-out husk of himself, and guilt gnawed at my insides like rats gnawing on stale bread. I was so often short-tempered with him, and I tried his patience constantly, even though I didn't mean to. Months earlier, I'd started thinking that Billy deserved a better wife than I was proving to be, and I couldn't shake the thought out of my head. The poor man was stuck with me. I vowed I'd try to be a better wife to him. I made the same vow almost every morning, and broke it every day.

Shaking and sweating with the aftermath of his terrible dream, he whispered, "Sorry, Daisy. I was fighting the damned Huns again, I guess."

"I know," I crooned, trying not to cry because Billy hated it when I did. "It's all right, sweetheart."

He groaned and I felt his body go stiff in my arms. When he flailed around in his sleep as he'd just done, his legs and his lungs suffered afterward. He lived with pain all day, every day, even when he didn't have nightmares. Although I worried constantly about his morphine use, I whispered, "Do you need me to get your medicine, darling?"

He tried to hide the extent of his torment, but I could tell how much he hurt because he gasped involuntarily when he opened his mouth to answer me. Then he said in his tight, pain-racked voice, "Yes. Please."

"Be right back." As carefully as possible, I unwrapped him and crawled out of bed. Without bothering to put on my robe, I ran to the bird's-eye-maple dresser on the other side of the room. I was shocked when I withdrew the bottle from where Billy kept it, because it was almost empty. I'd picked up a full bottle from Dr. Benjamin two days earlier. Could this be the same bottle? It was on the tip of my tongue to ask Billy if he'd had to use that much morphine syrup in two days' time, but I swallowed the question. Better he have the medicine, I reasoned, than live in anguish.

The fact that he'd taken so much of a potent opiate in two days' time frightened me, though. A lot.

He didn't need me nagging him about his drug use. He had sufficient hardships to bear without adding a pestiferous wife to the mix. I exasperated him quite enough already. That being the case, I took him the bottle and turned to go to the kitchen. "I'll get a glass of water." Dr. Benjamin had told me he should take the medicine with a full glass of water.

"Don't bother." He lifted the bottle to his lips and drank.

My mouth fell open and I spoke before thinking. "Billy! That's too much!"

"No, it's not."

He stared straight at me as he said it, and my heart hurt as if talons were digging into it. I pressed a hand over my bosom, and didn't know what to say. When he recorked the bottle and held it out for me to take, I shook my head slowly. "Oh, Billy."

"Yeah," he said. "It's a rough life." Then he let his head fall back against the pillows, still gripping the bottle.

Without any more fussing, I went to the bed and took the bottle from Billy's grasp. It was empty. After staring at my husband for several seconds, wishing there was something I could do for him and knowing there wasn't, I gave up and put the bottle back in the dresser drawer. Leaving Billy to recover on his own, I put on my robe and slippers and went to the kitchen,

feeling disheartened and hopeless and full of rage at
fate.

I guess I've had worse days—well, I know I have—
but I sure hope I never have to go through another one
as tense as that first Sunday in December 1920. The
weather didn't help. Fog had rolled in overnight and
now blanketed our neighborhood. Well, I thought, as I
had many times of late, why not? Might as well add
dismal weather to what was certain to be a horrid day. It
lived up to my expectations, too, with the exception of
a few bright spots.

Suffice it to say that I managed to sneak downstairs
to confer with Marianne before heading for church. She
was in a blue mood, which I appreciated and understood
although I think I might have been a bit short with her.
I'm not sure about that.

She'd always sort of reminded me of one of those
long-eared, baggy-eyed basset hounds, even when she
wasn't scared for her life and safety. There were good
reasons for her sadness, but that morning I was bone
tired and inclined to be snappish. I find helpless women
difficult to tolerate, probably because I've never been
allowed to be helpless.

In an attempt to redeem myself, I reminded her about
the coffee cake. If anything will make a discouraged
person perk up, it's Aunt Vi's cooking. "Wait until we're
out of the house," I said. "Then eat all you want."

"Thank you."

I guess I'd intimidated her, because she didn't say another word, and she stared at me as if she expected me
to rustle up a bullwhip and flay her alive. I sighed heavily and climbed back up the basement stairs.

I also succeeded in getting in touch with Harold Kincaid, discovering in the process that Harold isn't an
early riser. I apologized abjectly for telephoning him so

early on a Sunday morning, and he agreed to consider the Marianne problem and get back with me later on in the afternoon.

Surviving breakfast with my family turned out to be easier than I'd anticipated, mainly because there was an interesting article in the *Pasadena Star News*.

"By gum, will you look at this!"

We couldn't look, because Pa was the one holding the newspaper. But we all asked him what he was reading.

"A fellow named Marconi started a radio broadcasting station in England!"

"Really?" Billy was always interested in new inventions. He and Pa had been gabbing about radio-receiving sets for months. "I read where they broadcast a football game in Texas a while back."

"A football game?" My fork stopped its path to my mouth, and the piece of coffee cake I'd speared fell off. "How'd they do that? Do they tell you when the ball's in the air and stuff like that? Would you like to listen to ball games on a radio set?"

"Sure! I think it would be swell." Billy chewed a bite of bacon enthusiastically.

His eyes were bright, too, and I knew he wished he could still play football and baseball. Failing that, he'd have liked to watch some games. I had a hard time featuring how merely listening to somebody talk about football could be entertaining. Perhaps my state of exhaustion accounted for my failure of imagination.

"Gosh, Billy," Pa said. "Just think about it. If we got a radio-receiving set, we could listen to all sorts of events. And the news. By God, we could get the news firsthand instead of waiting until it gets from wherever it's happening to us here on the west coast."

"I don't know," I said, contemplating the nature of recent news events. "Do you really want to know who the rumrunners are killing every day?"

I'd been hell-bent on Prohibition before it went into effect. And really, when I thought about it on a personal level, I was still glad the country'd hopped aboard the water wagon, mainly because I was afraid Billy'd take to drink if he could—instead of taking to morphine, I guess. But the illegal liquor trade was becoming more vicious by the day, and I wasn't so sure any longer that country-wide Prohibition was even possible, much less a good idea.

"There's more to life than bootlegging," said Billy dryly. "I think it would be swell to be able to listen to ball games on a radio set."

Okay. After I brought Billy's dog home and bought a new motorcar, I was going to get the family a radio-receiving set. That depended, of course, on whether I could find one in Pasadena. Since Los Angeles had become the center of motion-picture activity in the nation, I didn't suppose it was too far-fetched to believe it would also become the radio capital of the world.

We hadn't talked radio to a standstill before we had to leave for church, so we were still yakking about it as we walked through the thick, cold fog to the First Methodist Episcopal Church, North, where perhaps the most miraculous occurrence of that day took place considering all the loose ends cluttering up my life: I remembered the alto part to "I Want a Principle Within." What's more, I sang the whole song without falling into a coma, which I think demonstrates remarkable determination under the circumstances. It's a truly boring hymn. Don't tell anyone I said so. I think it's some kind of sin to hate hymns.

During the church service, I kept an eye on Billy, unable to shake the vague horror that had bothered me since I saw him finish off that bottle of the morphine concoction Dr. Benjamin prescribed for him. I had a good view of the congregation from the choir stall behind the minister's pulpit. Generally I used the boring parts of Mr. Smith's sermons to take in the ladies' fashions and decide what I should sew next (I might not be able to cook worth a darn, but I could sew like a champ). Not that day. That day I stared at my husband and tried to spot signs of drug addiction. Since I didn't know what signs to look for, my scrutiny didn't serve to bring me to any conclusions on the matter.

My word, but he was a handsome man. He'd been tall, my Billy, and slim. That was before he'd been confined to a hospital overseas and then in Los Angeles for months after he'd been shot and gassed in France. When he came home to me again, he was a stoop-shouldered, skeletal wreck.

As I sized him up that day, I decided he looked more gaunt than slim nowadays. The hollows in his cheeks hadn't been there before the war, nor had the slouch to his posture. He found it difficult to sit up straight since the mustard gas had ruined his lungs, and any exertion brought on fits of painful coughing.

After a while of watching Billy and becoming more dismayed as the seconds dragged by, I gave it up and vowed that the next day I'd pay Dr. Benjamin a visit. I had a few hard questions to ask the good doctor, although I feared the answers were going to be as hard as the questions.

When we got home after church, I saw that some of the coffee cake was missing, although I'm sure I was the only one who noticed it. We Gumms and Majestys don't generally keep close tabs on our leftovers, but I paid special attention to the cake that day because I was worried about Marianne and wanted to be sure she ate. She had some weight to make up for in order to regain her full vigor— or her health, if vigor was too much to ask. She'd never struck me as the robust type on the few occasions I'd seen her before her escape from her father's house.

What I wanted to do then was take a nap, but I couldn't. Since I was already dressed in a nice, sober-hued Sunday dress, hat, and shoes, I said, "Gotta go up to Mrs. Bissel's house. Be back as soon as possible."

"Have your lunch first, Daisy," said Aunt Vi. "No sense rushing around and not eating."

"I'm not very hungry." Even as I said the words, I knew they wouldn't work. Nobody in Aunt Vi's life ever got away without eating a meal, and I'd already forgotten to eat once that week. The dear woman would be watching me like a hawk for days to come, forcing food down me any time she caught me.

As far as I was concerned, I could, and undoubtedly should, go without eating for a week or two, since the prevailing mode in fashion was for a boyish, slim-hipped and -bosomed, straight-as-a-string figure. Mine didn't qualify. I wasn't fat, but I had more curves than were strictly fashionable. I bound my breasts, but that didn't help much. I'd have fit right in during the Victorian epoch. But Queen Victoria had died in 1901, a year after my birth, and people had skinnied down since then.

The whole family was in the kitchen, Ma and Pa sitting at the small kitchen table, Billy angled in between the icebox and Ma's chair. He looked better than he had earlier in the day. Of course, he would, after having downed all that morphine. I wished it was Monday, so I could run right over to Dr. Benjamin's office and confide my worries to him.

"Come on, Daisy," Billy said. "Mrs. Bissel can wait until after you eat."

True, but I might not be able to. I had a mental image of me falling asleep behind the wheel of the Model T and crashing into an orange tree. I'd die there, battered to death by autumn oranges. Nevertheless, I gave in. "Okay. I guess I can eat something."

"Humph," snorted Aunt Vi. "I should say so, Daisy Majesty."

"Are you feeling well, dear?" Ma felt my forehead as I took a chair next to Billy.

God bless my family. At that particular moment, I wanted them all to vanish, but I knew I was only grouchy because I was tired. They were the best family in the world, really. "I'm fine, Ma. Honest. Just a little tired. I didn't get much sleep last night."

"Did you have any luck getting the ghost out of that lady's basement?" Pa grinned at me.

"Sure did." I winked back at him. "It was a cat. I forgot the darned trap again, but I managed to catch it and let it out down the street from our house."

"You ought to have brought it home, dear. I'm sure we could use a cat."

"I don't like cats," Pa said. "A dog, now . . . well, dogs are different. I like dogs."

That was merciful, considering I expected to bring one home that very day. I said, "I'm not much of a cat person, either. But I'm sure someone will adopt it."

On my behalf, I must state here that, had the cat been real and not imaginary, I probably would have brought it home. I'm not terribly fond of cats, but I'd never have allowed it to wander all alone in the big, cruel world with no one to care for it. I'm like the rest of my family in that regard.

I expected Billy to say something sarcastic about me having spent the night chasing ghosts and catching cats in somebody else's house, but he didn't. When he did speak, I almost wished he'd used his breath to scold me.

"Sam's coming over in a little while," he said. He took the plate Vi handed him and smiled at her. "We're going to spend a gloomy afternoon playing gin rummy. He claims he's going to win his fifteen cents back, but I doubt it."

Billy had a wonderful smile. It used to make my heart go pitty-pat and my knees turn to jelly. That morning, it made me want to scream and throw things. If there was one person on the face of the earth I wanted to see less than I wanted to see Sam Rotondo—especially with Marianne Wagner hiding just under his big flat feet in our basement—I couldn't think of who it could be.

"How nice," I said weakly as I, too, took a plate offered by Aunt Vi.

"You eat every bite of that sandwich, young lady," Vi told me sternly.

I saluted her. "Yes ma'am."

She flapped her hand at me. "Go along with you, Daisy Majesty."

Whatever that meant. Aunt Vi always said it when somebody did something amusing or annoying, so I guess it was an expression that covered a lot of bases.

Pa cranked the Model T to life for me after I'd finished my lunch—every bite of it—so at least I didn't have that chore to accomplish. The Ford groaned a good deal as it chugged up Lake Avenue, but I wouldn't let it quit. The fog had burned off by then, and I thought it was kind of a shame when the sun came out and shone benevolently down upon us. The ghoulishly groaning motorcar would have added a ghostly note to an already creepy atmosphere. It sounded out of place on a sunny day. I'd just about decided to buy an Oldsmobile by the time I got to Mrs. Bissel's house.

Mrs. Bissel and her entire household staff were awaiting me at the sun-room door when I parked the old Model T in the circular drive. They all looked happy. Even Ginger had a grin decorating her face. I bowed my head for no more than a couple of seconds as I thanked God that at least I'd earn a puppy from this wretched job.

While I was at it, I asked God to provide me with some kind of inspiration as to what to do with poor Marianne. I didn't allow myself too long a prayer, since I feared I'd go to sleep if I kept my eyes shut for very long. Anyhow, my experience with prayer has been that God is happy to receive thanks, but falls short when it comes to dishing out direct advice.

Which meant I had to think for myself, darn it. See?

This is where the pesky notion of free will comes into play. If God would only condescend to handle this problem, I could leave it up to Him. But no. Life doesn't work that way.

Mrs. Bissel actually trotted out to the car, which was something to see because every inch of her jiggled. "Daisy! You did it!"

I'd done it, all right. And it was probably going to land me in the slammer. I told my cynical side to give me a break and smiled back at Mrs. Bissel. "I'm so glad I could help." Out of curiosity (I mean, *I* knew I'd taken care of the noises coming from belowstairs, but how in heaven's name did *she* know it? It was only around one-ish on a Sunday afternoon, and my understanding of the problem had led me to believe the "ghost" only walked after dark), I asked, "Are you certain, Mrs. Bissel? I don't want to take credit for a job I haven't finished yet."

"Fudge!" she exclaimed. "I know you did it, because after that one hellish noise in the middle of the night— you know, when you told us all to go back to bed—we didn't hear another single sound all night long. Then we all went down to the basement together this morning before we went to church, and we could *tell* the thing was gone. Not a single one of us received the *hint* of an evil emanation."

Oh. Well, gee, I guess I had done it, then. Evil emanation? Heck, even *I* hadn't received any evil emanations from poor Marianne, except those my imagination had invented. On the other hand, I was the only one who knew it had been Marianne. With appropriate humility, I nodded my head. "I'm only glad to have helped you out."

"You did more than help! You got rid of the ghost!"

This astonishing pronouncement came from Ginger, whom I'd begun to think of as even more cynical than me on a bad day. Maintaining my demure mien, I murmured, "It was nothing."

"Let's not stay out here freezing to death," exclaimed

Mrs. Bissel. "Come inside, Daisy! Mrs. Cummings is so happy the spirit—or ghost . . . tell me, do you know what it was exactly, Daisy?"

She would have to ask. "It was a stray and restless shade from the Other Side, Mrs. Bissel. After some prayer and persuasion it was induced to relinquish its residence on this plane and move on where it can rest in peace forevermore." Rest was on my mind a lot that day.

Mrs. Bissel and her staff exchanged a series of befuddled glances. Then, one after the other, they nodded wisely. Mrs. Bissel said, "Aha. We thought as much."

"I knew it wasn't any old rat," said Susan, giving Ginger a light shove on the shoulder.

"Well, how should *I* know what it was?" Ginger asked grumpily. "I've never had anything to do with spirits before."

"None of us has," agreed Mrs. Cummings. Then she gave an eloquent shudder and rubbed her arms, presumably to get her gooseflesh to go away.

Mrs. Bissel continued where she'd left off. "At any rate, Mrs. Cummings was so happy to have the thing removed from the premises that she's made one of her wonderful chocolate-caramel cakes. Come into the breakfast room and have a slice, Daisy!"

"Thank you," I said, wondering where the cake would fit. I'd just eaten lunch. But chocolate-caramel cake is chocolate-caramel cake, and one should always seize opportunities that present themselves (my father told me that once after he won an entire pecan pie at an Independence Day celebration at Tournament Park).

"And I'm going to insist that you take your puppy home today, too," Mrs. Bissel said, fairly glowing at me. "You've more than earned it."

"Thank you!"

Thus it was that I not only returned home that day with the most precious puppy in the world, but Mrs. Bissel had also forced upon me twice as much money as I generally charge for my services. It might have been fair; I couldn't really say for sure, since I'd never attempted to rid a house of a runaway spirit—or a runaway girl—before. I aimed to tuck the money in a box I kept for money to buy a new motorcar. I'd already squirreled away over seven hundred dollars, which was almost enough to purchase a new Oldsmobile.

Ten

Thanks to the puppy, my mood had improved at least a hundred percent by the time I pulled the Model T up to the curb in front of our bungalow on South Marengo. I was grateful for the non-ghostly atmosphere now, since fog would have been out of place with the mood engendered by a happy-go-lucky, waggy-tailed, black-and-tan puppy who considered riding in even so shabby a car as ours a treat. His little paws could scarcely reach the window, but he put them there, hung his head over the sill, and barked at everything with sheer joy (I assumed it was joy, since he seemed awfully cheerful).

The sun had stayed put in the sky. No longer did it try to hide behind huge mounds of gray thunderheads and acres of fog. Rather, it shone down on the puppy and me from a gloriously blue sky decorated with puffy white clouds. The San Gabriel Mountains loomed over Altadena and Pasadena like benevolent monoliths, and I allowed myself to believe I'd actually be able to help Marianne overcome her problems without being arrested in the process.

Some of my self-assurance shriveled when I walked in the front door to see Sam Rotondo laughing it up with Billy and Pa. The three men absolutely adored playing gin rummy together on Sunday afternoons. Except that Sam and I didn't get along, I was glad for Billy's sake that he'd formed a friendship with Sam.

Well, and Pa's sake, too. Since he'd started having so much trouble with his heart, I was grateful to anything that kept him close to home, especially since he was always forgetting to keep a supply of nitroglycerine tablets on his person.

But I determined not to allow Sam to darken my mood that afternoon. I had the puppy in my arms, underneath my black coat. He was being pretty good about being hidden, although he wiggled a trifle at first. Then he discovered the buttons on my frock and amused himself by gnawing on them.

"Guess what I have," I said when the three men turned to see who'd invaded their masculine sanctuary. I presumed Ma and Aunt Vi were in the kitchen or had gone out for a walk, since they didn't greet me at the door.

Billy blinked at me a couple of times. "Guess? How can we guess?"

Pa played along. "Looks like it's something small. A revolver?"

"Pa!" I giggled.

"Or maybe a hand grenade," said Sam.

For once, he didn't look as if he suspected me of just having robbed a bank or murdered a neighbor. He even grinned slightly.

Sam Rotondo was a good-looking man, and if he wasn't forever doubting my integrity, I probably would have liked him. It was better this way. After all, Sam was a widower, and I was trapped in an unhappy marriage. Who knew what might have happened if we'd liked each other from the beginning of our association? I've always prided myself on being a good, upstanding woman, but even good people can be tempted. I hope I'll always do the right thing, even in the face of temptation, but I'm not altogether sure of myself.

"Come on, Billy," I said, grinning from ear to ear, "you have to guess, too. I won't keep you in suspense for too long, but make a stab at it, okay?"

His face, which had been pinched in disapproval—he always seemed to disapprove of me—relaxed. "Okay, Daisy. I think it's a . . . a set of keys to a brand-new Duesenberg."

I laughed outright at that one. "Good heaven, Billy! I know we need a new motorcar, but lower your sights, will you?" I turned my back to the men. "Okay. You all missed it." Whirling around with the puppy held aloft in both hands, I cried, "Voila!"

"What in the name of glory is it?" Sam said.

I gave him a well-deserved scowl. "What do you mean, what is it? It's a puppy!" I carried the pup over to my husband. "And it's for Billy."

"A puppy," Billy murmured dazedly.

With my heart thumping hard, I set the puppy on his lap and stood back. "I thought he could keep you company when I'm out working."

"Isn't he a beaut?" Lord bless my father. "Why, he looks like a real scrapper, Billy."

"I don't know about the scrapper part," I admitted, "but I think he's about the most precious puppy I've ever seen. He's one of Mrs. Bissel's pedigreed dachshunds."

Billy's sour expression lightened as he and the puppy gazed into each other's eyes, sizing each other up. When Billy lifted a hand and stroked the pup's silky fur, my tension eased slightly. I knew, because I'd known the pup almost since his birth, that his fur was soft and warm and felt like velvet.

"Gee, it's sure small, isn't it?" Billy lifted the pup and stared at it, and the pup's tail wagged like a pendulum. They were nose-to-nose for a couple of seconds before the pup licked Billy's nose, Billy's face broke into a huge smile, and I let out a whoosh of relief.

"Is that thing really a dog?" Sam sounded skeptical.

I turned on him, indignant. "What do you mean, 'is it really a dog'? It's not merely a *dog,* it's a *pedigreed* dog! It comes from better lines than *you* do, I'm sure!"

He laughed, and I realized he'd been ragging me. "I'm sure he does. My lines stink."

Everyone laughed then. Except me. I was embarrassed because I'd lost my temper at Sam for no reason. I consoled myself with the knowledge that I usually had a darned good reason for getting mad at him.

"He's real cute," murmured Billy, turning the puppy over onto its back and rubbing its tummy. The pup's tail swished back and forth like mad. Everyone was watching with rapt attention, and we all grinned when his hind leg started making scratching motions.

"He sure likes that," I murmured, enchanted.

"He's in puppy heaven," Sam said.

The telephone rang. It would. And just when I wanted to bask in the approval of my husband and father, too.

I left the puppy with the men and dashed for the 'phone in the kitchen, hoping to catch it before all the ladies on our party line picked up. I should have known better. A chorus of "Hellos" tickled my eardrum as soon as I lifted the receiver.

"Daisy Majesty, please," said the rather high-pitched masculine voice on the other end of the wire. I recognized the voice as belonging to Harold Kincaid.

"I'm here, Harold." I didn't want him to get frustrated with the other ladies and hang up on me. "Please, Mrs. Barrow, Mrs. Lynch, and Mrs. Mayweather, this call is for me, thanks."

Two clicks. I waited, trying to discern breathing on the wire. "Is anyone else there?" I didn't want any eavesdroppers on this call.

"I'm still here," said Harold.

"I'm glad of that, but I don't . . . Mrs. Barrow? This call is for me. Please hang up your wire." The old snoop held out for another second or two, but I knew she was there. "It's against the law to listen in on other people's telephone conversations, Mrs. Barrow." For the most part, I tried to be nice to the old bat, since I didn't want anyone, not even snoopy eavesdroppers, spreading nasty tales about me. Sure enough, a third click, louder than the other two, smacked our ears. "Ah, there it is."

"How many people share your wire, Daisy?" Harold asked. He was born into a wealthy family and worked in the motion-picture industry, thereby earning another fortune all on his own. Harold didn't have to share his telephone wire because he could afford the exorbitant fees the telephone company extracted from people who wanted a wire all their own.

"I don't even know for sure. There are at least three other families sharing it, and one of the women, Mrs. Barrow, is the world's biggest snoop."

"I'd be happy to pay for you to get a private wire, sweetie. You know I'm at your disposal."

That's because I'd been instrumental in getting Harold's father arrested and locked up for criminal activities. I know it sounds odd for a child to dislike his father, but if you'd known Mr. Kincaid, you wouldn't like him either. Besides all that, Harold was a truly nice man. So was his boyfriend.

I guess that goes to show you that preconceptions don't always hold true. Both Billy and Sam considered people like Harold and Del loathsome and unnatural. I suppose they were kind of unnatural, but they were both nicer than your average young American male. I'd decided months ago that I didn't care what they did together, as long as I didn't have to watch.

Anyhow, Harold had told me more than once that he hadn't had any control over his . . . what would one call it? Sexual proclivities? He'd gone on to say that he couldn't imagine anyone actually *choosing* to be hated and vilified by the ordinary people in the universe, and that if he'd had a choice in the matter, he'd have opted to be normal, too.

I don't know about any of it. All I know for sure is that Harold had become a very good friend of mine, and

I wouldn't have had him any other way than the way he was.

"Thanks, Harold. But you needn't do that. I don't usually have secrets to keep." I shot a glance toward the living room. The men were still occupied with the puppy, I guess, because I didn't see anyone staring at me in an attempt to figure out what I was talking about and to whom.

"Your present secret is quite a doozy," Harold said. "I suppose this one makes up for you not having many before it came along."

"Yeah." I sighed heavily. "I guess it does."

"At any rate, I sure hope you won't get too many more calls like this one."

"You said it." My spirits started to sag as I took Harold's comments to mean he couldn't help Marianne and me in our quest to keep her hidden from her father.

"But I think I have a solution for you, at least for the next couple of weeks."

"You do?" All at once I wanted to whoop with glee.

Then again, what did I know? I hadn't seen Marianne since early that morning. For all I knew, she'd flown the coop or died from boredom down there in the underpinnings of our house.

Unlike in Mrs. Bissel's house, there was no door leading from our basement to the outside world. We had but a single entrance and exit, a door situated below the staircase, between the hall and the kitchen. I guess only rich people can afford multiple basement doors. But Marianne wouldn't have needed an extra door. It would have been painfully easy for her to run away while we'd all been at church.

"I believe I do," Harold continued. "The poor thing can't stay here because my aunt from New Jersey is coming to visit next Tuesday. Mother's out of town for a couple of days, but she's coming back on Wednesday with outriders and will have a full house for a month, so I offered to put Aunt Matty and Uncle William up, and

I don't think I could keep Miss Wag—ah . . . your friend's presence a secret with people coming in and going out all the time. Mother and Algie Pinkerton are planning to announce their engagement the week after next at a ball to be held at Mother's place."

Harold's mother, Madeline Kincaid, was a very lovely lady, if not too bright. Algie Pinkerton, a long-time friend of hers, must have proposed. I thought the match was a good one. As already mentioned, Mrs. Kincaid's first husband had turned out to be a real stinker. Her daughter was a louse, too. She deserved a little happiness in her life, and Algie was a great guy, even if he had a silly name. What's more, he was already rich, so he wouldn't be marrying her for her money, as her first, despicable, husband had done.

Mr. Eustace Kincaid was in prison now, which is where he belonged, and I'd heard that Mrs. Kincaid had filed for divorce. She'd have to wait a year from the date of filing before she and Algie could tie the knot, but there was no law against long engagements that I knew about.

When her husband's nefarious deeds had been brought to light, Mrs. Kincaid had worried about what the world would think. Algie Pinkerton had been proved correct when he'd pointed out that the world would undoubtedly find her more interesting than ever, thanks to the scandal. I thought it was keen that Algie and Mrs. Kincaid were getting together.

"Oh, I'm so glad!" I said. "I'm sure they'll be happy together."

"Anybody would be better than my old man," Harold said, his voice as dry as old bones.

"I'm sure you're right." It had always distressed me that Harold's father was such a beast, because Harold rated a nice father. I sometimes had the urge to let him borrow my own for a few days. I'd bet Pa wouldn't call Harold a faggot.

"Anyhow, getting back to your problem, do you know George Grenville?"

"Sure, I know him." Although I couldn't fathom what Mr. Grenville had to do with the topic under discussion. He was a nice man, and he owned my favorite bookstore, Grenville's Books, on Colorado Street and Oakland Avenue. We'd gotten to know each other almost as soon as he moved from Boston to Pasadena. He was very good about ordering books for me, and we'd conducted many interesting conversations about various forms of spiritualism. George knew a little bit about pretty much everything, because he read so widely.

"Have you ever seen the cottage he lived in when he first moved here? Behind his store?"

"Er . . . no. I didn't know he lived behind his store."

"He doesn't any longer. He built himself a tidy little bungalow on Catalina, near Washington. He only stores books in the cottage nowadays."

"Oh." Gee, Harold sure knew a lot about George Grenville. I wondered if George was of Harold's persuasion. I didn't ask, believing such a question to be too personal (not to mention none of my business).

"He's agreed to take in Miss . . . ah, I mean, your friend, for a little while. She can live in the cottage behind his store until you and she figure out what to do with her on a permanent basis."

"How nice of him!"

"Yeah, he's an all-right sort of guy." As if he'd read my thoughts, he said slyly, "He's not one of us, Daisy. So you'd better be sure you trust him with your runaway."

"Harold!"

He burst out laughing, and I knew he'd caught me again. Harold was forever saying outrageous things, hoping for just such a reaction from me. He usually succeeded. I laughed, too. "You're horrid, Harold. You know that, don't you?"

"I do my best," he said modestly. "Listen, Daisy, the

bookstore's closed today, but George said he can be there by four this afternoon. Can you get your stowaway there at four?"

"Sure, that shouldn't be a problem." Except that I'd have to sneak Marianne past my family and drive her to the bookstore in the Model T, which didn't have a top, and it would still be broad daylight and anybody might see us. I'd think of something. I had faith in my powers of sneakiness. "Thanks so much, Harold."

"Thank George. I only provided the means of communication."

"I certainly appreciate it. It would never have occurred to me to ask Mr. Grenville to help out."

"I've known the man since he moved to California," Harold said. "I helped him set up his store."

"I didn't know that."

"He comes from money, but he was trying to escape a smothering family. I understood his problem, believe me. But he's made a success of the bookstore all by himself."

We ended our conversation shortly after that. Boy, you could never tell about people, could you? I wanted to rush right downstairs to the basement and tell Marianne the good news, but thought I'd better check on the living-room contingent first. I'd been hearing strange noises issuing therefrom for several minutes.

When I set foot in the dining room, I glanced at the living room again and knew why. "Good heavens!" I pressed a hand to my heart, which had all but shot out of my chest when I saw Billy's wheelchair fly across the room. Well, it didn't actually *fly;* it zoomed, I guess is a better word for it.

Pa and Sam were laughing so hard, they couldn't talk, and Billy was hollering as loud as he could, so I had to find out what had propelled the wheelchair by myself. By Jupiter, it was the puppy. Billy had hold of a piece of cloth—I learned later that it was Sam's handkerchief—

and the puppy had taken hold of the other end by means of his sharp little puppy teeth. He was growling up a storm as he pulled Billy across the room, his shiny black butt in the air and his tail wagging like a fiendish windmill blade.

Sam was on his hands and knees, his arms held out, attempting to steer the puppy in the right direction. Pa sat on a chair, acting as the cheering section, I guess. They were sure having fun. When the puppy backed into the wall, he let go of the cloth and spun around, barking at the thing that had dared halt his progress. I have to admit, it was a pretty funny sight.

"Shoot, Billy, do you think that's good for him?"

Wiping his eyes, Pa sputtered, "Why not? He's a strong one, and he's enjoying himself."

So was Billy. I hadn't seen him grin so hard in, literally, years. He even laughed a little. I hoped his lungs wouldn't give out on him. "I've named him Spike, Daisy. Because he's such a tiger."

"Spike?" I squinted at the puppy. He was as shiny as polished onyx and about as big as a minute. He didn't look much like a Spike to me. But he was, as Pa had pointed out, a strong one. And he was Billy's. I guess I could live with a Spike in the house. "Spike's a good name for him."

"Thanks, Daisy. This was a great idea of yours."

My heart glowed. "Super, Billy." It was so very seldom that I did anything Billy approved of. "I'm so glad you like him."

"He's a champ," Billy said simply.

"He's the smallest dog I've ever seen." Sam looked almost human kneeling there. Spike had picked up the handkerchief again and was now trotting around, looking as if he was searching for an appropriate hiding place for his treasure.

Sam made kissing noises to attract Spike, who left off dragging the handkerchief and went over to sniff Sam's hand. Sam rolled the pup over and allowed his fingers to be used as chew toys as he glanced up at me. "This was a great idea, Mrs. Majesty. A great idea. This little fellow's cute as a button."

"Thanks." I was as unused to receiving compliments from Sam as from Billy, and I'm afraid I sounded like it. Fortunately, nobody was paying much heed to me, the pup being the center of attention.

"He's a spunky little ruffian," Sam said. He sounded as if he approved of this character trait. If it had been a human ruffian, I'll bet he'd have arrested him.

"A real spitfire," agreed Billy, rolling his chair over and grinning down upon his friend and his puppy.

Sam stood up, creaking at the knee joints as he did so, and Spike sniffed at his shoes.

It occurred to me that Spike probably wasn't house-trained. "I'd better take him outside for a minute or two and let him do his duty."

I was just about to bend down to pick Spike up and take him outdoors, but I was too late. Lifting a little puppy leg, he squirted a tiny stream onto Sam's polished shoe.

"Hey!" Sam cried.

Pa started laughing again, hard.

So did Billy.

Even more amazing was that I, too, burst out laughing. Scooping the puppy up in my arms, I said, "What a discriminating doggie you are, Spike!"

"Hey," Sam said again, frowning at me.

I didn't mind his frown for perhaps the first time in our acquaintance. Spike had done what I'd longed to do for months: totally disconcerted Sam Rotondo. "There are rags in the kitchen," I said as I sailed out the front door.

I heard Pa whooping with glee even after the door closed behind me.

* * *

Spike fit right in with the rest of the family. In time, Sam forgave him for piddling on his shoe. As the three men played with the dog, with intermittent games of gin rummy tossed in while Spike caught his breath and napped, I slipped away to pack some things in a sack for Marianne.

I was having good luck that day, aside from the fact that I was probably going to spend the rest of my life in jail. But Ma and Aunt Vi had gone out visiting, and Spike was keeping my father, husband, and mortal enemy engaged in the living room. Without anyone noticing, I slipped down to the basement, carrying a sandwich and a glass of milk for the stowaway.

Marianne threw herself at me when she saw me. "Oh, Daisy! I was beginning to think I'd die down here!"

"Sorry. This house isn't as easy to hide in as Mrs. Bissel's." I laid the food out on a suitcase. "Here, eat up, Marianne. I have good news for you."

She'd already stuffed her mouth full of sandwich, but that didn't stop her from asking, "You do?"

"I do. Thanks to Harold Kincaid, you now have a place to stay while we figure out how to keep you safe from your father forever."

She swallowed before speaking again. "In Mr. Kincaid's house?"

I shook my head. "He can't keep you because he's got company coming, but another gentleman, George Grenville, has a whole entire cottage that's currently unoccupied. You can stay there for at least a couple of weeks."

She looked at me without speaking as she chewed and swallowed another bite of sandwich. I was glad she didn't talk with her mouth full again, mainly because I'd begun to think of myself as having an unfortunate influence on her. But I suspect she'd only been really hungry when she'd first spoken.

"Then what?" she asked. She didn't look as overjoyed as I thought she should.

"I don't know what then," I told her, a trifle put out with her attitude. "Golly, Marianne, let's take this one step at a time, all right? I've never tried to keep a human being hidden before. It takes some practice."

"I'm sorry." She looked repentant as she slugged back half a glass of milk. "I'm just so scared."

"I'm sure you are." I was, too, if it came to that, although I didn't burden the girl with my worries. "But Harold and I will be able to think of something, I'm certain." Liar. I was certain of no such thing, at least in regard to my own personal self. But I had great faith in Harold.

I left Marianne to her milk and sandwich and went back upstairs to tell Billy I was leaving him for the afternoon. I anticipated he would be less trouble than usual since he had not only Sam and Pa to play with, but Spike as well.

Claiming I had a séance to conduct—fortunately, Billy didn't bring up the fact that I never conducted séances on Sundays—I managed to get Marianne out of the house slightly before four that afternoon. It would have been a nice, easy walk to the bookstore on a late-fall afternoon, but I didn't want Marianne showing her face in town, so I aimed to drive her there.

None of the men mentioned the odd hour of the fictitious séance, either, I guess because they were involved in their gin rummy game and the puppy. I noticed several one-cent pieces stacked next to my husband's place at the card table, so I presumed Sam's game hadn't improved. I also noticed that Spike was curled up on Billy's lap, and my heart glowed. For the first time in a long time, I knew I'd done something right.

Ma and Aunt Vi were still visiting elsewhere when Marianne and I crept out of the house. Marianne hid behind a winter-bare hibiscus bush while I set the spark and throttle levers, turned the crank, reached inside to pull the spark lever down, then leaped into the machine and pressed the low-speed pedal, all the while praying that I would soon be able to afford a motorcar with a "start" button and a battery so I'd never have to fiddle with the lousy crank and levers again.

Once the Ford had sputtered to life, I scouted the area for intruders. I didn't see any, so I gestured at the hibiscus bush. Marianne dashed toward me, stooped almost double so the men wouldn't see her if they happened to look out the living room windows.

She scrambled into the car, huddled on the floor, and I threw a blanket on top of her. "Keep that over you, Marianne. I don't want anyone to know you're in the auto with me."

"I will," she said, her voice muffled.

You can imagine my feeling of relief as I pulled away from the curb, tootled up Marengo Avenue, and turned right on Colorado. We were almost in the clear! It was true that I still had to figure out how to ensure Marianne's safety in the long run, but at least I didn't have to keep her hidden in my basement any longer.

You never knew about people, either. It was always possible that Marianne herself would discover she possessed a modicum of ingenuity. I wasn't about to bet on it, but stranger things had happened. At least I thought they had.

Eleven

"I think I'm allergic to wool," Marianne said as I pulled up in front of Grenville's Books.

"Don't throw off the blanket yet," I advised. "I don't see Harold or Mr. Grenville."

"But it itches."

"Then scratch. Don't show yourself until I know what's going on." I fear my voice reflected my impatience with the girl. Here I was, putting my entire life and freedom on the line—not to mention the good opinion of my husband, if he had such a thing—and she was griping about an itch. "It's wool," I said, straining to keep my temper in check. "Wool's supposed to itch."

"I'd make a lousy sheep," she muttered.

That was a pretty funny comment. I'd have laughed if I hadn't been so all-fired nervous. I was, however, vaguely encouraged to think that Marianne might develop a sense of humor if allowed to remain apart from her father's domineering influence for long enough.

I let the Model T idle at the curb, hoping it wouldn't have to idle for long, because it tended to overheat if it wasn't moving. Actually, it tended to overheat anyway, although its behavior was better in cool weather than it was during the summertime. It was a good thing Marianne had waited until autumn before making her bolt for freedom.

Squinting east down Colorado Street, which was all but

deserted on this cool Sunday afternoon, I spotted a low-slung automobile speeding our way. "I think Harold's coming!" I sagged behind the steering wheel, not having realized until that moment exactly how edgy I was.

"Can I come out yet?"

"No. Keep scratching. I've got to talk to Harold about where to take you. I don't see Mr. Grenville anywhere."

"I hope this works," Marianne mumbled.

"You and me both." We'd discussed Harold's plan, and she'd balked at first when she learned that Mr. Grenville was a single gentleman. I didn't tell her that most men were beasts, married or single, because I didn't want to shock her. However, when I'd pointed out that she had no choice in the matter unless she wanted to return to her father's house, she gave up her protests.

When I glanced at the woolen lump on the floor, I noticed it was moving in spots, as if Marianne had taken my advice and was scratching her itchy skin. I'm not really heartless; I'd have been glad if the blanket hadn't been made of wool, but gosh, a body can't have everything, can she?

Sure enough, the automobile turned out to be Harold's snazzy, jazzy, bright red Stutz Bearcat. It was a great motorcar, although I didn't envy Harold too awfully much. A bright red Bearcat would seriously compromise the image I'd so carefully crafted of myself as a serious spiritualist—if that isn't a contradiction in terms. A sober-hued, closed-in Oldsmobile or Chevrolet would be better for my purposes.

Harold made a U-turn in the middle of Colorado Street. I held my breath and scanned the neighborhood, waiting for a copper to whiz out and give him a ticket. No such animal appeared, and I breathed more easily. After climbing over Marianne and trying my best not to step on her, I ran over to the driver's side of his machine.

"Harold! I don't see Mr. Grenville anywhere!" If he'd

backed out of our deal, I didn't know what I'd do with Marianne.

"That's because the cottage is behind his store," Harold said, pushing his goggles up so that they rested on top of his head. I've never felt the need to wear motoring goggles. The Ford couldn't go fast enough to whip up very much wind or dust, unless the Santa Anas were blowing, and when that happened, nothing helped. "Follow me."

"Right-o." I raced back to the Model T, jumped over Marianne's still-huddled form, and put the car into gear. With a cough and a chug, the old Ford pulled away from the curb, and I followed Harold around the corner and into the bumpy, unpaved alleyway. We pulled up in front of a tiny doll's house of a cottage.

After parking, Harold vaulted over the Bearcat's door and trotted over to me. "Where's the girl?"

I pointed to the woolen heap on the floor. Marianne's voice floated to our ears. "Is it safe to get out yet?"

"She's allergic to wool," I explained to Harold.

"Too bad," he said. "Wait just a minute longer, Miss Wagner. I've got to see if George is in the house. I don't have a key."

He walked up to the door of the tiny abode. Before he got there, the door was flung wide, and George Grenville stood there, smiling, his wire-rimmed spectacles gleaming in the afternoon sunlight. Darned if I didn't nearly swoon from sheer relief. "He's there!"

"Can I get up yet?" Marianne asked again. She was beginning to sound a trifle desperate.

"Just another little minute," I promised her.

George walked over to the Model T. "Good afternoon, Mrs. Majesty. I understand you have a delivery for me." He chuckled, as if he thought this was a good game. I thought that, as a game, the entire situation stank.

"Thank you so much, Mr. Grenville," I said with absolute sincerity. "We didn't know what to do."

"Glad to help a damsel in distress," he said gallantly, if a wee bit tritely. He peered into the automobile. "Er, where is the damsel?"

I looked up and down the alley. "Are you sure it's safe?"

"Sure," said Mr. Grenville. "The whole town rests on Sunday afternoons. There's nobody around for miles, and there won't be until around seven, when evening church services begin."

"Thank goodness for that." I leaned over and grabbed the blanket. "Okay, Marianne. Scoot."

She did exactly that, tumbling from the automobile, pushing off from the running board, and streaking to the open door of the cottage, crouched low for fear someone might notice her. Harold followed her into the cottage, and I got out of the automobile and folded the blanket. I was about to put it back in the rumble seat where we kept it, when I thought about something. "Will you need this, Mr. Grenville?" I sniffed the blanket. "It smells a bit like gasoline."

"I don't believe so, Mrs. Majesty. I've stocked the place with blankets and linens." He was enthusiastic and set to enjoy his part in our melodrama. I silently wished him luck and hoped he'd remain sanguine for as long as we needed him.

"Thank you awfully, Mr. Grenville." I guess tension and nerves had been keeping me alert because as soon as rescue appeared on the horizon, I suddenly felt as if I was about to drop in my tracks from fatigue. A yawn took me by surprise, and I slapped a hand over my gaping mouth, embarrassed. "So sorry. Didn't get much sleep last night."

"I can well imagine." Mr. Grenville rubbed his hands. "Please, Mrs. Majesty, let me show you the amenities. I fear there aren't many of them."

"You're a peach to allow Marianne to stay here. Believe me, the girl needs help."

I guess I sounded grave, because he lost his smile. He was an apple-cheeked fellow, slim and of medium height. He looked much too healthy and athletic to be a bookseller. His hair was dark brown, and he didn't cut it as often as he ought. At the moment, it curled around his ears and kissed his collar, looking as if it might tickle. His gray-green eyes owlish behind his specs, he said, "I'm sorry she's in distress. Can you tell me about it?"

Hesitating, I walked to the door of the cottage where I turned to face the port in Marianne's personal storm. "Maybe I'd better leave that to Miss Wagner. Please know, though, that she *really* needs your help. Heck, she wouldn't have run away without a good reason."

"I'm sure that's true."

"She's not flighty," I went on, fearful lest he believe Marianne to be one of those modern-day "lost youths" who were always defying everybody and getting into trouble. "She's not the sort of girl to do anything drastic without good cause." And if that wasn't the truth, I didn't know what was. "She's actually quite shy. She's definitely not one of your 'I'll-say-she-does' girls."

"I see." Mr. Grenville's gray winter suit was a trifle baggy, although it looked as if it had cost a pretty penny before he'd rumpled it beyond salvation. At the moment, he had his hands shoved into his jacket pockets and was staring at the ground, a serious expression on his face. "It's a shame she felt it necessary to run away from home." Lifting his head, he stared me straight in the eyes. "But if you believe her reason was adequate, I'm sure it was."

I nodded. "It was. Truly."

"Very good, then. I'll do what I can to help her." Reaching behind me to open the door like the gentleman he was, he gestured for me to enter, saying as he did so, "I must say, I don't care for her father, based on the few times he's been in the store."

"You're a discerning individual," I said darkly.

"Ah. I see. Her father, was it?"

"Her entire home life is rotten," I said, trusting Mr. Grenville to forgive me the slang.

He seemed to. He closed the door behind the both of us, and we stood there, looking at Harold and Marianne, who looked back at us, Harold with a grin, Marianne as if she were set to meet her executioner.

Thinking it might relax her, I made a small joke. "Heck, Marianne, I drove you here in a Ford, not a tumbrel."

Harold's grin broadened.

George Grenville chuckled.

Marianne continued to stare at me blankly, and I deduced she wasn't a big reader. "That's what the fellows in the French Revolution used to haul the aristocracy in when they took them to the guillotine."

"Oh." Her knees gave out on her, and she sat with a plop on the sheet-covered sofa behind her.

From the boxes of books stacked everywhere, I deduced Harold was right about the cottage being where Mr. Grenville kept new shipments and extra copies of the volumes he sold. The small sofa upon which Marianne sat had been shoved against a wall and had indentations in it that looked as if they'd come from boxes, undoubtedly also filled with books. There were bookcases, too, stuffed with books, and books lay stacked on the bar counter that divided the kitchen from the living room. From where I stood, it looked as if the man's whole life was built from books.

Thinking a formal introduction was in order, I said, "Marianne Wagner, please allow me to introduce you to Mr. Harold Kincaid and Mr. George Grenville. Harold is one of my very best friends. Mr. Grenville owns and runs Grenville's Books, which is, in my humble opinion, the best bookstore in Pasadena, if not the entire state of California."

"Happy to meet you," said Harold, grinning at Marianne, who stared back, wide-eyed.

After giving me an embarrassed nod, Mr. Grenville executed a polite bow. "It is my sincere pleasure to be of assistance to you, Miss Wagner."

She lifted her head slightly, but didn't seem to want to look directly at him or get up off the couch. In a tight voice, she murmured, "Thank you so much, Mr. Grenville."

Mr. Grenville swallowed and goggled slightly.

"And you, too, Mr. Kincaid."

"Any time," said Harold.

"Oh, no!" cried Marianne. "This will never happen again, I'm positive."

I decided then and there that a lack of imagination isn't exclusive to my mother.

"Are you absolutely certain you don't mind? Are you sure it's all right for me to stay here?" Marianne continued. She gulped and allowed herself to take a peek at Mr. Grenville. Her gaze fell immediately, and she started wringing her hands.

It was all right for her to stay there as far as I was concerned, at least in the short term. Thinking it was up to Mr. Grenville to reassure the girl, I glanced at him.

He gathered up the conversational tatters and ran with them, rather like Spike pulling Billy's wheelchair across the living-room floor by means of Sam's handkerchief. He went so far as to rush over to the sofa (approximately two long strides; it was a *very* small house) and plunk himself down beside her. "Please, Miss Wagner. It's perfectly all right that you're staying here. I gather you've had a rough go of it, and I'm more than happy to help."

She turned her baby-blues upon him, lifted her clenched hands to her bosom, and whispered, "Thank you *so* much."

He swallowed and gazed back at her. Shoot, the two

of them were gazing into each other's eyes as if they were long-lost lovers reunited after battling hordes of Cossacks and then trampling over a couple of swarms of Visigoths and Vandals for the right to be together. I took a peek at Harold, and I'm ashamed to admit that I cast a sarcastic glance at the ceiling. He looked back and winked, grinning like an imp the while.

"Please," said Mr. Grenville, "you needn't thank me. It's little enough I'm doing for you."

"Oh, no," she said, still whispering, sounding as if she were on her last legs and he'd just pulled her from the jaws of a ravening crocodile. "You're saving my life."

That was a teensy bit dramatic, but I'm sure she meant it. I didn't doubt but that she'd had an awful time, thanks to her scaly old man, although to dismiss my part in her rescue and devote her entire attention to Mr. Grenville was a bit much. I figured I was only tired; that's why I was crabby.

I cleared my throat, thereby breaking the spell. Both sofa-sitters jumped slightly and turned to look at me. "Would you like me to do some shopping for you, Marianne? I'm sure Mr. Grenville—"

"Call me George, please, Mrs. Majesty." He rose from the sofa, embarrassed, although I'm not sure why. Probably because I'd caught him gawping at Marianne. She'd been gawping back, so I didn't think he needed to fret that anyone might consider him silly. Frankly, I doubt if Marianne had an ounce of judgment in her. She'd been taught never to think for herself, she'd been an apt student, and I gathered that she was already beginning to look upon George as her hero.

"Only if you call me Daisy," I said with a smile. "Turnabout's fair play, after all."

"Of course. Daisy." He had a very nice smile; not quite as great as Billy's in his earlier days, but nice. Friendly.

Back to Marianne. "Anyhow, I doubt that George here had much of a chance to stock the pantry shelves.

I'll be happy to bring you some groceries and so forth."
I turned to Harold. "And what about clothes? Marianne
doesn't have a thing to wear, and she's a lot taller than I
am." It's kind of embarrassing, but my wardrobe was
extensive, thanks mainly to my skill with Ma's White
Side-Pedal Rotary Sewing Machine. I loved to sew, and
I'd have been happy to supply Marianne with duds from
my vast collection, but they wouldn't have fit her.

"I'll take care of that problem," Harold promised.
"I'm a costumer, after all. I have access to scads of
ladies' clothing."

Marianne rose from the sofa, and I saw her lower lip
tremble. She seemed to be a trifle shaky on her pins,
too. "Please," she begged, sagging a little and steadying
herself with a hand on the couch's arm. "I can't allow
you two men to go to this much trouble on my account."

Oh, brother. She'd never said anything like that to *me*,
the one who'd rescued her from Mrs. Bissel's basement.
I chalked it up to her having been browbeaten into believing men were the only truly capable people in the
world. And this was in spite of her own experiences
with yours truly, I might add.

"Please, Miss Wagner, don't give it another thought.
It's no trouble," George said. "It's no trouble at all."

Easy for him to say. He didn't have a husband at
home, wondering what he was up to and spoiling for a
fight as soon as he showed up. Not to mention a policeman sitting there with him, longing for a reason to slap
him behind bars.

"Absolutely," agreed Harold, sounding less heroic
than George, probably because his voice was high-
pitched and rather thin.

"Be that as it may," said I, trying to get everyone to
pay attention to the important matters before I collapsed
and died from lack of sleep, "do you need any foodstuffs, Marianne?" Because I knew Marianne to be

useless when it came to the practicalities of life, I turned
and directed a questioning glance at George. "George?"

"I've stocked the kitchen with bread and eggs and
milk," he said, proud of himself. "I'm sure Miss Wagner can make do until one of us goes to the grocery and
dry-goods stores on the morrow."

"Great," I said. "And you sure won't get bored with all
these volumes to read." I gestured at the tons of books.

George grinned broadly. "Absolutely. I'll be happy to
recommend reading material if you'd like, Miss Wagner."

Marianne bowed her head and blushed scarlet.
"Thank you. Please call me Marianne."

"Thank *you.*" George gazed at her as if she were a
chocolate ice-cream cone and he a starving man.
"Please call me George."

"Thank you," she whispered. "George."

I'd never considered George a particularly musical
name until that second. Marianne's tongue caressed it as
if it were a furry cat she was petting.

When I glanced at Harold again, I saw him staring at
the ceiling as if he found the two young people as
maudlin as I. Actually, I think I reacted negatively to
George and Marianne's obvious attraction to each other
because I was so darned pooped. All I wanted to do was
forget all about Marianne Wagner, drive home, and
crawl into bed.

"Okay," I said, a trace too loudly, making Marianne
and George, who'd taken to gazing raptly at each other
once more, start, "let's look around, shall we? We can
see what I'll have to bring tomorrow. I brought some
clothes." I lifted the small sack I'd packed. "My stuff's
sure to be too small, but I'm also sure you'd like a
change of clothes, Marianne."

"Oh, yes," she said, sounding as if she didn't mean it.
I knew she did; it was only that she was unused to having people other than servants hand her clothing. I'll bet

they never handed her used stuff in sacks, either. "Thank you."

"You're welcome. Harold can bring you more duds tomorrow." I made my way past the sofa to another room. "Say, this is a nice kitchen for such a small place."

"I used to live here," George explained. "When I first moved out to Pasadena, I did my own cooking. Marianne can fix some scrambled eggs and toast for supper tonight, and I'll stock the place more fully tomorrow."

"Sounds good to me."

When I glanced at Marianne, she was staring at the two of us as if we'd been speaking a foreign language. I sighed. "Um, that's right. I forgot you don't know how to cook very well. Have you ever scrambled an egg, Marianne?"

Slowly she shook her head. "I'm afraid I don't know how to cook anything at all," she said, clearly ashamed of this deficiency.

George blinked at her. "Oh. Well, I'll be more than happy to scramble some eggs for you this evening. In fact, I'll dine with you, if you can call eating such a meal dining." He laughed as if he thought that was a great idea.

I wasn't so sure. I mean, I was relatively sure George was a true gentleman and all that, but it was still kind of shocking for a young, unmarried woman and a slightly older, unmarried man to be sharing a house all alone without a soul to chaperone them. I didn't care what the bright young things in F. Scott Fitzgerald's books did with each other. This was Pasadena, California, where stricter rules prevailed.

"I have another idea," George exclaimed brightly. "I'll lend you a couple of cooking books! There are several of them in the shop, and maybe you can teach yourself how to cook!" He added, still smiling, "You probably won't have too much else to do for a while."

Again Marianne clutched her hands together at her bosom. When she did that, she bore a striking resemblance to Mary Pickford in one of her more insipid roles. "Oh, George, would you? That would be so kind of you."

"It's nothing, really." George dug the toe of his shoe into the braided rug under his feet. "I'll be more than happy to help you learn, as well. I'm quite the cook, when it comes to eggs and toast and cheese sandwiches and so forth."

"Thank you so much."

"Yeah," I said to George, attempting to sprinkle a dose of reality on their fairy tale. "That's great, George, but don't get too carried away. Marianne's in danger of being discovered, and your bookstore's situated on the busiest street in Pasadena. You've both got to be careful that nobody sees her. Her picture's been in the papers, and her family's got the police out looking for her, don't forget."

Considerably sobered, George nodded. "Of course. I shan't lose sight of our objective."

"Good." I walked over to Marianne and put a hand on her shoulder. "Are you sure you'll be all right, Marianne? I'll be happy to drive you back to your parents' house if you want me to."

Her blue eyes got even bigger, and she stared at me in horror. "No! Please don't do that!"

"I won't," I assured her. "Don't panic. I'm only offering you the option. I don't want you to feel obliged to remain in George's cottage if you're afraid or anything."

"I don't bite," George teased. "And I'd never do anything untoward."

From the blank expression on Marianne's face, I gathered she had no idea what we were talking about. I sighed heavily, wishing I'd assisted a slightly more worldly specimen of womankind to run away from home. Poor Marianne was liable to be found out because she didn't have enough sense to keep her curtains drawn.

That being the case, I opted to get rid of the gentlemen for a few minutes while I had a woman-to-woman chat with Marianne. "George, will you go hunt up a cooking book? Harold can help you."

"What?" George looked startled.

Harold, who was a good deal brighter, or perhaps merely more sophisticated, than George, took him by the arm. "Come on, George. Let's find a how-to-cook book."

"Oh." George's expression of befuddlement went better with his spectacles and his calling in life than his ruddy complexion. "I see. Certainly, I'll be happy to do that."

The two men skedaddled, and I gestured for Marianne to walk through the house with me. It didn't take long. The house consisted of four rooms: living room, bedroom, bathroom, and kitchen. The kitchen was about as big as a postage stamp, but I didn't suppose it mattered since Marianne couldn't cook anyway.

I couldn't cook worth spit myself, but there's a difference. You see, I'd at least been taught the rudiments of the cookery arts by my aunt and my mother (although Mother was a lousy cook, just like me). I knew *how* to cook, more or less; I just didn't *like* to cook. This was especially true because my aunt Viola was the world's best cook, so there was no real reason for me to trouble myself in the kitchen.

Marianne, on the other hand, had grown up being waited on hand and foot by a house full of servants. I had a feeling she didn't know how to wash her own clothes, either, or maybe even wash her hair. It sure needed a good scrubbing.

That being the case, I figured I'd better ask her a few pertinent questions. "You've never cooked anything at all before, have you, Marianne?"

We were standing in the tiny kitchen, perusing the stove, I with approval, Marianne with awe. It was a nice stove, actually, albeit small. But it was a self-regulating gas range, and it would be really easy to cook on, if one knew what one was doing.

She shook her head and murmured in a despairing tone, "I can't do anything."

"That's got to change, and soon, if you expect to learn how to live away from your parents' house. If you were to, say, get a job as a typist or a clerk in a department store, you could have your own room in a boarding house or an apartment building or something like that."

Her eyes got big again. "You mean live all by myself? Support myself?"

"Well . . . sure. Isn't that what you ran away for? So you could live by yourself?"

She stared at me. "Um . . ."

I sighed. "I think I understand. You didn't think about that sort of thing when you did it. You just wanted to get away. Is that about right?"

She nodded. "I was stupid, wasn't I, not to think about those things?"

Well, yeah, I guess she was. Since I didn't want to crush her, I said, "Not necessarily. You can learn how to do the things you'll need to do in order to subsist on your own." With a chuckle, I waved an arm at the mountains of books. "This is about the best place I can think of to do it in, too."

"Yes." She wasn't one teeny bit sure of it. "I wish I didn't have so much to learn."

"Okay, I can understand that. But now that you've made your escape, we have to think of some way for you to support yourself. Do you know how to use a typewriter, by any chance?"

"No."

I'd figured as much. "And you don't know how to cook."

She shook her head. "I can play tennis." There was a hopeful note in her voice.

Tennis? Good Lord. "I don't believe you can earn a living at that."

"Oh. I guess not."

Giving a thought to my mother, who was the head bookkeeper at the Hotel Marengo and made darned good money, for a woman, I tried again. "Are you any good with numbers?"

"You mean adding and subtracting?"

"Well, sort of. I was thinking of bookkeeping and accounting."

She remained silent for a couple of seconds. "Um . . . I'm not sure what those things are."

"But you can add and subtract, can't you?"

"Of course. I've been to finishing school."

How come was it, I wondered, that this child of wealthy parents had gone to school to be finished and ended up as useless as a bump on a log? My own alma mater was good old Pasadena High, and I could at least scramble an egg. Heck, I could even make potato soup, and I earned a darned good living on nothing more than my wits and other peoples' gullibility.

I don't know why things like that continued to astonish me. I'd known for years that life wasn't fair. Which didn't mean a blessed thing and never had.

"I only ask about addition and subtraction because sales clerks, like those who work in Nash's Grocery and Department Store or Hertel's, probably need to know a little bit about such things. You know, they have to write up sales slips and the like."

"Sales clerks? Sales slips?"

Her voice had sunk to a weensy little squeak. I could tell she didn't like the idea of getting a job, although I acquitted her of laziness. I think she was just scared and unaccustomed to the idea—which meant she was unaccustomed to using her noggin, too, as if I needed further proof of that particular quirk in her personality.

I tried not to let my frustration show. It wasn't really this poor dud's fault she didn't know how to do anything. "Have you ever given any thought about what kind of work you'd like to do if you had to get a job?"

Another head shake. "I never thought about working at all."

I couldn't help myself. I sighed again. "It would probably be a good idea to start thinking about it now. If you expect to keep away from your family, you're going to have to have something to live on, and that means you'll need to be able to earn some money. And it will probably have to be somewhere other than Pasadena, since you're not of age yet."

There went her eyes again, opening wide and goggling at me. "You mean . . . you mean I'll have to *move?*"

"How else do you expect to remain undiscovered by your family, Marianne? If you were to start working in a store in town, they'd find you, sure as shooting." I knew I was too tired to be doing this much rational contemplation when I blurted out, "Obviously, you've not put any thought into your situation. I'd suggest you consider what you're doing here. If you aren't willing to learn a skill that will enable you to take care of yourself, you'd probably better go back home and marry Mr. What's His Name. I doubt that George will want to support you indefinitely, and I *can't.*"

I felt rotten when her eyes filled with tears that overflowed and trailed down her cheeks. "I'm such a failure," she said, hiccupping, as she turned her back on me and covered her face with her hands. "I'm so sorry, Daisy. I don't mean to be a burden."

Heaving another weary sigh, I patted her on the back. "I'm sorry, Marianne. I didn't mean to snap at you. It's just that I'm so tired." And I'd been working for money since I was around six or seven years old. The Gumms and the Wagners didn't have a whole lot in common, in other words. "Don't worry about it tonight. Just take a warm bath and wash your hair and change into something clean. George will cook dinner for you, and you can start becoming self-sufficient by learning how to cook simple meals. We'll work on the harder stuff later. Okay?"

She whirled around and threw her arms around me. She was considerably taller than I; I am kind of a shrimp, but I didn't topple over backward. Instead, I braced myself, patted her on the back some more, told myself to shape up and show some sympathy for the poor goose, and said, "There, there. Everything will work out all right. I'm sure it will."

Lies, lies, lies. Unless Marianne learned to fend for herself, and quick, she was doomed. I'm sure that if I hadn't been so exhausted, I'd have been able to relieve her anxiety more appropriately.

Oh, well. Might as well leave the reassurance part of this fiasco to George, who seemed to want it. As for me, I was going home.

Twelve

You'd have thought I was an armed burglar intent upon mayhem from the reaction I got from Spike when I opened the front door of our tidy little home that evening. He'd been sitting on Billy's lap, but as soon as I poked my head in the door, he flew off as if he were a bird, his front and back legs spread wide, and raced over to me as soon as he hit the floor, barking as if he aimed to murder me from the toes up. He couldn't reach any higher than mid-calf, but that didn't daunt him.

Staring down at him, I murmured, "My word, Spike. You're sure a good watchdog." When I knelt in front of him, he jumped on me and started licking every part of my person he could reach, his entire body wiggling. I'd been feeling kind of glum when I drove home from Grenville's Books, but Spike made me laugh. Maybe I should have gotten a dog years before if they were this good for one's spirits.

"He's a scrapper, all right," came from the card table set up in the living room.

I glanced up and saw Pa, Billy, and Sam Rotondo all grinning at Spike and me. "He sure is. Has he been outside recently?" And that was another thing. Spike had piddled on my enemy's shoe. If that didn't show loyalty and a keen perceptive ability, I don't know what did.

"Better take him out again. He hasn't been outdoors for a half hour or so."

"Has he gone inside?" I didn't mean it as a joke, but the men laughed.

"Naw. He's been a good dog. But let's not press our luck."

"Good idea, Billy." So I scooped up Spike and carried him outside.

While Spike did his duty, I sat on the front porch steps, my chin in my hands, my elbows on my knees, and pondered what to do about Marianne. The situation was perilous, and not merely for her. If my role in her continued absence from her family's home was ever discovered, I was sure to be in hot water.

I wondered if the Wagners could sue me. Was there some sort of law to discourage people from helping out other people if the other people were underage? For that matter, *I* was underage, being only twenty. I was married, though, and I think that made a difference. So far, I hadn't found too many pluses to being a married woman, although I'm sure I would have, had Billy not suffered his grievous injuries.

If the Wagners *could* sue me, I wondered if they would. Probably. Dr. Wagner didn't strike me as an open-minded, forgiving gentleman.

And then there was Sam, who'd already threatened me with a charge of obstruction of justice. Could he do that? Exactly what kind of justice was I obstructing? Marianne hadn't been charged with anything, at least not to my knowledge, and in my own mind I had a hard time convicting her of breaking any laws. She didn't have the initiative. Not that I think criminals are to be admired, or anything, but . . . oh, never mind.

I suppose she had broken and entered Mrs. Bissel's basement, although she hadn't really *broken* anything except a jar of something. I'd forgotten to ask her about the mysterious crash in the nighttime. Anyhow, she'd swept it up and trekked out to the garbage cans by the garage in the middle of a violent rainstorm so as not to leave a mess for somebody else to clean up. Somehow I doubted that Marianne's tidiness would sway a judge. Or Mrs. Bissel, for that matter, although she was pretty easygoing as a rule. Marianne's problem was a knotty one, and I was getting nowhere close to solving it as I sat on the porch watching the puppy.

I think it was against the law for a father to use a child as Marianne's father had done, but I doubted that Marianne would be willing to set the law on Dr. Wagner. And I'm sure her mother would object. Nobody liked to have their dirty secrets laundered in public, even those of us who didn't have millions of dollars and society editors writing about us all the time. Marianne and her set hated scandal. She wasn't one of the rebellious youths, like Stacy Kincaid, who thrived on sensation and debauchery.

Spike had done his doggie duty and was scampering around the front yard sniffing at the hibiscus bushes and the hibernating daylilies and generally becoming better acquainted with his new home when the door opened behind me. I knew who it was even before I turned my head and looked, because I felt a chill crawl up my spine. Unless that was the weather. It was darned cold out there.

But it wasn't the weather. It was Sam. I was unable to contain a deep sigh.

"How's the pup?" he asked, sitting on the steps beside me. I scooted over a couple of inches. I'd have gone farther, but the porch rail was in the way.

"He's having fun getting used to his new home."

"How'd the séance go tonight?"

Holy cow, that's right; I'd said I was going to conduct a séance. I'd forgotten all about that particular lie, and now wondered if I'd allowed myself enough time before returning home. I thought I had, but wasn't positive. Not that Sam knew how long séances lasted.

That being the case, I said, "It went okay. I'm too darned tired to be conducting séances, though. Next time, I'll be sure to stay home the night before I have to give one." There. That should cover all bases.

"Where'd you hold it?"

All bases except that one. If Sam were just anybody, I'd have believed he was merely showing polite interest in my work. I knew better. He still thought I was somehow involved in Marianne Wagner's disappearance. The fact that he had become correct all of a sudden didn't make me feel more kindly disposed toward him.

Since helpful and generous Harold Kincaid at least knew what was going on, I decided to give him a bigger role in my knot of deceptions. "Harold Kincaid's place in San Marino. Some of his friends came over. You know, it was the same old thing. Summon dead relatives. Talk to them. Reassure everyone that all's well. That sort of thing."

Sam grunted. He didn't like Harold, not for any reason involving rational thought, but because Harold was what he was. I guess prejudices come in many forms. "I don't suppose you've heard anything about Miss Wagner, have you?"

I gave him a squinty-eyed stare. "No, I haven't, and I can't conceive of why you keep asking me about her. I don't know her from Adam. Or Eve. Anyhow, I expect she's buried in the foothills somewhere. Have you bothered looking there? Or in Dr. Wagner's garden?"

He was squinting back at me as if he hadn't believed a word I'd said so far and didn't anticipate the truth bursting from my lips any time soon. "Men are combing the foothills. So far, they haven't come up with any trace of her. There's not a shred of evidence pointing to Dr. Wagner being the means of his daughter's disappearance. Quite the contrary, in fact."

This time, it was I who grunted. Spike bounded over to sniff at Sam, and I thought about asking Sam to take his feet off the second step and put them on the walkway in the hope that Spike would decorate his shoe again. I decided it would be prudent not to.

"I," Sam went on, "am of the opinion the girl's hiding out somewhere in town."

"How do you figure that?" I didn't look at him, but picked up a twig and, after showing it to Spike, threw it across the yard. Elated, the puppy bounded after it. It's so easy to please a dog. I wished husbands were as easy to amuse.

"It's a feeling," said Sam. "That's all. When you've been a policeman long enough, you learn to pay attention to your hunches."

"Is that so?" I glanced at him. The porch light had been turned on while I'd been gone, probably by Pa or Ma or Aunt Vi in anticipation of my return home from my fictitious séance. Sam's face looked craggy, with the shadows of night battling with the illumination from the porch fixture. The light picked out the planes of his face and accentuated his deep-set, dark eyes. They were glittering now, those eyes, and he didn't stop staring at me. It was disconcerting, primarily because he looked big and solid and dependable, and I had a treacherous urge to throw myself into his arms and beg him to take care of me.

The very idea disgusted me. I mean, what kind of married woman, even if her husband is crippled, has thoughts like that about another man? The worst kind, is what. Moreover, this particular man was perpetually out to get me and didn't like me at all.

Because I was so irked with myself, I said sarcastically, "I hope the majority of your police work is based on considerably more than your hunches, or the citizens of Pasadena are in big trouble."

He didn't say anything for several seconds, which doesn't sound like much time unless you're the one telling lies to the copper. My heart started jumping around like it was doing Swedish exercises, and that line of Sir Walter Scott's slithered through my brain: "Oh, what a tangled web we weave, when first we practice to deceive."

Darn it, how come I remembered poetry at the most inconvenient times? Besides, none of this was my fault. My only sin so far was in being too tenderhearted for my own good. My temper climbed. "Don't look at *me* like that, Sam Rotondo! *I'm* not the one who kidnapped Marianne and slit her throat!"

That brief but impassioned speech took both of us aback. I couldn't believe I'd said it, and neither, evidently, could Sam. "Slit her throat? What do you know about someone slitting her throat?"

Totally out of sorts now, I picked Spike up and tried to settle him in my lap. He didn't want to settle; he wanted to play. Blast it, I ought to have known better than to get a male dog. Men are all alike. Perverse creatures. Never do what you want them to do. After wiggling like a fiend for several seconds, the puppy jumped from my lap and streaked across the grass once more, chasing God alone knew what.

Sam watched him go with more amusement than I. "What's he after, I wonder."

I didn't answer Sam's question, mostly because I was so cranky with him and mad at myself. Instead, I shrugged.

As I should have expected of him, he didn't let the prior subject drop. "What about that throat-slitting scenario, Mrs. Majesty? Do you know something the police don't?"

"Oh, for heaven's sake, call me Daisy!" I don't know to this day why I said that particular thing at that particular moment. I guess his calling me *Mrs. Majesty* in that accusatory tone of voice got my goat. "And I don't know a darned thing about Marianne Wagner."

"You just said—"

"I know what I said! I only said it as a possibility. I

hope nobody cut her throat; but if you haven't found her *yet,* she's probably dead somewhere." I glared at Sam. "What's more, I'll bet her old man did it, no matter what evidence you claim not to have."

"Hmmm."

We sat on the porch without speaking for another few seconds until I couldn't stand it any longer and broke the tense silence. "I wonder where Spike went."

"Thataway, I think," Sam said, pointing to the Wilsons' house next door.

"Ah." Pudge Wilson, who was eight years old, was in awe of me, and I adored him for it. He was always gazing at me as if I were a motion-picture star. It was comforting to know that at least one member of the male gender thought I was worth revering. Too bad I wasn't married to Pudge.

"Will he come back on his own, do you think?"

"I don't know." With a weary exhalation of breath, I got up from the porch. "I'd better find him. The Wilsons have a mean cat named Samson that's always chasing Mr. and Mrs. Longnecker's dog."

Sam rose, too. "The cat chases the dog? I thought it was supposed to be the other way around."

"Not in this case. Samson's a lot bigger than Spike, too."

Sam fell into step beside me, and I gave him what I hoped was a withering glance. "I don't need help to find a puppy."

He smiled. He would. It wasn't a friendly smile. "You never know. It might be hard to find a black dog in the dark."

"Maybe."

It wasn't difficult to find Spike because he trotted down the Wilsons' driveway, past their gardenia hedge (which smelled glorious during the summertime but it wasn't summertime, more's the pity), and greeted us as if we were paying him a social call. When he wagged his tail, the whole back end of his body wagged with it. He was the most precious puppy in the world, even if he was a boy. I squatted on the lawn and held out my hand to him. He ran over, wiggling, and I picked him up.

"He's a fine little fellow," Sam said, holding out his fingers for Spike to gnaw, which he did with gusto.

"I'm glad Mrs. Bissel let me have him."

"That's right. You exorcised her ghost, didn't you?"

I sighed. "It wasn't a ghost. It was a cat."

"Ah."

He didn't believe me. To heck with him.

We walked back toward our bungalow. Sam stopped beside his Hudson. "I'm off now," he said.

"I'm going to bed," I said. "I can't remember ever being this tired."

"Right. Must be tiring, ridding a house of a ghost and then conducting a séance to talk with several more of them."

"Don't be sarcastic," I advised bitterly. "It's how I earn enough money for Billy and me to live."

I'd turned up our walkway and had begun to believe I was going to escape relatively unscathed until Sam next spoke. "Mrs. Majesty? Daisy?"

Darn. I turned. "Yes?"

"I just want you to know that I don't believe you."

"No, really? What a surprise."

I'm sure he frowned, although it was too dark for me to discern his expression. "This isn't a joke, Daisy. I think you know something about Marianne Wagner. If you don't come forward with your information, you're liable to get into big trouble. I don't think Dr. Wagner is the type to let something like this go."

His words scared me to death. Nevertheless, I couldn't give Marianne up to her awful old man. "Dr. Wagner," I said, "is a villain and a louse."

"He's the girl's father, whatever else he might be."

"I don't care what he is." Oh, how I longed to pour

out Marianne's troubles into Sam's ears. *Then* he wouldn't threaten me with the law, I'll bet. He'd probably arrest Dr. Wagner, in fact. "I hope Marianne ran away to the Yukon Territory and never gets found."

Sam stared at me and I stared at him for I don't know how long. It seemed like an eternity—fully long enough for my knees to give out, if a Gumm's knees did such things. After what might have been forever or longer, he said, "Just remember what I've said, please."

"I will."

Couldn't do anything else. His threats positively haunted me.

He got into his automobile, pressed the self-starter—I was going to get us a new car come heck or high water so I never had to crank the Model T again—and drove off down the street. Holding on to Spike so that he wouldn't jump out of my arms and hurt himself, I watched the Hudson retreat, wondering where Sam lived.

"Oh boy, Spike. I don't know what I'm going to do, but I'm afraid I'm in big trouble."

Spike only wagged and wiggled. Figured.

The next several days passed without anything too ghastly happening.

On the Monday following Marianne's escape and my coming home with Spike, I put on my best bib and tucker. Actually, it was a tailored suit I'd made of navy blue tricotine, with the seams bound with braid. It was quite elegant, especially when I wore it with the turban-style hat I'd made of the same material, as I did that day. The skirt had one of those hems that went up and down, but even the highest part of it didn't go more than six inches above my shoes. I followed fashion. I knew what was considered acceptable and what wasn't. Whenever I left the house, I did my best to look modish, modest, and refined so that people wouldn't consider me more of an oddball than they already did on account of my spiritualist business.

The first place I headed after leaving the house was to Dr. Benjamin's office. I could have telephoned first to see if he was in, but decided it would be more circumspect to take a chance on his being in the office. I couldn't be sure a telephone conversation wouldn't be overheard, either by Billy, the operator at the telephone exchange, or by prying neighbors on our party line.

The weather on that December day might have been designed to buck me up. The day was brisk but sunny, and as I gently persuaded the Model T up Lake Avenue to Beverly Street, where Doc Benjamin's office sat, my battered soul drank in the glory of the San Gabriel Mountains and the clear, perfect blue sky. A few pillowy white clouds hovered over Mount Wilson, but they only added to the perfection of the scene. In my opinion, a sky without clouds is boring.

Dr. Benjamin's normal office hours were from one to five in the afternoon, leaving his morning hours free for making house calls. Luck was with me that day. Before even bothering to hang up my coat I walked over to Mrs. Benjamin, who acted as his nurse and office manager. She sat behind the counter, shuffling papers and looking harried. But when she glanced up to see who'd come in, she smiled. She also told me the doctor was in his office and would see me presently.

"Are you ill, Mrs. Majesty?"

"No. Thank you. I'm not sick. I'm here about something else."

Mrs. Benjamin brightened. "Oh, my dear, you're not . . ."

In those days all but the very young, who considered themselves too sophisticated for tact, used euphemisms for words like "pregnant." A lady was "expecting a blessed event" or "in the family way." She was never flat-out pregnant.

I anticipated the end of her question, primarily because I didn't want to hear it for fear I'd start crying. I was feeling pretty wobbly that morning. "I'm afraid not, Mrs. Benjamin. I need to talk to the doctor about Billy."

Billy couldn't sire children any longer. If I'd known what was going to happen to him after he left me to go to war, I might have jumped the gun on our wedding day and insisted on intimacy earlier. I suppose that sounds shocking—or it would have back then, anyhow.

The fact remains that I'd always wanted children and so had Billy. We'd talked about rearing a family lots of times before we were married. After he came home from the Great War, the subject hadn't come up once. Children weren't in the cards for me as long as Billy and I were married, and since I'd never, in a million years, desert him, I guessed I would remain childless. It was a bleak thought—almost as bleak as having a drug-addicted husband.

Mrs. Benjamin's happy smile crumpled instantly. "How is the poor boy, dear?" She reached a hand across the counter to me, and I took it, telling myself not to cry.

"He's not too chipper, I'm afraid. I'm worried about—" I had to stop and swallow the lump of tears clogging my throat. Then I blurted out the sordid truth. "I'm worried about his morphine use."

Shaking her head in sympathy, she said, "I'm sure the doctor will be able to advise you, Mrs. Majesty. He'll only be another little minute. The Mathison boy had to have his wrist set. He sprained it when he fell out of a tree."

"Boys will be boys," I said, wishing I had one of my own.

"Oh my, yes."

"I'll just take a seat, then. Thanks."

"It won't be but another minute or two."

I sat on the comfortable, old, overstuffed chair that matched the sofa in the same condition, and picked up a tattered issue of *The Saturday Evening Post*. My eyes blurred as I flipped through the pages, and I used my waiting time to try to control my rampaging emotions. I'd feel like a fool, blubbering in front of Dr. Benjamin, although I was sure he wouldn't have minded.

A few minutes later, a little boy and his mother exited the doctor's sanctum. The kid looked as if he'd been crying, but heck, he was only five or six years old. I smiled at him and felt bereft and incomplete and sorry for myself. He grinned back and held up his bandaged left hand as if the bandage was a mark of courage.

"I busted my wrist," he said proudly.

I said, "Ouch. That must have hurt."

His mother tutted. "It's not broken, Freddie. It's sprained."

"I mean it's spained," he corrected himself, still holding up his hand.

"Poor you. I hope it gets better soon."

The little boy shrugged as his mother fetched his coat and cap from the coat rack in the corner. After she'd helped her boy don his outer garments, she did the same with hers, went to the counter and opened her handbag, and took out a five-dollar bill. "The doctor told us to come back in a week, Mrs. Benjamin."

"That's fine, dear. Here's a lollipop for Freddie. He was a brave little soldier."

A brave little soldier, was he? Darn it, I wished Mrs. Benjamin hadn't used those words. My eyes filled up, and my throat started aching to beat the band. Brother, was I a mess.

"Your turn, Mrs. Majesty," Mrs. Benjamin said cheerfully. "Just go right on in."

"Thank you." I used the approximately fifteen seconds it took me to open the door and walk to the doctor's office to concentrate on not breaking down. It was no use. I was sobbing by the time I'd finished telling my tale to Dr. Benjamin.

He was such a nice man. He got up and closed the

door so that we could be private, and he patted me soothingly on the back as he went to his chair behind his big, scarred desk, cluttered with papers, powder packets, medicine jars, and his stethoscope.

"I-I'm sorry," I blubbered, feeling stupid and wretched and generally lousy.

"There's no need to apologize, my dear. Neither you nor Bill deserve what's happened to him and, by extension, you and your marriage."

After mopping my eyes and blowing my nose, I thanked him and asked, "Am I worrying for nothing, Dr. Benjamin? Is it safe for him to take so much morphine? I'm so afraid he'll become addicted—or, worse, take an overdose." I wish the subject of suicide had never been mentioned. It had been paying me visits ever since I'd spoken the word a few days earlier.

The sympathy in his kind old eyes almost made me cry again. "I can tell you three things, Daisy." He held up a fist and illustrated his points with his fingers. "The first is no, you're not worrying for nothing. The second thing is that your poor husband is, without the drug, in constant and severe pain. His legs are ruined, there was nerve damage to both of them from the shrapnel, and his lungs were eaten up with gas. The third thing is, I don't have any solutions for his problems and it breaks my heart. I also suspect he is becoming addicted to the morphine."

I think I gasped. I know I whispered, "Oh, no!" because the doctor held up his other hand to forestall further words from me.

"The thing is, my dear, that he—and you—have to choose between two evils: agony or addiction. If it were I, and I must say I'm glad it's not, I'd choose addiction. With the morphine, he'll at least be able to get around, which I'm sure I'd prefer over being bedridden and in constant pain."

Squeezing my handkerchief in my hands, I asked,

"Isn't there *anything* to give him for his pain other than morphine?"

He shook his head. "I'm afraid your husband is in bad shape, Daisy. You know that, but I'm not sure you understand exactly how perilous his condition is."

"I think I do," I murmured. Actually, it was more like a moan.

"Then you know he's more susceptible to pleurisy and pneumonia and many other pulmonary ailments than he was before he was so badly injured."

I nodded.

"And you also know that such an illness will probably take him one of these days."

After sniffling and vowing I wouldn't break down again, I nodded once more. "I was just . . . I don't know. Hoping, I guess, that there might be something else we can do for him."

"There's always hope, my dear."

"Do you really think so? For Billy?"

The tenderness in his eyes told me the answer to that one. I pressed my lips together so as not to blubber again.

"Take heart, Daisy. Researchers are making great strides in many areas of medical science. The best thing you can do for Bill is to love him."

"I do." The two words came out squeaky.

"I know you do, my dear." He heaved a huge sigh. "Sometimes, when I see men who fought for this great country in the late war—and especially those who were the recipients of the Kaiser's mustard gas—I wonder if they weren't the unlucky ones, instead of those who died in action."

I knew exactly what he meant. As somebody said, probably Shakespeare, because he said almost everything people quote—except for the few choice epigrams rendered by Oscar Wilde—"If wishes were horses, all men would ride."

"So I guess it's the morphine and addiction or bed and pain?" The idea of my Billy, who used to be so healthy and athletic, confined to a bed made my insides scream with fury and impotence. Darn it, this wasn't fair!

"I'm afraid that's about it. As I said, if it were I, I'd choose the morphine. And don't forget, too, that pain can wear a man down. I'm sure you view drug addiction as a social evil, as do most of us, and it is, except in certain special cases. The more debilitated by pain your husband becomes, the more liable he is to succumb to diseases. And melancholia. You might want to consider the morphine as preventing his falling victim to some other dire illness."

"That's a good point," I said, not quite certain I believed it.

Dr. Benjamin didn't rush me. I'm sure the compassionate fellow would have let me sit in his office and whine indefinitely, but a Gumm knows how to accept fate, even when she doesn't want to. At that moment, I wanted to gas fate with the same mustard gas that had ruined Billy's lungs and then shoot it, as the Huns had shot Billy. Damned coldhearted, indifferent fate; I hated it almost as much (and as unproductively) as I hated the Germans.

When I finally rose to leave, Dr. Benjamin handed me another bottle of medicine for Billy, opened his office door, and then walked with me down the corridor to where his wife sat, working on the books. It was a special courtesy on his part, and I understood and appreciated it. Dr. and Mrs. Benjamin watched me as I retrieved my coat.

"Good luck, dear," Mrs. Benjamin called as I opened the door.

Turning to give the couple a last wave, I said, "Thanks." I remember thinking it was a shame Marianne's doctor-father couldn't have been the Benjamin-esque type. She'd never have run away from home with a father like Dr. Benjamin.

After my discouraging meeting with the doctor, I was happy to visit Mrs. Frasier's house and read the tarot cards for her. I admired her duet of miniature pinschers, mentally comparing them to Billy's Spike. I suppose if I couldn't have a dachshund, I'd settle for a miniature pinscher, although they seemed a bit high-strung for my taste. We didn't need a dog that required more attention than Billy, for Pete's sake.

Mrs. Frasier, a tall, lean woman, lived on Orange Grove Boulevard, about three mansions down and across the street from Mrs. Kincaid's place. She and her husband entered dog shows all across the country, and they both lived and breathed miniature pinschers. As I've mentioned before, Mrs. Frasier had made it her mission in life to get her dogs recognized by the Westminster Kennel Club. I wished her well, and only hoped she'd not feel bored and aimless if she ever achieved her goal.

I always enjoyed driving through that neighborhood because it was so beautiful. Even in December the yards were green, and the whole street practically reeked of wealth and prosperity. Sleek automobiles were parked in driveways and on the street, and my rickety old 1909 Model T felt out of place. I patted it on its dashboard and told it not to pout. I didn't mention that I was aiming to trade it in on a new model because I didn't want to make it feel worse.

Since I was blue myself, I made sure the tarot cards predicted nothing but sunny skies and bliss for Mrs. Frasier. She was particularly concerned about how her dogs would place in the upcoming dog shows in which they were entered. I didn't know anything about dog shows, but I gave her an equivocal answer that could be taken any old way she wanted to take it. I was almost as good as a Jesuit when it came to equivocation.

Mrs. Frasier chose to take my predictions in a positive

light, which I considered sensible of her. I mean, face it, life is life. It's going to do whatever it wants with all of us, and there's no sense in worrying about things before they happen. I'd learned over the years, as I consorted with rich people, that they had problems, too. Besides, people liked to hear good news. Mrs. Frasier was pleased.

When I told her that I'd just given my husband a dachshund puppy, she exclaimed, "Oh, Mrs. Majesty! You should have asked me! I'd have given you one of my min pins. They're the best dogs in the world, you know."

Since one of her min pins had taken it into its head to disembowel my handbag, I thanked her and said I was sure we'd be happy with Spike. "But your dogs are wonderful, Mrs. Frasier," I added as I tried to grab the one who'd snatched my handkerchief. Every time I got close to him, he darted the other way. He was the quickest little dickens I've ever seen.

"Percy, stop that!" Mrs. Frasier said in a stern voice. She was about as much a disciplinarian as my aunt Vi and Ma, which means she wasn't one.

I swear to goodness, the dog grinned at her. Then he ignored her as effectively as he'd ignored me, and dashed off (with my handkerchief) to another room. Since there didn't seem anything else to do, I laughed.

"Oh, dear. He's such a tease. I'm so sorry, Mrs. Majesty."

"That's all right, Mrs. Frasier. I've got other hankies."

"I'll get it back for you, dear."

So, for ten minutes or thereabouts, Mrs. Frasier and I chased a little red dog around her house. It was an interesting way to get a tour of a grand mansion, and I almost appreciated the creature for it, although I was doubly glad I'd given Billy a dachshund after we'd finally cornered Percy in the laundry room and forced him to release my handkerchief. It turned out to be a waste of time, since the silly dog had pretty much shredded it by then.

After I left Mrs. Frasier's mansion, I tootled down to Grenville's Books to check on Marianne. I was accustomed to visiting the bookstore even before I took to aiding and abetting runaway rich girls, so I had no qualms about parking the Model T on Colorado in front and walking in as if I had every right to do so.

Thirteen

I found George perusing the small cooking section of his store and grinned. "Hey George. Hard at work on our project, I see."

He turned and smiled. He looked mighty happy for a man who was in almost as much trouble as I was—or would be if anyone ever found us out. "Good day to you, Daisy. Yes, indeed, I'm learning the rudiments of the cookery arts. I should take lessons from your aunt, I guess. According to Harold, she's the best cook in the world."

I joined George in the cookbook section. "He's right. Aunt Vi's a genius in the kitchen."

"I'm afraid our guest isn't."

From the expression on George's face, I deduced he didn't find this a flaw in Marianne's makeup, but rather an endearing character trait. I hoped he'd continue to consider her ignorance darling rather than infuriating if he had to put up with her for a while.

"I'm sure anyone can learn," I said, keeping my voice down. I also wasn't sure about the "anyone" part. I was a dismal failure in the kitchen. Then again, as I've said before, why should I cook? I had Aunt Vi.

"Our project is interested in sewing, too." George's face took on an expression of bright inquiry. "Harold tells me you're a champion seamstress, Daisy. I don't suppose you'd be willing . . ."

"Not right now, George." I don't know why it is, but I hate teaching anybody anything. I'm really bad at it, too. I couldn't teach a duck to quack. Also, I was disinclined to teach Marianne Wagner how to sew. Not that I didn't like the girl, sort of, but teaching her any skill at all sounded like more work than I wanted to tackle. I'd have been willing to bet she didn't even know how to thread a needle. "Maybe later. I've got too many jobs at the moment." That was also true, and it felt good not to have to lie.

"I have a feeling cooking's easier to learn than sewing," George said musingly, as he took a book about how to prepare and cook casserole dishes off the shelf.

"Not for me, it wasn't." That was the truth, too. Gee, my score was improving. That made two entire truths I'd told in less than twenty-four hours. I wasn't counting the ones I'd told in Dr. Benjamin's office.

Oh boy. I honestly, really and truly, never set out to become a criminal. I know my means of earning a living might seem unusual to some people, but it was paid work, I was good at it, and my services were valued by my clients. That's what I always told Billy when he ragged me about being a spiritualist, and that's what I believed. More or less. I was as proud of my skill as a spiritualist as my aunt Vi was proud of her prowess in the kitchen. The Marianne business, on the other hand, had me as nervous as a lobster poised over a kettle of boiling water.

"She's a whiz at cleaning."

"That's good."

"She's got the whole place swept and dusted."

"Great." Four whole rooms. Wonder what she'd do if she had an entire house with people in it to keep up, as I did.

I told myself to stop comparing myself to Marianne because it wasn't fair to either of us. I had skills Marianne lacked, and she had money, which I lacked. Actually, she didn't even have money any longer.

And it wasn't her fault she'd been taught to be a leech on society instead of a productive member thereof. George and I could probably teach her how to survive. And I'd even teach the girl to sew if I had to. It was the least I could do—and probably the most, as well.

"I think she's relaxing a bit." George squinted at the spine of another cooking book. "Aha. This one looks good." He took a copy of *A Thousand Ways to Please a Husband, with Bettina's Best Recipes* off the shelf.

It looked okay to me, except for the *Husband* part. I narrowed my eyes as I observed George. He was throwing himself into our scheme with wholehearted enthusiasm. I wondered if his only reason was to protect Marianne from the forces of evil—so to speak. Or could he have another, less savory motive underlying his helpfulness? I'd always thought of him as one of the world's more amicable specimens, and not a fellow who'd do anything of an underhanded nature to a poor, defenseless female, but what did I really know about him? Nothing; that's what.

"Is it okay if I go visit with her? Can I get there through the back of your store?"

"Certainly. Let me go with you." He must have detected something in my expression, because he hastened to add, "Just to show you how to get there from here. You've never been in the back part of the store before."

He was right about that. "Thanks, George."

So I followed him behind the counter and through the guts of his business to the back door. I could have found the way on my own, and without even bread crumbs to mark the path, but I didn't say so to George. I was curious to see him and Marianne together. If they appeared too chummy for my quivering antennae, I'd have to think of something else to do with the girl.

Golly, but helping girls to escape from their wicked parents was a lot of trouble! I decided then and there I'd stick to raising the spirits of dead people and chatting with them through Rolly from now on. Rescuing damsels in distress was for the birds.

When George knocked on the door to the cottage, we didn't have to wait more than a second before Marianne threw the door wide, a warm smile of greeting on her face, and one of my old housedresses draping her form. The dress had faded from blue to gray a couple of years earlier, and it was too short for her, but she didn't seem to mind. When she saw me, she gasped.

I shoved George inside the cottage and followed on his heels. Marianne released the doorknob when she saw us charging at her, and I slammed the door behind me. "For heaven's sake, Marianne, find out who's knocking before you open the door!"

Her eyes did their opening-wide routine. They didn't soften my attitude, and I went on, "It might have been anybody! It might have been your father!"

"Oh my," she whispered, backing away from me as if *I* were the demon of her life instead of her personal good fairy.

"Really, Daisy," George said in disapproval. "There's no need to scold the poor child."

I turned on George. "Like heck there isn't! If Marianne aims to be successfully rescued from her former life, the least she can do is cooperate!"

It looked to me as if George would have taken me to task if Marianne hadn't stepped into the breach, which was totally unexpected, at least by me. In a small, shaky voice, she said, "No, George. Daisy's right. I'm very sorry, Daisy. You've done so much for me, and I ought to have considered more carefully before I opened the door. I thought it was George."

I felt like hollering at her some more, but knew that was only my bad mood clamoring for release. It wasn't Marianne's fault she was an idiot. I sucked in approximately three acres of air and let it out slowly. George still looked sulky, and I decided I'd been perhaps the least bit precipitate.

Slumping down on the sofa—absent this afternoon of books and sheeted covering—I said, "I'm sorry, Marianne. I didn't mean to yell at you. But you have to take this seriously unless you want to get us all into deep trouble."

I'd managed to intimidate the poor girl. She stood there with her head bowed, clasping her hands and looking miserable. "No," she whispered. "You're right. It was foolish of me to open the door without peeking out first."

"I've already been threatened with jail by a policeman," I told her.

She gasped again, and rushed to sit beside me. Snatching up my hands in hers, she cried, "Oh, Daisy! How is that possible? Who threatened you? My goodness, nobody *knows,* do they?"

I squeezed her hands back to show her I was over my pique, although I wasn't altogether sure it was true. "I'm sorry, Marianne. No, nobody knows. A police detective who's a good friend of my husband suspects I know where you're hiding."

"No!" She dropped my hands and used hers to bury her face in.

"How could he suspect?" George asked skeptically. "Have you mentioned Marianne to him?"

"I didn't have to. He was already working on her disappearance. Anyhow, he suspects me of everything without my doing anything at all, ever."

Marianne lifted her head, squared her shoulders, and said, "I can't allow you to suffer on my account, Daisy. I shall go home." She sounded as if she meant it.

"No!" cried George.

Marianne's pose of noble self-sacrifice lasted approximately ten seconds before she collapsed and burst into tears. Shooting me a baleful glance, George rushed to her other side and wrapped her in his arms. The sofa really wasn't big enough to accommodate three persons comfortably, so I stood up.

I'm afraid I peered down upon the two would-be lovers without a whole lot of benevolence warming my bosom. "There's no need for hysterics," I said dryly. "Nobody knows you're here, Marianne, and nobody knows I have anything to do with your continued absence from your parental abode. All I'm saying is that you ought not open the door before you know who's outside knocking on it."

"Perhaps," George said stiffly, "it *would* be advisable to ascertain who's outside the cottage before opening the door." He looked up at me as he spoke, and his expression told me as clearly as words that whatever mistake his heroine had made, I was wrong to have become irked with her.

"Exactly," said I. "I'm sorry I yelled at you, Marianne. I'm a little tense about this whole escapade, I guess."

"Oh, Daisy!" Extricating herself from George's arms, Marianne jumped up from the sofa and made a dash at me, falling to her knees, her arms outstretched.

Startled isn't half strong enough to describe my state of mind. I'm not accustomed to people falling on their knees before me. Shoot, Billy hadn't even gotten down on one knee when he proposed. Come to think of it, if I recall correctly, I proposed to him. But that's neither here nor there.

"Oh Daisy, I'm *so* sorry! You're doing so much for me! I'll never answer the door again, I promise!"

Oh, brother. "Just don't open it before you know who's there, all right?"

"Of course. Of course."

After giving the matter another second or two of thought, I amended my request. "Actually, maybe you're right. It would be better if you didn't open the door at all." I tried to ignore her imploring position. She reminded me of a medieval mendicant begging favors from a saint.

She sat back, surprised. "Not open the door at all? But how will anyone get in?"

"That's the whole point," I said. "You don't *want* anyone to get in. No one except George, Harold, or me. And the way to assure that is to not open the door if anyone knocks." Glancing at George and silently praying that the silly girl would get up off her knees, I said to him, "When you visit, George, you can tell her your name. And if either Harold or I visit, we'll do so only in your company. That'll be safe, I guess."

Thank the good Lord, Marianne stopped worshiping me and got up, balancing on the arm of a chair to do it. The girl wasn't awfully graceful. "That makes sense," she said. She blinked her pretty blue eyes at George. "Don't you think so, George?"

He was still frowning a trifle, probably because he thought I was being hard on a sweet, innocent child, but he nodded. "Yes. I understand what Daisy's saying. I suppose that would ensure your safety better than having Daisy or Harold knocking all day long."

All three of us jumped when another peremptory knock came at the door. It was almost as if someone had been listening in on our conversation and had chosen the exact moment when we'd all be most unprepared in order to test our resolve. Marianne sucked in air and turned as white as paper. I rose from my chair, nerves abristle. George turned and braced himself with his feet apart and his hands bunched into fists, as if he planned to attack whoever had knocked.

"Miss Wagner. Miss Wagner, it's me, Harold."

A collective sigh of relief issued from Marianne, George, and me. "Harold," I murmured, pressing a hand to my thundering heart.

"I have clothes," Harold added. He sounded as though he didn't enjoy waiting in the alleyway with an armload of female clothing. Harold was sensitive about such things, since he was—well, you know.

"I'll get it," I said. Maybe I'd been reading too many detective novels (they're my favorite reading material, with the occasional western thrown in), because I envisioned Harold standing at the cottage door with Dr. Wagner behind him, holding a gun to the back of his head. "Marianne, go into the bedroom for a minute, please."

"Do you really think that's necessary?" George. Glowering at me again.

My nerves twanged, my temper snapped, and I said, "Yes, I do," in a voice I guess he didn't want to argue with, because he said only, "Very well," and gazed at Marianne's retreating back as if he were watching his last hope on earth desert him.

Things were getting pretty thick between those two. I renewed my decision to have a serious chat with George.

"Harold? Is that you?"

"Who the hell do you think it is?" He was getting crabby. "I already told you who it was."

"Is anyone with you?"

"Daisy, for the love of God, open this door!"

I opened the door.

"Good God," Harold muttered as he stumbled into the cottage.

I could see now why he was short-tempered. He not only held a pile of ladies' dresses and underpinnings, but there were boxes, too, heaped on top of the clothes. "Gee, Harold, what's in the boxes?"

"Shoes and hats. *Heavy* shoes and hats." His arms gave out over the small sofa, and the clothing and boxes fell out of them, sliding here and there, and making a mess. Shaking out the kinks from his arms, Harold turned to me. "For God's sake, Daisy, why'd you take so long opening the door?"

"I'm sorry, Harold. Maybe I was being too cautious, but Marianne has to learn not to open the door for just anybody."

That was the wrong thing to say. Harold stiffened up like a retriever eyeing a duck. "I am *not* just *anybody,* in case you've forgotten, Daisy Majesty. I'm one of the gentlemen attempting to help your runaway, if you'll recall."

My runaway? Well, really! "I'm so sorry, Harold, but Marianne had just opened the door to me without even looking first. I guess we're all a little jumpy."

Harold collapsed on top of a blue satin gown. The gown, carrying Harold with it, promptly slid off the pile of clothing, and Harold ended up on the floor along with a couple of boxes and several other dresses. "Darn."

Fortunately, Harold is an easygoing fellow. His predicament made him laugh. I was so relieved, and Harold looked so darned ridiculous, I joined in.

A small voice from the bedroom asked, "May I come out now?"

Crumb, I'd forgotten all about the heroine of the piece. "Sure, Marianne. Harold's brought you some clothes."

She appeared at the door, wringing her hands (she did that a lot) and looking worried. I considered her state of trepidation regarding entrants to the cottage somewhat late in arriving.

"Ah, Miss Wagner. Sorry about the eccentric greeting." Harold climbed up from the floor, trying not to step on any of the frocks, underthings, and boxes, and gestured at the heap. Eyeing the girl's poorly fitting housedress and wrinkling his nose, he added, "It looks as if I arrived just in time."

"Don't be snotty, Harold," I said. "I'll have you know that's *my* dress, and I only wear it to clean house."

He eyed me without favor. "And your husband doesn't object to this?"

"Cut it out, Harold." I wasn't in the mood to listen to jokes about my husband or my fashion sense. "Why don't you two men clear out of here, and I'll help Marianne change and hang things up."

Marianne turned her languishing blue gaze upon

George, where it lingered for a couple of seconds before she transferred it to Harold, where it belonged, in my humble opinion. "I don't know how to thank you, Mr. Kincaid," she said in a small, subdued voice. "You're all being so kind to me. I'm sure I don't deserve it."

"Nonsense," I said stoutly.

"It's nothing, really," said Harold.

"Oh no, Marianne," George said in a voice Saint George might have used on the virgin before he slew the dragon. "Anything. Anything at all. We're at your disposal."

I wanted to tell him to speak for himself, but didn't. I think my equilibrium was still a bit rocky because of the unpleasantness at home and my worry about breaking the law.

Not only that, but (and this is an awful thing to say) there was something about Marianne that generated within my usually tolerant bosom an urge to smack her soundly and yell at her to shape up. Don't ask me why. Maybe it's because she acted so darned helpless and kept looking to the men to rescue her, when *I* was the one who'd saved her silly hide.

One of Mrs. Kincaid's friends is an Episcopal priest named Father Frederick. He's one of the world's kindest gentlemen, and I've talked to him from time to time about my relationship with Billy. I'd never tell Billy this, or my mother, because they'd not only feel I'd betrayed them, but Ma's a die-hard Methodist who considers Episcopalians only slightly less pernicious than Roman Catholics.

However, some few weeks after the Marianne affair had finally ended, when I was at Mrs. Kincaid's house to conduct a séance, I asked Father Frederick if my attitude toward Marianne Wagner reflected poorly on my overall character and moral worth. I mean, I don't normally feel like smacking dumb animals, you know?

Father Frederick was a peach about it, patting me on the shoulder and assuring me that my reaction was normal. I guess I looked skeptical, because he went on to say that when somebody figuratively lies down in front of you and begs you to boot her down a flight of stairs, it's an unusual person who fails to oblige the beggar.

He also said that my own view of the world had been colored by my station in life and the responsibilities I'd been forced to carry. He didn't mean it in a snooty way, but in a way I understood, especially when he added, "You know, Daisy, there aren't many women as competent and smart as you. I'm sure the poor Wagner girl does her best, but I've yet to meet a woman to equal you."

Well, *that* shocked me speechless, you can bet. I must have goggled, because he grinned and said, "I mean it, Daisy. You're one of a kind. I think it's a shame, too. The world would be a better place—and probably considerably more interesting—if there were more women like you in it. But don't worry about your reaction to the timid Miss Wagner, because it was perfectly normal. Believe me." He chuckled. "You ought to have to hear confessions once or twice. That would *really* tax your restraint."

Shoot. I wanted to ask him to telephone my third-grade teacher, Miss West, and tell *her* those nice things about me. All Miss West ever did was whack my knuckles with her ruler and tell me to pay attention. She sure never told me I was smart. Quite the contrary, in fact.

But that was weeks later. Right then, I ground my teeth and told myself to remain calm and compassionate because Marianne wasn't as accustomed to fending for herself as I was.

After the men scooted off to the bookstore to wait for me to join them, the two of us gazed down upon the heap of clothing, Marianne with bewilderment, I with an eye to organization. Since I knew Marianne to be useless, it was I who said, "Let's sort everything out before we do anything else. Put the underwear over here." I gestured at the living room's one overstuffed chair.

"Then we can shake out the dresses and see if anything needs to be pressed before wearing."

A tiny voice said, "Pressed?"

I sighed. "You've never ironed anything, have you?" She shook her head.

"Well, don't worry about it now. If some things are too wrinkled to wear, I'll bring down some flatirons and show you how to press clothes."

"Thank you."

Her tone of voice led me to believe she considered the skill of pressing clothes beyond her limited abilities, but I knew that was only because her abilities had never been educated in how to handle the necessities of life. I'd bet you anything she could play tennis better than any other ten people, and she could probably make pretty little watercolor sketches and pour tea like a princess.

Digging into the pile of fabric, I forced a smile. "Don't worry, Marianne. I'll teach you how to survive in the big, bad world. It might take a while, but you can do it."

She reached down and lifted a pretty pink frock that was slipping off its hanger. "Do you really think so?"

"Of course I do!" I sounded more confident than I felt, but figured we both needed some morale boosting. "Lay the dresses over the back of the chair."

She did as I suggested, moving like an automaton, and it didn't take too much time to get Harold's offerings organized. I left Marianne to hang everything up and tuck the undies away, figuring she could use the practice, and I went to the bookstore.

I still had to have a woman-to-man chat with George Grenville.

Fourteen

"You *what?* I can't believe—I've never—how can you—" But George was too outraged to complete his sentence.

I thought about putting a hand on his arm to soothe him, but determined I'd better not. I didn't think George would strike a woman, but who knew? "I'm sorry, George. I didn't mean to offend you."

He stood before me, gasping, his usually ruddy face a vivid red, his fists clenched. "I—I—" Again, words failed him.

I heaved a sigh. "Listen, George, I'm not casting aspersions on you. I'm sure you're a fine gentleman who'd never dream of taking advantage of a lady in distress—"

"It doesn't sound to *me* as if you're sure of any such thing! And if you don't think that's an aspersion, I don't know what . . ." His indignant speech trembled off into incoherent sputters.

Oh boy. I'd been as delicate as I know how to be, which is pretty darned delicate. I mean, I didn't get to be a first-class, well-paid spiritualist medium by verbally behaving like a bull in a china shop. I guess there's no truly polite way of asking a fellow if he aims to seduce a girl, however, and George had taken my attempt at judicious inquiry amiss. In spades.

"Listen, George, I've always thought of you as a true gentleman. But these are unusual circumstances, and I want to be sure Marianne comes to no . . ." Darn. I'd done it again. George was blowing up like a hot-air balloon.

Bravely daring, I put a hand on his arm. He didn't shake it off or hit me, so I guess it was okay. "I'm sorry, George. Please just know that my concern for Marianne is genuine and is based on deep worry about her and her situation."

"And you believe mine *isn't?* "

It had never occurred to me that George Grenville, of all people, could be so touchy. "I'm sure it is." I wasn't entirely sure what "it" was in this instance, but I wanted to placate him.

"I want only the very best for Mari—" he broke off and cleared his throat. "For Miss Wagner."

"I'm sure of it, George. And I certainly didn't mean to upset you. But the situation is one of the utmost sensitivity. We're conspiring to keep Miss Wagner from her family, after all, and that might be looked upon askance by the general public, not to mention the police." Surely, even *George* could comprehend that.

He seemed to. Deflating a trifle, he said, "I suppose I can understand that."

Thank God for small favors. "So I'm sure you can also understand that my questions aren't intended to accuse you of anything the least bit unsavory. But . . . well . . . it seems to me that you might be becoming, maybe, a little bit interested in Marianne." There. The truth was out. "And I don't want anything else of an upsetting nature to happen to the poor thing. She's been through enough."

"I know that," George said. He still sounded rather surly. "And I'd never do anything to hurt her, either mentally or . . . or physically." At the last word, his face positively glowed with embarrassment.

"I'm sure of it."

"As if I'd ever hurt Miss Wagner! Why, she's the loveliest . . . the most wonderful . . . the most precious . . ."

Oh brother. "You admire her, I gather." I tried not to sound tart.

"*Admire* her! Why, she's the most perfect . . . the dearest . . . the . . ."

I got the picture. "I see."

We'd bidden a fond farewell to Harold several minutes earlier. Harold had tootled off in his Bearcat, aiming for Los Angeles and the Sam Goldwyn Motion Picture Studio, at which he worked. I'd thanked him heartily, but he'd brushed off my gratitude, telling me he was more than happy to help, especially after seeing Marianne in my fright of a housedress. I pretended to stamp on his foot, and he laughed at me, and I think everyone felt better after that.

My good mood hadn't lasted longer than the beginnings of my conversation with George. We now stood in the back room of his bookstore, having left Marianne contemplating a closet full of frocks that, if not brand-new, were at least cleaner than the dress she'd been wearing for the past two and a half weeks—and, if I'm to be honest, were certain to be a good deal more becoming to her than my faded blue housedress. Harold knew ladies' clothes. He'd brought a selection designed specifically for Marianne's insipid blond coloring.

I don't mean insipid. I mean . . . Oh, heck, I do too mean insipid. The girl was such a mouse, she drove me nuts. The bravest thing she'd ever done in her entire eighteen years was run away from home, and I guess that one outrageous act had sapped her supply of guts. Fortunately, I had enough for the both of us, and probably a couple of other people, too.

That didn't negate the fact that I wished Marianne had a backbone. If she were a girl of strong character, I wouldn't have had to insult George as I was doing. If he'd tried anything on her, Marianne would have belted him across the chops, and that would have been the end of it—if she'd had a backbone.

Eyeing poor George keenly, I said, "You admit that your admiration of Marianne is growing, then?"

"Admit it? Of course, I admit it! I mean, no, I don't admit—Dash it, Daisy, there's nothing to admit! Admit is such a—such a—negative word. You make it sound as if I've committed a crime!"

I pressed a palm to my forehead, and wondered if my tongue belonged to me, or if I'd picked up someone else's by mistake that morning. I generally chose my words more carefully than this. "Calm down, George," I said wearily. "Forget the verb if you don't like it. You admire Marianne? You're becoming fond of her?"

"Fond? Fond? Why, I—"

"A simple yes or no will do, George." Good Lord in heaven, maybe the two deserved each other. If ever there was a damsel in need of a strong knight to rescue her, it was Marianne. And while on the surface George bore no resemblance whatever to the saint whose name he bore, he was behaving like a darned knight of the darned round table. What's more, he was treating me as if I were the dragon instead of his faithful Sancho Panza—although I think he belonged to Don Quixote and not Saint George.

George didn't like it, but at last he managed to splutter, "Yes."

"Good. I'm happy to hear it. Then you'll take care that no damage to Marianne's reputation occurs."

His eyes started bulging, but I lowered my eyebrows and gave him one of my better steely-eyed stares, and he swallowed his indignation. "Yes."

"Very well. In order to do that, you must make sure that no one sees her or even suspects that she might, by some remote chance, be hidden away in your cottage."

"I understand that, of course."

"Good. Marianne herself seems a little shaky on that part of our melodrama, so I'd appreciate it if you'd impress upon her the importance of staying out of sight at all times. Will you do that?"

"Of course. And I resent your implications that Marianne—Miss Wagner is—isn't—"

I was getting tired of this. "Cut it out, George! She swung the door wide open in my face not an hour ago! Watch her, will you? And make sure she understands the importance of keeping out of sight!"

He sucked in about seven gallons of air and let it out in a whoosh before he said, "Certainly," and left it at that.

"Good. I'm going home now, but I'll be back later. I do have a family to care for, you know. My sole responsibility in this life doesn't begin and end with your sweetheart."

"She's not—" Again, he caught himself. "I beg your pardon, Daisy. I know you have other responsibilities."

"Very well." Because I truly didn't want George to hate me or consider me some kind of hard-hearted Hannah, I produced a smile from where I keep a few in reserve for when I can't offer a client a genuine one, and gave it to him. "I didn't mean to scold you, George. I hope you know that. I'm only concerned for Marianne's safety."

I think that did the trick. His frosty demeanor crumbled like breaking ice, and he laid a hand on my arm. "I'm sorry I took your solicitude the wrong way, Daisy. But please be assured that I will never, ever, in any way, do anything improper as regards Miss Wagner. She's—she's—"

I braced myself for another long list of laudatory comments on a girl I considered as bland as custard. Fortunately, George decided to stop before he'd stuttered himself into a deep hole.

Catching his breath on a third "she's," he said simply, "I will do my utmost to shelter her from life's storms."

This sounded serious, but I was too tired to question him further. I left him to his books and Marianne and coaxed the Model T home again. The poor motorcar was becoming crankier and crankier (so to speak) with each passing day.

Not that my duties ended there. After first attempting and failing to placate my husband, who begrudged every moment I spent away from him, I changed out of my spiritualist suit and into a woolen skirt and a white waist decorated with navy-blue flowers, an ensemble that not even Harold could disparage.

Then I found a length of cord in my sewing basket and fashioned it into a combination collar and leash. After throwing a sweater on over my waist and helping Billy into his jacket, he and I and Spike set off to Nelson's Five and Dime Store on Colorado Street to purchase a regular collar for Spike. Billy held Spike's homemade lead, and I pushed Billy's chair.

Billy's mood got better when he understood that I intended to spend the remainder of the afternoon with him. The crisp December air gave him a boost, too. The day was glorious. No devil-winds tried to blow me off my feet, no fog clogged Billy's lungs, and no rain threatened any of us. Clouds with gray centers and white edges hinted of storms to come, but the weather was perfect for walking, and we all three enjoyed it.

Spike had never been for a walk on a leash before, naturally. After a few false starts, when he attempted to chase after something interesting and the leash stopped him with a jerk that flipped him over backward, he got the picture.

"He's a smart little guy," said Billy, his voice ripe with pride for his new puppy.

His approval tickled me for a second before it made me sad. Billy would have been *such* a good father. It was a crime that all of his fatherly instincts had instead to be lavished on Spike. Granted, Spike was a cutie-pie and would ultimately prove to be less trouble than a child, but one can't really compare the two.

"Smart enough to know how not to get himself strangled," I agreed, laughing at Spike's antics. We'd walked approximately two blocks when this conversation took place, and I don't think Spike had lifted his nose off the sidewalk more than twice, the first time when he'd tried to hare off after the Wilsons' cat, Samson, and the second time when he'd attempted to rush across the street and attack a dog that was at least ten times as big as he was. Spike might, as Billy claimed, be smart, but he had a rotten sense of proportion.

Shortly after that, Spike's energy started to flag. He was only a puppy, after all.

"Put him in my lap," Billy suggested.

So I did. As we walked, several people smiled at us and stopped to praise the adorability of Spike, thereby giving Billy more reasons to appreciate his new pup. It made me happy to know that I'd done something right for once.

In other words, we had a pleasant walk. Not a sharp word passed through the lips of either of us, and Spike was a wonderful companion.

In those days, shops and stores didn't bombard their customers with Christmas merchandise until after Thanksgiving had come and gone. That day, shopkeepers were hanging holly branches and mistletoe, and the idea of Christmas made Billy and me both feel jollier than usual. I think Spike had something to do with our good moods as well.

Christmas music is my favorite. Mr. Hostetter had already begun rehearsing the choir for our Christmas cantata, and I imagined Aunt Vi would start making Christmas cookies soon. My mouth watered at the thought.

As we approached Nelson's, I thought about the ice-cream sodas Billy and I used to take together at their soda fountain. Maybe we could get one today. Billy's chair prevented him from comfortably reaching the counter, but perhaps he wouldn't mind sitting at one of the little round tables at the side. As I contemplated whether or not to ask him about it—you could never tell how Billy would take things—he interrupted my musings.

"What color collar do you think we ought to get for Spike, Daisy?"

"Do they make them in different colors?"

"Sure they do! Sam and I talked about it last night. I don't suppose they sell colored collars and leashes in far-off, rural villages, but in big cities like New York and Pasadena, where lots of rich people live, they even sell them with diamonds."

"Good Lord." Sam and he *would* have talked about it, wouldn't they?

Well, I suppose I shouldn't be grumpy just because Billy had talked to Sam before he'd talked to me. Anyhow, he sounded positive regarding the collar issue, so I guess he—or Sam—knew what he was talking about. I squinted at the puppy with an eye to style. "I think he'd look quite spiffy in red. What do you think?"

"Red's good," admitted Billy. Sometimes he opposed anything I said just to be contrary, but that day I guess he'd decided to be agreeable. "Better than blue, I guess. Or maybe he'd look good in green."

"Green's good," I concurred, although I thought Spike would look much more Spike-ish in red, because red would set off his glossy black coat so beautifully. The color of the dog's collar wasn't worth arguing about.

Billy was absolutely right about the different colors available in collars and leashes. We got Spike a lovely red leather collar (I made sure Billy thought it was his own idea), and a cunning, woven, red-and-green plaid leash. He looked quite dashing as he trotted out of Nelson's, his tail held high, and his shiny black doggie ears flopping. He was all dressed up for Christmas.

I couldn't help smiling. Spike had such a *presence*

about him. He was definitely king of our own small Pasadena hill.

When we got home, wonderful food smells greeted us as soon as I opened the front door. Good old Aunt Vi was on the job—and our meals didn't have to take a detour through Mrs. Kincaid's house first, either, for the next couple of days. Ma and Pa had both come home, and they were delighted with Spike's new clothes.

"Now all he needs is a little red Santa hat, and he'll be perfect for the season," Pa said, grinning as Spike showed off his pretty new collar by chasing the knotted sock Billy threw for him. He was sure an energetic little guy.

"Oh boy, wouldn't *that* be a sight," Billy said, also grinning.

So far the afternoon was progressing nicely. Billy hadn't said a single snide thing to me since shortly after I had returned from Grenville's Books, and he'd remained relatively cheerful during our entire walk and all the way home. Also, he hadn't taken any morphine that I'd seen—and I'd been watching. I hoped I wouldn't spoil his good mood when I left him to drive back down to Grenville's in order to visit Marianne after supper. I didn't dare not go, since I still had my doubts about leaving George and her alone together.

Not that I had the slightest doubt that George had meant his passionate declaration of chivalrous intent. But shoot, even booksellers are human. Given the circumstances, what with his apparent adoration of Marianne and hers of him, anything was likely to happen, no matter how strong George's moral fiber.

Marianne herself was built of such weak stuff that she'd bend in the merest breath of a breeze. It wouldn't take even a full-blown storm to crumble her defenses. I just wanted to make sure, is all.

"That nice policeman came by a little while ago, dear, and I invited him for dinner."

My gaze whizzed from Spike, who was growling and shaking the sock as if he was trying to kill it, to Ma, who'd spoken. "What nice policeman? Sam Rotondo?" What the heck was the matter with my family, anyhow, that they all thought Sam was such a nice guy? Were they all blind that they couldn't see how sly the man was? He was forever poking and prying into other people's business.

Okay, I know Sam was a detective, and I suppose it was his job to snoop into criminal activities, but the darned man was always suspecting *me* of evil deeds, and I didn't think it was fair. Granted, this time there might be the tiniest little reason for Sam to suspect me of having something to do with Marianne Wagner, but he didn't *know* that.

"Yes, that nice man who took us all out to dinner last week. I'm so glad you got to know him, Billy. He's such an asset to the family."

Saints preserve us, as my aunt said occasionally.

"Yeah," said my husband. "Sam's a nice guy. What's even better is that he's a lousy gin rummy player."

Pa laughed. I didn't, but I did come up with a smile. It was a struggle. "I'm going to change clothes," I told my treacherous family as I headed to our bedroom.

I don't mean that. My family wasn't treacherous, even though they were singularly blind when it came to Sam Rotondo. As I hung up my skirt and waist, I decided that if Sam could be sneaky, so could I.

The relationship between George and Marianne might ultimately prove to be Marianne's salvation. I wasn't sure what the laws were in the state of California, but I thought a woman could get married without her parents' permission at the age of eighteen. I knew you had to be twenty-one before you could vote, and you used to have to be twenty-one before you could buy booze (before it became illegal for anyone at any age to do), but I wasn't sure about the marriage deal.

Then again, if they *could* get married without Marianne's parents' permission, the *Star News* published notices of applications for marriage licenses once a week. Did they print all the names, or just some of them? It would be a terrible thing if notice of pending nuptials between George and Marianne appeared in the newspaper before they could tie the knot. Her father would see it for sure.

Wasn't there some sort of waiting period between the issuing of a license and the time the marriage could take place? I couldn't remember from my own wedding.

Of course, I might be jumping the gun. For all I knew, George intended to love Marianne from a distance, like Lancelot should have loved Guinevere if he'd given half a hang about Arthur and his kingdom. George seemed to be a terrible romantic. Sometimes romantics had a hard time dealing with reality.

Egad. I didn't need Sam Rotondo to drive me crazy; I was doing a great job on my own.

If there's anything I love better than Aunt Vi's pork roast or roast beef or roast chicken (or a dozen other of her wonderful meals), it's her roast leg of lamb. And to dine on leg of lamb on a Monday night was particularly special, since we generally had to wait until Easter, or at least Sunday, and then get it left-over from Mrs. Kincaid's dinner. I almost didn't mind having Sam there, the food was so good.

Besides, I aimed to pump him. I'd read plenty of detective novels. Surely, I could question somebody without him cottoning on to my motives for doing so.

I suppose I could have been wronger (if that's a word), but I'm not sure how. I was trying so hard to sound guileless, too.

"Why do you want to know that?" he asked in response to my question about the legal marrying age in California. He'd already gone squinty-eyed, the rat.

"Just curious," I said with a sprightly grin.

I was not, it turned out, sprightly enough. As Sam continued to squint and Aunt Vi sliced lamb, Billy aimed his pretty brown eyes my way, too. "Yeah, Daisy. Who're you aiming to marry this time?"

Fiddle. Turning to Billy, I tried to maintain my bright demeanor. "Nobody. I'm happy with the husband I have, thanks." It wasn't much of a lie, really. I loved Billy. I wanted us to be happy. I *wished* we were happy.

"That's right," said Pa, merrily accepting a plate piled high with lamb, roast potatoes, green beans, and Aunt Vi's delicious popovers. "We Gumms are lucky in love." He winked at Ma.

"Lucky you," said Billy.

That hurt my feelings, but I didn't say so. Since I'd already begun my attempted pump of Sam, I continued. Spike wasn't the only dogged individual in the family. "I was just thinking about ages today. You have to be twenty-one to vote, and you used to have to be twenty-one to drink, but can you get married when you're younger than that? Without your parents' permission, I mean."

"And this is just because you're curious?" Sam smiled at Aunt Vi as he accepted his own fully loaded plate. He had a nice smile when he wasn't being sly. So far I'd never been the recipient of one of his plain old non-sly smiles.

"Yes," I said. My stomach growled. How come the men always got served first in this family, was what I wanted to know. Among other things.

Sam eyed his plate hungrily. He was polite enough not to dig in until we were all served and Pa had said grace, so he answered me. Not that he wouldn't have otherwise, but sometimes I thought he only tolerated me because he couldn't shoot me. "Eighteen is the legal age of consent in California. A person doesn't need a parent's permission at eighteen."

"Ah. I thought so." I acccpted my plate with gratitude.

After we were all served, Pa said grace, and we dug in.

"This is delicious, Mrs. Gumm," Sam said affably. He was always nice to my relatives. It was only my humble self toward whom he expressed reservations.

"It's wonderful," I concurred.

"Aunt Vi's the best cook in the United States," Billy said.

This was a normal conversation for us during the first few minutes of a meal. We all appreciated Aunt Vi more than we could say, and we didn't want her to think otherwise. It would be awful if she got mad at us and moved away or refused to cook our meals. Not that she'd do that, but still, she deserved as much praise as we could heap on her, so we heaped it high.

I think we all feared some man would snap her up one of these days and carry her off to cook for him instead of us. She wasn't a spring chicken any longer, being about Ma's age, which was fifty or so, but any man would be a fool not to value her just because she was kind of plump and not in the first blush of youth. Then again, most men *are* fools. Too bad there aren't more men like Pa around.

I wanted to work my way back to the subject of marriage, but discreetly. I didn't want Sam to suspect my purpose. Not that he didn't already, but I didn't want to give him any further motive to press me regarding the Marianne Wagner situation. "Say, did I tell you that I'm going to meet a Russian count this coming Friday?"

"A Russian count?" Ma stared at me as if she thought her little girl was coming up in the world.

I nodded. "Yep. Mrs. Wright's giving a party for him, and wants me to conduct a séance. He's interested in psychic phenomena and mysticism and so forth, and is hoping I'll be able to communicate with the late Tsar Nicholas via Rolly."

That this was true, and that I was a little nervous about it, didn't make Sam's response any more welcome.

"Do you ever worry that one of your clients will consider you a fraud?"

Sam was of Billy's opinion regarding the way I earned our living. I frowned at him, which is less than he deserved, but as much as my mother and aunt would tolerate. Not to mention my father and husband. "Heavens no. I'm a mistress of my craft." So there.

"She sure makes good money at it," said my husband. I smiled at him, since that was perhaps the nicest thing he'd said about my work in a year or more.

"That's right," I agreed. "And that's because I'm an excellent practitioner of my art, Sam Rotondo. If you don't believe me, you can just go ask my clients."

"I already did," said Sam glumly. "Mrs. Kincaid thinks you belong on a pedestal. Maybe with a golden crown."

I think I smirked. At least I didn't voice the, *She's right,* that danced on the end of my tongue.

"My little girl would look darned good on a pedestal with a golden crown on her head," said Pa, bless his heart. "She's the cat's meow, and that's the truth."

"Daisy's always had such a way about her," said Aunt Vi, smiling fondly at me.

This was another one of Aunt Vi's sayings. I don't know why, but she always said these vague things that were meant kindly, but which I never quite understood. I mean, what does "she has a way about her" mean, anyhow? What kind of way? A good way? A bad way? It was kind of like her saying, "go along with you," which is something else I've never figured out. When I told Billy about my reaction to these equivocal statements of Vi's, he only laughed and said I was being too literal. That didn't help, but at least I knew what it meant.

"Yes indeed," said Ma, beaming at me.

"Do you have to speak Russian?" Sam asked. He appeared truly curious, but I didn't believe it. I knew he was only trying to catch me out somehow.

"No. Rolly is Scottish, and he interprets for me."

He eyed me skeptically, but I only lifted my chin and chewed.

"You should hear her accent when she's got Rolly going," Billy told him. I think he would have laughed if his lungs were still healthy. It was the first time in a long time that he'd spoken of my job and me in so friendly a manner. I stared at him hard, but could detect no indication that he might have taken more morphine than was good for him.

"She's really something, my Daisy," said Pa. "She could probably speak Russian if she had to."

"Or if somebody paid her enough." Sam. With sarcasm.

I sniffed significantly, but didn't snap back. At least my family liked me. I decided it wouldn't hurt to ask another marriage question. "Say, Sam, when a couple gets a marriage license, is it always reported in the local newspaper, or just sometimes?"

"What's this obsession you have about marriage licenses, Daisy?"

Darn it. I tried not to glare at my husband. "I'm not obsessed with marriage licenses. I just wondered, is all."

"But why? You're already married."

Okay, the thing is, I know now that I approached this thing totally the wrong way. I ought to have thought of a good lie to account for my interest in marriages before I'd dared broach the subject. However, I've always been of the opinion that it's never too late to correct a mistake, if you have enough imagination.

That being the case, and since I have an agile imagination (and was feeling kind of desperate), I shrugged and said, "I ran into Laura Berry today. She said she and Roger Markham are getting married in June. It got me to thinking about it, is all. Our own wedding was only three years ago, but I can't remember what we did to prepare for it." I gave the assembled diners a careless laugh.

That was a big whopper, and I hoped Billy never ran into Laura and asked her about it. He probably wouldn't, since he couldn't get around very well, and I think Laura had moved to the Altadena area.

"Yeah," said Billy. "A lot's happened since then."

Boy, was *that* the truth. I sighed and smiled at him. "I guess when we got our license there was a notice about it printed in the paper."

"There was," Ma said. "I have it in the album I kept at the time." She sighed. "You were both so young and happy then. You made such a splendid couple."

As Billy had said, a lot had happened since then. I think I sighed too, remembering how happy we'd both been. "I'd like to look at the album, Ma. I'd forgotten all about it."

"I'll get it out after dinner."

"Thanks."

I decided to wait until then to ask more marriage-license questions. As I ate, I thought about Marianne and George and how they could be married secretly. Maybe a couple could go to another town and procure a license without the information being reported in the *Star News*. Was there a waiting period? Did you have to have any sorts of tests before they gave you a license? I doubted it. I didn't remember taking any tests.

Or maybe I was totally off base. Maybe George just had a Prince Charming complex and a compulsion to save silly women from catastrophes of their own devising. I'd read about Napoleon complexes; why not Prince Charming complexes? Lots of people were interested in psychology in those days, although only the rich ones could afford to go to psychiatrists. The rest of us had to muddle along on our own.

Fifteen

Ma, Aunt Vi, and I had cleaned up the dishes, and I'd taken Spike out to piddle and poop before Ma got the wedding album down from the bookshelf in the back room, where we did the sewing and I read palms and Ouija boards and tarot cards. I'd hoped that in the interim between dinner and the album, Sam would have left for his own house. I was beginning to wonder if he even *had* a house, he was at ours so often.

As usual, he didn't oblige me. When I handed Ma the album (I'd had to climb on a chair to get it), and we walked into the living room, he was there, chatting with Pa and Billy, and looking as if he aimed to stay. And stay, and stay, and stay. Drat the man.

Looking at the wedding album made me teary-eyed, and I felt like a fool. When I lifted my head to peek at everyone else (they were all standing behind the sofa, leaning over my shoulder, except for Billy), I noticed that Ma and Aunt Vi were surreptitiously wiping their eyes with their fingers. I guess I wasn't the only one who felt sorry for Billy and me.

When I made the mistake of peering at Sam, his face might have been carved out of granite. That was okay. I hadn't expected to find sympathy in that quarter.

"You were so beautiful that day, Daisy." Ma sniffled.

"She still is," said Aunt Vi dreamily.

"That's why I married her," said Billy. When I grinned at him, he winked back.

Now why, I wondered, was he in such an all-fired good mood all of a sudden? Could Spike have had such a benevolent influence in only one short day? He was napping in Billy's lap while we glanced at the album, and I think it was at that moment that I began to look upon him as a miracle dog. Until then, I hadn't properly understood the value of pets in a person's life. It occurred to me that Rolly might suggest pet ownership as a valuable means of coping with grief in my clients. Boy, you just never know when inspiration will strike, do you?

Returning my attention to the album, I pointed at another picture. "Oh, Billy, look at you in your uniform. You were so handsome in it." I gently pried the photograph out of its corner holders and handed it to him, hoping he wouldn't get depressed by looking at himself as he used to be.

He gazed at the picture with a pensive frown. "That seems like a million years ago, doesn't it?"

I nodded. "Yes. But it was only a little over three years ago."

He handed back the photograph, and I carefully replaced it in the album. When I glanced up at the audience again, I saw that Ma and Aunt Vi were weeping for real now, and both had pulled out their hankies. Even Pa had a funny, sad look on his face. Sam looked as if his entire body had been carved from stone instead of just his face, and I wondered if he was thinking about his deceased wife.

Suddenly I wanted to ask him if *he* had a wedding album. Had he and his wife wanted children, as Billy and I did? Did he know about colored dog collars because they'd had a dog? What kind of dog had it been?

I pressed a hand over my eyes and decided I was going crazy. There couldn't be another reason for me to want to know about Sam Rotondo's life, either before or after he'd invaded ours.

With another deep sigh, I shut the album, hoping it hadn't been a mistake to take it out. Billy didn't need any reminders, other than his daily life, of how much he'd lost by serving his country. Neither did I. "Thanks, Ma. We sure had a beautiful wedding, didn't we?"

"You did. Even Reverend Smith said it was a special wedding."

"He did, didn't he?" I smiled, remembering.

Everyone sort of wandered away from the couch, sat down willy-nilly, and stared off into space. Since we were already on the subject of weddings and nobody else seemed inclined to talk, I figured I might as well take advantage of the lull in the conversation. "Say, Sam, is there anywhere a couple can go to get married other than the city in which they live? I've heard people can get married in Reno."

The question brought him out of his stone-statue pose, and he squinted suspiciously at me. Figured. "There's a residency requirement in Reno."

"Oh." That wouldn't work. Marianne didn't have anything else to do with herself except sit around and wait to be rescued, but George had a bookstore to run. Besides, it would be most improper for them to go to Reno alone together. If that's not a contradiction.

"Why?" he asked with more intensity than I deemed healthy for my own personal welfare. "Are your friends eager to tie the knot?"

"Yeah," I said, striving to remain casual. "They don't want to make a big deal out of it."

"Shucks, I think a girl's parents deserve to see their little girl into a new life with all the pomp and circumstance they can afford."

I smiled at Pa. "Thanks. You and Ma sure did a wonderful job for Billy and me. And Vi." I gave my aunt an especially bright smile, because she deserved it. "That cake was spectacular."

Vi muttered a denial, but we all knew what I'd said was nothing but the truth.

I went on, "But Roger lost his mother to the 'flu, and Laura lost both her parents, and she doesn't have anyone else to give her away. I think they're worried about money, too." I was going to have to pay a visit to Laura Berry pretty darned soon, if I could find her, just in case any of my family happened to run across her and ask her questions that would ultimately be embarrassing for me.

Sam didn't relax his squinty-eyed stare significantly. I could tell he still suspected me of dire dealings, but he answered my question. "A couple can go to Mexico to get married, but it's a two-day drive from here, and some states don't recognize Mexican marriages."

"Mexico?" Good grief. I was absolutely certain neither George nor Marianne would care for that. "How come in books, couples can pop into a judge's office and tie the knot? Do you still have to go through all the preliminary rigmarole?"

"What rigmarole?" Sam narrowed his squint.

"You know. Licenses and that sort of thing."

"A couple needs a marriage license, no matter where they marry. A judge's office is quicker than a preacher, I suppose."

"Can somebody drive to another city and use its judge? I mean, you don't have to be married in the city in which you live, do you?"

"No." Sam was sitting on the edge of his chair, frowning at me for all he was worth. "Are you sure you're only interested in these things for the sake of your friend?"

"Yes! Why else would I be asking?"

"I don't know." He might as well have said "because I don't trust you," to judge from the tone of his voice.

"Hmmm." I needed to know more, but was afraid to

continue my inquiries. Laura had worked as a reason to ask the first few questions, but Billy knew we weren't great friends; he'd be as suspicious of my motives as Sam if I kept prying. Darn it, I needed to know this stuff! In an effort to divert suspicion, I said, "Working on any interesting cases, Sam?" I gave him one of my most winning smiles.

It didn't win him. "Can't talk about it."

Irked, I said, "How come you talk to Billy and Pa about your cases, but you won't tell me anything?"

"I never talk to them about my work until the cases are concluded," he said sternly.

"That's true," said Billy. "No matter how hard I pump him, he won't blab."

Nuts. I didn't know what to say then. What I wanted to do was go back down to the bookstore, but I feared my departure would not only infuriate my husband, but induce Sam to follow me. If he discovered Marianne, the game was up and my goose was cooked, although what hiding a girl from her parents had to do with obstructing justice, I still couldn't figure out.

I know it sounds awful, but I sneaked out of the house that night after everyone else had gone to bed and I was sure Billy slept. I felt like an idiot, too, both for sneaking and for going to the bookstore at so late an hour. It was ridiculous, I told myself, to check up on Marianne and George just because I was troubled that they might be starting to like each other more than I believed was good for them. Or me.

Have I mentioned that the Model T didn't have headlights? Well, it didn't, and the sparsely spaced street lights didn't provide much illumination. I might as well have gathered a bunch of lightning bugs and used them to light my way, except that we didn't have lightning bugs in Pasadena.

As I squinted into the darkness, I mentally berated myself all the way to the store, wondering what would happen when I crashed the car into a tree or a fence. If I lived through the accident, would Billy ever forgive me? If I didn't, would he think I'd been sneaking out to a secret rendezvous with another man? He probably would, and his opinion would have been grossly unfair. Heck, I didn't have time to meet other men, even if I'd had the inclination, which I didn't.

I'd managed to work up quite a state of self-righteous indignation by the time I reached Colorado and Oakland, although my feathers smoothed out once I realized I'd been worrying myself unnecessarily—at least until the drive home.

For all my sneaking and worrying, I didn't learn a darned thing that night. The bookstore was dark, the cottage was dark, and I didn't have nerve enough to knock at the door. After the scolding I'd given Marianne that morning, she'd probably die of fright if she heard somebody knocking on the cottage door in the middle of the night.

It seems stupid now, but I walked clear around the block, searching for George's automobile. I knew, because I'd seen it, that he drove a dark gray Cadillac. Since the night was pitch-black, I had to do a lot of squinting, and I think I remembered every single one of the gruesome detective novels I'd read in the past five years. I didn't find a dark gray Cadillac, although how I could have told if it was dark gray, black, or navy blue in the dark, I have no idea. On the other hand, I didn't get mugged by a heat-packing mugger, either, or slashed to death by a modern-day Jack the Ripper, so I guess my late-night adventure might have turned out worse.

After I'd walked around the block, I stuck my nose against the front window of the cottage and saw nothing, but nothing. The weather was freezing and I was afraid my nose would stick to the glass, so I decided I'd snooped enough for one night. I wasn't comfortable, though. As much as I trusted George, the situation seemed mighty darned perilous.

It was with an uneasy feeling in my innards that I drove back to Marengo. The Ford didn't appreciate our evening out. It barely made it home. I think I prayed it home, actually, although I'm surprised God listened to me since I'd been telling so many fibs lately. Then again, I hadn't noticed God paying much attention to what we humans did on earth anyhow, so maybe the car would have made it home even without my prayers.

The house was quiet when I tiptoed up to the door. That state of affairs lasted until I turned the key in the lock and pushed the door open. I'd forgotten about Spike.

You'd have thought a crazed ax murderer was trying to sneak into the house to kill everybody. I scooped the pup up and clamped a hand around his long snoot, but the damage was done. Lights flared on all over the house, and Billy called out in a shaky voice, "Daisy? Daisy, where the heck are you?"

Doggone it! Literally. "Darn you, Spike," I muttered, knowing it wasn't his fault. He was only doing his job—a state of affairs that sounded a lot like my own, actually. I called out, "It's okay, Billy. It's only me. I . . . uh . . . went out for a little walk because I couldn't sleep."

Okay, I suppose it was fortunate that God *didn't* pay too much attention to us poor human creatures here on earth. If He were more attentive, he'd probably have struck me dead with a lightning bolt a year or so before that evening's pack of lies.

"A walk?" Pa stumbled down the hall and into the living room, rubbing his eyes, his bathrobe flapping. "Daisy, are you nuts?"

"I wouldn't be surprised." With a sigh, I sagged against the door frame. "Sorry for the uproar, Pa. I forgot about Spike." Thinking fast, I fumbled to come up with some way to substantiate my latest lie. "I . . . uh . . . should have taken him with me, I guess."

Pa looked at me strangely, but only said, "I guess."

"Is everything all right?" Ma appeared at Pa's side, looking bewildered and sleepy-eyed. She had to get up early in the morning and go to work, and I felt so guilty, I darned near blurted out the truth. Since the truth would probably be even harder on my family than a pack of lies, I didn't.

"Everything's okay, Ma. I'm really sorry."

"Daisy!" Billy. Roaring. "Daisy, what are you up to now?"

Oh Lord, I didn't want Billy to have to get up and get himself to his wheelchair. Moving around was agony for the poor man. My guilt soared like the mercury in a thermometer on one of our hot Pasadena summer days. "I'd better get to Billy," I told my parents apologetically. "I'm awfully sorry for waking you up."

Pa yawned. "That's okay, Daisy-Belle."

As I hurried toward our bedroom, I said over my shoulder, "It was Spike. I forgot he was such a good watchdog."

"Good night, dear," said Ma. I'm sure she was still confused. I relied upon Pa to explain everything to her.

It wasn't until I entered the bedroom that I realized I still held Spike. He didn't mind. His tail was wagging up a storm.

"What the hell are you up to, Daisy?"

Because I didn't want to blind him, I turned on the small lamp on the dresser. My heart crunched when I saw him sitting up in bed, and I rushed to his side.

Dropping Spike on the bedspread, I hugged Billy gently. "I'm so sorry, Billy. I didn't mean to wake the whole house. I forgot Spike was such a terror."

He wasn't acting too terrible at the moment. After an initial moment of confusion, he liked the soft covers and started burrowing around in them. Ignoring the puppy, Billy scowled at me. "What's going on, Daisy? I don't believe that trash about going for a walk."

"But I did!" I couldn't come up with an ounce of indignation to color my statement. It was kind of the truth. I *had* walked around the block that night; it just hadn't been our block. "See? Feel my hands."

I put a hand on Billy's cheek, which was another bad mistake, since my hands were cold. He jumped, which made his muscles tense, which made him cry out. I really hated myself in that instant.

"Oh, Billy, I'm so sorry!"

"Damn it, Daisy," he muttered through clenched teeth.

I burst into tears. I guess the strain of the past several days had gotten to me. Sinking onto his lap, I repeated, "I'm so sorry, Billy. I'm so sorry."

He gave one of his shallow sighs and put his arm around me. "I can't stand this, Daisy."

Sniffling pathetically, I said, "You can't stand what?"

"Being lied to."

I cried harder. In between sobs, I said, "I'm not lying to you, Billy."

"Right."

Okay, here's the thing: I was lying to him, but not in the way he thought. But I didn't dare tell him the truth about Marianne Wagner, because I was afraid he'd tell Sam, and then I'd be in truly deep water. But more than that, I didn't want Marianne to have to go back to her father's house. Her father was a terrible man, and I honestly believed I was doing a good deed in continuing to hide her from him. It was bad luck that was turning all my good intentions inside out.

I tried hard to stop crying. "It's the truth, Billy. I would never, ever lie to you." *About anything important to you.* Naturally, I didn't add that part, since he wouldn't have understood, and it would have made things even more confusing, if that was possible.

Another small, raspy sigh issued from his ruined lungs. He kept his arm around me, and I wiped my eyes on the sheet. I couldn't see Spike any longer. Without getting up, I asked, "Where's the dog?"

"Huh?" Billy's eyes had been closed, but he opened them at my questions. "Spike? Hey, Spike, where are you?"

We both saw a wiggle under the bedspread, and Billy chuckled softly. He used to have a hearty, loud laugh. "I think he's just found my foot. He's nibbling on my big toe."

"Good grief." I lifted the counterpane and peeked under it. Sure enough, there was Spike, tail wagging madly, chewing on the lump that was Billy's left big toe. "I'll take him outside to piddle once more."

"Bring him back. It might be nice to have him in bed with us."

Billy sounded so wistful, I darned near started blubbering again. If this Marianne Wagner situation didn't resolve itself pretty soon, I didn't know what I'd do, although I feared for my sanity—not to mention that of my family.

I took Spike out the back door and let him snoop around for a while as I sat on the back porch steps and shivered. It was no more than I deserved.

When I got back indoors, Billy was standing by the dresser, putting a bottle away. I stopped at the door, holding Spike, and bit my lip, telling myself to remember what Dr. Benjamin had said. An addiction to drugs was a small price to pay for freedom from pain. I wanted to know if that was the bottle Dr. Benjamin had given me. I wanted to know if he'd picked up another bottle somewhere. I wanted to know if he was seeing a doctor other than Dr. Benjamin. I'd heard that drug addicts were awfully clever when it came to securing their poison.

Instead of asking him any of those questions, I went over and kissed him, hoping my kiss conveyed even half the love I felt for him. Then I threw Spike onto the bed, thrilling him and making Billy chuckle again, changed into my nightgown, and crawled into bed. I think I went to sleep before Spike, who was a championship sleeper.

I spent the entirety of the following morning with my husband. Anxiety gnawed at my insides, and I had to suppress the urge to telephone Grenville's Books approximately seven hundred and fifty times, but Billy deserved a wife, and I was it. He, Pa, and I decided to walk to the dry-goods store on the corner of Marengo and Bellevue to buy some dried pea beans which, according to Pa, he was going to make into authentic Boston baked beans. In order to do it properly, he claimed, we'd have to make a detour to the butcher's shop for some salt pork. Since I'm game for trying anything at least once, I agreed to this scheme.

"What do you know about fixing Boston baked beans, Pa?" Billy wanted to know.

So did I. "Yeah, Pa, what's going on with this sudden urge to cook? Do you know something about Aunt Vi that we don't?"

He looked so horrified, both Billy and I laughed. "Good gosh, no!" Slapping a hand on his chest, he said, "Don't scare me like that, Daisy. I have a weak heart, remember."

That was supposed to be funny, so I laughed. The truth was that the thought of Pa having another heart attack scared the living daylights out of me.

Billy saved the situation. "I didn't know you liked to cook, Pa."

"I don't, but I remember eating my aunt Grace's baked beans when I was a kid, and I found this recipe in one of last year's *Good Housekeeping* magazines." He flapped a folded periodical at us. "Just thought I'd give 'em a try. They're good with sausages or frankfurters."

I covered Spike's ears. "Don't listen to him, Spike." The puppy had been frolicking at our feet, trying to persuade us to take him with us. As much as I hated to disappoint the little fellow, I didn't think a trip to the butcher's shop would be a good idea for a piggy little puppy. He licked my hand.

Billy grinned at me and said to Pa, "Sounds good to me."

"My Massachusetts relatives still eat Boston baked beans every Saturday night. It's tradition."

"I thought they lived in Auburn," said I, handing Billy his overcoat. It was a struggle for him to get it on, because it was long, but the weather had taken a downturn, and his legs hurt in cold weather even worse than they normally did. I wasn't going to take a chance on him catching a chill, either. Dr. Benjamin's warnings about pneumonia and other lung ailments were clear in my mind.

Pa shrugged. "Auburn's close to Boston."

"Ah."

"It might be fun to see the eastern states someday," said Billy. It was the most optimistic comment to come from that quarter in, literally, months.

"Yes, it would," I agreed. "Isn't Sam from back east?" I knew he was. I was only making conversation.

Billy nodded. "New York."

"Massachusetts is better," said Pa with conviction.

Billy and I exchanged a glance and then we both laughed.

We used the back-door wheelchair ramp, then I pushed Billy down the long drive to the sidewalk in front of the house. Our across-the-street neighbor, Mrs. Killebrew, waved a bouquet of chrysanthemums at us. "Morning, Mrs. Majesty! Mr. Majesty. Mr. Gumm. I'll bring you a bouquet when you get back home."

"Thanks, Mrs. Killebrew. The flowers are gorgeous." That pleased her. It pleased me, too, since I love to have flowers in the house.

It was, all in all, an auspicious beginning to our day. I made Billy put a lightweight rug over his legs, since I didn't want any part of him to get chilled, and we all three strolled along, chatting companionably.

"The only thing I didn't like when I was back east," said Billy after contemplating the weather for a bit, "was clam chowder."

"Where'd you eat it?" Pa demanded. "If you ate it in Boston, you didn't eat the real stuff."

"I can't remember. Why? What's the difference between Boston clam chowder and everybody else's?"

"They put tomatoes in it in Boston," Pa said in a disgusted voice, with a shudder to match.

"Oh." Gee, I liked tomatoes. "Er, tomatoes don't go well with clams?"

"No." Pa was as positive as I'd ever heard him.

"As far as I'm concerned," Billy said, "it's the clams that don't go with the tomatoes. Clams don't go with anything that I care to eat."

"You've never had 'em fried," said Pa, virtually licking his chops. "Fried clams are ambrosia."

"Ambrosia? Isn't that a little excessive?" I was giggling, though. Couldn't help it. Pa loved his food—too much, according to Dr. Benjamin. He pulled out a cigar, and another admonition of the doctor's made my giggle dry up. "Put that smelly thing away right this minute, Pa! You know what the doctor said."

With the air of a person enacting one of Shakespeare's more tragic scenes, Pa heaved an enormous sigh and complied. "Darned women are always trying to spoil a fellow's fun."

"Nuts to that," I said, perhaps a trifle sharply. "I want the men in my life to last a while, thanks."

Billy turned to glance back at me. He had a funny smile on his face. "I'm glad to hear it."

I didn't know what he meant by that, but it made a shiver run up my spine.

* * *

After we got back from the butcher's and the grocer's, Pa put the salt pork in the icebox and the beans in the cupboard to await Friday night to be put in water to soak overnight (the only way to do it, according to Pa, whose pronouncement was affirmed by Aunt Vi), and I went across the street to get some of Mrs. Killebrew's chrysanthemums. She gave me a huge bunch, orange, yellow, white, purple and tan, and perfect for late fall.

"Thanks so much, Mrs. Killebrew."

"You're more than welcome, Mrs. Majesty. Your aunt Vi brought me over a loaf of her French bread yesterday, and I've never eaten anything so wonderful in my life."

I nodded and smiled warmly. "Aunt Vi's the best cook in California, if not the United States."

"She sure is. She gave me her raisin pie recipe, too." Mrs. Killebrew's brows furrowed. "I hated to ask Vi because she's such a good cook and I'd feel stupid, but . . . well . . . do you know what a capital T means?"

"It means tablespoon," I told her kindly. I didn't let on to Mrs. Killebrew, but I wanted to turn a handspring in joy at actually knowing the answer to a culinary question. It might be a small question, but *I*, Daisy Gumm Majesty, who couldn't even brew a decent pot of coffee, had answered it!

See? There's another example of the benefits of being middle class. You can take pleasure in the small victories life presents you.

After I'd arranged three lovely bouquets of chrysanthemums and put one in the living room, one in the dining room, and one in our bedroom, I made lunch. I could fix sandwiches and open cans of soup without doing much damage to the kitchen or the people dining. Besides, we had Aunt Vi's leftover lamb to put between her fresh, homemade bread, and even I couldn't ruin those two commodities.

When we'd finished lunch, Pa went to his and Ma's bedroom to rest. I washed up the lunch dishes. A copy of *National Geographic* had been delivered in the morning's mail (in those days, first-class stamps cost two cents, and mail was delivered twice a day), and Billy settled in to read about Siberia, a place that sounded horrid to me.

I went to our bedroom to change into something more appropriate for afternoon visiting. I was only going to be visiting Grenville's Books, but Billy didn't have to know that. Maybe if he thought I was going about my spiritualist business, I wouldn't have to lie about my destination or the reason for my leaving home.

As I settled a sober brown hat over my dark red hair and tugged the jacket of my brown-and-white, cotton-and-wool-blend, ankle-length, shepherd-checked suit into place, I contemplated what a despicable woman I must be to consider a sin of omission preferable to a sin of commission.

Oh well. I grabbed my small brown handbag, transferred the contents of that morning's bag into it, and braced myself to tell Billy I was leaving him, trying to console myself with the knowledge that we'd had a pleasant morning. That didn't work, so I gave it up.

Billy glanced up from his magazine. His face didn't change expression when he asked, "Going out?"

I went over and kissed him on the cheek. "Not for long." I prayed it was the truth. "I'll be back soon."

"Reading the cards and boards?"

He would have to ask. I sucked in air and lied yet again. "Yup. Both of those things." What the heck. With luck, this situation would soon be resolved.

I wished I believed in luck.

"You look beautiful, Daisy."

"Thanks, Billy. I made this suit with a bolt end I got at Hertel's Dry Goods. I'm glad you like it." I gave a little twirl to show off the total ensemble. "It's got a new ankle-length skirt."

His grin was a trifle lopsided. "I kind of liked the shorter skirts on you. You have pretty ankles."

What in the name of gracious was the matter with the man? He *never* complimented me several times in less than six or seven months. "Thanks." I kissed him again. "Need anything while I'm out?"

"No thanks."

So I left him there, reading about Siberia. According to the cover of the magazine, there was also an article about Haiti in December's issue. I'd rather have read about a tropical island than a frozen Bolshevist country with bread lines two blocks long. Standing in a bread line was inconceivable to me then, and I devoutly hoped I'd never have to find out what it was like.

Sixteen

I parked the old Ford at the curb in front of Grenville's Books. Then I walked in the door as if I had every right to be there, which I did, although I didn't feel like it.

Because it's what I usually did, I browsed through the new books George had put on display. I noticed Booth Tarkington's latest contribution to American literature and decided I didn't need to read it. If I wanted to be depressed, all I had to do was wake up in the morning. *The Magnificent Ambersons* had just about done me in. If Mr. Tarkington ever got himself analyzed and cheered up, I might tackle another one of his books.

There weren't any new books by Mary Roberts Rinehart, darn it. A lady named Agatha Christie had written a terrific mystery story a couple of years earlier, featuring a dapper Belgian detective named Hercule Poirot, but George didn't have any of her new books on his shelves, if she had any. She was British, and I guess it takes a while for books to travel from there to here.

People were still buying *This Side of Paradise*, by F. Scott Fitzgerald, I presumed, since George had three copies of it. There's another book that had left me cold, since it was filled with bored young people who didn't have enough real work to do and who passed their time by being blasé, drinking too much, thinking life wasn't worth living, and getting into trouble. Nuts to them. I didn't care for people like that.

Fitzgerald had a new book out, as well, a compilation of short stories called *Flappers and Philosophers*, neither one of which excited me a whole lot. I didn't have time to fuss with philosophy, and had too many responsibilities to be a flapper. It seemed to me that Mr. Fitzgerald and I were destined to differ, which I'm sure was okay by him. And, since he was rich and I wasn't, maybe he had the right idea. I've never claimed to be brilliant.

Shoot, how'd I get on that subject? Oh, yes, the book-store. There were a couple of Arthur Crabb's detective stories, which featured a guy named Samuel Lyle. I liked them pretty well, but I'd read the ones George had.

Then I noticed a book called *The Strange Case of Mortimer Finley*, by someone named Louis Tracy, which sounded interesting. I'd just picked it up to scan when I heard a murmur from George's back room. I froze for a second and my blood ran cold. Then I slammed the book down on the shelf and raced to the counter.

Marianne was in George's back room! And she was talking! Flinging up the countertop, heedless of the terrible noise it made, I raced into the back room.

Sure enough, there was Marianne. And George. And he was showing her what looked like an accounts book. "What's going on here?" I regret to say I shouted the question.

Marianne jumped a yard, uttered a shrill "Eee!" and dropped the accounting book. George grunted and would have fallen off his stool if he hadn't thrown out an arm and braced himself on the table next to him.

Marianne's blue eyes were as round as jawbreakers. She slapped a hand over her heart which was, presumably, thundering. As well it might.

Assuming what must have looked like full fighting stance, I bellowed, "What the heck are you doing out of that cottage?" I pointed to the back door. I was so furious with them both, I wanted to batter them with several of George's larger volumes. Perhaps atlases of the United States. Or even the world.

George recovered first (Marianne had started crying, which is no more than I'd expected of such a poor specimen of womanhood), rose from his stool, and put a hand on my rigid arm. "Calm down, Daisy. I can explain."

I whirled on him. "You'd darned well *better* explain, George Grenville! I brought Marianne here to *protect* her! She's not supposed to be out of the cottage. In case you've forgotten, she's trying to *hide!*"

"I haven't forgotten anything." George was getting miffy—and for no good reason, if you ask me.

"No? Then what's she doing here, practically out in the open? Didn't you say her father visits your establishment from time to time? What are you trying to do, George? I thought you were trying to help her, not hinder her escape."

I don't get really angry very often. When Billy and I fight, I'm usually more frustrated and unhappy than angry. Boy, was I ever mad at George that day. And Marianne, although I'm sure she was less to blame for this idiotic lapse than George, since he had a brain and she didn't.

"Calm down, please," George said again, getting heated. "There's no need to yell."

I turned to Marianne. "Listen to me, Marianne Wagner. Do you want my help or don't you? Because if you do, I'm going to insist that you obey a few simple rules. If you don't, fine. I'll just leave you to George's tender mercies, and you can dally in the bookstore all day, every day, until your father comes in and finds you and hauls you back home."

She covered her eyes. "No! No, I don't want that!"

"Daisy!" George roared. "There's no need—"

Again I spun around. I was *furious*. "The hell there isn't!"

Now, I never curse. Not only am I a good Christian

girl, but swearing is unladylike and vulgar. It's a testament to my state of mind that I cursed that day.

George swallowed hard. Marianne squeaked again. I didn't care. "Lock up your shop, George," I said in a less vociferous but more threatening tone of voice. "We need to talk."

Without another word, George turned on his heel and stomped to the front door of his bookstore. He flipped the OPEN sign to the CLOSED side with a vigor that clearly expressed his exasperation with yours truly, and stomped back to us.

Marianne was sobbing softly, her hands covering her face. I made no move to comfort her, believing she didn't deserve it. George went to her, put a gentle hand on her shoulder, and glared at me. "Really, Daisy, there's no need for this."

"Yes," I said, pushing the words through my grinding teeth, "there's every need for it. Now get her to the cottage."

It occurred to me that George was so angry with me, he might just hustle her over there without looking, so I added, "I'll check to make sure the coast is clear." Turning to give George a glare even hotter than his own, I barked, "Is the cottage door unlocked?"

"Yes." He was terribly huffy now. Too bad. I was mad enough for any six people.

"Well, it shouldn't be," I snarled.

There was no one in the alleyway, so I waved George and Marianne forward. He held her tenderly and scowled at me as he walked her past me and aimed her across the alley. She, naturally, was still crying.

I slammed the back door as I exited the bookstore. The childish gesture felt good. What was the matter with those two? Didn't they *care* about Marianne's welfare? I almost wished George sold china or pottery, since I'd have loved to smash something.

As soon as I set foot in the cottage, I locked the door.

Then I aimed a deadly stare at the pair of feeble-witted conspirators. "All right, what's the meaning of this? Haven't we already talked about how important it is to keep Marianne out of the public's eye? Do you think her problem is trivial, George? Is that why you're exposing her to the risk of discovery?"

"Now wait a—"

"No, darn it, I won't wait a minute! Has she told you what her father's done to her? Do you *know* why she ran away?"

Marianne warbled a feeble, "No-o-o-o!"

So, I turned on *her.* "Why not, Marianne? If there's no other way to make you two behave, you'd better tell George exactly what your life's been like at home. I'm about to give up on you. You don't seem to have an ounce of sense between you when it comes to self-preservation."

"Now see here, Daisy, there's no need to be—"

"Yes, there is!" Since there wasn't anything breakable in it, I slammed my handbag on the small table next to the sofa. "I'm sick and tired of being the only one who gives a care about Marianne's welfare, George Grenville! Do you think I'd risk being arrested on a whim?"

The word caught Marianne's attention. She lifted her head from her cupped hands and stared at me, her eyes looking like two blue marbles in a clear mountain pool. "A-arrested! What do you mean, Daisy?"

"I mean I've been threatened with arrest and imprisonment if I help you elude your parents!" It wasn't much of a fib.

Her face as pale as rice, Marianne swallowed. "Imprisonment?"

George, who might have been expected to give thought to my words, frowned. "How did that happen? It's all well and good for you to scold me for being careless, but how does anyone else know you're involved in this mess, unless you told somebody?"

"Nobody knows. My husband's best friend is a detective, and he doesn't trust me. He keeps asking prying questions about Marianne, and he's told me more than once that if I'm hiding her, I'll be in trouble with the police."

"Oh no!" I swear to heaven, if Marianne's eyes had gotten any bigger, they'd have fallen out of their sockets, especially as they were slippery with tears. Her voice was a quavery whisper.

"Oh yes." Mine, on the other hand, was as hard as rocks and flint and other like matter. "Now, are you two going to behave, or shall we just give your father a ring and tell him where to find you, Marianne?"

Evidently stricken speechless by the threat of danger to my own humble self, Marianne shook her head.

"I wish you wouldn't talk to her like that," George said querulously. "She's a gently reared young lady who—"

I stamped my foot, effectively squashing the rest of George's sentence underfoot. "I know *exactly* what she is, George! I'm trying to get *you* to understand her danger! What don't you understand about it? Do you think we're lying to you? Exaggerating to you? Do you think we're making up a story for your amusement? We're not, you know."

He had the grace to look slightly—only slightly, drat the man—abashed. "I know that."

"It's not George's fault, Daisy."

This astonishing—astonishing because it was so unexpected (and because I didn't believe it)—declaration came from Marianne. I turned a skeptical eye on her. "No?"

"No. I asked him to teach me about the bookselling business. I . . . I thought maybe I could get a job here."

Squinting as I made my way through her thought processes, which were kind of murky, I said, "Here? You can't work here until you're twenty-one. Do you know of another bookstore in another city that needs help?" Maybe the girl was more resourceful than I'd given her credit for.

She shook her head, confirming my opinion that resourcefulness wasn't one of her more prominent characteristics. "No. But I thought perhaps George . . ."

I didn't blame her for not finishing *that* sentence. What had she been going to say? That she thought George could give her a job in three years? That she hoped to hide out in his cottage, eluding her father and the rest of the citizens of Pasadena, not to mention the Pasadena Police Department and who knew how many private investigators the Wagners might possibly employ, until her twenty-first birthday? I had an urge to pound my head against the wall. Or maybe it was Marianne's head I wanted to pound. I must have appeared as doubtful as I felt, because she bowed her head, folded her hands in her lap, and clammed up.

A moment of silence ensued. I tried to gather the shreds of my composure together, catch my breath, and not start picking up odd books lying about the cottage and hurling them through windows.

At last George cleared his throat. "We don't have to wait that long," he said.

Marianne lifted her head and blinked at him. The trails of tears on her cheeks made her appear even more pathetic than usual, and her blue eyes still looked as if they'd been dunked in a woodsy pond. Her rosebud mouth opened slightly, as if she was waiting for an awe-inspiring, problem-solving, and perhaps earthshaking declaration from her hero, Saint George.

I'm afraid that I eyed him as if he were the devil or one of his minions. "Oh?" The one small word held approximately six hundred pounds of sarcasm, and George must have felt every one of them, because he winced.

"Yes," said he. "I mean, no. I mean . . . Oh, curse it, I don't know what I mean."

"I figured as much." Taking a deep breath, I silently counted to ten and then said, "All right. Until we figure out what to do, will you both *please* not tempt fate by flaunting Marianne in the open?"

"We weren't—" George caught my eye, which was probably extremely flinty by that time, and didn't continue. If you ask me, it was a good thing. "Never mind."

"Thank you. Then you'll remain in the cottage, Marianne? You won't go to the bookstore? And you especially won't go into the bookstore in broad daylight when anyone might see you?"

"No," she whispered. "I mean, yes, I'll remain in the cottage, and I won't go to the bookstore. I promise." She looked beseechingly at George, who nodded.

"That's right," said George. "Marianne will stay in the cottage until you tell us it's all right for her to leave it."

I felt a little better after that, although not a whole lot. I still didn't trust those two. I was also feeling plenty depressed about having to lie so much to Billy and my family. I was beginning to think Marianne Wagner wasn't worth my peace of mind. However, I'd started this rescue operation, and I supposed I had to finish it. It would be too cruel to abandon Marianne at this point.

It would sure help if she and George cooperated, though.

During the next few days, I began to harbor hopes that if I hadn't yet come up with a resolution to Marianne's problem, at least I wouldn't have to fight George and Marianne in order to keep her hidden. I fretted occasionally about what I perceived as the increasing warmth of their relationship, but I had too many other things to worry about to spend much time on it. If they crossed the line, they could face the consequences on their own.

I know, I know. Big talk. But I really *did* have one or two other things to think about than Marianne Wagner and George Grenville, although I did my duty by them and visited Marianne at the cottage at least once a day, in between my other responsibilities. It was a real bother to do so.

Mrs. Wright's séance on Friday night went without a hitch, and I even had my hand kissed by a Russian count, which you must admit doesn't happen every day. He was an odd duck, although Sam said he didn't sound any odder than most of the Russians he'd met since their revolution. I wouldn't know about that. I also suspect Sam only said it to be contrary.

The party was swell. I wore my favorite black silk dress with a dropped waist and a patch of beaded embroidery on the side, and felt quite elegant among all the diamonds, emeralds, pearls, furs, and glitter. I never wore jewelry, primarily because I couldn't afford to, but also because the stark plainness of my evening garb accentuated my pallor and my vocation. I stood out in the crowd, and people started feeling creepy even before they got herded into the séance room, joined hands, the lights went out, and my one red lamp, lit by one small candle, became their only source of illumination.

Rolly didn't speak to Czar Nicholas that evening Rather, he had a chat with one of the czar's late daughters. They'd all been killed by Bolshevists in 1917, an incident that had given me a poor opinion of Bolshevists in general.

In my estimation, it's all well and good to revolt against an oppressive government, but there's no reason to take it out on the kids. Heck, it wasn't the children's fault their father was a czar any more than it was their fault their mother was a nitwit who believed in that wicked charlatan Rasputin.

Not that I consider all charlatans wicked, mind you. If I did, I wouldn't have a leg to stand on in my arguments with Billy. But from all I've ever read about the Mad Monk, he was crazy, and a drunk to boot, and the czarina was an idiot to believe a word he said—not that her being stupid was any excuse to murder her. Boy, I tell you, having scads of money and power doesn't necessarily mean you also have brains.

Of course, there were lots of people in Pasadena, California, who believed in my own fictional psychic powers, and I didn't deplore their naïveté. But there's a difference between Rasputin and yours truly. Rasputin was only out for himself, in my opinion. I, on the other hand, was trying to support a family.

Besides that, darn it, my work helped to comfort bereaved people. Believe me, in those days there were tons of people who had lost relatives and lovers and husbands in the war or in the 'flu pandemic, and they all needed solace. I did my small best to provide it, thereby helping them cope with the remains of their lives, in spite of what Billy thought.

I didn't mean to rant again. All I meant to do was explain the séance for Count Ivan Romanov (if he really was a Romanov which, I gather, is the name of the Russian royal family. Sam said he doubted it, but Sam doubted everything).

I felt a good deal of tension in the room as everyone took their places. After all, it wasn't every day I performed before royalty, even the deposed variety. The people who attended the séance had met each other in Mrs. Wright's ultra-fancy drawing room before the séance began, which was a normal procedure. I'd been kind of hoping that Harold Kincaid would be there, although I hadn't expected it. My expectations were met, which meant I'd have to go through the whole evening without the support of one of my best friends.

But everything went quite well after I got started. Nobody fainted. Nobody screamed. Rolly spoke in his best, most mellifluous Scottish burr, letting the count know that the czar was coming to terms with what had happened to him and his family. Rolly also said that the czar continued to care about Russia and his former people.

I let everyone know that poor Nick was worried about the Bolshevists. *Everyone* was worried about the Bolshevists in those days. You'd think there was a Bolshie hidden under every bush and behind every tree, waiting to pounce on passersby, from all the hair-raising articles published in magazines and newspapers.

Personally, I don't know if I've ever even met a Bolshevist. If there were any living in Pasadena at the time, they were keeping a mighty low profile.

You know, when I'm doing séances, I never really know what's going to come out of my mouth. I'm not claiming any kind of rapport with the spirits; I'm only saying that I must be able to sense people's feelings and expectations, because I alter Rolly's words to fit the way I gauge the emotional environment at the time, and I take my cues from what I sense about the company I'm in—if that makes any sense.

That night I knew, without knowing how I knew, that the count wouldn't believe me if I had Rolly interpret for the czar. I knew the names of Nicholas and Alexandra's daughters because I'd read about them. The name that popped out of my mouth when Rolly was talking through me was Tatiana. As soon as her name hit the air, I felt the count, who sat next to me, jerk slightly, and heard a soft exclamation leave his lips.

Ever since those terrible men killed the Russian royal family, there'd been speculation about Anastasia, one of the daughters. Women had been turning up all over Europe, practically from the first, claiming to be her. That night, for some reason beyond my ken, I made Rolly tell the count that Anastasia was with her family. Or, in other words, she was dead.

Maybe the thought of a poor princess wandering alone in a world that had murdered the rest of her family was more painful than I could bear. Maybe I'd been concerned with Marianne for too darned long and was thinking of her and Anastasia as cut of the same cloth. I do know that I could perceive similarities between the two, neither of whom was fit to live in the world without plenty of help. I'm not sure. All I know is that the count broke down and sobbed at the end of the séance.

At first (after I'd spent some time coming out of my "trance") I felt awful about his unhappy tears. Then, after he'd composed himself, taken my hand in both of his and kissed it, I realized that between us, Rolly and I had managed to give him some kind of peace in his soul. Does that sound pompous? It's not meant to. It's the truth.

Since it was a Friday night, when I finally left the Wrights' mansion and went home again, Sam was there, playing gin rummy with Pa and Billy. I had anticipated this, and was, therefore, prepared for his ill will when I walked into the house. Ma and Aunt Vi had already gone to bed, since they were used to early hours.

Naturally, Spike started barking as soon as he heard the Model T pull into the driveway. I had to spend the first few minutes of my return home petting him and telling him what a good doggy he was.

Dogs are so soothing. At least the kind you can pick up and cuddle are. The evening had been stressful; I was feeling keyed up when I got home, and I'd have given almost anything not to have to put up with Sam, but I could practically feel my rampaging nerves settle down as I stroked the dog.

"Hey there, Daisy," Billy said. He'd looked up and smiled at me when I opened the door, which was a distinct improvement over what I'd anticipated his greeting would be. "How'd it go tonight?"

"Pretty well, thanks. How long are you guys going to stay up losing your money?"

"Not much longer," said Pa. "Sam's got to work tomorrow."

"On Saturday?"

"A detective's work is never done," Sam growled, slapping a card on the discard pile.

Still holding Spike, I moseyed over to the card table. It's probably stupid, but the fact that I didn't dare tell the men that I believed I'd served a useful, not to say kindly, purpose that night annoyed me. They'd only have laughed at me. So, after resettling the puppy in Billy's lap, I told them inconsequential things about the séance: the fancy clothes all the people had been wearing; the monocled, bearded count; and the gist of Rolly's conversation with Tatiana.

Billy, who'd taken to studying his rummy hand, peered up at me again, his eyes wide, I presume in wonderment. "How on earth do you come up with that sort of stuff, Daisy?"

I shrugged. "Beats me."

"Does it hurt?" Sam's contribution. He was trying to be funny, I suppose, because Pa laughed.

"My little girl has a way about her. She knows what to say to people."

I kissed him on his balding head. "Thanks, Pa."

"You're probably right." Billy. Grudgingly. "She sure seems to know what to say around rich people, and whatever it is, it convinces them to keep throwing money at her."

Sam only grunted.

Feeling feisty, I said, "Whatever I do, it works. I make *very* good money at it. Besides that, how many times has *your* hand been kissed by a Russian count, Sam Rotondo?"

He darned near dropped his cards, and his face took on such a horrified expression that *I* laughed. He shook his head, muttered, "Good God," and went back to his game.

Before I took myself off to bed—I was bone tired—I went to Billy and kissed him on the cheek. He put an arm around my waist, which was unusual, and I appreciated it. "Winning?" I asked, as a rush of love for him galloped through me.

He grinned. "You bet."

"Good." Because I hoped—ridiculous, but true—that it would help Billy come to terms with my job, I said, "Mrs. Wright paid me a lot of money. And the count gave me a piece of jewelry that looks as if it's covered in diamonds. I tried to refuse it, but he wouldn't let me."

"Why'd you try to refuse it?" Pa wanted to know.

"I didn't think I deserved it. But the count disagreed. He wouldn't take it back when I asked him to."

"I'll just bet he didn't," said my husband, although he didn't sound cross.

"It's true," I said, indignant. "I was actually shocked when he handed me the thing. I think it's a bracelet."

That got everyone's attention, except for Spike, who had evidently run himself ragged that day, because he'd curled up on Billy's lap and was sawing logs like nobody's business.

Pa put his cards facedown on the table and stared at me. "You *think?* You mean you haven't even *looked* at it?"

"No. It was . . . I don't know. I felt funny about it. I didn't want to accept the gift, and then it would have been awkward to gawk at it. It looks awfully expensive."

"I sure hope it is," said my husband, his beautiful brown eyes sparkling, which was something they didn't do often. "Where'd you put it?"

"In my handbag. Want to see it?"

They all said yes, so I opened the bag and dug around in it until I felt the piece of jewelry. When I pulled it out, it was trailing my hankie, which I disengaged gently. The gem-encrusted bauble darned near blinded me when I held it out over the card table and the jewels flashed in the light. I'd been right: it was a bracelet. And it was jammed with so many precious stones, I could only blink at it.

It seemed to have the same effect on everyone else in the room. No one spoke for several seconds as their eyes adjusted to the light glinting off the jewels. I finally broke the silence. "Gosh, it looks even more expensive now than it did then. Do you think the gems are genuine?" If they were, maybe we'd be getting a new automobile sooner than I'd expected.

"It would be a mighty shabby trick of the count to play, to give you something like that and have it turn out to be paste," Pa said after another few seconds.

"May I see it?" Sam held out his big hand, palm up.

I frowned at him. "Why? Has somebody reported a Russian bracelet having been stolen? If you think I pilfered the darned thing, Sam Rotondo—"

He interrupted, "No. I just want to look at it up close. My uncle was a jeweler in New York, and I know something about stones."

"Really?" Billy brightened. "Maybe you can tell us if Daisy's count gave her a fortune tonight, or only a child's plaything."

"Heck," I muttered. "No kid's going to play with that if I have anything to say about it."

"Maybe you ought to take it to Arnold's Jewelry Store," Pa suggested. "I expect they can tell you if the stones are real or fake."

Sam had been turning the bracelet in his hand, holding it up to the light, and squinting at it hard. It was the first time I'd had a chance to feast my eyes on the thing myself. It was really something.

Diamonds and emeralds had been set in a gold design that resembled vines twining together. Rubies twinkled on the ends of stems that trembled, catching the light in a way I considered truly amazing. As I've already mentioned, I don't wear jewelry. If I did, I doubt that I'd wear anything that flashy, but it was a marvelous piece of work.

"It's Russian, all right," Sam at last. "And I'd say the stones are genuine."

"You can tell Russian jewelry from American jewelry?" I don't think my tone of voice held scorn.

"Sure. A trained jeweler can tell if a piece has been

made by craftsmen from France or Germany or Russia or most other places that have particular conventions in the art of jewelry making. This," he held up the bracelet, sending multicolored sparks flying through the room, "is Russian. It was either made there, or it was made by a Russian in this country. Or any other country, I should say. After the revolution, thousands of Russians made a bolt for it, and most of them took up their old professions in their new countries."

"After what I read today about Siberia, I don't blame them for scramming out of there," murmured Billy.

Sam sighed. "No, I don't, either. There are hundreds of Russian Jews living in New York City. Many of them are skilled artisans." He looked up at me and handed me back the bracelet. For once, he didn't appear contemptuous or disapproving. "Looks to me as if you have yourself an honest-to-goodness treasure here, Daisy. Take care of it. Or," he said, breaking into a grin, "sell it and get yourself a new motorcar. I think the Ford's about to call it quits."

Boy oh boy, I wished he wouldn't smile like that. He doled his smiles out sparingly, and between one smile and the next, I always forgot what a difference they made in his demeanor. When Sam Rotondo smiled, he looked almost affable. And he definitely looked handsome.

Not that he could ever have rivaled my Billy in good looks. Or that I cared.

Seventeen

In those days, most stores were closed on Saturday, and all of them were closed on Sunday, so I didn't get to take my Russian bracelet to Arnold's Jewelry Store until Monday. You can bet I showed it to Ma and Aunt Vi, though. They were as awed as I had been—especially when I told them Sam said the gems were genuine.

Aunt Vi had to return to work at Mrs. Kincaid's house that morning, and Ma worked half days on Saturdays at the Hotel Marengo, so I had to get to them early.

As soon as I heard Vi in the kitchen starting the coffee brewing, I bounced out of bed, shoved my feet into my old floppy slippers, flung on my robe, and scooted out of the bedroom, leaving Billy to take his time about getting up. It usually took him a while, because his muscles would relax overnight and then hurt like fury when he tried to move his limbs the next morning. He also had to cough a good deal to get the phlegm out of his ruined lungs. Poor Billy.

As Ma and Vi stared at the bracelet I'd put on the kitchen table, I stood back and grinned. "I'm going to take it to be appraised at Arnold's on Monday. If it's worth what Sam thinks it's worth, I'm going to buy us a new motorcar sooner than I'd planned."

I guess Ma was still trying to take in the glory of the gemstones because she didn't shut her mouth, which had fallen open in surprise. It was Vi who spoke first.

"Are you sure you don't want to keep it, Daisy? It's not every day a body is given something like this. This valuable." She shook her head, as if she couldn't quite believe it was true.

To be honest, I couldn't, either. In fact, I'd thought about it a lot during the night, since I hadn't slept well. If Arnold's Jewelry Store confirmed Sam's assessment of the bracelet, I decided I'd better hold on to it for a while, just in case the count decided he hadn't really wanted to part with it after all. I don't suppose he'd have been the first person to regret a generous act and then accuse the recipient of theft. I didn't aim to get caught up in anything like that.

So although the notion didn't thrill me, I'd come to the conclusion that I'd better wait and save up my money, without using the bracelet, before I bought a new car. My statement to Vi had been for entertainment's sake.

"Actually, I'm not going to sell it. At least, not right away."

"My goodness, Daisy, I've never seen anything like it," said Ma at last. "May I pick it up?"

"Sure! Pick away. If you hold it to the light, better shade your eyes, because the shimmer will blind you."

As if she were lifting a newborn baby out of a bassinet, Ma raised the bracelet in her fingers. "Oh my, it's heavy, isn't it?"

"Sure is. And I'll bet those little shaky stems would catch on your clothes if you didn't take care." I clasped my hands behind my back and beamed upon my two favorite ladies in the world. They'd been best friends since their school days. Vi had married Pa's brother way back in ninety-two, a few years before Ma married Pa. They were as different as night was from day, but they were still the very closest of friends.

I was happy to have brought something interesting into their lives. Not that they were bored or unhappy with the roles they played on a daily basis, but face it, they were both working drudges, just like me, only I had a more interesting job than either of them. What's more, my job was one that occasionally, as it had that day, provided intriguing sidelights.

In a way, I looked upon the count's bracelet rather as if it were a treat for all of us, if only because it was unusual for such an item to appear in the Gumm household. And if the count one day rued his generous impulse and demanded the bracelet back, that would be interesting, too.

How many other people would have turned a talent for manipulating a Ouija board into a fascinating, full-time, and very remunerative job? Not very darned many, I'll bet. Even if you didn't approve of how I earned my living, you had to give me credit for ingenuity.

The word made me think of Marianne, who didn't have any, and I sighed. Ma, who had been staring at the bracelet as if it were a holy vision, tore her gaze away from it and glanced at me. "What's the matter, dear?"

"Not a thing, Ma." I tried to look as perky as I made myself sound. "Just thinking about what I'm going to do today."

I usually didn't have to work during daylight hours unless people made appointments to come over for tarot or Ouija-board readings, so I took it upon myself to keep the house clean and tidy. As a rule, I did the job on Saturday, with occasional forays into various rooms with the dust rag, mop, and vacuum cleaner during the week. Once every six months or so, we all washed windows. Even Billy got into the act during window-washing time, because he could reach the lower ones from his wheelchair.

That day, after Ma and Vi had admired the bracelet until they were both almost late for work, I put it away, threw on my oldest housedress, tied a big white apron over it, wrapped a scarf around my head, put on my ugliest and most comfortable shoes, and grabbed the dust mop. I actually enjoyed cleaning house. The chore made me feel like a real housewife instead of a phony spiritualist whose husband didn't appreciate her.

The day didn't work out exactly as I'd planned. I should have anticipated as much, since my days seldom went the way I wanted them to. I was actually humming the choir's Sunday choice, "We Three Kings," when the phone rang, almost startling me out of my skin.

Although it was our ring, I was in the living room and didn't make it to the kitchen until the entire herd of party-line people had already picked up. Billy grinned over his toast and eggs as I shooed them off the line. Mrs. Barrow was particularly tenacious that day, but eventually even she hung up.

With a wink for my husband, I finally got to talk to Mrs. Kincaid, the calling party. I was surprised to hear from her, since she'd only just come home from wherever she'd been visiting, and I knew she was preparing for a large engagement party in a few days' time. The fact that she was practically hysterical jarred my composure.

I've already mentioned (probably too often) that Mrs. Kincaid's daughter, Stacy, is a first-class drip. Stacy fancies herself a member of the "lost generation" when she isn't fancying herself one of the "bright young things" everyone was talking about in the early twenties. As far as I was concerned, she was a pain in the neck, and the USA's favorite expression, "I'll say she does," might have been coined for her alone. She did just about everything she could think of, as long as it annoyed her mother.

That day, Mrs. Kincaid sobbed at me about how Stacy had been drinking and carrying on (her words, and I'm not sure exactly what she meant) at a speakeasy on South Fair Oaks Avenue. The place had a Pasadena address, but was technically in the county, so the Pasadena Police Department didn't have jurisdiction over it, according to Mrs. Kincaid, as if the news would interest me, which it didn't.

I also didn't know what she expected me to do about it, but I listened. Couldn't do anything else, since she was one of my best clients and a lovely lady, if the tiniest bit dim.

"And oh, Daisy, she's taken up with a female named *Flossie!* Can you imagine it?"

"Um, I believe Flossie is a nickname for Florence, Mrs. Kincaid."

"Flossie? Flossie? What kind of woman calls herself Flossie?"

I couldn't answer that one, although I suspected I knew what Mrs. Kincaid assumed. In the gently soothing tone I adopted when attempting to calm down bereaved or hysterical clients, I purred, "Would you like me to read the cards for you, Mrs. Kincaid? The spirits might offer some suggestions or a bit of comfort."

She sniffled loudly and swallowed. "Yes. Oh yes, if you can, dear. I'd so appreciate it. I'm so worried about Stacy."

"I understand." Which was true. Stacy'd been causing Mrs. Kincaid palpitations of one sort or another for years.

"I wish one of your spiritual contacts would suggest something to be done about her."

I've never voiced my own personal suggestion, that Mrs. Kincaid should deliver a couple of hearty smacks to Stacy's rear end, and I never would. Mrs. Kincaid would have been shocked and appalled. Not only that, but if she took my suggestion and started treating her daughter like the bratty kid she was, Stacy might reform, and that would cut into my Kincaid business.

All right, so maybe Billy might have had some small reason to worry about my overall moral character, but I wasn't *that* bad. Anyhow, it was probably too late for Mrs. Kincaid to begin acting the stern parent. If she started in on Stacy now, the monster child would probably just run away from home. Unlike Marianne Wagner, Stacy wouldn't have felt the slightest qualm about breaking her mother's heart.

"She asked me to call you."

This bit of news so astounded me, I nearly dropped the receiver. Billy had been watching, grinning, and I guess he saw my eyebrows shoot up, because he tilted his head and stopped grinning. I shook my head to let him know there was nothing for him to worry about.

"Um . . . Do you mean Stacy asked you to call me?" I gave Billy an incredulous grimace. I thought of something that was probably stupid but not quite as unbelievable as the notion of Stacy Kincaid asking her mother to telephone me. Stacy didn't like me any more than I liked her. "Or do you mean Flossie asked you to call me?"

"Flossie?" Mrs. Kincaid shrieked the name. "Good heavens, no. I don't know the woman and don't want to."

"I see." Needless to say, I didn't see a thing.

"Stacy asked me to call you because a man named Jenkins—oh, Daisy, Stacy calls the man *Jinx*—wants to hold a séance, and she recommended you."

Nuts to that! If there was one thing on God's green earth not even *I* would do, it was hang out in a speakeasy and conduct a séance for a bunch of lousy, murdering bootleggers. I didn't yell at the woman because I liked her and needed her business, although I refused her request so firmly, I doubted even she could misinterpret my feelings on the matter.

"I'm afraid I can't do that, Mrs. Kincaid. My spirit guide is extremely particular about the ambience in which he reveals himself. The atmosphere in such a den of iniquity wouldn't be appropriate." It wasn't the first time I'd wished I'd chosen a more elegant name than

Rolly for my spirit control. But what can one expect from a ten-year-old?

Another sniffle. "I told her that," said a subdued Mrs. Kincaid. A pause ensued, probably because I couldn't think of anything to say, and she was trying to come up with some way to persuade Rolly that it would be perfectly all right for him to show himself in an illicit gin joint. I knew Rolly better than she did, though, and I knew she couldn't do it. "Are you sure, dear?"

"Absolutely," I said firmly. I resisted the urge to say something about speakeasies already being full of spirits and not needing mine.

"Very well." Now she sounded sad.

I thought that was a shame, given the fact that she was getting married to a really nice man soon, and almost wished Stacy were present so I could slap her for her mother's sake. I couldn't wait to tell Harold about this. Harold had about as much use for his sister as I did.

As soon as I hung up after having my ears abused by poor Mrs. Kincaid for several more minutes, I told Billy all about the call. He shook his head. "This isn't the first time I've thought one of your clients needed a psychiatrist more than she needed you," he muttered dryly.

I sighed. "You're probably right."

I'd no sooner resumed dust-mopping than the doorbell rang, so I trotted to the door and scooped up Spike before he could chew a hole through the door and attack the foot of whoever was standing there (he couldn't reach any higher than that). You can probably imagine my embarrassment when, clad in my house-cleaning clothes, I encountered an entire regiment of Salvation Army members, holding out their tambourines in the hope that I'd donate to their cause.

Mind you, I appreciate the Salvation Army. Not only do they serve a truly noble purpose, but they provide the community with a lot of music, and I love music. You couldn't walk down Colorado Boulevard in those days without encountering a Salvation Army band playing up a storm on some street corner or other.

Also, my late cousin Paul's best friend, Johnny Buckingham (who was leading the contingent at my front door), had just been promoted to captain in the Salvation Army. Paul and Johnny had gone off to war together. Johnny had come home. For the first couple of years after that, as had happened to so many other young men, he'd gone to the dogs—no disrespect to Spike intended.

It was the Salvation Army that had dragged Johnny out of the gutter and given him a new purpose in life. I honored any institution that didn't give up on people. Besides all that, I'd always liked Johnny and was glad to see him, even if I was also embarrassed by my dowdy appearance.

"Shoot, Johnny, you caught me at my absolute best, as you can see." I patted the scarf tied around my head as if I were a showing off the latest fashion in chapeaus.

He chuckled. "It's all right, Daisy. I know you're a hardworking girl." He must have spotted Billy behind me, because he waved and said, "Howdy, Billy. We're just out collecting for the Army."

Billy returned Johnny's greeting. "Happy to donate to your army, Johnny. The one I joined, I'm not so sure about." He dug in his pocket even as I ran to the kitchen to get a couple of dimes out of the sugar bowl.

After I'd dropped them into the tambourine and shut the door, the phone rang *again*. This time it was Mrs. Bissel. As soon as I heard her voice, I froze, the awful possibility that she had yet another visitor in her basement having struck me. Hard. Thank God, it wasn't that. She only wanted me to conduct a séance for her.

Rolly had no misgivings about appearing to a house full of silly people and dachshunds, so we arranged a date, and I resumed cleaning . . . and the telephone rang.

I dropped the dust mop and uttered a low growl,

which startled Spike, who ran, yipping, under the sofa. I guess Billy had heard us, because he said, "I'll get it." It wasn't easy for him to reach the telephone, and I wondered why he was still being nice to me. This was the fifth or sixth day in a row during which he hadn't been snide or fussy or grumpy once.

A terrible notion occurred to me, and I vowed to check on Billy's supply of morphine syrup before the day was out. If I found that he'd either started hoarding it or drinking even more of the stuff than I already knew he drank, I was going to have another talk with Dr. Benjamin.

Maybe—Sweet Lord have mercy—I'd even talk to Sam. Billy liked Sam, and Sam liked Billy. What's more, and as much as I resented Sam's almost constant presence in my life, I knew he'd have a better chance of talking sense into Billy than I'd ever have.

The possibility that Billy might be saving his medicine in order to do away with himself scared the wits out of me. It was infinitely worse than the possibility that he was becoming addicted to the stuff.

But Billy would never do that. He was . . . he was . . .

Oh Lord, he was a shell-shocked cripple who had no use for the life he was forced to live, and I loved him more than I could bear.

I was standing in the living room, the dust mop at my feet, staring through the dining room into the kitchen and wondering how to protect my husband from himself, since nobody'd protected him from the damned Germans, when Billy rolled his chair from the kitchen to the dining room. Seeing me standing there, staring at nothing, he stopped rolling and gazed at me quizzically. "What's the matter, love? Anything wrong?"

Yes, there were tons of things wrong. I forced myself to smile. "Nope. Just wondering who was on the 'phone."

"Don't know, but it's for you."

"It would be." Leaving the dust mop on the floor, I

went to the kitchen, my heart hammering in my chest like a funeral march. I *wished* I could stop imagining horrible things.

This time the caller was George Grenville. My heart did another sickening dip, and I prayed that Marianne hadn't done anything stupid. Anything *else* stupid, I suppose I should say. "What's up, George?" I asked.

My voice must have betrayed my worry, because George hastened to reassure me. "Not a thing, Daisy. I only wanted to know if you believed it would be out of line if I dined with Mar—with the person in—oh, you know what I'm talking about."

"I know." Jeepers, I guess he'd taken my tantrum of a few days before to heart. He'd never asked before if he could take a meal with Marianne; he'd just up and done it. "I should think so, as long as everything remains on the up and up." I expected him to take exception to my condition, and he did.

"I am *not* a scoundrel," George declared.

"I never said you were." Actually, if one were merely to look at George, about the last thing in the world you'd expect him to be was a scoundrel. A football player, maybe. A teacher, even. You'd probably even come up with bookstore owner before you'd think *scoundrel*. The fact remained, however, that he was supposed to be protecting Marianne Wagner, an unmarried female with no worldly skills, and I didn't want there to be a hint of scandal attaching to either one of them.

"You act as though you consider me the lowest of the low," George said sulkily. "That's why I called you today. I didn't want you to jump to any unsavory conclusions."

I glanced around to see where Billy was in the overall scheme of things. I didn't want him to know about Marianne, because then he'd be part of the conspiracy. Collusion. Whatever it was. He wasn't too near, but I still thought better of naming names over the telephone.

"I'm sure you're a virtual knight in shining armor, George. But the person we're talking about is a babe in the woods, and she needs our help. She doesn't need more problems to contend with, even those that come about through misinterpreted kindness."

"Granted." His tone was resentful, but at least George was admitting that I might have a valid point, which was a step in the right direction.

"That being the case, and knowing you to be a gentleman, I'm sure that your dining together would be appropriate."

"Wonderful!" Relief blew through the telephone wires along with the word. "And tomorrow, too?"

I sighed again. "Tomorrow, too." What the heck. If they were destined for each other, perhaps proximity would prompt George to spring the question. That would get the girl out of my hair quite nicely.

Of course, there was also the possibility that continued socializing with each other would give George a clue as to how much work he'd have to do if he aimed to marry the wench. She didn't know how to do a darned thing, and he'd have a job of it to bring her up to snuff. I could have told George how difficult it would be for him to earn the bacon and keep house, too, because I did it all the time. And I even had Aunt Vi to cook for me.

After that, I managed to get through the remainder of my house-cleaning duties without any more interruptions. When I was done cleaning house, Billy and I took Spike for a walk, and then I took a jaunt to the bookstore to check up on my charge. It was a fair hike, but the day was beautiful, and I felt like walking.

A brisk breeze blew the leaves around, and I noticed that the cheeks of my fellow pedestrians were pink with the weather and exertion. Everyone was in a Christmas mood, and everyone I passed greeted me. I returned the compliment. Cheer was in the air, by gum, and I had a hard time worrying about anything, even Billy.

Marianne was fine. George was fine. Heck, even I was fine. After I returned home, I became even finer when Aunt Vi came home with our supper, left over from the dinner she'd fixed for Mrs. Kincaid. That night it was chicken à la king. God bless my aunt. If I ever had to cook for Billy and me without her, we'd surely starve.

The next day after church, I took another toddle to the bookstore. I was pleased to find Harold there, measuring Marianne's frocks with an eye to making them fit better.

"Daisy, my love!" Harold cried around a mouthful of pins. He was on his knees on the rug, taking tucks in a creamy-white bodice. "Long time, no see."

"It's only been a few days, Harold." I missed him, though, when I didn't get to talk to him all the time. Harold Kincaid was the only person in the whole world to whom I could confide anything and everything. He was the only one besides Dr. Benjamin who knew how much I worried about Billy.

"True, true," said Harold. The fabric slipped and he muttered, "Get in there, you little fiend." I loved to watch Harold work. He treated fabrics as if they were naughty schoolchildren. Being quite the seamstress myself, I understood.

"Where's Del, Harold? I thought maybe he'd come visiting with you."

I liked Del Farrington, although Del and I weren't as close as Harold and I. You'd think it would be the other way around, since Harold could be critical and sarcastic, while Del was never anything but polite and sweet. Or maybe Harold's biting side was the reason we got along so well. He thought my line of work was a hoot, he appreciated me for being good at it, and he also knew how difficult life could be if your situation was out of the ordinary. So there you go. Who can tell about these things?

"Del's attending mass at Our Lady of Perpetual Malice." Harold glanced up and winked at me.

I'm sure I looked as astounded as I felt. "He's *where?*"

Grinning, Harold elaborated. "Actually, he's at Saint Andrew's. I like my name for the place better."

"Oh. I didn't know Del was a Roman Catholic."

"Mercy, yes. He'd go to mass every day of the week if he could. He can't, because he has a bank to run, but he's *tres* religious, you know."

Goodness gracious. "No, I didn't know." And I'd never have guessed in a million years, either.

Delroy Farrington, a perfectly gorgeous young man, had been born in Louisiana. He had moved to California after the war, and had secured a position as cashier in Mr. Eustace Kincaid's bank. He and Algie Pinkerton had taken over the bank when Mr. Kincaid did a bunk. But Del was a homosexual, and for some reason I never considered that people like that would go to church, or be welcomed there if they did. Wasn't there some sort of rule against it? I didn't ask, although Harold would have been totally unembarrassed to tell me. Marianne's presence held my tongue.

Harold went on, stabbing pins in the bodice at approximately one-inch intervals along the seam. "I keep telling him that being Catholic is ill bred and that he ought to transfer his allegiance to the Episcopalians, which are almost the same but not quite, and infinitely superior socially, but he won't hear of it. He was an altar boy in New Orleans, and he won't switch for anything."

"Oh." I have to admit that Harold's glib attitude toward religion grated on my sensibilities a teensy bit. I cherished my association with our Methodist Episcopal church, and not only because it helped to keep my reputation aboveboard. Nevertheless, I knew better than to object, because Harold was perfectly able to become even more caustic than he already was being. Besides, he was entitled to his opinion.

During this conversation, Marianne sat on the tiny sofa, her hands folded in her lap, looking upon Harold and me with eyes as big and as blue as the sky outside. I deduced she wasn't accustomed to people being flippant about churches and churchgoing. I wasn't, either, if it came to that.

She dared drop a tidbit into the conversation. "I haven't been to church for over a month now."

"What church do you normally attend?" I asked politely. I intended to check the larder for supplies, but didn't want Marianne to feel as though I considered her a burden, even though I did, so I chatted with her first.

"We go to Westminster Presbyterian. I—I like it all right." As if she couldn't stand not dropping his name every chance she got, she added, "Mr. Grenville attends the First Congregational Church. I think they call it the Neighborhood Church now."

"Ah. Unitarian," said I. I kind of liked the Unitarians. They took in everybody, not unlike the Salvation Army people, although I had a hunch the Unitarians preferred their souls accompanied by a good deal of money, while the Salvation Army didn't care.

"Wise choice," said Harold. He slipped the last pin into the bodice and stood, creaking slightly. Harold was a trifle overweight, and I didn't get the impression that he favored vigorous exercise. "If I went to church, I think I'd attend the Unitarian church."

"You don't care for church, Mr. Kincaid?" Marianne asked timidly. I think she was shocked.

"Church is all right. I'd rather sleep in on Sunday mornings."

"Oh." She gazed at Harold, seemingly lost in wonder that somebody would admit aloud to such a preference.

"You're going straight to heck, Harold. You know that, don't you?"

He winked at me. "I've known it for years, Daisy dear." He flung the bodice over his arm, scooped up several other items of dress that he'd marked for alteration, and looked around for his hat.

Marianne whispered, "Oh my."

I felt kind of sorry about having dismayed her, but honestly, the girl had no sense of humor at all. Before I could apologize, a knock came at the door. Marianne jumped to her feet, and her cheeks flushed becomingly. Obviously, she expected the knock to be George's. Their relationship, if they had one, was clearly progressing like wildfire.

"I'll see who it is," said I, suiting the action to the words. Marianne stood beside the sofa, her hands clasped, her eyes eager. For her sake, I hoped it was George.

It was. George stood outside the front door of the cottage, bearing in his arms several covered dishes. He must have picked up enough food for an army battalion. I swung the door open. "Howdy, George."

He was startled to see all of us, but I reassured him. "I'm just leaving. I only came by to inspect the cupboards and see if Marianne needed anything."

"And I'm going to take these things home, stitch them up, and bring them back. It shouldn't take too long." Harold showed George the pile of clothes.

George stared blankly at them. "Oh." His eyes narrowed as he lifted his gaze back to Harold.

As he moved into the house and set the dinner dishes on the living room table, I knew what he was thinking: *real* men didn't alter clothes.

Honestly, I just didn't understand men. Harold was a wonderful person: funny, kindhearted, generous, smart, and rich. But the *real* men in the world couldn't get past his homosexuality to appreciate all of his fine qualities. Men. There was no doing anything with them.

I think Harold understood George's squint, too. His smile was even more cynical than usual when he took his leave of us.

"I'll check on supplies," I told the remaining two people. "Then I'll get out of your hair."

George caught my arm. "There's no need for that, Daisy. I've taken on the responsibility of making sure Miss Wagner has everything she needs."

It was my turn to squint. "Oh?" I wasn't sure that was such a great idea. Because I didn't want to shock Marianne (again), I didn't say so, although I vowed then and there to have another chat with George as soon as I could.

Shoot, by the time this problem was solved, George was going to be so sick of me, he'd never allow me to enter his shop again. And it's not that I really doubted his gentlemanly intentions; it's only that I knew we had to be careful.

George understood my hesitation. He frowned quite balefully. That was okay by me. Better to make an enemy of George than compromise my own principles or Marianne's virtue—I suppose. At that point, I was so tired of the whole affair, I only wanted it to end.

Eighteen

The next few days passed uneventfully, thank heaven. Billy and I continued to take Spike for walks every day. I continued to try to train the puppy and clean up after him when training didn't work. He was so precious, I couldn't get angry at him for making mistakes, especially as he was genuinely contrite when I pointed out the errors of his ways.

Would that *people* would try so hard and repent their mistakes so sincerely. But people have never lived up to the standards set by dogs, and I don't suppose they ever will.

Sam continued to consider me a prime suspect in the disappearance of Marianne Wagner, although I didn't know why. Still don't, for that matter. What did he think? That I had spirited Marianne away from her family home in the dark of night via a rope ladder and then secreted her in the attic of a crumbling medieval castle in France?

Heck, until I discovered her in Mrs. Bissel's basement, I didn't even *know* the girl. I had enough responsibilities already and would never willingly embroil myself in other people's Gothic dramas. I was only embroiled in this one by accident. Sort of.

However it had happened, I knew Marianne now—too well for my convenience. Anyhow, I didn't mind awfully much trotting to the bookstore every day to check up on her, because I got to browse through all the new books when they arrived.

I wasn't that much of a book-buyer in those days, being a frequent patron of the Pasadena Public Library on Raymond Avenue and Walnut Street. Not only did I not have the money to be buying books all the time, but our little bungalow was already bulging at its seams. There wasn't room for millions of books and us too. Visiting George's bookstore so often allowed me to see which new books I wanted to check out from the library, so I could have first dibs on them.

Harold brought the altered frocks back to Marianne on Monday afternoon, and Marianne and I passed a pleasant hour, during which she tried them on and I made approving comments. As long as we could talk about clothes (about which I knew a lot, given my interest in sewing), we got along fine. If I ever changed the subject to, say, popular fiction, presidential politics, anarchism, Prohibition, or anything other than clothes, Marianne had no conversation.

On Tuesday night, I visited Mrs. Kincaid, read the Ouija board and the tarot cards, and she claimed to feel better when I was ready to depart. I don't know why; I hadn't told her a darned thing except, more or less, "this, too, shall pass." The passing part referred to her daughter's foul behavior, of course, and I wasn't sure about that. I had a feeling that as long as Stacy lived with her mother, her mother would be troubled by her daughter's behavior.

Anyhow, the only sure solutions I could think of to the Stacy problem would be too drastic for Mrs. Kincaid's peace of mind. If someone *else* were to, say, shoot Stacy through the heart or shove her off the roof of a fifteen-story building, Mrs. Kincaid could mourn her daughter, and then get on with her life. I'm sure Stacy wouldn't do anything so obliging as to meet up with a murderer.

Gosh, I must dislike Stacy even more than I thought

I did to come up with such ghastly scenarios. Please forgive me for my lapse.

Thursday night at choir practice, we started going over a slew of Christmas and leading-up-to-Christmas hymns. Our offering for the upcoming Sunday was going to be "Lo, How a Rose 'ere Blooming," which was pretty and old and sounded great when all four parts sang the right notes. We usually did.

On Friday night the pleasant routine that had held for almost an entire week ended. With a big, fat, frightening—not to mention extremely distressing—bump.

I passed up going to a special prayer meeting at church with Ma and Aunt Vi (the congregation had decided to pray for the children, worldwide, who had been orphaned by the war and in the influenza pandemic) in order to conduct Mrs. Bissel's séance. I didn't really mind missing the prayer meeting. I'd rather have stayed home and read a detective story, but at least I had an excuse other than personal pleasure to skip the meeting.

Mrs. Bissel had locked up the hounds for the duration of the séance. I was sure she'd let them all in later, since she was such a softie. Besides, it had grown quite cold at night, and dachshunds don't have coats thick enough to enable them to endure chills. In other words, in case you hadn't already noticed, Mrs. Bissel treated her dogs better than lots of parents treated their children.

She and her guests all claimed to be fascinated by and appreciative of my efforts, including—who would have guessed it?—Mrs. Everhard Alan Wagner, Marianne's mother. I wasn't overwhelmingly gratified to see her when I met the séance attendees. To tell the absolute, unvarnished truth, I darned near fainted dead away on the spot.

I was also surprised, since I didn't think Dr. Wagner ever allowed her out of the house without his supervision. She seemed nervous enough to have ripped a page from her daughter's book and run away from home, although I doubted she had. At least, if she had eluded the bad doctor's eagle eye, she wasn't trying to hide the fact.

Her daughter's disappearance was common knowledge, and I felt sorry for the woman. She looked as if she hadn't slept since Marianne took off. That being the case, I shook her hand, gave her one of my most sympathetic and understanding smiles, and said, "Have you had heard anything about your daughter, Mrs. Wagner?"

Her eyes filled with tears, and I felt like a rat. She quickly snatched a handkerchief from her handbag and dabbed at her eyes with hands that trembled. Shaking her head, she said, "N-no. Thank you, Mrs. Majesty. There's been no word of Marianne."

"I'm very sorry."

"Thank you."

Because I was so curious as to why she'd come that night, I said, "You don't normally attend my séances, Mrs. Wagner. I'm happy to see you here."

I think—but I'm not sure—I saw a flash of defiance in her eyes. It only lasted a split second if it was there at all, so I might have been mistaken.

"Dr. Wagner didn't want me to come."

"Ah." I'd suspected as much. I didn't say so.

"But I deserve to attend functions if I want to," she went on, sounding like a child defying its parent.

I murmured soothingly, "Of course."

"I'm a grown woman. I have rights."

"Of course you do. And Mrs. Bissel's functions are always most respectable."

"That's exactly what I told Dr. Wagner. He finally allowed me to come as long as our chauffeur drove me here and picked me up afterward."

Good Lord. I'd hate to be her when she went home that night, if she'd had to work herself into this state of truculence before she went out for an evening with the girls. She must have driven herself into a frenzy before she'd defied her old man, and I had an uneasy feeling he'd pay her back for it. I only smiled graciously.

Her boldness fled as fast as it had come. She stuttered, "Mrs. Majesty, I-I'm hoping you can give me some kind of . . . of . . ." Her voice faded away, as if she didn't want to finish the sentence.

She didn't have to. I knew what she was going to say. "I'm sure we will be able to ease your heart," I purred in my comforting spiritualist's voice.

The woman swallowed and whispered, "Thank you so much."

I smiled and squeezed her hands tenderly. I was the worst kind of hypocrite, standing there, spouting platitudes about a girl whose whereabouts I knew, to a mother who was in such an agony of worry and despair that she'd risked the wrath of her brutal husband. Because I was so sorry for her and felt so guilty, I said, "You're welcome, Mrs. Wagner. Please don't despair. The emanations are positive for a response regarding your daughter."

"Oh, I do hope so," she said on another sob. Then her grip on my hand tightened and her eyes, which were as blue as Marianne's but sunk in dark rings, opened wide, and she recanted. "No, I don't mean that! If you hear from her, that will mean she's—she's dead, and I don't think I could stand that."

Nuts. Even when I tried to be supportive, I made a mess of things. I squeezed her hands again and murmured, "Rolly will be able to tell us if Marianne is there, however. It's better to know, don't you think?" I sure thought so, mainly because I was going to have Rolly reassure the poor woman that her daughter hadn't yet made it to the Other Side.

Mrs. Wagner cried into her hankie for a minute or two while I murmured softly and reassuringly and wished I hadn't become entangled in her daughter's affairs. I could cheerfully have thumped Marianne

Wagner just then. The least the girl could have done was take her mother with her when she ran away from home. Or leave a note, for Pete's sake.

The pre-séance gathering didn't last long. As soon as everyone invited by Mrs. Bissel to participate had arrived, she bustled us all into the breakfast room. The table in the dining room seated fifty people and was far too huge for six of us to hold hands around it. I hoped Mrs. Cummings wouldn't make a lot of noise in the kitchen while we were communing with the spirits, because the clangings of pots and pans were disruptive of the atmosphere I strove to achieve.

I'd been contemplating the use of incense during my séances, but hadn't tried it yet and wasn't sure I would. With my luck, somebody would have a sneezing fit and ruin everything.

It was the first time in the history of my work as a spiritualist that I became impatient with the conventions of my craft. I didn't want to sit in a dark room with a red lamp and spend ten or twenty minutes warming everybody up so I could spring my act on them. I wanted to get straight to the point, which by then had become reassuring Mrs. Wagner that her daughter was alive and well.

I wanted to tell her that she'd see Marianne soon, too, but didn't dare, mainly because I didn't know it was the truth. For all I knew, Marianne would decide to move to London, England, and spend the rest of her life there working as a chambermaid to a princess or a duchess. I doubted it, but since I didn't know, I didn't risk saying anything about Marianne's possible return to her mother's home.

Of course, I could have had Rolly say that if Mrs. Wagner left her evil husband, she'd see Marianne in a jiffy. That idea didn't occur to me at the time, however, and even if it had, I doubt that I'd have voiced it. I've never considered it my place, as a medium, to urge drastic action on anyone. And if divorcing a spouse isn't drastic, even if he's an abusive so-and-so, I don't know what is.

In those days, divorce was still considered something of a scandalous procedure, especially in Pasadena, which was really a kind of high-class, not to say stodgy, place. Movie stars and flappers might be divorcing their spouses right and left, but the rest of us didn't take our marital commitments so casually.

Because I am, first and foremost, a practical woman (not to mention an expert at my art), I didn't allow my impatience to affect the séance. I went through the usual routine: first I had all the attendees sit at the breakfast-room table and made sure the room was as dark as we could make it. One lamp with a cranberry-colored globe was placed in the center of the table with a lighted candle in it.

After everyone had entered and sat down, and Ginger had closed the door, I asked everyone to hold hands and be quiet (only I was more diplomatic than that). This set the tone: mysterious and a little eerie.

No séance I've ever conducted has been silent. Somebody always coughs or sneezes, chairs scrape, sometimes people giggle, groan, or cry. I even had a woman faint on me once. I strove for silence, however, and usually achieved a fairly decent facsimile thereof.

A few moments after I went into my trance, Rolly showed up (figuratively), speaking with a Scottish burr in a voice an octave lower than my natural tone. He always spoke in affectionate accents, mostly because I enjoyed pretending that a man, even a fictitious one, liked me enough to be nice to me.

Before tackling the Wagner dilemma, I had to dispense with the main purpose of the séance, the reason Mrs. Bissel had hired me to conduct it in the first place. She wanted me to get in touch with—of all things—a deceased dachshund breeder from New York City.

It was lucky for me that I'd learned all about dachshunds from Mrs. Bissel. Rolly was able to communicate with the dead breeder, one Mrs. Wilfred Hartland Rice, who assured Mrs. Bissel that her dogs were the crème de la crème of the dachshund world, and that if dog-judging politics didn't interfere with the natural order of things, one of her hounds would certainly be represented at Westminster one of these years. Believe it or not, vague predictions like that almost always satisfy my customers. You figure it out; it's beyond me.

Also (and I *really* hate to admit this) I was able to give Rolly's contact on the Other Side a fairly good New York accent, thanks in part to Mrs. Barrow, our party-line snoop, but mainly due to my association with Sam Rotondo. I'm sure it was the first time I'd ever been glad I'd met the man.

After the hooey concerning Mrs. Bissel and the dogs was over, I took a detour into what I considered the truly important part of the evening. I made sure everyone was primed for it by sinking more deeply into my trance (I'd explain how I do that, but it would take too long) and creating a series of eerie raps and moans.

When I was sure all the séance participants were on pins and needles wondering which spirit, out of all the people in the world who had lived and died in however long mankind had inhabited the earth, would pop up next, I held another conversation with Rolly.

"Rolly," I said in my most spooky of mediumistic voices, "I want to ask you about a girl whose spirit might have crossed over to your side. The girl has disappeared on this plane, and we don't know what has become of her. Her mother is extremely worried about her."

Mrs. Wagner choked out a sob. I knew it was she because the sound had come from her end of the table. Besides, nobody else at the table had a crying interest in a vanished child at that moment, if you understand what I mean.

"Aye, lass," said Rolly (well, it was really me, but it

was supposed to be Rolly), "I understand. What is the wee lassie's name?"

"Marianne Wagner."

Another sob from Mrs. Wagner's end of the table. I felt truly terrible for her, and had a sudden and—thank God—transitory urge to leap to my feet and confess everything. I couldn't do that without betraying my entire family, and I'd rather betray hers than mine. Does that make me a bad person? I have no idea, but I know what Billy would say. In any case, I carried on in true Gumm fashion.

"Och, her poor mither," Rolly said, genuinely sorrowful—and for good reason, as noted in the above paragraphs. "Let me see now."

By this time, there were snuffles coming from all around the table, and I was afraid people would break their hold on each other and start reaching for handkerchiefs. As I was supposed to be in a trance, I couldn't very well ask everyone to stay put and be still, but I prayed they'd not break the circle. I know what you're thinking: Why would God listen to a fraud like me? And I have no answer. They kept holding hands, though, in spite of their emotional reactions and my equivocal position with God.

At last Rolly spoke again. Or I did. Nuts. I only know that I sensed the appropriate time for an answer. I'd become an expert at timing by then. "Tell the lassie's mither that Marianne Wagner still walks on the mortal plane, love. She's not crossed over to this side yet."

The reason Rolly called me "love" is that he was supposed to be a long-lost flame of mine from the eleventh century. By the time I held Mrs. Bissel's séance, I'd had the story straight for a decade, so I never forgot any of the particulars: Rolly and I were wed in what's now Scotland in 1050-ish. We'd produced five sons together, and Rolly had been a soldier.

The most important part of the whole story, as far as I was concerned, was that Rolly and I were soul mates.

We'd shared a deathless love; the kind of love every woman dreams about and most of us never achieve. I'd wanted to, with Billy, but it didn't work out that way.

But enough of that. I'm sure I conceived the Scottish angle for my spiritual control because I'd been reading *Rob Roy* at the time. At least Rolly was different from your run-of-the-mill spirit guide. Most spiritualists back then used red Indians or Egyptian pharaohs or Hindu princesses for their controls.

That, however, is neither here nor there. I thanked Rolly for the information he'd imparted to Mrs. Bissel's guests, and especially Mrs. Wagner.

"Och, love, a mither needs to know her child's safe." I hoped Mrs. Wagner believed in my skills more than I did.

What she did then was break down completely. As bad as I felt for her, I couldn't comfort her since I was supposed to be in a trance. I slumped dramatically to let everyone else know that they were free to take over the job for me. And they did, bless them.

By the time I uttered a few moans and groans, blinked vaguely several times, and pretended to have difficulty lifting my body into an upright position, Mrs. Bissel and several other compassionate ladies were tending to Mrs. Wagner. I passed a pathetically trembling hand across my brow, and smoothed my skirt (I was wearing a lovely, deep green silk evening suit that night that went swell with my dark red hair and pale-as-a-ghost complexion. I worked on that pallor, believe me, and lived in fear of developing more freckles).

As soon as she saw that I was out of my "trance," Mrs. Wagner got up from her chair and staggered shakily to the head of the table, where I sat. Once she got there she shocked the heck out of me by falling on her knees before me, as her daughter had done a week or so earlier. I concluded they'd learned the behavior from Dr. Wagner, who probably demanded they worship him. Personally, I absolutely *hate* when people do that.

"Oh, Mrs. Majesty," she whispered through her tears. "I can't thank you enough for what you've done tonight."

I know it sounds petty, but I hoped her salty tears wouldn't make stains on my silk skirt. In fairness to me, I must say that wasn't my first worry; I was mainly concerned for her.

"Please," I said, "I did nothing. It was the spirits, speaking through me." Leaning over, I put a hand under her elbow and exerted gentle pressure in an effort to get her to stand up again.

She resisted. "No, no. You did it. It was you who gave me the comfort of knowing my little girl is alive."

I'd make a lousy god. When people kneel in adoration before me, I only get embarrassed.

That being the case, I rose from my own chair, bringing her up from the floor with me. "Come along, please, Mrs. Wagner. I think you could use a cup of strong tea."

The other ladies were fluttering (or lumbering, in the case of Mrs. Bissel) around us by that time. Mrs. Bissel, whose heart was as big as she was, said, "Yes, yes. Oh my, yes, Diane (Diane being Mrs. Wagner's first name). Let me get Mrs. Cummings to rush the tea to you. And a chocolate éclair. I'm sure an éclair will work wonders."

Éclairs always worked wonders for me. I hoped they'd do as well for Mrs. Wagner, so I smiled and nodded at Mrs. Bissel.

She thundered out of the room, aiming for the kitchen. I guided Mrs. Wagner to the huge front parlor where Mrs. Bissel always had her guests take sustenance after my séances. The woman was generous to a fault, always feeding folks. I adored her for it, too, because I liked to eat almost as much as a dachshund. That's why my body didn't fit the slim, boyish shape in fashion at the time.

That had never stopped me from enjoying a meal or a snack, however. I sewed all my clothes. If I got fat, I'd just sew bigger ones.

I spoke with Mrs. Wagner for quite a while after the séance concluded—until her husband's hired bully-boy called for her much sooner than she was ready to go. As you might expect, she didn't tell the man to wait until she felt like leaving the party, but ran out of the room like a scared rabbit so as not to "annoy Dr. Wagner. He's so busy, you know."

Huh. I walked with her to Mrs. Bissel's back door, assuring her that the spirits don't lie, which was a lie itself, but I didn't care by that time. I wondered if she'd told her husband she was going to attend a séance that evening. I doubted it. If he'd known a séance would eventuate, I'm sure Dr. Wagner wouldn't have allowed her to attend. He hadn't wanted to let her out of the house at all.

As I drove home, nearly freezing to death in the chilly December weather in spite of my black wool coat, I vowed that the next day I'd report what had happened at the séance to Marianne. And I was going to recount a vivid and detailed version of Mrs. Wagner's reaction to learning her daughter was alive. Darn the girl, how could she *do* that to her mother?

Then again, how could Mrs. Wagner allow her daughter to be abused in her own home—and by her own husband? The problem was a knotty one, and too convoluted for someone like me to evaluate and solve.

To be fair, in those days there weren't many women in Pasadena as independent as the ones in my family, and most of those were working stiffs like us. Most of the rich women I knew back then—and I knew a bunch of them—had never learned how to do anything useful. They were primarily decorative and served as their husbands' social secretaries, broodmares, and hostesses, with occasional ventures into charitable work and dog shows.

But, gee whiz, even a rich woman can leave her husband if he's a monster. Sure as anything, if a kid of mine was ever beaten (or worse) by her father, you can bet it would only happen once—and that the man would never be able to perpetrate such villainy again.

Not that Billy would ever beat a child, especially not one of his own. Not that Billy could ever *have* a child, but . . . oh, never mind.

Billy wanted to go Christmas shopping the morning following Mrs. Bissel's séance. Wouldn't you know it? How often does your average husband want to go Christmas shopping? In case you don't know the answer to that one, I'll tell you: never.

I'd actually have been pleased that he was taking an interest in something so mundane as Christmas shopping if I weren't champing at the bit to get to Marianne. I longed to spill my guts about her poor mother and shame the girl into doing something with herself; preferably either going home or leaving town. But I went along with Billy's wishes, willing if not eager to champ a little longer.

Between us, we got presents for Ma and Pa and Aunt Vi and Spike. Yes indeed. We bought a bright red India rubber ball for the puppy. I got the impression the ball wouldn't last long enough in its pristine condition to be wrapped for Christmas, but would be put into play much earlier; probably that afternoon. But that was all right. We could get him another present to wrap and put under the tree. Preferably food; Spike was an amazing eater.

"Say, Daisy, let's go to the foothills after church tomorrow and chop down a tree for Christmas."

Billy felt pretty good that day and was guiding his wheelchair under his own steam. I'd bundled him up well, with a tweed jacket, woolen scarf, hat, and a lap blanket, but the sharp wind kept lifting the edges of the blanket. I'd have put the packages in his lap to hold the blanket down, but the weight would have hurt his legs.

So I carried the packages and worried about my husband and his legs and lungs and possible drug addiction, and wanted to race to Grenville's books and either force George to marry Marianne or force Marianne to move somewhere else. I'd pretty much decided marriage would be the best solution to our pickle, although I had no idea how to get the idea out of my head and on to fruition.

"Sounds like a good idea to me. You and I can pick it out, and Pa and I can cut it down."

"Sam can go with us. He can chop it down."

Ah, yes. Sam. He would have to intrude on our weekend, wouldn't he? "Oh. Sure, that would be fine."

"Damn, I hate being a cripple."

Billy seldom growled right out loud and on a public street like that about the state of his health, and he seldom used profanity, either. It scared me. It made me think again of suicide, as if I didn't already have enough crises to contemplate. "I know, sweetheart. Life isn't fair. It's been downright cruel to you."

"You're telling me." He'd been hunched over slightly, but straightened and glanced at me, grinning. "Don't pay any attention to me, Daisy. I'm only griping for the heck of it. Didn't mean to spoil the day."

Goodness gracious, what *was* the matter with the man? He *never* apologized for being crabby! "You're not spoiling anything," I told him. I'm afraid my voice might have wobbled slightly because I was so alarmed by Billy's recent behavior. "What happened to you was brutally unfair, and you have every reason in the world to resent it."

"Resent it," Billy murmured. "Right. I guess I do resent it."

"I know." I sniffled and felt stupid. "So do I."

"I'm sorry you're stuck with a cripple, sweetheart."

"Stop saying things like that!"

"Okay."

And he did. He didn't say another sour word the whole time we were out of the house.

His behavior was driving me crazy. Something was terribly wrong. I vowed that as soon as I got rid of Marianne Wagner, I'd have a heart-to-heart chat with Dr. Benjamin and—Lord help me—Sam Rotondo. My stomach tightened at the notion of talking about personal matters with Sam, but I'd endured worse in my life.

"Could you push me for a while, Daisy? My arms are getting mighty tired." He didn't mention his lungs, but the wind was bitter, and I'm sure they were hurting, too.

"Sure, sweetheart. Let me put the packages in the basket." Pa had attached a basket to Billy's wheelchair for exactly this purpose. Pa could do darned near anything. He was such a helpful man.

"It's a beautiful day," Billy opined.

I stared at the top of my husband's head, bemused. Billy never commented on the weather. He was right, though. "It sure is."

The sky was as sparkly a blue as I'd ever seen it. There were clouds piled up around the San Gabriel Mountains, covering their peaks in mounds of white flannel.

Billy said, "Bet we see snow on those peaks tomorrow morning."

"It's sure been cold. Wonder if it will snow down here."

"I doubt it. It never snows in Pasadena."

"It might snow in the foothills, though."

"Maybe."

"It would be kind of fun to pick out a tree in the snow."

"You think so?" Billy sounded skeptical.

"Sure. It would be so—so—seasonal."

He chuckled.

"It would be nice if it snowed here, though." Trying for a smidgeon of optimism, I added, "Every now and then we get sprinkles of the white stuff."

"Not very often."

"True. But I wouldn't mind if it snowed a little bit in town. I think our bungalow would look very pretty in the snow."

"I don't know. It might look pretty, but it wasn't built for heavy weather. It'd probably be frigid indoors."

I shrugged. "I could build a fire in the fireplace. That would be cozy."

"Don't get your hopes up," Billy advised.

Matters more important than snow were plaguing me that day, and it occurred to me that I might take care of the most pressing one while we were on our Christmas-present-buying jaunt. "Say, Billy, as long as we are out, why don't we walk to Grenville's Books? I want to get a collection of Sherlock Holmes stories for Pa."

"Sounds good to me, if you don't mind pushing me."

"I don't mind, Billy." I wanted to cry, but I didn't mind pushing his chair.

"Great. I want to see if they have any books about Siberian history."

This was so surprising, it dried up my tears. "Siberia! Good heavens, Billy, why do you want to read more about Siberia? It's a terrible place, isn't it?"

"Well," he equivocated, "I wouldn't want to live there, but that article in the *National Geographic* was interesting. Siberia's a fascinating place. If I were able to get around, I'd like to travel there someday."

"Siberia. Good Lord. Now, if it had been the article on Haiti that had fostered an interest in tropical islands, I could understand it. But . . . Siberia?" I couldn't help it; I laughed.

Nevertheless, I was happy to oblige his urge, hoping I'd have a chance to slip over to the cottage and tell Marianne about her mother.

Nineteen

We heard the commotion before we got to the store. My heart jumped to my throat. In an instant, my mind filled with visions of policemen surrounding the joint with their guns drawn. Those images faded as soon as they'd come, only to be replaced by visions of Marianne's brothers tearing up the bookstore and beating George to a pulp.

"Golly, listen to that," Billy said. "I always thought bookstores were quiet places."

"Me too." I hurried up, but couldn't go too fast for fear of hitting a bump and spilling Billy out of his wheelchair.

I knew the sounds of altercation signified another problem. My life was already filled as full as it could be with troubles, and I didn't need this one, whatever it was. As if that mattered.

As soon as I opened the door, I saw what was wrong. My heart, which had stuck in my throat half a block back, sank downward and lodged in my sensible walking shoes.

It was over. I was doomed. I would spend the rest of my life behind bars—and then what would happen to Billy? Speaking of whom, Billy craned his neck to see around me and inside the bookstore, so I took a step back and pushed him the rest of the way in. Might as well; there was no use running away from it. My sins had found me out.

I didn't want to face them. But I'd stepped into the breach of my own free will when I'd aided and abetted Marianne, so I had to. Billy would hate me now. My stock with Ma and Pa and Aunt Vi would plummet straight to heck, too.

Because I'd rather have been struck by a bolt of lightning, boiled in oil, and/or hanged from the tallest tree in Pasadena than to have shown how scared I was, I walked up to the scene of the brouhaha, leaving Billy's chair a few feet from the back counter.

Facing the problem was more than Marianne had done. My lips tightened as I featured how she'd come to this pass: she and George had flouted my orders. I knew it. And now we were all in the soup. Marianne had crouched down in front of the counter, her fingers twisted into claws and pressed to her face, hiding her mouth. Her eyes were as round as blue golf balls and radiated terror.

George, on the other hand, had adopted a fighter's stance, fists clenched, feet spread wide, cheeks blazing with ire, eyes furious behind his sparkling eyeglasses. His jaw bulged because he'd clenched his teeth so tightly, and sweat bedewed his forehead. Poor guy. I sure wouldn't want to confront Dr. Wagner—although I figured it was my duty to do just that.

That being the case (and knowing this was at least partially my fault), I walked up to Dr. Wagner and stuck out my hand. "How do you do, Dr. Wagner, my name is Daisy Majesty."

He was a good-looking man; tall, stately, with a head of thick gray hair and a little goatee and moustache that were always well-trimmed. I know clothes, and I could tell that Dr. Wagner's dark woolen suit had been tailored to his measurements. He could have posed for a fashion plate.

All the other times I'd seen him, he'd been acting the part of a wealthy, sophisticated doctor, all smiles and oily aplomb. Not that day. That day, his eyes bulged, his face had turned brick red with fury, his usually princely moustache and goatee bristled, his hat had tilted askew, there were flecks of foam at the corners of his mouth, and his gloves, which I guess he'd ripped off in order to slap George's face, had fallen to the floor. He pivoted to confront me as if I were a charging rhinoceros. It was a good thing he wasn't armed. It was also a good thing I was prepared, or I'd have turned tail and skedaddled out of there so fast, nobody would even have seen me.

"What do you have to do with this?" he bellowed.

I blanched but didn't back down. As far as I was concerned, it was past time somebody stood up to this beast. "Not a thing until this minute. I don't like it when people bullyrag my friends."

"Bullyrag?" he roared.

"Yes. I refuse to talk to anyone who yells at me, and I don't allow people to yell at my friends, either."

"Daisy, it's probably—"

Dr. Wagner interrupted George's feeble attempt to get me to shut up. "And exactly what does that mean?"

He was still hollering, so I folded my arms over my chest and clammed up. His face got redder and veins bulged in his forehead. I reflected wistfully that he might have an attack of apoplexy and die, but knew he probably wouldn't. My problems are never solved that easily. "Stop yelling," I commanded. "If you want to learn what happened with your daughter, you must calm down."

Dr. Wagner spun on his daughter, who flinched away from his heated stare, virtually squashing herself against the counter. She looked as if she were trying to disappear. "My daughter is coming home with me right now!" he stormed. "This is scandalous! How long have you been living in sin with this man?"

"Living in *sin?*" Now it was George who roared. Marianne covered her ears.

"Stop it!" I said—rather loudly, I fear. Oddly enough, they did stop it, for a second or two. It was long enough for me to say, "There's been no sinning done here. The only sinning was yours, and it prompted your daughter to run away from home!"

"Good God." That was spoken in a low, tight voice, and by Billy, but I didn't have time to soothe my husband at the moment. If such a thing could be done, there would be plenty of time for it later, when he visited me in jail.

I wondered if Dr. Wagner would get dizzy from all the precipitate whirling he was doing. This time he whirled on me. "Stay out of this, you! This has nothing to do with you!"

"It does now," I retorted. "And quit yelling right this minute."

To my surprise, he did. At first I thought it was because he'd decided to obey my command, but I was wrong.

Sam Rotondo marched up to us. I hadn't heard him enter the store—well, who could hear anything with Dr. Wagner bellowing at the top of his lungs? I was not happy to see him. Neither was anyone else, to judge by the expressions on their faces. I glared at him. He glared back at me, so we were even and things were progressing normally.

"What's going on here?" he demanded. "We got a report of a disturbance."

"So they sent a detective?" I asked. Sarcastically.

"Yes." Sam wasn't sarcastic. He was as frigid as an iceberg. I decided it would be better not to goad him.

"I," said Dr. Wagner, "am Dr. Everhard Wagner. This young lady is my daughter." His face started to lose a little of its high color, and my hope for a deadly fit or a heart attack faded accordingly. "I intend to take her home with me."

Marianne cried, "No!"

So did I.

"Let's calm down here," Sam suggested. He glanced at Billy, who only grinned and shrugged, to let Sam know that all this was new to him.

"I will not calm down!" howled the doctor. "I intend to collect my daughter right this minute and get out of here! I've never heard of such a thing!"

"How old is Miss Wagner?" asked Sam, although he already knew the answer to that one.

"She's eighteen years of age. She's a minor. I am still her legal guardian, and I intend to exercise my authority right now."

Okay, that was too much for me. My biggest fear was that Sam would go along with the wretched man because, without knowing the full story, he would perceive no other action possible on his part. I took a giant step and slid myself between Sam and the ogre. I mean Dr. Wagner. It was a tight squeeze, but I'm little.

"Oh no, you don't," I said boldly (more boldly than I was feeling, if you want to know the truth). "Marianne ran away from home because you beat her—and worse. I'd never even heard of a father actually doing those things to his own daughter until I learned about *you!*" I turned on Sam, whose mouth was slightly open, as if he'd been going to say something before I preempted him. "Isn't it a crime to beat a child, Sam? And to touch a child in . . . in . . . er, inappropriate ways?"

That took care of Dr. Wagner's complexion. It passed up red entirely and turned a bright fuchsia pink. *"How dare you!"* he screamed.

So I turned on *him.* "I dare because it's the truth. Marianne told me so." Back to Sam. "Well? Isn't it a crime? Marianne is, as Dr. Wagner himself admits, underage. Not to mention his own daughter. Isn't that a crime, Sam?"

"Um . . ." For the first time since I'd met him, the mighty Sam Rotondo looked uncomfortable.

It didn't matter, since Dr. Wagner didn't wait for an answer. His color deepening by the second, he roared, "I've never heard such outrageous allegations in my life! Who are you, young woman, that you can cast aspersions on me, a highly respected surgeon? If you think you can get away with such slander, you'll discover your error! I'll sue you until you don't have a pot to—"

"Stop it!"

This unexpected command issued from the throat and lips of none other than Marianne Wagner, who'd apparently reclaimed her backbone at last. When I turned to gape at her, she'd straightened to her full height, which was taller than mine, although not by much, and had her hands bunched into fists at her sides. George tried to take her arm, but she shook him off.

In the resulting silence, Marianne continued. "Mrs. Majesty is right, Father. You know she is. Don't you *dare* talk about lawsuits! *You're* the one who's in the wrong. *You're* the one who drove me from home! You beat Mother, you beat me, you did . . . other things. You're a brutal, horrible monster!"

Wow. If somebody had offered to bet me that Marianne Wagner would one day stand up for herself against her old man, I'd have turned him down—and not merely because I don't gamble. I honestly, really and truly, didn't believe Marianne had an ounce of spunk in her. Shows how wrong I can be without half trying, doesn't it?

She was quivering with wrath and indignation. Dr. Wagner stared at her, his mouth hanging open. George's eyes were bulging with surprise. Billy was totally enthralled.

Sam, as might have been expected, was the only one who wasn't influenced by Marianne's affecting performance. Breaking the silence, he said, "All right, let's all calm down." It was the same suggestion he'd offered before, but this time we all took him up on it.

His color still high, Dr. Wagner huffed. I guess he didn't dare say anything more for fear that either Marianne or I would drag some more of his sins out of the swampy darkness and dump them into the light of day. It's *got* to be a crime to beat your spouse and child, never mind the other things he'd done to Marianne. I probably should have asked Sam before this present crisis, but I hadn't wanted to make him any more suspicious of me than he already was.

Sam went on. "Can someone please tell me what's going on here?"

Once more I leaped into the breach. "I can."

He gave me a sour look. "I expected as much."

I wasn't put off, mainly because I was used to his sneers and snide remarks. "What you've heard is the truth, Sam. Marianne ran away from home when Dr. Wagner made living there too harrowing for her safety and sanity."

Dr. Wagner gurgled but didn't speak. Sam shot him a "shut-the-heck-up glance," so I continued.

"Mr. Grenville was kind enough to allow Marianne to remain in the cottage behind his store until Marianne decided what she should do from among a variety of options." I didn't let on that we hadn't come up with those options because Marianne was a totally useless human being, since it didn't have any bearing on the situation at hand.

Rather, I took a deep breath and an even greater chance, and said, "Miss Wagner and Mr. Grenville have come to know each other during the past couple of weeks. They are now deeply in love and plan to marry posthaste." There. I'd not only committed myself, but George and Marianne, too. Lord help us all.

Dr. Wagner found his voice. "I forbid it!" By this time his face was purple. "She's not twenty-one yet!"

Marianne took another bold step and faced her father. "You can't forbid it, Father. I'm eighteen years old. That may not be old enough to vote or to live on my own without your permission, but it's old enough to marry." She lost some of her spirit and turned to Sam. "Isn't it?"

Sam nodded.

Marianne was now blushing furiously. "That is, if George—Mr. Grenville, I mean—cared to . . . I mean, unless he thinks we should wait three years . . ."

The ending was pretty feeble for a speech that had begun with such pluck, but her reasoning was sound. As luck and my insight into his character would have it, George knew what a chivalrous gentleman should do in such a case. Stepping up to the bat—or to Marianne, in this instance—he got down on one knee and took Marianne's limp (and probably damp from all the tears it had wiped away) hand in his and spoke directly to her, ignoring the rest of us in the audience. "I don't want to wait three years, and we don't have to."

I knew what was coming, but didn't want to spoil his grand moment by speaking. If George proved to be the hero I'd pegged him for, everything might turn out all right after all—except for me having to spend the rest of my life behind bars. I used to be a pie-in-the-sky optimist, but events in late years had knocked me around some; therefore, I held my breath and watched.

"If Marianne will do me the honor of becoming my bride, we can be wed as soon as possible. I love her, and I believe she returns my regard."

Marianne nodded and mouthed the word, "Yes." That was all right; none of us needed to hear it to understand.

"What?" Dr. Wagner. Bellowing. Again. *"What?"* He yanked the hat off his head and slammed it to the

floor. I expected him to kick it or jump up and down on it, but he didn't. He seemed to swell up before he jerked around and faced me. He was a scary sight, all bright purple and fuming like a steam engine. I didn't blame Marianne or her mother for being afraid of him if he got like that very often. However, before I'd show him he frightened me, I'd fly to the moon, so I lifted my chin and glowered right back at him.

"This is all your fault!" he bellowed. "If you hadn't interfered in my daughter's life, none of this would have happened!"

But I, unlike the other women in his life, was no shrinking violet. I snapped, "You're wrong! This is *your* fault! If you'd treated your daughter the way any decent man should treat his child, she'd never have run away!"

I'm almost certain he would have punched me in the jaw, exactly the way I'm sure he'd punched his daughter and wife on more than one occasion, except that Sam caught his fist and held him back. Sam was darned strong, and as much as it pains me to say it, I appreciated his strength and quickness right then.

"That's enough from both of you," he growled. Some of my appreciation wilted. Darn it, everything else might be my fault, but Dr. Wagner's being an ogre sure wasn't. "Calm down, Dr. Wagner. And you too, Mrs. Majesty."

I frowned at him, but he didn't pay any attention to me. As soon as he got Dr. Wagner under control, he turned to George and Marianne. George had scrambled to his feet when Dr. Wagner started hollering and clutched Marianne in a protective embrace, even though it was I whom the doctor was threatening at the moment. "What about it, you two? Are you willing to marry?"

"Willing?" George asked, astounded. "I adore this woman. If she'll agree to marry me, I'll be the happiest man in the world!"

I wondered how long that would last, but not out loud.

"And I love George," Marianne whispered. "I would be so happy to be his wife."

I gave that declaration a longer life expectancy.

"But . . . but . . ." As he sputtered, Dr. Wagner's gaze went from George to Marianne and landed on me. His face screwed up in an expression of such outrage that I'd have shrunk back if I were, say, Marianne.

Since I'm not, I scowled at him. Then I did something that was unworthy of a woman with my reputation for graciousness, not to mention the ability to commune with spirits from beyond life's pale. I stamped on his hat. I thought for sure he'd bust an artery or something, but he didn't. He recommenced swelling up until he resembled a dapper but outraged toad.

Again, Sam stepped in to prevent homicide (or whatever the doctor had planned for me). "That's enough, you two. What we need to do now is have a calm chat with the couple and see if we can't get this problem solved."

"I won't have it!" shouted Dr. Wagner.

"I'm afraid you don't have any say in the matter," Sam said coolly. "Not if your daughter is eighteen years old and she wants to marry this gentleman. He's clearly amenable to such an action."

"I am," George said sturdily.

"And I," said Marianne.

"Then I'm afraid there's nothing you can do, sir." Sam smiled slightly at Dr. Wagner, who didn't return the gesture.

Instead he stood, rigid and trembling, for approximately ten seconds, before he spun on Marianne. Secure in George's arms, she didn't cower. He pointed a quivering finger at his daughter. "You are no longer a member of my family," he declared in the voice of doom.

As he swooped down and picked up his crunched hat, Marianne spoke. "Thank God for that!"

Dr. Wagner looked stricken as he walked out of the bookstore.

I felt like applauding.

After the door closed behind Marianne's father, Billy *did* applaud. We all turned and gawped at him but, by gum, he was chuckling!

We agreed that George would drive Marianne to the courthouse and Sam would join them there. He promised to hurry them through the process of securing a marriage license and so forth, pulling whatever strings might be necessary, while I took Billy home. He didn't feel up to attending the nuptials. Then I would drive down to the courthouse and stand as a witness for the happy couple.

"I was afraid you'd be mad at me," I confessed as I pushed Billy and our Christmas presents along Colorado Street, heading west toward Marengo.

"I probably would have been if I hadn't witnessed that scene at the bookstore," Billy admitted. "But you were right about Dr. Wagner. He's a louse."

"He sure is. I just couldn't send Marianne back to him. When we're alone, I'll tell you some of the things he did to her, Billy. You won't believe it."

"Yes I would, and I don't want to hear about them, thanks anyway." He shuddered. "I can't imagine a father doing that to his own child. Or anyone else's, for that matter."

"Me neither." It was either really cold or shudders were contagious, because I shuddered, too.

I kept waiting for him to blow up or say something nasty to me, but he didn't. I didn't have any idea what had come over him, but I hoped it lasted—as long as it didn't presage something horrid. As I have no precognitive powers and couldn't tell, I remained nervous.

Spike was so happy to see us, he piddled on the floor of the living room. I didn't scold him; it was excitement that had made him do it. Billy only laughed. I got more nervous.

Since I was going to a wedding, even if it was going to be at the courthouse, I changed into a nice blue suit. It wasn't as elegant as my black wool dress, but I didn't think black would be appropriate for a wedding, especially under the circumstances.

Right before I walked out the front door, Billy stopped me. "Wait a minute, Daisy."

My heart thudding, I waited. But Billy surprised me.

Digging into his pocket and withdrawing a couple of dollars, he handed them to me. "Get a posy or something for Grenville and Miss Wagner. They'll be the only flowers the blushing bride will get, I reckon."

"Oh, Billy!" I was so touched, tears sprang to my eyes. "Thank you so much." I leaned over and kissed him.

He blushed a little. "It's nothing," he muttered. "Just some flowers."

But it wasn't just some flowers. It was a tender gesture from the man I loved, and I knew it if he didn't.

The Ford balked at being started. I have no idea what was wrong with it, and I worried that it would break down completely before I could replace it. But I didn't want to walk to the wedding, so I took a chance on the Model T.

There was a flower vendor on the corner of Colorado and Fair Oaks, so it didn't take much time to pick out a pretty bouquet of white roses and yellow chrysanthemums. It might not have been wedding material under normal circumstances, but I figured we'd all make allowances.

The weather was frigid. The wind hitting me in the

face gave me more color than usual (I know it for a fact, because I glanced in the little mirror I kept in my hand-bag before climbing out of the motorcar). Clouds covered the mountains, and I wondered if it was snowing up there.

The old Pasadena City Hall, which was destined to be replaced in 1929, had been erected in 1877 on the corner of Fair Oaks Avenue and Union Street. By 1920 the old wooden building was kind of shabby, but my heart was light as I parked at the curb in front of it. I saw Sam's big old Hudson and George's gray Cadillac already there, and when I ran up the steps and pushed the door open, the three of them were waiting for me.

"Hope I haven't made you wait too long," I said breathlessly.

George rose and walked over to me, both hands extended, a smile a mile wide on his face. "We just got through with all the preliminaries," he told me. "You're right on time."

"Huh," said Sam.

When I looked at him, he was peering at his pocket watch. I figured he was only being unpleasant for the heck of it, so I paid him no mind and rushed over to Marianne after I'd given George a big hug. "I'm so happy for you, Marianne!"

She'd stood up when she saw me. When I handed her the flowers and said, "These are from Billy and me," she threw her arms around me and started crying. Why do I have this effect on some people?

"Oh, Daisy, I can't thank you enough for all you've done for me. You even spoke back to my father!"

I'd done more than talk back to her old man, but I didn't mention it. In Marianne's mind, standing up to her father was the bravest thing a person could do. Risking imprisonment didn't even show up on her list, I'd wager. I glanced at Sam over Marianne's bowed head, but he hadn't hauled out the handcuffs, so I figured I was safe at least until the ceremony was over.

"It was nothing," I purred. "Anyhow, you stood up to him, too."

"Yeah, yeah," said Sam, as cross as ever. "Let's get this show on the road. We were only waiting for you. The judge is ready."

Since it didn't seem appropriate to snap at Sam with Marianne and George, madly in love and eager as anything, standing there watching, I smiled graciously. "Of course. Let's go."

It took very little time to tie the knot; much less time that I remembered from my own wedding. I guess that's because this one took place before a judge at City Hall. Marianne and I both cried, of course. What's the point of attending weddings if you can't cry during them? Sam eyed me as I dabbed at my eyes, but I only lifted my chin and tried to pay no attention. He was big, though, and hard to ignore.

When it was over, I wrote my name on the form the clerk handed me. The judge and the clerk and Marianne and George and I were all grinning like mad. Sam signed his name, too, looking as sober and unmoved as ever. I felt like a mother hen watching her chick grow up when George took Marianne's hand and they began walking down the corridor toward the front door of the building.

Sam and I flanked the happy couple. "What do you plan to do now?" I asked. "Or do you even know? This was kind of sudden."

George laughed. "I think what I'll do right now is drive Marianne to her new home and carry her over the threshold. I left the store so abruptly, I don't think I even remembered to turn out the lights, so I'd better go back and lock up."

"I'm so happy," Marianne whispered.

"I'm glad, darling," George told her lovingly. "So am I."

I vaguely recalled Billy talking to me in that sappy tone of voice once or twice before he left for France. After heaving a huge sigh, I said, "I hope you two will have a wonderful life together."

"I'm sure we will," said George, sounding as if he believed it.

"I'm so happy," Marianne repeated. She, on the other hand, sounded as if she was in a trance—a real one, as opposed to the ones I used in my job.

Sam and I walked them to George's Cadillac and stood there, waving, until the motorcar got lost in the traffic. I sighed again. "Well, that's over."

"Yeah," said Sam. "I don't suppose you'd like to tell me about it."

I glanced up at him and chewed my lip for a second. "Um, there's nothing to tell. Nothing more than you already know. Honest." My gaze fell to his hands, just to make sure he wasn't reaching for his gun or the handcuffs or anything else of a restraining nature.

"Huh." He turned, stuffed his hands in his trouser pockets, and walked toward his Hudson.

Was I really going to get off that easily? I took a step after him, intending to ask if he planned to arrest me, but stopped. What was the matter with me, anyway? Might as well accept good fortune when it presented itself, even if I didn't believe it would last. Still a little shaky, I went to the front of the Model T and grabbed the crank. I really hate cranking cars. I couldn't wait until I could replace the old clunker.

The blasted car wouldn't start. I cranked and fiddled with the choke wire and the high-speed pedal and the low-speed pedal, and the Model T sat there like the chunk of metal it was, and wouldn't even cough at me. Standing back, I put my fists on my hips and glared at it. Glaring at the Ford was approximately as effective as glaring at Sam Rotondo, which means not at all.

"Need a lift?"

It was Sam. Of course. With a sinking feeling in my heart, I gave up. I knew my escape from justice had been too good to last. "Thanks, Sam."

He got out and opened the door for me, a courtesy I hadn't anticipated from this source. Since his car didn't require a crank or a choke wire or a high- or low-speed pedal, all Sam had to do was press the starter button and drive. What freedom!

Concluding I'd best not think about freedom, since I was probably going to lose mine soon, I sat sedately and stared out through the windshield. Sam didn't speak. So I didn't, either.

It wasn't until he pulled up in front of our bungalow on Marengo that he turned to me. I braced myself. "Are you going to tell me what happened?" he asked.

"There's nothing to tell," I said. I knew the cuffs were only seconds away from my wrists.

Sam didn't move. He only stared some more. I stared back. He knew I was lying. I knew he knew. He knew I knew he knew.

And still he said nothing.

At last I said, "Listen, Sam, are you going to arrest me or not?"

"For what?"

"*I* don't know! You said something about obstructing justice, although I have no idea what justice I obstructed."

He didn't speak. My nerves began to jump around like water on a hot griddle.

After what seemed like forever, he released a huge breath, shook his head, and said, "You're home."

I knew that. After a moment, I said, "That's it?"

"That's it."

I swallowed and decided to pretend it really *was* it, at

least until something awful happened. "Thanks for the ride, Sam."

"You're welcome."

He didn't get out to open the door for me. I didn't push my luck and did it myself.

Spike was overjoyed to see me. Billy seemed happy, too.

Twenty

We went up to the foothills and chopped down a Christmas tree after church on Sunday. The weather was as crisp and clean as anything, and we had a great time.

Pa and I sawed down the six-foot fir tree that Billy and I had picked out, and the two of us laid it in the pony cart. Although Pa had gone down to the courthouse and fiddled with the Model T until it started, we'd decided the motorcar was too untrustworthy to be taken into the mountains. Brownie, our stubborn old cart horse, was unreliable, too, but at least he didn't have to be cranked (being plenty cranky to begin with, according to Pa, who liked his puns).

Aunt Vi and Ma met us at the door when we returned and brought the tree in. We drank hot cocoa and ate Aunt Vi's delicious Christmas cookies while we decorated the tree.

I've always treasured the memory of that afternoon, because it was so wonderful to be in the bosom of my family and to have no more than the usual problems hanging over my head. No longer did I have to worry about Marianne or her bestial father or whether she'd be discovered hiding in George's cottage. All I had to worry about was Billy, my morals, and Sam coming over all the time to irk me. I was accustomed to those problems, so I was comfortable again.

Along about five o'clock, a knock came at the door.

This wasn't an unusual happenstance, since we were a sociable family and it was the season for visiting one's neighbors. I trotted over and opened the door, scooping up Spike along the way, since I didn't want him barreling outside.

A special-delivery messenger stood at the door in his gray uniform and cap, holding out a parcel. I thanked him, tipped him, and took the parcel indoors, thinking it was probably a Christmas present from one of our relatives back east, even though it was extremely unusual for them to spend money on special delivery and a *Sunday* special delivery was unheard of in my family.

The package was addressed to me. I nearly dropped it when I read my name.

"What is it?" Billy wanted to know.

For that matter, everyone wanted to know what it was. They gathered around me as if I were a magnet and they were steel shavings.

"I don't know."

"Is it a Christmas present?" asked Ma.

"I don't know."

"Why don't you open it and find out?" my practical husband suggested.

Because I was afraid of it, was why. I couldn't say that. I turned the package over in my hands. It didn't *look* like a bomb. It didn't look like a Christmas present. At last I said, "What the heck," and untied the string. And then I sat with a *whump* on the sofa, staring for all I was worth at the contents of the package.

"Daisy, what is it?" Billy sounded worried.

"What's wrong, darling?" Ma.

"Is it something bad?" Vi.

"Say, little girl, what's going on?" Pa.

I held up several greenbacks. They were fifty-dollar bills. "It's . . ." I had to swallow. "It's money."

My family uttered a collective gasp and stood mute, as if they were all unable to speak. I was in the same condition myself. With shaking hands I lifted the card and opened it. It read, *Thank you so much,* and it was signed, *Diane Marie Cutler Wagner.* I held up the card for all to see.

I couldn't accept the money. I didn't need to be paid for doing a good deed. Leaping to my feet, I rushed to the bedroom, snatched my coat out of the closet, stuffed the money into my handbag, and raced to the door. "I'm going to have to take the Ford. Wish me luck."

They all knew where I was going, because I'd told them about George's participation in the Marianne affair. I didn't know if they'd be at the bookstore. In fact, I was pretty sure they wouldn't be, but the store was closer to our house than George's house on Catalina, and I didn't dare show up at Dr. Wagner's house. If the bookstore failed me, I'd try to coax the Model T up Catalina Avenue.

For once my luck was good. Lights glowed in the store as I parked the Model T. I ran to the front door and whacked on it until George unlocked it and pulled it open.

"Daisy! For heaven's sake, what's wrong?"

I pushed past him into the store. My hands were almost frozen solid. "Is Marianne here?"

"Marianne? Sure, she's here. So's her mother. We were just showing her around the store."

I probably looked like a raving lunatic when I turned on George. "Mrs. Wagner's here? Now?"

"Daisy, what's the matter? Has something happened to Billy?"

"Billy?" I stared at him. "Why should anything have happened to Billy?"

"I don't know, but something's obviously wrong."

"No. No. But I need to talk to Mrs. Wagner. Now."

Shaking his head as if he were giving me up as a lost cause, he said, "Of course. Come with me."

Marianne and her mother sat together behind the

counter, holding hands. Mrs. Wagner looked even worse than when she'd attended the séance. She looked as if she hadn't slept for a month, there were huge circles under her eyes, and there was a big bruise on her cheek. I could guess who'd put it there. Somebody would be doing the world, not to mention Diane Wagner, a big favor if he shot Dr. Wagner dead.

Rising from her chair, Marianne glowed at me. "Daisy! I'm so glad you came! You know my mother, don't you?"

Mrs. Wagner got up, too, and gazed at me shyly. "How do you do, Mrs. Majesty?"

"I'm fine, thanks. It's good to see you, Marianne." I sucked in a huge breath. I hadn't even counted the money, and we could sure use it, but I hadn't earned it. I fumbled a bit, but managed to pull the package out of my handbag. Thrusting it at Mrs. Wagner, I said, "Thank you very much, Mrs. Wagner, but I can't accept this."

She didn't take it, but only smiled sadly. "I won't take it back, Mrs. Majesty. It's yours." She gestured at the package.

My hand started to tremble. I *really* didn't want to give it back, darn it, and she was making it awfully hard to do so. "But . . . You must take it back, Mrs. Wagner. I can't keep it. It's too much. I didn't earn it."

"You did earn it, and it's not enough, you mean. You saved my daughter from my own fate. If I could give you millions, I would. That's the best I can do."

"But . . ."

"Take it, Daisy," said George. "If I could add to it, I would." He gave Marianne a smile that darned near gave me a stomachache, it was so sweet. "But I have a wife to provide for now."

Marianne blushed charmingly. It's a good thing she was so pretty. I've noticed that men forgive pretty women a lot more easily than they do ugly ones, and I had a feeling George was going to be getting lots of practice in the area of forgiveness. Marianne would be a long time in learning how to keep house for herself and George.

"Oh yes, Daisy," she said. "Please accept the money. You were the first person in the whole world who ever tried to help me."

It's a good thing she wasn't watching her mother when she said that, because Mrs. Wagner looked stricken.

Okay, I kept the money. I couldn't fight *three* of them, could I? I was as gracious as anything about it, too.

As I drove home in the dark, trying my best not to hit anything, I thought over what Mrs. Wagner had said about me rescuing Marianne from her mother's fate. I guess I'd had a hand in it, all right, but I didn't buy her reasoning. As far as I'm concerned, even female people have a duty at least to try to direct their own fate. But I was born and bred a Gumm. Maybe rich people are different. Well, heck, I *know* they're different.

Nuts. It was too complicated for me. But now I had a lot of money to compensate me for my confusion.

The next day, I kissed Billy before I headed out the door. He eyed me suspiciously. "Where are you going?"

"You'll find out," I said, winking. I don't wink very well, being inclined to include both eyes in the gesture.

Frowning, Billy said, "What are you up to now, Daisy? If you're going to exorcise another ghost . . ."

"No!" I laughed. "No more ghosts, Billy. Promise. I'm just going out for a little bit."

He still appeared skeptical, but he didn't argue. Maybe his recent even temper wasn't anything to be nervous about. It seemed to me, when I contemplated it, that he was less argumentative now that he had Spike to keep him company when I was gone during the day. It was a comforting thought—considerably more comforting than the notion that Billy had given up on life and stopped fighting because he aimed to commit suicide.

Billy's skepticism vanished when I drove home in our

brand-new, shiny black, closed-in, battery-powered, four-cylinder Chevrolet automobile (one with a door on the driver's side as well as the passenger's). In fact, he was thrilled.

So was everyone else in the family, even Spike, who enjoyed going for rides with us.

And I hadn't even had to sell the count's bracelet!

Christmas was special that year. The Christmas cantata at church went without a hitch, and I even saw Mrs. Dearing, a long-time member whose doctor husband also sang in the choir, wipe her eyes during "Silent Night."

Billy remained relatively civil during the whole season, and even though Sam was a more or less constant presence in our lives, I managed to avoid him pretty well. I talked with Dr. Benjamin again, and he downplayed my worries about Billy possibly committing suicide. I couldn't make myself talk to Sam. Eventually, I decided to believe the doctor—sufficient unto the day, and all that.

Spike helped unwrap our presents, even though we hadn't intended him to. Nobody cared.

In short, life was good with a couple of minor exceptions, the main one being Sam Rotondo, and I could stand him much better now that I didn't have to fuss with a cranky policeman as well as a cranky motorcar.

I'm sorry. You can blame appreciation of puns on Pa.

Romantic Suspense from
Lisa Jackson